Claudia Carroll was born in Dublin, where she still lives and where she has worked extensively both as a theatre and television actress.

CLAUDIA CARROLL

Love Me or Leave Me

AVON

AVON

A division of HarperCollins*Publishers*
77–85 Fulham Palace Road,
London W6 8JB

www.harpercollins.co.uk

A Paperback Original 2014

A catalogue record for this book is
available from the British Library

ISBN-13: 978-0-00-752087-9

Set in Minion by Palimpsest Book Production Limited,
Falkirk, Stirlingshire

Printed and bound in Great Britain by
Printed and bound in Great Britain by Clays Ltd, St Ives plc

This book is warmly dedicated to Moira Reilly

With love and thanks, always

THREE YEARS AGO . . .

Chloe.

'Shh, shh, shh,' I can hear my best friend Gemma saying, as she hands me a fistful of Kleenex and purposely avoids hugging me, so as not to crumple the wedding dress. Even though it makes shag-all difference now. My perfect wedding dress too; the one I spent long months trawling just about every bridal shop the length and breadth of the country to find.

'It's all right, sweetheart. Just try to tell me what happened.'

Right then, I think, staring dully back at her. You asked for it. So here it is; here's what I can remember from just minutes ago, before the skin got ripped off the surface of my life, exposing nothing but raw flesh underneath.

The killer is, I'm just a nice, ordinary, normal girl. This isn't the kind of thing that's supposed to happen to nice, ordinary, normal girls, now is it?

So I took a deep breath and began. Gemma says nothing, just nods silently and waits till I've finished.

'You'll be okay, you know.'

'Will I?'

She paused for a beat and I was so grateful to her for at

least answering me honestly. But then, Gemma is one of those people who physically gets heartburn when required to lie.

'I only wish I could say yes.'

*   *   *

'And two hearts will beat as one.'

Dawn Madden and Kirk Lennox-Coyningham
Would love you, as one of their dearest friends,
To celebrate their fusion
At Mount Druid,
On the feast of Midsummer, June 21st.
Blessing in the unconsecrated chapel
At two o'clock.
Feasting at The Old Gazebo,
Followed by a tree dedication ceremony on the grounds.

Please don't RSVP by post, as we believe all paper is wasteful. And know that vegetarians, vegans and all on a gluten-free or lactose intolerance diet will be well catered for.

Organic and unfermented wine freely available.

No gifts please. Donations only, if necessary, to the National Forestry Society.

Accommodation isn't a problem at Mount Druid. But please let us know if you'd prefer a Mongolian yurt, a shepherd's hut or a self-catering cottage (running water available here. And eco-loo facilities).

(This invitation has been printed on 100% recycled organic paper and no trees were harmed in its manufacture.)

*   *   *

Jo and Dave

Cordially invite you

To celebrate their marriage

On fifteenth of February

ST MARY'S CHURCH, 2.45pm sharp, for a prompt
3pm start.

Dress code: strictly black tie, floor length dresses for
ladies. Absolutely no cocktail dresses please.

Reception to follow at the Radisson Blu hotel punctually at 7pm.

Full wedding list available at Brown Thomas (no
off-list gifting permitted).

Kindly note:
1. Coaches will be on hand at the church to transport
   guests to the hotel. Please clearly tick the box
   below if you require transportation.
2. All coaches will leave the church punctually at
   4.30pm. This is essential in order to facilitate an
   on-time arrival at the hotel.
3. Kindly RSVP before December 31st if you have any
   dietary requirements. Please note, this is essential.
4. Seating plan will be available to view at *www.
   It'sJo's_Big_Day!.com,* from January 1st.
5. No confetti or rice to be thrown at any stage.
6. Guests requiring overnight accommodation, see

attached list, which is arranged in order of comfort and budget, from five star standard, downwards.
7. All queries concerning the day should be addressed directly to Jo Hargreaves at Jo_Marketing_Director @digitech.com

Thank you for your prompt reply and looking forward to seeing you on our special day!

*   *   *

Lucy and Andrew
Are getting married!!!
And they request the pleasure of your company,
At the mother of all parties to celebrate
On New Year's Eve,
Pichet Restaurant, Trinity St., Dublin.

Sorry, but the actual wedding ceremony will take place privately, on the Twenty Fourth of December, at the Moon Palace Hotel, Cancun, Mexico.

With apologies and please don't kill us!

No gifts please. We have everything we could possibly need in each other . . .

YESTERDAY . . .

Chapter One

London
Chloe.

Last night, the old nightmare came back to haunt me.

I don't actually know if it's day or night. All I know is that it's still my wedding day – or rather the day I was supposed to get married – and I somehow allowed myself to be led out of the bathroom where I'd locked myself, and laid down on top of the fluffy hotel bed. Still in my confection of a wedding dress, crumpled to bits now, like some kind of latter-day Miss Havisham. And they must have given me a sedative the equivalent of a horse tranquillizer, because instead of the heartache that's to come, all I feel is groggy and sluggish, like I've been out cold for hours.

The curtains are drawn and it's semi-darkness in here, but suddenly I'm aware of someone breathing and a big blurry silhouette perched on the bed beside me. Frank? Could that by some miracle actually be him? For one wonderful, fleeting moment, hope overrides everything my sane mind is trying to tell me. By some miracle, was today just some kind of hallucination and this is actually my wedding night? But I poke round at the slumbering

11

figure a bit and realize that it's not Frank at all; it's my best friend Gemma, now out of the gakky bridesmaid's dress, the one that I practically bullied her into wearing and back into her normal, standard issue jeans with a swingy, summery top.

Still here. Still watching over me, bless her, like the guardian angel that she really is.

'Did I dream it all?' I croak over to her.

She shakes her head.

''Fraid not, love.'

'So where is everyone?'

'Well, a lot of his side just buggered off when . . . well, when they realized that there wasn't going to be any . . . emm, you know. But your parents, plus most of your family and pretty much half of your mates from work all decamped to the Cellar Bar downstairs. More private for everyone, I think they all felt, given . . . you know.'

'Yeah,' I say dully. 'I work here. Believe me, I know.'

Doubtless still all reeling in astonishment at, well, let's just say, how the day actually panned out. I'd be kidding myself if I didn't think this wouldn't be the talk of the town for years to come. Poor Mum. And after all the bother she had finding shoes to match her dress for it too.

'So . . . what happened? I mean, afterwards . . .'

'Now that's absolutely nothing at all for you to worry about, sweetheart,' Gemma says firmly. 'That scary wedding planner one, whatshername . . . dealt with everything beautifully. God, you should have seen her. Worth every penny you paid her just for the massive damage limitation job she did. Your Dad made a short speech at the church and it was all very . . .'

'Very what?'

She looks back at me, as though weighing up whether or not I can be trusted with the truth. But then I know she'll tell me everything. Gemma always has and always will.

'Well . . . I want to say dignified, but I do remember him using the phrase, "I'll kick that bastard's arse if he ever comes near my daughter again." Oh and then, he chased Frank all the way downstairs to the underground car park, then threatened him with court action for breach of promise. I nearly thought your Dad would have to be held back by burly security men. I was only thankful he didn't have a set of golf clubs to hand; he'd have sent Frank straight to an intensive care unit.'

I surprise myself by actually smiling. But then Dad's a barrister; he's always threatening people.

'Did you talk to Frank?' I manage to get out groggily. Jeez, what did they slip me earlier anyway? A valium sandwich? The same kind of tranquillizers you'd use to anaesthetize a rhinoceros?

'Briefly. He was loading up suitcases into the boot of his car and told me to tell you he'd call.'

'What?' I say, suddenly wide-awake now. 'You mean that was it? That was all the fecker said? The guy breaks my heart, completely humiliates me in front of the world and its sick dog, and all he can come out with is, "tell her I'll call"?'

'Well, in fairness, it was all he could say. I left out the bit where I was physically walloping him with the wire metal bit off my bouquet and only praying it would inflict lasting damage on the cowardly git.'

I squeeze her warmly, silently blessing her loyalty, then slump back against the deep hotel pillows. And now that I'm actually awake, here it comes. What I've been postponing all day. I've been forcing myself all this time not to relive today's horrors, but now, like on oncoming car-crash, there's no avoiding them.

So where did it all go wrong? What in the name of God did I miss? Then, slowly, my stomach starts to twist as it all begins to come back to me. The excruciating rehearsal dinner last night for a start, I suddenly think. That was the start of it. Definitely the first time I got that slightly sick feeling right in the pit of my solar plexus that something was slightly off-centre.

Frank has this slight poker tell, you see. Whenever he's a bit uncomfortable, he gets twitchy and finds it difficult to make direct eye contact, particularly if you happen to be the one he's uncomfortable around.

But at the time I thought he was just a bit nervy, nothing more. I even remember looking across the dinner table at him naïvely, lovingly even, more fool me. There's one hundred and twenty people landing on top of us today, I figured, so who could possibly blame him? Have to admit, I was feeling a bit tetchy myself. I spent useless hours worrying about utter crap, like would the flower arrangements wilt at the reception tables, before everyone got the chance to admire them? And knowing my mates, probably try to nick them later on. But never in my wildest imaginings, did I think this would come to pass.

Suddenly, violent flashbacks start to crowd in on me. I get a pin-sharp memory from this morning of the make-up artist, a lovely girl called Zoe, hysterically screeching, 'Mother of God, the groom! What the hell is he doing here?! Would you ever just get OUT!' as Frank gingerly tapped at the door of my hotel room while we were all still getting ready.

'Frank! You know right well it's bad luck to see the bride just before the ceremony!' I can remember my niece Emma screeching over her thin, emaciated shoulder blades, in between lashing on more bronzer than you'd normally see on a *Strictly Come Dancing* finalist. At that, a sudden, disconnected thought ricochets round my addled brain. Poor Emma. God love the girl, she was so looking forward to being a bridesmaid today. Even joined Weight Watchers especially, then went and lost a whopping eleven pounds. She was the envy of her whole class in school, apparently. And is now so stick-thin, I honestly don't know whether to feed the kid, or else make soup out of her.

And yet still Frank didn't budge. Instead, he just stood there, taking us all in with flat-fish eyes. Dead eyes, I'm now thinking.

'Ehh . . . sorry to interrupt you all, but by any chance Chloe, would you have a minute?' he said directly to me, and just in case I'd missed last night's subtle clues, there it was yet again for all to see. That telltale twitching.

'Oh, isn't that sooo romantic,' I can clearly remember Mum having to practically shout at the young one who was blow drying her hair, raising her voice so she could be heard above the blast of the hairdryer. 'Bet Frank wants to give her a lovely wedding present before the ceremony. Bit of jewellery, probably, he's a good lad like that. Wait till you see, our Chloe has him well trained!'

I can remember being a bit taken aback when he suddenly appeared out of nowhere like that, but nothing more. Some last minute problem with buttonholes or seating arrangements, was my ridiculous guess. Because how could I have possibly foreseen what was to come?

A sudden wave of nausea sweeps through me as the

whole thing hits me square in the face again, its impact getting more and more painful each fresh time. I'm sweating now, cold and clammy, shivering and shaking weakly, wondering when my life will finally stop spinning out of control.

'Chloe?' says Gemma softly through the gloom of the hotel room. 'I'm right here if you want to talk about it.'

'Do you want to know what Frank's last words to me were?' I eventually manage to croak back at her.

'Tell me.'

'He said, "I'd better go now. My left buttock is getting numb from sitting on this tiled floor."'

'Well, my oh my, what a diehard romantic he is.' And even through the darkness, I can sense her rolling her eyes up to heaven. 'Seriously Chloe, you couldn't have married Frank,' she goes on, hauling herself up on one elbow now and looking down at me. 'I mean, come on, all the signs were there . . . I did try to warn you . . .'

'Sorry,' I interrupt, staring up at the ceiling, 'but I can't do this right now. Please bear in mind this is supposed to be my wedding night.'

Gemma looks steadily down at me.

'Any point in my mentioning great romances of the past that have all crashed and burned? Charles and Diana? Liz Taylor and Richard Burton? Jennifer Aniston and Brad?'

I manage a weak shake of my head, then turn away from her, savouring the cool feel of the hotel pillows against my thumping head.

'For God's sake, look at you, you're completely drained,' she says, eyeing me steadily. 'Now how about you just go back to sleep, and have a nice little snooze, love? And just wait till you see, everything will be so much better tomorrow. Trust me. I'll leave you in peace and make sure no one disturbs you.'

She tiptoes out the room, like I'm a convalescent recovering from major heart surgery who can't even handle the stimulation of a door being closed gently . . . and finally I'm alone again.

With my mind racing.

What to do? Go back to sleep, then get up tomorrow and somehow try to piece my whole life back together again? Go back into work and face everyone? In the very hotel I was supposed to have my wedding reception in? To make matters worse, where Frank and I have worked shoulder to shoulder together for the past few years?

Then comes a sudden straw of hope which I wildly clutch at. Maybe I could try to laugh it all off? Side-step all the humiliation by pretending it was mutual and that Frank and I are actually good friends?

But even if I had the energy, I know deep down that it just can't be done. Because how am I supposed to come back here to work and just act like nothing happened? How could I look across a function room at him and smile, like he hadn't just ripped my entrails out and mashed them up against a wall? How can I just pick up the threads of my old life and somehow struggle on? Even in my semi-drugged state, I know I can't do it.

Not. An. Option.

And then suddenly, from out of nowhere, an idea.

You don't have to, a tiny voice inside me prompts. *You don't have to face any of them, not if you don't want to. Who says you even have to? You can just pack up and go. Start a new life, start over. Start right now.*

Suddenly I'm sitting bolt upright, heart walloping

17

cartoon-like in my chest, as I really start to give it serious thought.

London, I could go to London, couldn't I? Not too far from Dublin that my family would think I've completely lost the plot and yet distant enough for me to get some perspective. I even have an old pal there who couldn't make it over for the wedding, maybe she'd look after me for a bit? We did hotel management together in college, so who knows? She might even know of a few job opportunities I could go for.

For the first time all day, I feel a surge of fresh energy coming over me. Just the thoughts of a new life in a whole new city, where I wouldn't forevermore be branded as the girl who got dumped on her wedding day, and suddenly I'm on my feet and already unhooking the back of my wedding dress. I've already got loads of luggage in packed suitcases here, full of clothes I needed for the honeymoon. Admittedly, most of it is fancy-schmancy underwear, but I know at least there's a pair of jeans and a warm jumper in there somewhere.

Ten minutes later and I'm out the door, pulling a small wheelie bag after me, tiptoeing down the deserted corridor like some kind of fugitive from justice. I know all my family and pals are still downstairs in the hotel's Cellar Bar, which is in the basement, so with any luck, chances of my running into any of them are slim.

I check my phone and am astonished to see it's actually still early; just coming up to six in the evening. And I know there's always late evening flights to London, so with all going well and if I can grab a last minute seat, I might just make it.

Then a sudden dilemma. How do I get out of here unseen

by the rest of the staff, by my colleagues, maybe even my boss? If I'm spotted, they'll just drag me back, tell me I'm not acting rationally and possibly call a psychiatrist to give me the once over. And if I use the staff entrance like I always do, there's no way on earth I won't be spotted.

Main door then. No choice. Just like any other guest. Best shot all round. I take the precaution of using the stairs in case I bump into anyone I know in the lift who'll physically try to haul me back, but thankfully, my luck holds; I've the whole stairwell to myself. I make it all the way downstairs and apart from distant voices wafting up from the Cellar Bar, I don't start running into any other guests until I make it to the busy, packed foyer.

Please, please, please, I find myself praying to a God I barely believe in, don't let anyone I know see me . . .

And for the first time throughout possibly the shittiest day known to man, the heavens actually send me a break. The Merrion Hotel is a real weekend hotspot, so the drawing rooms by reception are packed with the fake tan brigade out in stiletto-heeled force and a clutch of hunky looking men wafting around them. Heart palpitating, I spot two lounge staff that work for me, but thank you God, they're so busy weaving in and out of the throng that they don't seem to even notice me.

Chest hammering cartoon-like, I weave my way through, slip out the main door completely unnoticed and in the blink of an eye I've escaped outside, clattering my wheelie bag behind me.

Mercifully, the air outside the hotel is cool and I allow myself a few deep, comforting gulps of it, feeling exactly like I've just escaped from Alcatraz. I make a silent vow to call Mum and Dad as soon as I'm safely booked onto a flight, because let's face it, last thing I need after the day I've had are any of my family going to the cops and filing me as a missing persons case.

Mind's made up and this girl is not for turning.

The Merrion Hotel is just round the corner from Stephen's Green, which I race towards as fast as humanly possible, all the while scanning right, left and centre for a cab.

And then, a miracle. Just at the junction of Kildare Street and the Green, with immaculate timing, a taxi turns the corner. I instantly let out an almighty yell at the driver and am just about to shove my way through the crowd to get to him, when a voice from behind suddenly stops me dead in my tracks.

'Any spare change for a hostel, love?'

No, no, no, no, no! Please, please, please don't let it be someone I know, come to haul me back . . . not now! Not when I've got this far! But even through the befuddled haze clouding me, a tiny part of my logical brain says . . . hang on just a sec. Your wedding guests are hardly likely to be out on the streets looking for change for a hostel, now are they?

'I don't drink or do drugs, love, I'm only looking for a bit of spare change.'

I turn sharply round to see a homeless guy just at my feet, huddled under a sleeping bag and shivering, even though it's a warm, balmy evening.

'Even just a few coins would help,' he adds, eyeing up my handbag.

Instinctively, I open the bag to fumble round the bottom of my purse for a few coins . . . and that's when my eye falls on it.

My engagement ring. The one that Frank flew me especially

to New York to buy, just so we could always say it came from Tiffany's. I take a good look down at it. Three tiny neat little diamonds. And much as I loved it, I know I can never look at it again as long as I live.

In an instant, I whip it off my finger and without a second thought, hand it over to the homeless guy.

Will we both be okay, do you think? I wordlessly ask him as our hands momentarily lock.

I don't know, he seems to say, looking lifelessly back up at me.

Two minutes later and I'm in the back of the taxi, speeding out towards the airport. And for the first time in my entire life, I don't have a single clue what tomorrow may bring.

Chapter Two

London, the present.

'Miss Townsend? Miss Chloe Townsend?'

'Yes, indeed,' I smile brightly back. But then I'm a firm believer that when nervous, just look and act confident and effervescent on the outside, and sooner or later, the rest of the world will eventually believe the lie.

'Rob McFayden from Ferndale Hotels,' he nods back, giving me a firm, businesslike handshake. Strong, confident grip.

'Good to meet you and thanks so much for coming along today, especially at short notice. Here, grab a seat.'

I do as he says, but then Rob McFayden from Ferndale Hotels is someone you just automatically do what you're told around. Even guests who've paid handsomely for the privilege, I'd hazard a guess.

'Okay if I call you Chloe? Sorry, but as you probably know, I'm not so big on formality.'

'Yes, that's fine.'

Not so big on formality? I think. *Ha!* Rob McFayden is famous for coming to work in jeans and trainers; almost like he was in such a rush to get there, he ended up sprinting. Rumour has it he's frequently acted as impromptu doorman/receptionist and even barman on the rare occasions when he feels things aren't being done snappily enough in his hotel chain. Received myth is that, at a wedding in his Parisian hotel, he once jumped in and acted as a sous-chef for the night, on account of they were one man short in the kitchen.

Yup, an unpredictable man, by all accounts.

'Great,' he nods curtly back at me. The mighty Rob McFayden doesn't even bother to sit behind his desk either, I notice, like would-be-employers usually do in interviews. Instead, he just rolls up his sleeves and perches casually on the edge of it, as if he's already decided this meeting will take no longer than three minutes, so the application of his bum to the seat is just a waste of time.

'So, I have your CV here, Chloe, and my HR team tell me it's all looking pretty good. Well,' he throws in briskly, 'obviously it's a glowing CV, otherwise, you'd hardly have got through my door in the first place.'

'Well, emm . . . thank you,' I smile tautly, although I'm not actually certain he meant it as a compliment.

Suddenly, the nervy tension between us is shattered as his phone rings. He whips it out of his pocket, checks the number then rolls his eyes.

'Sorry, but do you mind if I take this? It's my Locations Manager in Italy and it's more than likely an emergency.' Then with a wry smile, he adds, 'It inevitably is.'

'Of course not,' I smile overly brightly to compensate for sheer antsiness. 'Please, go right ahead.'

He takes the call, giving me the chance, for the first time, to really get a half-decent look at the guy. A lot younger than I'd have thought, is my initial impression. Early forties at most, salt and pepper slightly greying hair, long, skinny build. Well travelled, lean, all angles. One of those ectomorph body types you'd almost automatically take a dislike to, on account of they can probably eat all they like and never gain a single gram. Well, either that, or the man lives off fags.

Then with a quick, businesslike, 'well, let's set up a meeting with the architect and I'll see you in Milan on Thursday. We'll pick this up then,' he's off the phone.

'Apologies for that,' he says, though not looking at me, instead totally focused on the CV in front of him, eyes darting busily up and down the page. 'So I see you've been working at the Bloomsbury Square Hotel here in London for the past couple of years.'

'Emm . . . yes,' I answer brightly.

'And you're Reservations Manager there . . .' he says absently, still scrutinizing the CV closely.

'That's right!'

'In other words, Chloe,' he says, pointedly using my name, 'you've basically spent the last two years looking after high maintenance guests, unhappy that they weren't allocated a panoramic view and dealing with complaints that the en-suite's not big enough. That sort of thing, yeah?'

I bristle a bit at this, mainly because my job involves a helluva lot more than just basic housekeeping.

'Well, of course, that's *some* of what my work entails, yes,' I answer him, 'but the job isn't just about troubleshooting staffing issues and rotas, but ironing out countless unforeseen guest-related issues on virtually an hour-by-hour basis.'

And don't even get me started on the guests that needed to be 'handled', in much the same way that you'd handle

24

nitroglycerine, I'm about to tell him. But no such luck; he's already moved on.

'But before that, I see you were Functions Manager at the Merrion Hotel over in Dublin,' he says, impatiently tapping a biro off the CV. 'Now that's good, that's more like it. In fact, that's the main reason I wanted to meet you personally this morning. Having an in-depth knowledge of the Irish hotel system would be hugely helpful for this particular job. As I'm sure you'll appreciate.'

'Yes,' I say, 'I thought that might be of interest, alright. Plus as you know, the Merrion is part of the Leading Hotels of the World group, so it was fantastic to gain first-hand experience working in that environment. I loved my time working there,' I tell him, growing more and more confident now I'm talking about what's essentially my passion. What I know and love best.

'Go on,' he says blankly.

'You see, I saw my job as so much more than just making a function such as a wedding, run smoothly. I took it as my personal mission to see that every single bride's dream day was utterly magical in every way that we could possibly make it. After all, every bride deserves her perfect day, doesn't she?'

Good girl, you did it Chloe! You actually managed to get it out. I allow myself a tiny sigh of relief now. Mainly because it took many, many hours of rehearsing that last bit in front of a mirror at home to finally get the wobble out of my voice, but somehow, I think I pulled it off.

'Well, I wouldn't know myself, never having actually been a bride,' says Rob dryly, looking right at me now. 'But if you've brought any back-up with you, I'd love to see it.'

'Of course,' I smile, but then I've come fully prepped

25

for this. Out of my briefcase, I whip a full list of every wedding, fiftieth birthday party and corporate black-tie shindig that I've ever organized and worked on. Back-up photos, the whole works.

'As you'll see here,' I tell Rob, handing it over, 'there was absolutely nothing I wasn't prepared to do for any of our guests, no matter what their budget. I've arranged for doves to be released at midnight, just as one couple asked; I've even organized themed weddings too, from a Caribbean indoor beach theme, to a couple who wanted the hotel dining room transformed into a scene from Hogwarts.'

'Hogwarts? Seriously?' he says, raising an eyebrow.

'Believe me, that was the tip of the iceberg,' I say. 'When the happy couple asked for a fleet of owls to fly in carrying emails from well-wishers in their beaks, that was when we ran into difficulty.'

'I can only imagine,' he says, shaking his head.

'But if you ask me, I think you can sum up any manager's mission statement in a single word. WIT.'

'Which stands for . . .?'

'Whatever it takes,' I say, really feeling in control now. 'Whatever a guest wants, I'll personally jump through hoops to ensure we secure it for them. No matter what.'

'I see,' Rob nods at me, then goes back to scanning through the file I've just presented him with. Now I worked hard on it and am bloody proud of what's in there, but I have to say, so far he looks completely unreadable and not at all bowled over and impressed as I was hoping he would be.

'So you've worked on weddings, functions, birthdays, I get it,' he says again, just that bit unenthused. 'But you see, this particular hotel I'm planning on opening in Dublin will, as you'll appreciate, appeal to a quite specific niche market. So, you want to tell me exactly why you think you'd be right for the job of General Manager there?'

I smile brightly, but then, boy am I ready for this.

'Firstly,' I tell him, taking care to meet the slate grey eyes boring into me now, 'because you see, I'm from Dublin. I know the city upside down and particularly the area around Hope Street, where the hotel will be situated. I've devoted my entire career to working in boutique hotels and have so many ideas I'd love to share with you.'

'Such as?' he says, and I could be mistaken, but swear I pick up just the tiniest spark of interest now. So I really go for it.

'As you say, this will be very much a niche hotel, so let's really appeal to that niche. As well as all the regular function rooms they'd get at any five-star hotel, let's give them so much more. We really have scope to go the extra mile here, so let's do exactly that.'

'Go on,' he says, folding his arms and looking interested now.

'Well, given the emotional intensity of what our guests will be facing, I'd suggest a relaxation room or maybe even a quiet room, for calm reflection. Equally, I'd love to see a games room where more boisterous guests could let off a bit of steam. And the gardens around the Hope Street area are all so quiet and serene, so let's really make a feature of that. We could possibly have a beautiful meditation area outdoors, as well as a water feature.'

'A water feature?'

'The sound of flowing water is really soothing outdoors,' I tell him confidently.

'I'll take your word for it.'

'And we could also have some decking and a barbecue

area, maybe for a final goodbye lunch, when all business has been conducted and before we send our guests on their way.'

'Good, good,' Rob is nodding away at me now and for a brief, shining moment, I think this might just swing things my way. 'But just for the moment, I'd like to get back to your CV,' he says, suddenly changing tack and referring back down to it, inspecting it closely.

Shite. Or maybe not.

'So it seems you worked at the Merrion Hotel for over seven years?' he asks, scrutinizing the CV forensically.

'Emm . . . yes, that's right.'

'Ah, but hang on here a second,' he says, suddenly spotting something that seems to jar with him. 'According to this, you left the Merrion three years ago, but didn't start work here in London months afterwards. Now for a CV like yours, that's quite a lengthy gap. So, I guess my next question is, why?'

'Well, you see,' I begin and for the first time, my voice is now starting to sound just that bit smaller than it has up to now. 'I had come to a point in my career where I felt working abroad would really benefit me on a number of levels.'

But predictably, he's zoned straight into this and won't let up.

'Yeah, but why the long gap? Pretty long time for someone who'd just finished up at the Merrion. Surely if you were planning to work abroad, you'd have locked a new job in place before jumping ship, as it were?'

He's looking at me unflinchingly now. Slate grey eyes, unblinking; the CV in front of him his sole focus.

'The reason being,' I begin nervously, taking a deep

28

breath, and locking eyes with him, then diving into my over-rehearsed answer. 'It just took me some time to find a post that was the right fit for me. As you can see, I'd gained invaluable experience at the Merrion and was anxious to expand my CV even further. I wanted to cover all managerial aspects of the job and if possible, branch out from a Functions Manager's role.'

Can't we just drop this and move on?

'Yeaaaah, but what you're saying still doesn't quite make sense,' he says, lightly tossing my CV aside, almost like he's lost interest in it now. 'You see, I know the Merrion, know it well; I've stayed there. Functions Manager in a hotel like that is a terrific gig anyone your age would kill for. Yet you left to go to London, and then took a lower grade job at a significantly reduced salary. Which strikes me as an incredibly odd thing to do, for someone with all your experience. It seems like a backward career move. Particularly for a manager as highly thought of in the industry as you are. And yes, Chloe, before you ask, please know I've done my homework on you before you even got this meeting.'

I don't say anything, just sit there, ramrod tense; bolt upright in my good work suit from Reiss, too-tight shoes and borrowed handbag, stomach clenched tight, frozen.

I probably blink. And all that's running through my mind on a loop is the one thought. I thought I was doing okay. I actually thought I was handling this. And then one probing question about my past, and I'm suddenly pole-axed.

For the love of God, Rob McFayden, please don't ask me any more . . . don't delve into it . . . just LEAVE it . . .

No such bleeding luck though. He's like a dog with a

bone trying to ferret it out of me now.

'So,' he persists, 'maybe you'd like to elaborate a bit? I guess what I want to know is, what exactly happened to you three years ago to make you leave?'

But my mouth's completely dried up. I lean forward and take a sip of water from the glass in front of me, aware that he's watching me intently, waiting.

Bum-clenchingly awkward silence now and all I can think is, *answer him, you eejit, you want this job, this is your dream job! So just look him in the eye and tell him the truth.*

Can't though. Just not possible. I think back to the searing pain, so sharp that even thinking back to it now, from a safe distance of years, I can still recall every detail on an almost cellular level.

Then I remember those first few dismal weeks in London, staying with an old college pal who I must have driven demented with the depressive state of me. I remember what a bloody struggle it was to get any kind of gig in the hotel industry at all back then, but how I just knew that hard work and lots of it would somehow pull me through. The only antidote that would have any kind of an effect on me.

And so yes, I accepted a lower grade job on a reduced salary and you know what, Rob McFayden? I was more than delighted to. Frankly, I'd have done anything that came my way; scrubbed pots and pans, scoured toilet floors if they'd asked me to. I worked and slaved behind my desk, doing every spare hour of overtime that came my way. I became the best, most devoted Reservations Manager in the Northern hemisphere. Christmas, New Year's Eve, bank holiday weekends; you name it. I basically volunteered for all the time slots that no one else wanted. I've had virtually next to no life here in London, it's just been a never-ending rota of either working, sleeping or catching up on laundry I allowed to pile up, on account of I was working. Wow, what a whopping big surprise.

And then miraculously, out of the blue and just when I was at my lowest ebb, I was headhunted for this job. My ideal job. The chance to manage my very own hotel, a tiny boutique one that appealed to a small, niche market. A very particular niche market as it happens, one that just happened to suit me down to the ground. And it seemed like everything I wanted all at once. A better job, a salary more in line with what I was used to, the chance to return home, back to Ireland and best of all, the chance to really prove myself. Because if I could make a hotel like this one work, then boy, I'd be ready for anything.

I'd lived with humiliation and pain for long enough now. I missed my family and pals. Enough with the punishment, time to move on. No more of this self-imposed exile, I'd had enough. And yes, I'm sure what happened to me was the talk of the town for a while, but it's in the past now, so why should I let that stop me pursuing what pretty much is a dream job on a decent salary? I may have been dead-ened on the inside, but one thing was certain: I was as ready to go back as I ever would be.

I eyeball Rob McFayden, take a deep breath and go for it.

'I had to leave my old job,' I tell him, 'for personal reasons that trust me, you don't need to know about. Besides, a single phone call to the Merrion Hotel will doubtless fill

31

you in on everything you want to know. But if anyone is qualified to run a hotel where broken-hearted people come to put their lives back together and move on, then believe me, I'm your girl.'

Chapter Three

A divorce hotel. Where you check in married and check out single. And yes, you did read that right. 'A safe sanctuary to go to when you suddenly found your whole life was in shreds and you were no longer able to see the wood for the trees,' just like the blurb said.

But it was envisaged to be an awful lot more; this was to be somewhere supportive, non-judgmental, healing even. A place where people who'd long ago ceased to love each other could meet in a calm, stress-free environment with trained professionals on hand to help and offer guidance.

For starters, there'd be a full team of industry professionals on hand to ease the soon-to-be-ex-couple through the process and to make it as fast and efficient as could be. Family lawyers, financial advisors, counsellors, you name it. There'd even be an estate agent on site, just in case jointly held property needed to be valued and subsequently sold. Absolutely everything had been thought of and nothing had been left to chance. This would be a place where two unhappy souls could quickly tie up loose ends and where something that had long been a source of acute pain to both, could gently be eased out of its misery. Kind of like Dignitas, except for the married.

At least, that was the general idea.

Of course I thought I was hearing things when I first stumbled across the whole concept. 'Stone mad lunatics,' I'd muttered to myself way back then, when I'd read about the opening of the world's first divorce hotel over in Amsterdam.

For starters, who in their sane mind would ever want to stay there? Let alone work in the kind of place where not a single guest even wanted to be in the first place? Just wait till you see, this daft idea will end up the laughing stock of the whole industry, I'd thought way back then, doubtless cackling like the wicked witch in *The Wizard of Oz*.

But that was then and this is now, and pretty soon I discovered the bittersweet taste of having to eat my own words. Because how wrong was I?

The divorce hotel concept is only about two years old now, virtually still a tiny baby in nappies, in hotelier terms. And yet in that relatively short window of time, it has not only met every single one of its financial targets, but managed to astonish the industry as a whole by actually exceeding them. No mean feat, in the middle of the biggest global economic meltdown since the Wall Street crash had everyone out queuing up outside soup kitchens, circa 1929.

The original divorce hotel which had opened on the outskirts of Amsterdam, was virtually minuscule by industry standards, with a bare twenty-five rooms. And yet occupancy had never once dipped below full since it first began trading. No other word for that in this day and age except un-be-fecking-lievable. So there was nothing for me to do, bar shake my head in astonished admiration, same as everyone else, while wishing like hell I could somehow inveigle myself onto the bandwagon.

So of course, it was only a matter of time before the up and coming Rob McFayden, with his finger ever on the pulse, got in on the act. A rival hotel group had already pitched to unveil a divorce hotel in London, so he began to look a little further afield. And thought, why not open one in a thriving, cosmopolitan city like Dublin? Which, thank you Ryanair, is easy to access, no matter what corner of Europe you happen to be in. A country famous for its hospitality and charm. And more importantly, as Rob told me at my initial interview, with a calculating glint in his eye, where he could negotiate a lease on a building for approximately a third of what he'd probably end up paying in central London.

I read that you can always remember exactly where and when you were whenever a life-changing phone call comes. But in my case I happened to be in Asda, buying loo rolls and a tin of Whiskas for a stray tabby cat that comes in to visit me whenever the mood takes her.

My mobile rang suddenly. Ferndale Hotels. I remember getting instant heart palpitation, shortness of breath, the works.

'Miss Townsend? Chloe Townsend?' came a crisp, efficient voice down the phone.

'Emm . . . speaking,' I stammered nervously as an irritating automated machine wailed 'Unidentified item in the baggage area.'

'Congratulations,' she said. 'Rob McFayden would like to offer you a contract as General Manager and we very much look forward to welcoming you to the Ferndale Hotel team.'

I think they must have heard my whoops of joy all the way to the back of the deli counter. Finally, finally, finally my life was turning around. And given what I'd been through, could there ever have been a job more tailor-made to suit me? Rob McFayden, I knew, was taking a huge chance on giving me the GM's job and over my dead body was I about to let anyone down. To make a hotel like this work anywhere on the planet would be a dream come true, but to make it work in Dublin, on my home turf meant so much more.

But, as was painstakingly outlined to me during my initial orientation training, there were many hard and fast rules to be observed. Rule one, though, was particularly hard for me to get my head round, seeing as how it was in flagrant contradiction of every other hotel on the face of the planet, where as long as a guest a) had cash enough to pay their bill and b) didn't look like they were physically going to trash the room and nick all the light fittings, then, as far as management were concerned, everyone was welcome.

But not at a divorce hotel, it seemed. Here, it was like the Alice in Wonderland of standard practice, where received wisdom was turned upside down. Strict protocol here was that only a couple who were on 'cordial terms' could be allowed to come and stay in the first place. And how could you possibly hope to do that, if you'd two exes still at the stage of wanting to hurl furniture across the room at each other?

Another hard and fast rule was that all couples had to be interviewed, either separately or together, just so that, as General Manager, I could be certain that this was the right place, at the right time for them. After all, no divorce hotel was to be confused with a marriage guidance coun-sellor's office. This procedure was all about neat and final closure, not accusations and recriminations and rows and bitterness and who got the lawnmower/flat screen telly/ leather sofa from IKEA.

Rule three was discretion. Utter and total discretion from all staff, at all times, about what went on within the four walls. And of all people, I understood all too well the acute need for fat gobs to be swiftly silenced, when you were going through something so private and acutely painful. Are you kidding me? I could probably teach a course in it by now.

On the plus side though, here was what newly separated couples got for their buck at your standard divorce hotel. No matter where you happened to live in the world and no matter what jurisdiction bound you legally, there's one 'truth universally acknowledged' that you can absolutely put your house on.

For anyone who finds themselves in the position of looking for a divorce, you've basically got two options. Either you go to court, have a lengthy, protracted – and doubtless expensive – case, where every single detail of your personal family life would be aired in a public courtroom. With absolutely no dirty linen left unexamined.

Humiliating, mortifying, prohibitively expensive and the end of it all, what would the net result most likely be? By and large, you'd get one third of the couple's joint assets, he'd have a third and the lawyers ultimately would make off with the final third.

And now suddenly here's a viable alternative. Given that this is undoubtedly a process both parties will want to get over and done with as quickly as possible, why not check into discreetly luxurious surroundings and get the whole thing sorted out in a single weekend? And with cocktails on the side? After all, there's nothing to be gained from dragging out the whole process. This way, instead of lawyers carrying off a vast chunk of the couple's joint assets, everything would be split fifty-fifty, fairly and equitably down the middle.

Best of all, no matter what stage a couple happened to be at in their separation, they could still check into a divorce hotel and at least get the final settlement set in stone. Then all the couple need do would be to bide their time and live their separate lives apart, until such time as they could appear before a judge, hand over their agreement, a gavel was walloped and they were formally granted a decree nisi. Easy as that.

A divorce hotel strove to make something complicated, simple.

Best of all, the premises that Ferndale Hotels had leased for their hotel in Dublin might as well have been purpose built for the job. Elegant and utterly discreet, it was one of those four-storey Georgian redbricks on Hope Street, just off leafy Fitzwilliam Square, surrounded by accountants' and lawyers' offices. The hotel's name wasn't even written on a canopy over the door, instead there was just a neat brass plaque saying, 'Ferndale Hotels, Hope Street.' Subtle and inconspicuous, its message clear. No one need ever know you're a guest, not unless you want them to.

'The Hope Street Hotel,' as it quickly came to be known.

*

So I'm officially based back in Dublin now and oh thank you God, it feels so good to be home! Even if I've been so run off my feet that I've barely had the chance to spend any quality time with my best mate Gemma or any of the old gang. Somehow just being here, doing a job that's challenging and yet that I really feel can and will take off, is firing me up and propelling me through each busy day until we formally open for business.

Plus of course, being this overloaded with work means I've absolutely zero time to think about the one and only blight on the horizon. The all-too-real possibility that I might just be standing in the vegetable aisle in Marks & Spencer's with greasy hair and no make-up, turn a corner and then walk slap bang into the whole reason why I high-tailed it over to London for as long as I did.

Frank. Or as Gemma refers to him, He Whose Name Shall Forever Remain Unspoken. Now, my spies tell me, promoted to Assistant General Manager at my old stomping ground, the Merrion Hotel, barely a stone's throw from Hope Street. I imagine bumping into him with such punishing frequency it would scare you. But I stop myself from going any further. After all, this business venture is about helping others through their broken relationships. And not dwelling on my own troubles. At least not now. Not yet.

But he'll be watching my progress here, I know he will, as will half the industry. So this is it then; my one and only chance not to be the girl who bolted from a perfectly good job because of what I went through. This is my shot at proving not just to Frank, but to all our old colleagues and not least to myself, that I can make this work. That I can make a success of this; that I can make it fly.

'I think it's amazing what you're trying to achieve here,' Gemma says to me over a hasty lunch break I manage to snatch. 'But I just have one question for you.'

'Fire away,' I say, between mouthfuls of takeout sushi.

'Don't get me wrong, the Hope Street Hotel sounds like a great concept and everything,' she says, shaking her head in puzzlement. 'But mother of God, given that all of your guests will be going through marriage break-ups . . .'

'Yeah?'

'Well, sweetheart . . . exactly what kind of dramas are you going to end up having to deal with?'

Chapter Four

Dawn.

Still in total shock, but at that numb stage where you can somehow function purely on automatic pilot, Dawn took one final moment to have a last, quick look around the tiny little shoebox of an apartment she and Kirk had been sharing, ever since they'd first been married. A poky flat above an Indian takeaway in town that permanently stank of garlic and onions, no matter how many cans of air freshener she went through.

The tiny part of her brain somehow getting her through the hell she was stuck in, reminded her that of late, the place been starting to drive her insane anyway. The constant stench of grease from the takeaway mixed with prawns well past their use-by date. And how noisy it got from about midnight onwards, when drunk revellers would nip in for a cheap vindaloo, then start calling each other wankers at the top of their voices on the street outside.

For as long as she and Kirk had lived here, they'd always planned to move on, just as soon as they could properly afford to, but of late, all the chats they used to have about their ideal pad had fizzled out. Almost as though each of them silently recognized it was pointless, because this day would inevitably come.

Just not like this, Dawn thought suddenly, shaking from head to foot, as the enormity of what she was about to do really hit home. Not this way. They'd been happy here. In many ways, they were still happy. Kirk was her best friend, her right hand, her go-to person. This would devastate him, but then he'd devastated her first, and like a child that knew no other way of expressing hurt, all she could do was try and inflict the same degree of pain right back instead.

So are you really prepared to do this? she asked herself for about the thousandth time that miserable day. *Just run away from the problem and not at least try to work through it?*

Yes was the answer. Because what he'd done had completely broken them forever. How could she possibly stay in this now? Just what kind of a doormat would that make her?

Suddenly overcome by a crashing wave of exhaustion, Dawn slumped down onto their tiny sofa bed and tried her best to sit still for a moment, at least until her head stopped spinning.

For a split second, her eye momentarily fell on a wedding photo on top of the bookshelf and she found herself dithering for a minute, wondering what she should do with it. Leave it where it was to remind Kirk that he had actually made a solemn vow that day? After all, he was the one who was forever saying that, 'a vow was a promissory note against your soul.' That that's how much getting married had meant to him way back then. Okay, so most of the time he was stoned off his head when he did come out with it, but still, the sentiment was there. Or would she just angrily fling it into the bin, so he could gauge for himself exactly how she felt about what had just happened?

She took a last second to really look at the photo. Her dream wedding. Or 'that hippy-dippy, tree-hugging fiasco' as her mother liked to refer to it. Hard to believe that it had been taken just a few short years ago. Has it really been that long, she wondered, her heart suddenly twisting in her ribcage as she thought back to that young, hopeful girl, so in love with this guy that she'd have happily walked through flames for him.

Yet there she was in the photo, in that cheap little maxi dress from Penny's, long bedraggled hair down to her bum, arms locked tight around Kirk, looking adoringly into his gentle, brown eyes. With their whole lives in front of them, rolling out like a red carpet.

Feck's sake, sure we're just a pair of kids in this photo, she thought, sudden anger flooding through her. And the problem now is we're all grown up, just in two very different directions.

Dawn even looked a bit different these days. While Kirk still looked exactly the same today as he had in the wedding photo, the past few years had changed her dramatically. Well, she'd had to evolve a bit, didn't she? After all, there was only so much tree hugging and chakra realigning a person could do, without realizing that was hardly going to pay the rent and keep them both in mobile phone subscriptions and Sky Plus.

Besides, Dawn had by now been promoted to manager of Earth's Garden, the health food store she worked in and was pulling in a not-too-shabby wage these days. So of course, she needed to look the part. Plus she'd recently discovered a tiny niche in the market for spelt muesli, to

43

great encouragement from Kirk, who'd help out with the business whenever he wasn't teaching his yoga class. And now she was importing it in herself and selling it through the store for a nifty return.

NLE Enterprises, the two of them jokingly called her tiny, fledgling company. Nice Little Earner. Kirk had even talked her into donating a hefty percentage of their profits towards a goat farm outside Nairobi. Mind you, left to Dawn, she'd have been far happier using the cash to move to a better flat, but then Kirk did have a point. After all, one goat farm in Africa could keep a whole village going. And it was the right thing to do, the ethical thing.

Wasn't it?

Anyway, these days Dawn acted and dressed like what she'd grown into, an up-and-coming owner of a small but steadily growing business. Out with all the hippy-dippy long, flowing clobber he used to love on her and in with neat work trousers and crisp white shirts from Zara.

In the early days, Kirk used to laugh at her and tell her she looked a bit like she was going out to repossess a house, but she'd noticed even that gentle teasing had completely ground to a halt of late. Like he barely even noticed her now. Yet another sign something was up. Just her bad luck, she thought bitterly, that it wasn't what she'd automatically assumed. The first conclusion any wife in similar circumstances would jump to.

Dawn allowed herself one final glance down at her wedding photo. With almost digital clarity, she could remember how stung she'd been that day at all the nasty, sniping comments streaming incessantly from 'her side'; her mother and sister Eva, not to mention all her mates from work. The way they kept on griping because nothing about the commitment ceremony had been right for them; all they could do was find fault wherever they looked.

But right at this moment, if she could go back in time, Dawn honestly thought that instead of allowing them all to get to her, instead she'd have berated the lot of them from the bottom of her hot little heart for letting her go through with it in the first place. Jesus, she'd only been twenty-two years of age! She hadn't the first clue what she was letting herself in for! Instead of moaning about the hemp wine, the lack of a DJ playing Beyoncé and the general crappiness of the sitar music, her mother and sister, not to mention all her pals, should have physically arm-wrestled her to the floor rather than letting her go through with it.

As for her? She must have been out of her mind not to realize this day would eventually dawn. Just not in this way. And not for the love of God, like this.

Peeling herself off the sofa, Dawn began to haul her packed suitcases as far as the door so she'd at least be ready when her taxi arrived. Then a quick, last minute spot check around the place, to make sure she hadn't left anything important behind. She tried to distract herself with petty, inconsequential stuff, like checking whether she'd remembered to pack shampoo, the charger for her phone and the last of the Hobnobs, just because they were Kirk's favourites and it would bloody well serve him right.

But whether she liked it or not, shockwaves kept searing through her like some kind of laser. She couldn't keep it out; it wouldn't stop intruding.

Of course, she blamed herself for not bloody well copping on sooner. For not guessing the truth, before it had to be spelled out to her. For God's sake, it had been exactly ten months, three weeks and four days since Kirk had even looked at her as anything other than a flatmate and pal! She could quite literally pin the last time they'd slept together down to a date. Was she really naïve enough to think that the two of them were sailing blissfully towards their silver wedding anniversary?

Even though her brains were like mince right now, that particular date still stuck like a limpet in her addled mind on account of it had been his birthday. Not many people could tell you exactly when they first suspected something was seriously up with their marriage, but she'd been able to sense as far back as then, that something wasn't right. She could practically smell it.

After all this was Kirk, who'd at one stage been so unbelievably passionate, exulting in her body, barely able to keep his hands off her. He wasn't even particularly bothered if the two of them happened to be out in public, something he tended to view as little more than a challenge to be overcome and nothing more. (Quite literally. And Dawn just thanked Christ the deer in the Phoenix Park wouldn't ever talk and left it at that.)

Ten months, three weeks and four days for a man who'd always been so physical and loving and . . . no other word for it . . . *experimental* in bed, she thought sadly. And God knows, it wasn't as though she hadn't made an effort. Over her dead body was she just allowing the two of them to slide into this new routine of long bedtime chats, laughs, giggles and then maybe a friendly cuddle before drifting off to sleep. Like some kind of middle-aged 'auld ones who'd slid into not having sex any more and instead just worried about their two point four kids and the variable mortgage.

Not a chance, this gal wasn't going down without a

protracted fight. She'd more than done her bit to try and spice things up between them, hadn't she? She'd tried her level best to recapture their first heady days and months together, when it was all sex and talking and still more talking and then rolling over for yet another bout of furious, unquenchable lovemaking. Surely no counsellor or therapist could fault her on that score?

Flushing a bit in mortification now, Dawn thought back to what a naïve eejit she must have seemed back then. How she'd forked out on all that highly uncomfortable hooker underwear, then shoehorned herself into it, in the vain hopes that the sight of her kitted out like something from a porno movie might reignite that old spark in Kirk. After all, before they'd ever met, he'd had legions of girlfriends and a tiny part of Dawn always worried that sex-wise, she didn't quite measure up.

But no, nothing doing. Instead, he'd just look her up and down, smile lazily up at her and ask whether or not those knickers felt like wrapping her nether regions up in dental floss and why wasn't she howling in agony anyway?

Then of course, Kirk would do what he was starting to excel at lately; turn it all into a joke and pull her in for a cuddle, as the two of them just slid companionably back into their old routine. They'd always been best friends, but whereas back in those incredible early days, they'd been lovers first and best friends second, lately they'd settled into being just each other's closest pal. And that was where it ended.

Back then though, Dawn had known no better, so she fought and kept on fighting. She winced to think about it now but at the time, sheer desperation drove her to act like she was up for anything. At one point, in a blood rush to

47

the head, she'd even contemplated suggesting a threesome. Last thing she herself would ever have wanted, the whole idea completely repulsed her, but then Kirk used to be up for anything sex-wise, and if this was what it would take to reignite things . . .

Took her all of about ten seconds to completely scrap the idea. Sorry, but sharing Kirk with some nameless faceless one from the internet or worse still, with someone they knew and knowing Dawn's luck, would more than likely bump into in the aisle at Tesco's, was just unthinkable.

But she'd lost count of the number of romantic nights à deux she'd tried to plan in their tiny flat, just for the two of them. Candles dotted around the place, romantic dinner, wine, sure you know yourself. With any luck, that would turn into one of those wonderful nights they used to have back in their early days, when Kirk would gently massage her and things naturally developed on from there.

For the past few months, Dawn had been trying this tactic as often as she could, yet every single time without fail, you could be bloody sure Kirk would try and find some way to weasel out of things going any further than companionable hugs and cuddles.

No, Dawn wasn't blind and she certainly wasn't stupid.

What happened was just the final proof she needed.

She was zipping up her wheelie bag and just doing a last, final spot check to make sure she hadn't left any of her face creams behind in the bathroom, when suddenly her mobile rang.

'Taxi for Dawn Madden?' growled a twenty-a-day smoker's voice down the phone.

'Be downstairs in two minutes,' Dawn told him, before hanging up.

Do it quickly, she told herself. *Just go now, fast while you still have some ounce of resolve in you.*

Trembling weakly, she grabbed hold of the last of her wheelie bags and slammed the door behind her.

And just like that, she thought, my marriage is over.

*

'Jaysus love, that's a fair amount of luggage you have,' said her taxi driver, as he helped Dawn load up the boot of the cab with one stuffed case after another. 'Taking a trip, are you? Airport, is it?'

'Emm, no actually,' Dawn said weakly, praying he wouldn't try to draw her out any further. No rudeness intended, but she just hadn't the strength to go into it, not now. She hopped into the back seat and gave him Eva's address, praying he wouldn't try to probe her much more.

'Ahh, I get it, you're moving flat then, are you?' the driver said in that gravelly voice, two slitty eyes glancing at her reflection in his rear-view mirror as they sped off into the traffic.

Dawn just about managed a tiny little nod and hoped against hope he'd take the hint that she wasn't really up for small talk. As it happened though, she was in luck; just a few more monosyllabic answers from her about the general crapness of the weather/direness of the traffic, and thankfully, he seemed to take the hint. Switching the car radio on, he tuned into one of those early afternoon moany phone-in shows, where callers ring in to rant about the general rubbishness of the health service, or else their dole being cut, etc.

Nerves still on edge, Dawn took a deep breath and looked out the window, for the moment at least tuning out the incensed voices bleating over the radio about the price of wheelie bin lifts. And that's when she saw it.

Suddenly, right beside her, a wedding car pulled up at the traffic lights. A sleek Bentley, with white ribbons fluttering at the front. And there, in the back seat, directly opposite her was a beautiful young bride, with a stunning white veil and what looked like a fabulously expensive dress on underneath. There was an elderly man right beside her, whose face looked flushed with either whiskey or pride, it was hard to tell. Her Dad, Dawn figured with a pang, there to give her away.

For a momentary second as both cars were stopped side-by-side, the bride locked eyes with hers. Ordinarily, Dawn would have waved and smiled and given a thumbs up, but somehow she couldn't bring herself to. Not today. Not after what she'd just come through.

Wish me luck? the bride's eyes seemed to ask her nervously.

I'm sorry but . . . please understand – I just can't, Dawn answered simply, looking right back at her.

The traffic lights changed, the wedding car glided gracefully on and now, Dawn found herself thinking back to another young, hopeful bride on another grey, drizzly day just like this; full of love and happiness and optimism about what lay ahead. Her eyes misted up a bit and suddenly, she found her thoughts drifting.

*

'I Kirk, take you Dawn, to be my beloved spouse and partner in life, to stand with you always, in times of celebration and in times of sorrow, times of joy and in times of pain, times of sickness and in times of health. I will live with you, love and cherish you, as long as we both shall live.'

Slight ripple of polite applause, which the High Shaman immediately silenced with an authoritative slamming of his ceremonial stick off the rickety wooden floor.

Scary looking git, Dawn thought, from out of nowhere. Where did Kirk find him, anyway? He'd nearly put you in mind of Professor Dumbledore from Hogwarts, right down to the heavy bushy white eyebrows, which from where she was standing, looked exactly like guttering that would overhang a building.

With a jolt, she realized Dumbledore was nodding in her direction that this was her cue. The Big Moment.

Concentrate Dawn, she told herself. You're about to get married here.

'And I Dawn,' she began in a wobbly voice, 'take you Kirk as my beloved spouse and partner in life, to tenderly care for you and to respect your individuality, to cherish you just as you are and to love you with complete fidelity. Always.'

A few 'oohs' and 'ahhs' from around the blessing area as Kirk beamed happily down at her; that gorgeous, dimply smile that never failed to completely knock the wind out of her.

'Then Kirk and Dawn,' the Shaman boomed on, sounding not unlike Darth Vader as his voice reverberated around the tiny, enclosed blessing area. 'By the power vested in me which derives over centuries from the ancient druids, I now declare you life partners joined in spiritual union, from this day forth!'

Massive round of applause as Kirk leaned down to kiss his brand new bride and Dawn stood up on tiptoe to whisper in his ear.

'I love you, so, so much.'

'And I'll love you always.'

Even though it had been a barefoot ceremony, Kirk still towered above her; tall, wiry, lean and so ridiculously handsome with the long, waist-length black hair and flowing white linens; God, Dawn almost wanted to laugh every time she looked at that beautiful face. I'll never be as happy again, she thought, as I am today. Just wouldn't be possible . . . sure, how could it be?

Hard though, not to be aware that at that very moment, her mother, up in the very front row, had abandoned dabbing away at the odd tear and was by now sobbing violently in full-blown floods.

'Ehh . . . happy tears, would you say?' Kirk had whispered softly, shooting her Mum a look of concern.

No, her mother's tears definitely weren't happy ones. But it had still been a beautiful commitment service in spite of everything, Dawn forced herself to think, smiling bravely. If you could momentarily just leave aside the tsunami of negativity she and Kirk practically had to wade through, just so they could stand in front of each other that day. All the endless, countless objections from her family, because they were both so ridiculously young.

Not that age even mattered, Dawn had spent at least six months before the wedding trying to convince just about everyone she knew. Like Kirk said, your age was just your number! Besides, when you knew, you just knew. And this was for life. She knew. Just knew.

'It's all just too much, too soon!' her Mum had wailed, when Dawn broke the news that she was committed. (Kirk didn't believe in the word 'engaged'; too many negative connotations.)

'And what in God's name, I'd like to know, are the pair of you going to live off?' she'd added crisply. 'His earnings as a yoga instructor? The land? Good luck with that, my girl!'

Implication heard and understood loud and clear. You're only twenty-two years of age, missy, and you haven't the first clue about either life or love. Wait and see, you'll come running back quick enough just as soon as you start missing all the cushiness of home and having an M&S within a two-mile radius of the house. And when you realize that modern conveniences like electricity, heating and Sky Atlantic can't be paid for by offering to send free Reiki and homemade yeast-free cookies into the ESB head office.

A far greater disappointment though, had been Eva, who hadn't exactly been leading conga lines around tables either, when she was first told the Big News.

'Oh honey,' she'd said worriedly, 'I know you've always bought into that whole mind, body, spirit thing, but . . .'

Dawn braced herself, instinctively sensing what was coming next.

'But the thing is, I really have to speak my mind here or forever hold my peace. And the truth is that you're rushing headlong into this. For God's sake, you and Kirk only met a few months ago, this is complete insanity! So there now, I said it. It's out there.'

'Totally untrue, not to mention unfair!' Dawn retorted defensively. 'Besides, Kirk always says no one can measure the depths of love just in units of time . . .'

'Yeah, right,' Eva had muttered under her breath, as she sipped at her Pinot Grigio and angrily nibbled the bar nuts in front of her, tight-lipped. 'I'll bet he does.'

Instinctively, Dawn had gone to diffuse the tension by hopping down off the stool she was perched on and giving Eva a spontaneous, tight bear hug.

53

'Ah here,' said Eva, impatiently shoving her away, 'what's with you suddenly hugging people for absolutely no reason? You nearly made me spill red wine all over my good suit!'

'Just dispelling the negative energy between us,' Dawn smiled, 'that's all.'

'You never used to be like this,' Eva said tersely, with her chin jutted out like she was gumming for a good, air-clearing row.

'Like what?'

'Like . . . well, you know.'

'No,' said Dawn, genuinely puzzled. 'No, I don't know.'

'Alright then, you never used to behave like the way you're carrying on these days. Like such a bloody flake-head.'

'What did you just say?'

'Come on, Dawn, surely you must see that guy has totally changed you! You used to be . . . normal. You know, fun to hang around with. But now all you want to do is sit around talking about what a fabulous soul Kirk is, or else telling me that my chakras are all out of alignment. And now you want to throw your whole life away before it's barely even started, with someone you barely even know? For God's sake, it's almost a bit like Kirk and that shower of nutters he's related to have sucked you into some kind of religious cult! You'll be shaving your head, wearing orange robes and dancing up and down Grafton Street next, you mark my words.'

Love and forgive, Dawn had to work very hard at remembering, biting back the instinct to defend the man she'd once adored so much. She and Eva had always been close, in spite of a five-year age gap, even more so since their

Dad had passed away years ago, when they were just kids. Eva had always been the perfect older sister, always watching out for her, always being there for her, no matter what. A thumbs up from her meant the world to Dawn.

And yet here it was, the single biggest thing ever to happen in Dawn's life and now all Eva could do was shake her head, wag her finger and tell her she was off her head insane. Hard to sit there and take it and pretend that it didn't bloody well sting. Even if looking back now, all her dire predictions had all proved one hundred per cent on the money.

Still though, in spite of all the many, many objections from far, far too many people to list, the whole wedding really had been magical from start to finish. At least, so Dawn had thought at the time.

After the initial blessing ceremony, everyone sat in a 'circle of harmony', as the High Shaman referred to it, and an Apache tribal poem was read out, to much sniggering from Sheila and Amy, Dawn's pals from the health food store where she worked. The pair of them kept nudging each other and loudly asking when someone would start playing a bit of Beyoncé, same as at any normal wedding. And whether or not there was a minibar anywhere close by?

'Try the elderberry wine,' Dawn had smiled encouragingly over at them. 'Exact same effect, far less of a hangover!'

'And for God's sake,' she remembered her mother audibly hissing, 'why do we all have to sit cross-legged and barefoot on the floor for this nonsense, anyway? My outfit is getting completely ruined!'

'Mine and all,' grumbled her Mum's best friend Maisie,

who they'd had to invite too. 'And when I think of all the trouble the pair of us went to, just to find shoes to match our outfits! Then they make you leave them at the door? Ridiculous carry on.'

'Just chill out and try to enjoy it all,' Dawn had told them both soothingly. 'Here, try some organic papaya tea, you'll like it.'

'I'd give anything for a normal cup of tea, but I'll pass on that green stuff thanks,' her mother sniffed. 'I'm not a huge fan of dishwater, as it happens.'

Dawn wisely chose to let it go. Yet another life lesson she'd been conquering, thanks to how masterful a guide Kirk was. And God knows, she'd certainly had plenty of practice of banishing all negativity to the ether where it belonged, in the run up to that wedding.

But however bad things got for her – and they only went from bad to worse – Kirk had always been there for her.

'Remember it's only because your mother loves you so much,' he'd gently remind Dawn. 'You're her youngest child and she's like a mother tiger protecting and defending you. Besides, in time, she'll see that we're doing the right thing. After all, there's nothing wrong with meeting your soulmate young, now is there?'

Kirk's family, at least had been a little more on board about the whole thing, but then the Lennox-Coyninghams could be accused of being many things, but erring on the conservative side when it came to marriage would hardly be one of them. Kirk's Dad, Dessie, who went around in Jesus sandals and flowing kaftans even in the depths of winter, was already on his fifth 'life partner', and had fathered no fewer than eleven children.

An eccentric family, the Lennox-Coyninghams, to put it mildly.

At the wedding, Dawn remembered the part she'd looked forward to most, when the High Shaman brought an end to all the bonding rituals and finally said Kirk 'could now kiss his beautiful bride and life partner'. To this day, she could still vividly remember him leaning down to her, brushing her waist-length hair away from her face, then really going for it. Tongues, feeling her boobs, the whole works. Not even caring that a whole roomful of guests were staring right at them, most of them clapping and cheering happily. Most of them.

Jesus, Dawn thought, pulling his beautiful body in tightly to her, would tonight ever come and would it ever be just the two of them finally alone? Just for one moment, she wished she could fast-forward through the rest of the whole day and cut straight to the wedding night. And from the sexy way Kirk's tongue was teasing hers, he seemed to be on exactly the same wavelength as her too. Wasn't he always? Back then, at least.

Sex you see, was where Kirk really excelled; Mother of Divine, Dawn had never known anything like being in bed with him. With him it had been breathtakingly unbelievable . . . acrobatic, even Olympian at times. Okay, so maybe a tad exhausting, but still beyond fabulous. Sure, who wouldn't envy her with a husband and lover like that, she remembered thinking.

Oh, the blessed irony.

Then, after their final blessing, they'd had the gifting ceremony, a truly magical experience, where Dawn and Kirk sat cross-legged in the centre of the Circle of Giving, as well-wishers queued up to give the newlyweds a little something. And the parade of gifts they were presented with really went no end towards cheering Dawn up a bit.

It was so touching, she'd thought, tuning out all the negative vibes, just how generous people had been with gifts, not to mention so imaginative. They'd been given a backpack picnic basket from Willow and Dave, matching his 'n' her tie-dye linen shirts from Shiloh, a two-foot-high lemon tree from Poppy ('so when life gives you lemons, you can both make lemonade!'), a 'fruit of the month' club subscription from Josh and Sammie and last but not least, a coffee maker from Kirk's Dad, Dessie. Which he then proudly whipped open to reveal a three-kilo bag of weed inside.

'So you kids can really enjoy tonight!'

'He grows his own!' Kirk had proudly announced to the room, exactly the same as if he was talking about his Dad's prize-winning petunias. 'And it's the best!'

'Sweet Mother of Divine!' Dawn overheard her Mum muttering, fanning her flushed face with the order of service.

'Ehh . . . and that's his idea of a wedding gift?' Eva hissed back at her. 'Out of curiosity, have these people ever come across an IKEA catalogue?'

Probably the only time all day her Mum had even cracked a smile.

Dawn flashed the pair of them a lightning quick warning look, for all the good it did her. Why did her side all have to be like this, she'd thought disappointedly, as a shadow suddenly fell across her happy day. So relentlessly rude about everyone and everything? Constantly putting the whole celebration down and finding fault every single place

58

they looked? Why couldn't any of her family or friends just chill out, relax and celebrate her happiness, like at any other wedding? Why, she wondered for the thousandth time, couldn't they just be a bit more like Kirk's family?

The Lennox-Coyninghams were all so cool, so laid back, so free and easy. Drinking the elderberry wine, munching on the yeast-free, gluten-free, non-dairy nibbles, laughing, celebrating, actually enjoying themselves. Like you were supposed to at a wedding. None of them were openly sniping and griping about the day in front of the newlyweds, now were they?

Disappointedly, Dawn snuggled into the crook of Kirk's arm and he locked her tight in his arms.

'Just let it all float away, sweetheart,' he whispered down to her, correctly reading her thoughts. 'Just remember, we're life partners now and that's all that matters.'

Then at midnight, there had been a very moving tree dedication ceremony but the warm, happy glow on Dawn's day dimmed even further when she realized her Mum wasn't even there for it. Eventually, she found her in the eco-loos, sobbing her heart out.

'Oh Mum, please don't,' Dawn had said, instinctively going to hug her. 'This is a happy day!'

'I can't do this,' her mother sobbed, not even bothering to dab away the tears now that had completely destroyed all her carefully applied make-up. 'I can't sit back and watch you make the biggest mistake of your life. I can't and I won't.'

'But it's not a mistake, Mum. I love Kirk, you know that. And this is forever.'

'Forever! What does a twenty-two-year-old understand about the word forever? You haven't the first clue what you're even talking about!'

'Don't do this, Mum. I'm so, so happy and I want you to be too.'

But Dawn was wasting her time and she knew it. Still and all though, she thought, as the night began to wind down, she'd somehow still managed to have a magical day, in spite of her side's best efforts to sabotage it all.

And then, finally, finally, finally, come about 2 a.m., she and Kirk were at last left alone in the Mongolian yurt they'd been given especially for the night.

Dawn was perched at the edge of the bed, shaking loose her plum-tinted, scraggly hair and unhooking the back of her plain white dress, when suddenly Kirk was over beside her, arms locked tight around her waist, jet black mop of his long, silky hair buried deep into her neck.

'Thank you, my love,' he murmured.

'For what?'

'For doing this. For committing to me today. For loving me the way I love you.'

'Always,' she'd whispered back, slipping out of her dress, kicking it aside and abandoning it on the floor. What the feck. It only cost fifteen euro in Penny's anyway.

'Just remember,' she told him lovingly, 'this is for always.'

'For always.'

What a lovely, lovely word, Dawn thought, as Kirk's hands slowly and expertly slid down her naked back.

Always.

*

'This the address you want then, love?' the taxi driver said, interrupting her reverie.

Dawn snapped to and realized that they'd already arrived at Eva's apartment building, right beside Grand Canal Square.

60

She found cash to pay him, even found the manners to thank him and managed to make it all the way up to Eva's apartment before collapsing into tears so violent, she even frightened herself.

Chapter Five

Jo.

From: Jo_Marketing_Director@digitech.com
To: davesblog@hotmail.com
Re: The last of your things.
April 17th, 8.05 a.m.

Dave,

Strongly feel for both our sakes that it's best if we don't communicate face-to-face right now, but restrict it to emails instead. Besides, I'm just too angry to even look at you right now and would find it a strain not to start flinging ornaments around the place were we to, 'attempt to solve this,' as you so naïvely suggest. Sort what exactly, Dave? There is absolutely nothing left for us to talk about.

I assume you're staying at your mother's, as I know how fond you are of all your home comforts such as Sky Sports and getting your laundry done, not to mention having home cooked dinners served up to you every night.

However, if you haven't cleared out the last of your stuff from my flat by the time I get back from London, then please understand; I'm hiring a skip and you can fish your entire vinyl collection, your collection of David Mamet plays (none of which you ever actually appeared in), your raggy, knackery underpants and those vile leather jackets that make you look like a pimp, from the bottom of said skip.

Please Dave, this is the probably the last thing I'll ever ask of you.

Jo.

From: davesblog@hotmail.com
To: Jo_Marketing_Director@digitech.com
Re: The last of your things.
April 17th, 8.44 a.m.

Dearest wife of mine,

A delight, as always, to be on the receiving end of one of your early morning emails. My, my, what a wondrous mood we're in today!

What is it with you anyway; do you wake up in bad form, then wonder who you can possibly take it out on? And seeing as how you can't exactly heap verbal abuse on all your minions in Digitech, because they'd rightly haul your arse through the courts for bullying in the workplace, you think, ah ha! My worthless husband can get a tongue lashing from me and that'll set me up for the whole morning!

Because it's always just all about you, isn't it? Let's never forget, we're all just extras in the Jo Hargreaves show, designed purely to snap to your beat.

Your ever-loving hubbie,

Dave.

PS. Lucky guess. Yes, I am staying at Mama's. Purely because, fond as I am of Bash, his idea of a nutritious meal is a) one that can be shoved into a microwave for three minutes or under and b) comes in a container that is reusable as an ashtray.

PPS. As for clearing out the last of my things, I'll do it when it bloody well suits me. Which as it happens, is this weekend, when you're back home.

PPPS. Because we have to talk, Jo. Be reasonable. You must, somewhere deep down beneath that thorny bracken that surrounds your heart these days, be aware of this.

PPPPS. See you when you're back.

Safe trip. Thinking of you. And in spite of what you may think, sending you love.

Jo was power walking through the airport when that particular email pinged through and after she read it, had to take several deep breaths to try and get her blood pressure back to normal. *In for two, out for three*, she told herself, *in for two and out for three.*

But it wasn't working. Christ, how did Dave always manage to have this effect on her? And did he think insulting her was going to make this any easier?

Don't answer it, she told herself. *Rise above it. Be the bigger person here.* But it was no use, two seconds later, her fingers were busily tap tapping away on her iPhone.

From: Jo_Marketing_Director@digitech.com
To: davesblog@hotmail.com

Re: The last of your things.
April 17th, 8.56 a.m.

Oh feck off with yourself, Dave. What gives you the right to start having a go at me?

Please understand that I really do mean it. If I come home to my flat (which I own, which is in my name and mine only, may I remind you), with your shite still littering the place, then I'm changing the locks and flinging the last of your junk out the window. The way I feel right now, I can't tell you the pleasure it'll give me. Plus it'll certainly give the neighbours a right good laugh to get a look at your last anniversary present to me. Because FYI, a print of a red Ferrari is my idea of cheap, tasteless tat.

(Look it up in the dictionary. You'll find it right there, under, 'Dave Evans: arsehole'.)

About to board my flight.

Don't bother contacting me again till you've done exactly as I ask. And can you please stop leaving voice messages on my phone the length of a radio play? I get the message. But you know what?

Sometimes being sorry for everything just won't cut it.

Jo.

From: davesblog@hotmail.com
To: Jo_Marketing_Director@digitech.com
Re: The last of your things.
April 17th, 9.15 a.m.

Christ Jo, you really should take a moment to read back on some of your more stinging emails. Just take note though, this is the result of what we're going through and how it's affecting you. Even though I'm the only one brave/foolhardy enough to say it to your face.

Ever stumbled across the phrase, 'misdirected anger'?

Suggest you look it up in the dictionary. You'll find it right there, under, 'Jo Hargreaves: nut job.'

See you this weekend.

In spite of what you think, I'm still prepared to work things out.

Yours,

Dave.

(Your husband, just in case that minor little factoid had slipped your mind, my pet.)

PS. Will now spend the rest of the day wondering what in the name of all ye Gods happened to that gorgeous, loving girl I married.

Just so you know.

Jo had just boarded her flight when that particular gem pinged through and was about to switch off her phone and let it go, when a sudden hot flush of anger swept right over her.

'Misdirected anger'? Did Dave really say that? And had she been seeing things or had he actually used the phrase, 'still prepared to work this out' after everything that had happened?

She checked the phone again, but there it was, in black and white. Then just as an air hostess made an announcement asking that all portable electronic devices be switched off, she went back to typing furiously, phone hidden under her coat, so no one would see.

From: Jo_Marketing_Director@digitech.com
To: davesblog@hotmail.com
Re: The last of your things.
April 17th, 9.22 a.m.

Dave,

Out of idle curiosity, you're prepared to work out what exactly? How you can inveigle your way back into living with me? It's clearly not because you actually want to be with me, so dare I suggest, because it's nice and handy for your dole office? So you can continue to sponge off me and live the life of an eternal student, while calling yourself an out-of-work actor?

As for all this utter crap about my 'misdirecting anger', frankly, you can take a running jump with yourself. My anger is pretty direct and well aimed, as it happens.

You know what you sound like? A child who thinks every problem in their little life is everyone else's fault bar theirs. You may have played the part of a head shrink in a show once, but that certainly doesn't make you one. If you really want to psychoanalyse someone, suggest you start a little closer to home. Oooh, off the top of my head, say for instance, a thirty-eight-year-old man in long-term unemployment, who's back living with his mother?

Now piss off and leave me alone. Some of us have real work to do.

Jo.

PS. As for 'this is the result of what we're going through and how it's affecting you'? Cop yourself on, Dave. You're *not 'going through' anything that I can see. Other than six cans of Bulmers a night, that is.*

From: davesblog@hotmail.com
To: Jo_Marketing_Director@digitech.com
Re: The last of your things.
April 17th, 9.35 a.m.

Dear Queen narky moody-pants,

You know why you're acting like this and saying these things. Because this isn't you, at least, not the real you. You're just acting out and looking for a convenient punchbag. So enter Dave, long-suffering husband, stage left.

That is, at least, I fecking hope it's not the real you. Otherwise never mind about your threats of wanting a divorce. *I* bloody want one first. So there. So how do you like it, when it's thrown back into your pretty and freakishly unlined face?

In spite of what you may think, dearest insane one, I still wish you love and luck on your trip and look forward to seeing you on your return.

Because I'm here for you. And the day may yet come when you'll need to remember that.

Dxxx

PS. You told me you liked the red Ferrari print. Shattered that you lied. Oh, the deceit of womanhood, etc.
PPS. As for your vitriolic comment re: my

employment status, you know I could be in a job right now if I wanted to be. I'll have you know, dearest one, that I was offered a telly commercial only last week, playing the part of a speaking Sky Plus box, but chose to take the principled stand of telling the casting director where he could go and shove it. Because in spite of your oft-repeated 'career advice' to me, I refuse to compromise my art for mere lucre.

PPPS. I don't really want a divorce. I don't want one at all. In fact, I want to stay married to you forever and ever, if only to annoy you. I want us to grow old and grey together, then be the one who wheels you around the nursing home, when you're stroke-ridden and need someone to wipe your arse. That's a measure of how much I'm staying married to you, sweet spouse of mine.

From: Jo_Marketing_Director@digitech.com
To: davesblog@hotmail.com
Re: The last of your things.
April 17th, 9.42 a.m.

Dave,

As it happens, I think you'd have made a fantastic speaking Sky Plus box. Shame you weren't offered something made of wood though, then you really could have had a chance to show off your range.

Have to go, flight taxiing now.

Am greatly looking forward to coming home to a lovely, empty flat, free of any and all reminders of you.

Jo.

PS. Please don't tell me the subliminal reasons behind my behaviour. I know there's nothing easier for you in the world than to conveniently blame what I've been dealing with personally for the breakdown of our relationship.

But trust me, it's broken and unfixable. It's over.

From: davesblog@hotmail.com
To: Jo_Marketing_Director@digitech.com
Re: The last of your things.
April 17th, 11.10 a.m.

Sweet-natured angel of mine,

Has your flight landed yet? Because I've a few further points I'd like to make and given the humour you're in these days, it'll be more than my life's worth to say to your face.

Firstly, may I remind you that I've done absolutely everything you ever asked of me? You were the one who wanted to get married in the first place, when we'd only been seeing each other for about a year. And I use the term, 'seeing each other' loosely, given that you were off on business trips more often than not. So I did what you wanted and proposed.

Then you were the one who bloody well insisted on a three-ring circus of a wedding, which was basically anathema to me, but I kept my mouth shut, just so you could have your dream day. Even though the sight of myself in the wedding photos, beaten into that poncey-looking morning suit still makes me want to vomit.

Thirdly, you were the one who made the decision that if you were ever going to have a child, then now was your chance. Again, I had virtually feck all say in the matter, but still went along with it. I actually wanted us to have a family of our own, and for the record sweetheart, I thought we'd have made grade A parents. You've have instilled discipline in our kid, whereas I'd have taught them when and where it was okay to wave two fingers at anything remotely resembling authority.

Not only that, but may I point out that I've stood by you through everything else that's been heaped on us since? I'm blue in the face at this stage reminding you that what you're soldiering through, I am too, as it happens. I know that minor, inconvenient fact tends to be overlooked by you, but just take a moment to really dwell on it, my love.

Why would you think that a miscarriage followed by several failed IVF treatments would be any less painful for me? Where's it written that you get to have the monopoly on disappointment and heartache and just what a fucking nightmare we're both stuck in here?

As an aside, on that very point, I spoke to Bash's pal Emma about what we've been going through. She's a maternity nurse and says your behaviour and the way you're acting so unlike your usual self is actually perfectly normal. It's just all those shagging hormones and fertility drugs they've been pumping into your body for the last eighteen months. That's all and it will pass.

Lastly, dearest love, you asked me to move out. Ergo, I did.

But over my dead body am I going to make this divorce easy for you. No, you don't get away from me that easily.

Your ever-loving husband,

Dave.

Jo had landed in Heathrow by then, having spent the entire flight doing all the lovely calming exercises she'd been taught at the clinic she'd been attending as an outpatient. But the very second she switched her phone back on and read that particular gem, somehow every bit of the deep breathing and meditation went right out the window.

Don't reply, she warned herself. If Dave wants the last word that badly, then let him have it. But try as she might, she couldn't stop herself and a few seconds later, her fingers were busy tapping away.

From: Jo_Marketing_Director@digitech.com
To: davesblog@hotmail.com
Re: The last of your things.
April 17th, 11.17 a.m.

Dave,

If you ever even think about discussing the ins and outs of my medical history with some random stranger ever again, I'll not only hit you with a divorce petition, but also I'll personally see to it that you're hauled through the courts for breach of privacy.

Jesus Dave?!! What next? You going to start standing on street corners, handing out flyers with photos of my lady bits on them?

And just so you know, this is categorically NOT hormones. It's you, driving me insane. End of.

Jo.

Chapter Six

Lucy.

'So you've really left him then?'

'Be more accurate to say we left each other,' Lucy answered, knocking back the dregs of the margarita in front of her and crunching loudly on an ice cube. It was her third and she probably should have left it at that, but somehow she found herself waving over to the barman for the same again. To hell with it anyway, she thought. My marriage just ground to a shuddering halt this week, why the hell not?

'Oh Lucy,' her pal Bianca said, shaking her head sadly and dabbing at the corner of her eyes with a Kleenex. 'I just can't believe it. I mean, this is *you and Andrew* we're talking about. You were like the gold standard of happy couples! If you guys can't make it, then what hope is there for the rest of us?'

Lucy managed a weak, watery smile back at her. Bianca was a sweet, lovely girl who meant well, but who actually did nothing but make Lucy feel guilty, for having the bare-faced cheek to have marital problems in the first place.

Bianca, it had to be explained, was a die-hard romantic,

who'd watched one too many romcoms starring Jennifer Aniston, and was convinced that once you sealed the deal with a bloke and had a ring on your finger to show for it, it would inevitably lead to happy ever after. And the sad thing was that at one time, Lucy had bought into all that too.

Whereas now she thought, what a load of my arse.

Besides as far as Bianca knew, what she believed was the absolute truth. After all, she and Andrew had once been loved up and happy together, hadn't they? So happy; Hollywood-ending happy. In fact, that was the whole bloody tragedy of it. Lucy had honestly thought this was her soulmate; the man she'd happily grow old with. The two of them should have ended up old and grey, worrying about their cholesterol and going off on Nile cruises, with a prescription for Viagra stuck in his back pocket on account of the age gap.

Not, for the love of God, with her sitting on a barstool, with the hangover from hell, yet already onto her third margarita and wondering how many more it would take for her to get so completely hammered that it would somehow numb the pain a bit.

Lucy had never really been much of a drinker, but these days booze was the only thing getting her through this. Lovely, lovely booze and lots of it. It was completely unlike her, not her normal carry-on at all, but then she figured, if this wasn't a dire emergency, then what was?

'None of this was your fault, you know,' Bianca told her firmly. 'If it hadn't been for . . . well, you know. Circumstances.'

'I know, sweetheart,' said Lucy, squeezing her hand, flushing with gratitude to have a genuine pal like this in her corner. 'Circumstances. That's all it came down to in the end really, wasn't it?'

But she certainly didn't need reminding of the circumstances that had suddenly propelled her out of her beautiful marital home with a husband she loved, to sleeping in Bianca's spare room and effectively living out of a suitcase.

'Well, all I can say is, I hope Alannah and Josh are finally happy with themselves now,' said Bianca, nibbling crossly on the bowl of peanuts in front of her.

'Are you kidding me? You can bet the pair of them are out celebrating getting rid of their beloved stepmother tonight with a bottle of Cristal . . .' Lucy broke off here a bit, but then when it came to Andrew's grown-up children from his first marriage, it was bloody hard going, keeping an even temper.

Sweet Mother of God, where to start about Alannah and Josh? They were twins and at twenty-eight, just two years younger than Lucy herself, so initially when Lucy first came into their lives, she'd made the critical error of trying to befriend them both. *I'm dating their father,* she'd naïvely thought back then. *So can't we all just get along and be friends?*

Right from day one, she'd really gone the extra mile with both of them. She constantly put herself into their shoes and realized how incredibly awkward this whole icky situation had to be for both of them. After all, wasn't this the oldest scenario in the book? A fifty-something divorcee, suddenly dating a new and considerably younger girlfriend? *To his kids,* she figured, *I must look like the mid-life equivalent of a Porsche.* Lucy had been around the block enough to know how utterly shite it must have been for the twins, and had genuinely bent over backwards trying to blend them all into one big happy family.

But in spite of all her proffered kindness and numerous olive branches, their rudeness back to her knew no bounds and it was honestly like the more of a superhuman effort she made with them, the more they despised her for it.

On countless occasions, she'd gone out of her way to invite Alannah to fashion shows that she was working on, or else to highly exclusive sample sales most girls would have sold a kidney to get into, mainly because fabulous designer gear straight off a catwalk was usually flogged off for half nothing. Not only that, but Lucy had regularly made a point of inviting Josh along to the flashy fashionista cocktail dos she was always getting plus ones for, where he could spend the whole night surrounded by beautiful women. Sure, what normal fella his age wouldn't kill for that?

Out of the goodness of her heart, Lucy had genuinely meant well. In spite of everything that had happened since and in spite of all the pain that had been caused, she'd desperately wanted them all to get along, but Alannah and Josh only sneered at her and dismissed her because she was a 'just a model'. And of course, the two of them had her pigeon-holed as some kind of brainless, vapid party girl who'd been lucky enough to meet this older, wealthy, distinguished guy and somehow cajole him down the aisle.

Heather Mills, they'd nicknamed her behind her back (she knew for a fact; she'd accidentally overheard), and it bloody well stung.

But then, that was the thing about Lucy. People were always reading about her in the papers or else seeing her on photo shoots in glossy magazine ads and had her down as tough and flinty, a girl well able to take care of herself. And yet, underneath all that, she might as well have been a big, soft marshmallow. So Josh and Alannah and their never-ending petty little slights got to her on a daily basis. How could they not?

And they never, not for one millisecond, seemed to let up. They'd never forgive her for what had happened to their family and by God, from day one they'd been determined to make Lucy pay with her heart's blood. Whether it was her fault or not.

Back at the bar, Bianca was now rummaging round the bottom of her handbag.

'Oh . . . by the way, I've got something here you probably should see, sweetheart,' she said. 'I thought it would be best to show you after a couple of drinks, to . . . well, to lessen the impact a bit.'

'Ehh . . . I'm guessing it's a decree nisi that Alannah and Josh made Andrew sign, with a gun pointed to his head?'

'Not quite that bad, but . . .'

Apologetically, Bianca held up a copy of that evening's *Chronicle*. And there it was in glorious Technicolor for all the world to see.

LUCY BELTER AND HER SUGAR DADDY HIT THE ROCKS! EXCLUSIVE.

'Oh, you're kidding me,' Lucy groaned, head in her hands.

'Sorry. Thought you'd be better off seeing it with a few drinks on you.'

'Oh for God's sake, I'm way too sober for this. Where's the barman with our refills?'

Bianca looked at her worriedly. 'Do you really think that's a good idea, love? It's just you've got that huge photo shoot first thing in the morning and you really need to look the biz.'

'Just one for the road then,' said Lucy, though she wasn't even sure she meant it. Alcohol was just about the only thing getting her through this whole nightmare.

'Right then, if you insist,' said Bianca doubtfully. 'Though I'm warning you, I'm making you drink buckets of water with it too. You need your beauty sleep.'

Bianca was a stylist and acutely aware of how important it was for models to look fresh and camera-ready at all times. As she headed off to the bar, Lucy smiled fondly after her and silently blessed the girl for being such a stalwart. God knows, she needed her mates around her now. Then her eye fell on the headline and in spite of herself, she winced again.

There was a downside of living your life in the public eye and Lucy was very well-known, not only as a model, but thanks to a regular slot she had on *Good Morning Ireland!* as a 'fashionista and trend commentator'. In other words, after any major red carpet event, Lucy was your go-to personality to sit in a hot TV studio and pass comments like, 'If you ask me, all Angelina Jolie needs is a nice, light spray tan and a Supersize Big Mac meal in that order.'

And amazingly, TV gigs really started to take off for her. Producers told her she was a born natural and audiences seemed to relish her gutsy, down-to-earth, no-nonsense approach.

Lucy loved what she did and most of the time was happy to see stories about herself in the papers; after all, it was part and parcel of her job, she reckoned. A job she'd worked bloody hard at since she'd first been 'discovered' at the tender age of fifteen. Her family wasn't wealthy and privileged like Andrew's; she'd had to graft for everything that came her way in life. But amazingly, right from day one, her career seemed to just take off. Six feet tall, with Nordic good looks and cheekbones you could nearly slice ham on, she was a natural. In next to no time, she was earning some serious money for herself, between catwalk shows and magazine shoots.

But Lucy was shrewd and streetwise and took absolutely nothing for granted, knowing that a model's sell-by date was short and a dole queue was potentially just a heartbeat away from her. So she took on every single modelling gig that was offered to her, slogging, slaving and grafting for everything that came her way.

You need a model to stand shivering in a bikini in the middle of Grafton Street in February to advertise sun holidays? Lucy was your first port of call. Or you need a glamour gal to climb naked into a giant vat of cold beans, just so you could promote some new reduced fat range? She was your gal. No job too big, too small or too mortifying. And recession or no, miraculously the money kept rolling in.

Of course the downside of having a public profile was that for months now, all sorts of sleazy tabloids were running features speculating on the state of her marriage. As far as possible, she did her level best to avoid reading any of that crap, but still. Hard not to feel like your nerve endings were lying jangled and exposed every time you glanced at a byline that screeched into your face,

THEY WERE A MISMATCH FROM THE WORD GO!

Alannah and Josh, she thought bitterly, must be having a bloody field day with all this.

80

Just then, a song came on the bar's music system. 'True Love' by Cole Porter. And completely unbidden, a memory surfaced, something Lucy thought she'd buried deep inside and worked bloody hard at keeping there. But in spite of her best efforts, the recollection still bubbled to the surface.

No, she warned herself, feeling her bottom lip start to wobble. *Don't sink under. It's just a silly love song; DO NOT let it get to you. You're doing so well. All you've got to do is stay strong.*

But it was no use.

Because the fact was, the last time Lucy heard that song had been on her wedding day. At the tiny little reception dinner afterwards, to be exact. She and Andrew had got married barefoot on the beach, at sunset in Cancun, and it was initially supposed to have been just the two of them and no one else. After all, getting married abroad seemed like the most elegant way of side-stepping all the attendant drama that they'd have had to deal with, had they got married quickly and quietly in the registry office at home, as had been their original plan. After all, Alannah and Josh wouldn't have liked it and the last thing Lucy wanted to do was cause any offence on her wedding day.

No doubt about it; the best way to avoid being accused of insensitivity around his first family was just as Andrew rightly said, 'to get married miles away from everyone on the beach of some tropical island, at sunset. Just you and me, darling, and not another soul. I don't want a three-ring circus like I had the first time round, for all the good that did me. Just the woman I love and a priest to marry us. As long as you turn up to marry me, then that's all that matters.'

'I think it's a fabulous idea!' Lucy had told him delightedly at the time, feeling like a burden had been lifted from her shoulders.

'And you're sure you don't mind missing out on doing the whole big white wedding thing?' he'd asked her, a bit worriedly. 'It's perfectly alright for me, you know, I've done all this before, I've had the whole shindig. But this is your big day, sweetheart, and all I want is for you to be happy.'

'I couldn't give a damn where we do it, you know that,' Lucy whispered into his chest, snuggling into him, loving the feel of his arms locking tightly around her. 'As long as we're together, isn't that all that matters?'

'Excellent,' he twinkled, lightly kissing her forehead. 'Then it's settled. Apart from the family, let's say nothing to anyone. Let's just book it and then think of how surprised everyone will be when we come back as man and wife?'

'You see?' she'd laughed happily at him. 'This is why I love you! You've just solved so many problems in one fell swoop and no one can possibly take offence at our going away now!'

'And of course there's something else,' he'd added, leaning in to kiss her properly now. 'Technically, our wedding will actually be our honeymoon too . . . so . . .'

'So . . . what you're saying is . . .' she teased, nibbling on his ear, knowing right well the effect it had on him. 'The minute we're married, we can go straight from the boring church bit, skip the whole reception part and really start putting our honeymoon suite to good use?'

'Well, now you just read my thoughts.'

Lucy didn't remember much more about that night after that.

Mind you, it hadn't been easy, breaking it to her own mother and the rest of her family that there wouldn't actually be some big fancy-schmancy wedding at home. Instead, just a tiny, strictly private beach wedding abroad, followed by a New Year's Eve dinner back home instead. Lucy hated seeing the hurt in her Mum's red, rheumy eyes at the news that she wouldn't be able to go to her adored youngest girl's wedding, but she still held firm. After all, she and Andrew had a deal; just the two of them and no one else.

But of course at the very last minute, and as soon as they heard the wedding just happened to involve a freebie trip to the Caribbean, Alannah and Josh had managed to inveigle themselves along. Lucy was tight-lipped with fury about it, but figured, this is the man I love and these, after all, are his kids and I'm about to be their stepmother. So what can I do?

The song played on as yet more memories resurfaced. Getting worse and worse it seemed, each and every time.

There had been the wedding dinner, with tensions around the table almost ready to skyrocket. They'd made a dismal little party that night; just herself and Andrew, side by side, clutching hands with Alannah and Josh at the table opposite them, glowering on. Just the four of them.

And the killer was that it could have been perfect. It *should* have been perfect. It should have been relaxed and romantic, just the two of them in this tropical paradise, just like they'd planned. But it was hardly likely either Lucy or her husband of barely two hours would look back on this day without shuddering, Lucy remembered thinking, glancing round the table in the Mexican restaurant and trying her level best not to vomit at what was going on around her.

'So anyway Dad,' Alannah harped across the table at

83

him, while poor, patient Andrew listened on, glancing between Alannah and Josh. Both of them, by the way, with faces like thunder on this, the happy occasion of their Dad's second marriage. Almost as though they'd been forced to come all this way to this fabulous, five-star resort hotel on a sandy white Caribbean beach with guns pointed to their heads, when in fact the exact opposite was the case.

'If you could just see your way to fixing up for my hotel room, Dad, I'd be very grateful,' Alannah was trying to cajole Andrew. 'I'm just a bit cash strapped at the minute, you see. What, with all the expense of Christmas and then having to buy an outfit for this wedding . . . well, you know yourself. Chi-ching. Anyway, you don't mind stepping up to the plate a bit here, do you? Come on, you wouldn't begrudge me today of all days! After all, I did travel out all this way, just to be here for you.'

Lucy stayed tight-lipped and managed to say nothing. At the very least, she thought gratefully, the sound of the restaurant's mariachi band playing some long-forgotten song the Gypsy Kings had a hit with approximately fifteen years ago, went some way towards drowning out the conversation a bit. *Just look out the terrace onto the sea*, she told herself, shivering slightly against the cool of the restaurant's air conditioning and pulling her wrap tightly round slender, tanned shoulders.

Forget about this tortuous evening and instead think about how sparkly the distant Caribbean looks in the moonlight. Focus on the warm, tropical breeze that's gently wafting through the restaurant's open terrace doors. Focus on Andrew, her soulmate, lover and now brand new husband. Focus on just about anything except Andrew's two adult children.

'Oh yeah . . . and another thing,' Alannah was still droning on in that nasally, whining voice that was not unlike listening to nails being dragged down a blackboard. 'Just to let you know, Dad, I seem to have built up a serious load of room service charges. Only telling you so you don't have a heart attack when you see the final bill! Oh . . . and by the way, for Christmas, I saw the most fabulous sapphire ring in the jewellers . . . not dropping hints or anything, just pointing you in the right direction, that's all!'

Give me strength, Lucy thought, flushing like a forest fire from a combination of the warm, tropical breeze, the huge meal she'd just gorged herself on, and the very real sensation that she could strangle Alannah with her bare hands, wedding day or no wedding day.

And no, it wasn't the bloody money, of course it wasn't. Andrew's cash was his to spend in any way he saw fit and Lucy would have been the last person to begrudge him splashing out on his two kids. After all, why shouldn't he? He was a wealthy man with pots of money to go around and Lucy wasn't the type to give two hoots what he chose to do with it. He could have gone and blown the whole lot of it on Mars Bars and she'd just have laughed.

No, what got to Lucy more than anything were Alannah and Josh's never ending list of demands towards their Dad, almost like they were extorting guilt money. And at the end of the day, guilt over what? Andrew had split with his ex well over five years ago, surely time to put all that behind them and move on?

And oh dear God, did the pair of them know so well how to pick and choose their moment. Perfect timing now for them to lay yet more demands on their father, when he was sitting back at the end of his wedding day; relaxed, chilled out, glass of brandy in one hand, cigar clamped to the other.

'Oh yeah, and another thing I've been meaning to say to you, Dad,' Josh chipped in, sitting with the full of his long, bony back to Lucy, patently ignoring her and putting Andrew square on the spot now. On the man's wedding day.

'You have to understand that having the reception in that fancy restaurant Pichet, when we all get back to Dublin next week is kinda upsetting for Mum. It's just that she often goes there for lunch with the girls and she feels it's really insensitive towards her. I mean like, the maître d' is a *really* close pal of hers. And after all, it is, like, the season of goodwill and everything. I mean, it's Christmas Eve and Mum's probably all on her own at home right now . . .'

Josh, by the way, was all of twenty-eight years of age and still living with his Mammy, with all the attendant comforts that entailed. And who'd turned up to the wedding cere- mony today dressed in a pair of Bermuda shorts and looking exactly like a Shane McGowan song. Almost as though he was trying to feign maximum disdain for his father's second marriage.

'Bit much, flaunting it right in front of Mum's face, don't you think?' Josh was still hammering on, no matter how hard Lucy tried to tune him out. 'It's just really hard on her, you know. So is it too late to . . . you know . . . like, just cancel the wedding thingy at the restaurant and back out of the whole thing?'

'Ehh,' Andrew mumbled, flushing a bit as he always did whenever his ex-wife was dragged up in front of Lucy. 'Well actually, it might be a tad awkward at this late stage, you see . . .'

'Come on Dad, you're already officially married! You've had the ceremony, you've done the deed and it's all over and done with now. Surely you don't need to invite everyone you've ever met in your life to some posh dinner when you get home as well, do you? It's just I'd hate for Mum to feel her nose was being rubbed in it. I mean, it's actually really insensitive, when you think about it.'

'Ahh, well you see . . .' Andrew began genially, but Lucy interrupted, unable to contain herself much longer.

'It's more than awkward to cancel our wedding celebration now, Josh, I'm afraid,' she fired back, not even giving a shite if she sounded rude. 'The party is all booked for New Year's Eve, we've reserved most of the restaurant and invited over fifty guests. Including my own family, who really wanted to be here today, as it happens. And this is the only chance that we both get to celebrate with them, not to mention all my close pals and your Dad's colleagues from work. To call the whole party off now would be the height of rudeness, not to mention that it could probably break the restaurant.'

Besides, she added silently, if either you or your mother had a bloody problem, then why didn't you tell us when we were first booking it? All of two months ago! Why leave it till the week before to start griping? And if you're so worried about your Mum being alone and upset over Christmas, then what are you even doing here in the first place? Why not stay home with her, if you're all that concerned?

Andrew slipped a supportive arm around his new bride's waist while Josh stopped all his sniping and just settled for glaring moodily at his new stepmother instead, temporarily silenced. But then Lucy knew the drill all too well by now.

She may have won that tiny battle, but she was still fighting a losing war. And make no mistake, this was all-out war.

Then after an interminably long, drawn-out dinner, Andrew gently ting-tinged the glass in front of him and rose to his feet to make an impromptu little speech.

'First of all,' he began hesitatingly, 'I'd like to thank both of my beautiful children for being here on this very special day.'

Funny, but Lucy could still remember thinking how handsome he looked in his white linen suit, tanned and relaxed and so sexy, in a silver-haired, moustached, Tom Selleck-y way. And good-naturedly, she began a tiny ripple of applause, to back him up. But no one, she noticed, joined in with her.

'And now if I may turn for a moment to my beautiful bride . . .'

Alannah called over the waiter and ordered another glass of wine, looking anywhere except at her Dad's beautiful new bride.

'I first clapped eyes on this gorgeous young girl at an awards ceremony my bank was hosting and thought she was the most attractive woman I'd ever seen . . .' Andrew gamely went on.

'And then he went home and told his wife all about it,' Josh muttered.

Both Andrew and Lucy heard him loud and clear, it was impossible not to, but both stayed tight-lipped. Not the time and certainly not the place.

'. . . Though in a million years, it never occurred to me that this vision of loveliness would ever have anything to do with an aul' fella like myself!' Andrew continued. 'I persisted though, didn't I, Lucy, and eventually got you to agree to go on a date with me . . . do you remember, darling?'

Lucy had to smile. Course she remembered. Andrew had somehow got hold of her number to ask her out to dinner not long after the awards do and her heart had just gone out to him. He'd told her about all the trouble he'd been having at home and how his marriage was effectively over, in all but name.

'. . . Of course it wasn't the easiest time in my private life,' he was saying, with just a tiny nod of acknowledgment towards Alannah and Josh. 'But I do think that over time and with great perseverance on my part, true love eventually won the day. And so without further ado, can I ask you all to raise a glass to the new Mrs Lowe? My darling Lucy, you're the love of my life. After my first marriage broke up, I never thought I'd smile again, laugh again, be happy again. Then you came along and with a simple wave of your hand, you changed everything. In my wildest dreams did I ever think I'd be blessed enough to find a soulmate at my hour of life? And yet it happened. So now, it's my supreme wish to make every day of our new life together absolutely magical. To my breathtaking bride!'

Lucy beamed warmly back at him and toasted him back, but it seemed Andrew wasn't finished yet.

'And now would anyone else care to say a few words?' he added, looking hopefully from Josh to Alannah. 'Maybe to welcome Lucy into our little family?'

No takers though. Instead, just stony, mortifying silence.

'After all, she is now officially a member of the Lowe family,' he added, flushing just a bit.

Still nothing. Just the sound of the mariachi band playing

'True Love'. Odd and discordant, Lucy remembered thinking from out of nowhere, to hear it sung in a Mexican accent.

'Josh? Alannah?' Andrew persisted, with just the tiniest edge creeping into his voice.

Say something, Lucy tried to madly telegraph over to the pair of them. Not for me, for your Dad. It would mean so much to him today of all days. For God's sake, he paid for your entire trip, would it kill you to string three sentences together on the man's wedding day?

'Okay, Dad,' Alannah said, in a dangerously low voice that Lucy instantly recognized meant trouble. 'Here's a few words for you.'

And suddenly, it was like no air moved.

'You broke our family,' Alannah said in a low, even voice. 'While you were busy moving on at the speed of light after you'd separated, you broke Mum's heart. And for the record, you broke us. So there you go. Enjoy your wedding night. And I hope you can live with that. But if you think I'm hanging around to hear more about how happy and in love you are now, then you're wrong. I'm out of here. You know I came all the way here for you, I wanted to be here for you, to try to support you if I could. But I've officially had enough. I tried Dad, but you know what? Turns out it's just too bloody hard.'

The air pulsed, as her words just seemed to hang there. Andrew, glass in hand, froze, just staring at her. This is exactly what it feels like, Lucy thought, to be punched right in the solar plexus.

*

Back on her lonely barstool all of three years on and it looked like Alannah had actually cursed her that day, like some kind of wicked fairy at a feast. Because there were four things Lucy knew now with absolute certainty.

That Alannah and Josh had set out to sabotage her marriage from day one.

That never in her wildest dreams could she could have foreseen the lengths they'd go to. The depths they were prepared to crawl to, just to be rid of her.

That she'd underestimated them at her peril.

And lastly, she thought, downing her shot in one gulp, just to stem the nausea, it was purely a matter of time before she and Andrew would be divorced.

Chapter Seven

Chloe.

'Welcome to the Hope Street Hotel.'

Oh God, I love saying it so much! Can't stop myself; every workman, interior designer, plumber and carpenter that crosses the threshold, is warmly welcomed to the Hope Street Hotel. We've got just two weeks to go before show-time and even though there's a mountain of work to do before we officially throw our doors open for business, I couldn't be prouder or happier of how it's all pulling together. This is the single biggest challenge I've ever faced into, and by God, I'll move heaven and earth if I have to, to make it work.

The hotel industry here in Ireland is actually starting to sit up and take notice of us too. There was even a piece about us in a trade magazine, naming me as General Manager and giving a bit of a blurb about our mission statement. I went a bit jelly-legged reading it, with pride, yes, but mainly because all I could think was, Frank will see this. And then he'll *know*, won't he? He'll know I'm back here, less than a five-minute walk from where he works.

I get a quick, momentary stab of insecurity combined with nervousness like I've never known. Sudden flashbacks keep coming back to me just at the thought of Frank, and I half wonder if he'll get in contact to wish me luck maybe? I'm just trying to figure out if I find that either terrifying or hopeful, when I'm quickly hauled out of it by yet another last minute snag at the hotel that needs troubleshooting.

Because there's still so much to be done before we officially open our doors, there's barely time to give thought to much else. Every morning, I'm at the desk in my cosy little basement office at the hotel by 7.30 a.m. and the whole day seems to go by in a complete blur. Meetings with accountants, interior designers, not to mention Ferndale's Human Resources manager who's over from the UK to headhunt and interview prospective staff. Believe me, it doesn't end. And I'm absolutely loving every minute and although I crawl back to my parents' house every night bone-tired from exhaustion, I can honestly say this is the most optimistic and forward-looking I've felt in a long, long time. In fact, ever since I first got that phone call to tell me I had this job, something is slowly starting to shift inside of me. Almost like all this hard work is slowly starting to erode the rock of pain that was locked away inside me. Which can't be a bad thing, right?

Anyway, it's just coming up to lunchtime one day, when I'm dashing out of one meeting to get back to my desk and catch up on emails. I'm padding my way down the softly carpeted back stairs, leading into the rabbit warren of tiny basement offices that's a bit like the nerve centre of the whole operation, when suddenly I notice a dramatic shift in the atmosphere round here. Hard to describe, but it's almost like the health inspectors or else some contrary restaurant critic has unexpectedly dropped in on us unannounced, for an early spot check.

'You okay?' I ask Chris Smyth, my assistant manager and general right-hand woman round here. Now Chris is normally the personification of long blonde coolness; she's worked for Ferndale for years, was seconded over from the UK weeks ago and I've yet to see the girl anything other than composed, efficient and bursting with energy. Whenever things get on top of me, she's that rational voice of calmness in my ear that says, 'It's fine. You can do this. Just take it all one step at a time.' Even at half seven in the morning, when the rest of us are still struggling to look alert on six hours' sleep, she's one of those people who are perpetually bright-eyed, alert and generally an all-round ray of sunshine.

But not now.

'Chloe, you're needed upstairs, quick,' the poor girl almost hyperventilates at me. 'He's here! Actually here. Now. One of his spot checks. And I had no idea we were even to expect him . . . I mean, nobody rang me from the UK to warn me, or anything, and the place isn't nearly ready! So what are we going to do? The decorators are still working in the bar area and it's a total mess . . . and then there's the garden that still isn't landscaped fully . . . and don't get me started on all the snags we're still dealing with . . .'

'Shh, shh, Chris,' I tell her as soothingly as I can, while half looking round my desk for a brown paper bag I can get the girl to breathe into. 'For starters, who exactly has just landed in on us anyway?'

Either President Michael D. Higgins, from the way she's going on, or possibly one of U2 with the full entourage? And then it dawns on me.

'Chris, by any chance are you trying to tell me that Rob McFayden is here? Upstairs? Right this minute?'

'Waiting for you at Reception,' she nods breathlessly. Almost with 'and sooner you than me' tattooed across her forehead.

I gulp and try very hard just to breathe. This is okay, I tell myself, this is fine. I haven't actually seen him since the day he first interviewed me, but of course I've been in almost daily contact with him over the phone. He has a habit of calling me at the oddest times and from the most unexpected corners of the globe, checking in on our progress. Hard not to get the impression that he still isn't quite there yet when it comes to fully trusting me, but there you go.

He was in Dubai, I know, last week. Paris before that. Then Rome the week before. Last time we talked, he said something about Milan. The guy must just live out of a suitcase and survive on plasticky airline food and little else. And all his calls are brisk, businesslike and generally all over in under four minutes.

Of course, I've been keeping Rob McFayden fully updated. And okay yeah, so maybe I have painted a slightly more positive picture than I should have. Maybe I have, ahem, glossed over the cracks a little more than I should have done, but come on. Who doesn't, when their boss calls demanding updates?

Everything's coming together beautifully, I've been calmly telling him. We're as close to being on track and on target as it's possible to be at this point. After all, someone as busy as Rob McFayden doesn't need to be bothered with details about light fittings in the bedrooms and a bit of mud out in the back garden, I figured.

But did I really, honestly think he wouldn't land in on us to see how the place is coming together for himself? Course not. Just assumed I might get a bit of advance warning first, that's all.

Taking a deep breath, I squeeze Chris's arm, say 'Wish me luck!' as brightly as I can, then trip up the main staircase that leads from the basement maze of offices up to Reception.

Do NOT let nerves get the better of you, I tell myself sternly, clipping along as fast as tight shoes will allow. He hired you because somewhere deep down he must believe in you, so all you have to do is just believe in yourself. You CAN do this. And yes, agreed, the hotel is currently a work-in-progress and of course, Rob McFayden could find holes to pick with a thousand things if he really wanted to. But after all, we're all working flat out here, aren't we? How can it be humanly possible for us to do much more?

I reach the top of the back stairs and sure enough, there he is, the man himself. Tall and lean, with salt and pepper hair, dressed like he just rolled out of bed in his own personal 'uniform' of a Gap t-shirt, jeans, trainers and a light blue sweater. Like it's permanently dress-down Friday round here.

Don't get me wrong, I like my uniform, but the sight of Rob McFayden looking so Sunday morning casual instantly makes me feel like a right prissy frump, in my Ferndale Hotels navy blue suit, with name badge neatly pinned to it. Tall and authoritative, he's chatting easily on his mobile with his full back to me. He hears the clickety-clack of my work high heels though, as I briskly walk along the marble tiled floor behind him, and turns round to face me.

I mouth 'Hi!' and give a quick, nervous little wave,

thinking, *Do not, under any circumstances allow yourself to be intimidated. Just walk tall, act confident and sooner or later, the whole world will believe the lie.*

After all, it's the first time I've seen him since the day he interviewed me, feck it, I'm entitled to be a bit antsy.

'Just gimme one sec,' he mimes back at me, with a quick half-wink and a 'winding up' gesture, as if to say he's trying his best to end the call.

Right. So obviously I'm expected to hang on then, and try and not look like I'm earwigging. Which is awkward, to say the least, given the conversation he happens to be having.

'Yes, darling,' he's saying in a low voice down the phone. 'Well, if that's what you want, then that's absolutely fine by me. You're the boss!'

Ahem. Well, you're certainly not onto the bank manager, I think, eyes darting down and pretending to busy myself with much pointless tapping at the computer behind Reception. Tell you one thing though, whatever woman he's talking to right now, she certainly knows how to keep the likes of Rob McFayden well and truly under her thumb.

'Now you're absolutely sure about this, love?' he's saying. 'I just want you to be completely happy wherever we go, you know that.'

Wow. Suddenly, it strikes me just how completely different his whole tone of voice is, even since the last time I met him. Right now, he sounds absolutely nothing like the intensely focused, businesslike whirl of energy who first interviewed me, all those weeks back. Instead, if anything, he sounds tender to whoever he's onto, gentle even. Loving and warm. The exact polar opposite to what's received wisdom within the industry about the mighty Rob McFayden.

97

Wonders will never cease. Got to hand it to whoever this particular girlfriend is. If you can keep an alpha male like this in check, then world domination probably wouldn't present too much of a challenge afterwards.

Jeez, wait till I tell Chris, is my immediate, tacked-on thought.

'Alright, say I pick you up on Saturday, usual time?' Rob asks softly, like he doesn't want me to hear. But even though I'm madly trying my best to pretend that there's urgent business under the shelves behind the reception desk that needs my attention, it's just impossible not to.

'Alright, love,' he says, finally wrapping it up. 'That's a date. Till then. Yes, me too, you know that.'

Eeugh. Overhearing that almost feels like I'm invading his personal space. But he appears to have no such qualms though, just clicks off the phone and strides over to where I'm standing, hand outstretched.

'Apologies about that. Had to take that call, you understand,' he says, meeting my gaze with all the cool confidence of someone just off the phone to their stockbroker.

'Of course, emm . . . Mr McFayden,' I smile back, brightly as I can, hoping against hope that I'm not flushing and sweating like a wino.

'I told you, it's Rob.'

'Sorry, Rob. I have to warn you though, we weren't expecting you to be in Dublin so soon. And as you can see, we still have a few snags we're sorting out right now.'

No sooner are the words out of my mouth than a power drill goes off in the background, which I practically have to shout to be heard over.

'But you know we're pretty much on schedule,' I half yell at him over the racket, 'I mean . . . obviously . . . give or take just a few last minute odds and ends round the place. Rest assured though, I'm pretty confident that we'll be ready in plenty of time . . .'

'Chloe?' Rob interrupts, as the din from the power drill dies down.

'Yes?'

'You're starting to sound nervous. Should I be worried?'

'Oh, well, you know!' I say in a voice that's approximately half an octave higher than normal. 'We're just all a bit pressured round here today, what with builders and everything . . . and of course, if we'd known you were coming, then it goes without saying we'd have been . . .'

'You think I haven't seen the inside of a hotel that's overrun with builders before?'

'No, course not, I just meant that . . . well, we are two weeks from opening and I'd hate you to think we weren't going to be ready in time, because you know, we're all completely confident . . .'

'Well, then. In that case, it seems my reputation as a complete bastard has gone before me,' Rob says dryly, mouth twitching down at the corners. 'I'm not here to fire hard-working staff because you're all working flat out on last minute snags.'

Okay, there is just no fecking response to that. So I just stand there, casting around wildly for some change of subject.

'Well, you'll be delighted to know I can't even stay for long, actually,' he says with a half-smile, like he's actually enjoying my discomfort. 'I'm actually en route back to London.'

'Oh?' I ask stupidly. 'You mean, you're not going to be around here for a few days, at least . . .?'

'Not this time, I'm afraid. I've been in Milan since yesterday you see, and just happened to have a chink of time between flight connections today, so I arranged to catch my flight back to London from here. I wanted to see for myself just how the place is shaping up.'

'Well . . . in that case, let me give you the full tour.'

'Lead the way.'

You're in control here, Chloe, don't forget that, I tell myself firmly. And yes, so maybe this is a work-in-progress and maybe there's a pile of tweaks and snags that we're still working through. Like the coffee tables we ordered still haven't arrived for the drawing room yet. Plus the fact that the plumbers are still working on the bathroom fittings, in at least three of the en-suites upstairs. And the electricians, who still haven't quite finished yet, have left so many wires and cross cables strewn across the floor of the dining room, it looks like someone spilt ten plates of spaghetti in there.

I could go on and on, but come on, it's a brand new hotel and we don't even open for another two weeks yet! Surely even as notorious a perfectionist as Rob McFayden has to make allowances here? It will all come together in time. Because it just has to. It's a good, sobering thought, and the more I keep telling myself that, the more I actually believe it.

Wordlessly, like he's on a very tight schedule, he strides a few paces ahead of me as we make our way from the elegant hallway where Reception is, to the lounge area just on the left. It's an old drawing room that our interior design team have worked wonders on. They've completely converted it from a slightly cold and forbidding Georgian reception room into a relaxed, warm and welcoming space, with a huge open fireplace, bookcases stuffed with leather-bound

100

books and a stunning Louise Kennedy chandelier that never fails to take my breath away. The furniture is fabulous too, sofas covered in gorgeous lavender damask fabric, long cream silk cushions and curtains to match and tastefully chosen paintings dotting the walls. The designers really have thought of everything; even the fabrics have been carefully covered in protective plastic, till the builders finally leave us in peace.

The Lavender Room, as we've taken to calling it and I'm bloody proud of what we've done here; it's elegant and graceful, yet so comfortable and inviting too; the kind of place designed to chill out in. Just perfect for the clientele we're hoping to attract. An awful lot of work went into it, but instead of having a good, thorough nose around, Rob just strides around the perimeter, checks the view from the window, plonks down on one of the sofas, as though testing it for squidginess, and then is straight back up on his feet again. Like he's seen all he wants to and is anxious to move on. Fast.

'So,' I tell him, flailing my arms around like a tour guide, 'you'll notice the fireplace in here has been completely restored and the chandelier was specially ordered in from . . .'

'Yeah, yeah, yeah. Lovely. Great. Purple walls, whatever.'

'Eh, actually they're lavender.'

'You'll have to forgive me,' he says dryly, 'but then I doubt there's many guys who'd successfully be able to distinguish between purple and lavender. Okay to keep moving?'

'Emm . . . riiight. But, you know there's still an awful lot in here I'd like to point out to you . . .'

'Apologies for this, Chloe,' he cuts across me, 'but I

haven't got long till I've to get back to the airport, I'm afraid. For the moment at least, this needs to be just an initial whistle-stop tour. So come on, impress me.'

'Well sure, but don't you want to know when the painters will finish the skirting boards in here? Or why the . . .'

'Do I look like the kind of guy who's interested in skirting boards?'

There's just no right answer to that.

'I haven't time to be a micromanager,' he goes on, striding for the door so fast, I nearly have to sprint to keep up. 'Which is exactly why you're here, you see. Your job is to worry about all the ins and outs for me. Mine is to oversee it as and when I can, and to bollock everyone out of it, if necessary. And here, so far at least, I can see I don't have to. So come on, show me the bar now.'

I'm just trying to figure out if that was an actual compliment or not, but there's no time. Two seconds later and we're on the move to the fabulous bar area, which is also just off Reception, right behind the Lavender Room. It's old-fashioned in style, completely in keeping with the age of the house, mahogany and wood panelled. Which, with full credit to the design team, is looking remarkably well. Deep, plush green leather sofas are dotted around with a pale green silk fabric covering the walls. It's going to be stunning, completely breathtaking and yet once again, Rob says nothing, just strides around, taking it all in and nodding every now and then. Jeez, I think. All the money this is costing him and he's not inspecting it more closely?

Tommy Kennedy, our ridiculously attractive barman is in situ, unloading crates and setting up behind the bar, so I introduce him to Rob.

'Howaya,' Tommy grins cheekily as they shake hands,

but then Tommy's just not the type to get remotely fazed by the fact that his boss's boss has just landed in on top of him.

Tommy is by far the youngest staff member we've got round here, just twenty-four, built like a rugby prop forward and with a Kerry accent that makes absolutely everything he says sound adorable. Chris and I interviewed him a few weeks back and hired him on the spot. He's a fantastic mixologist and it's always a bonus, as she wisely pointed out, to have a barman who looks like something out of a Gillette ad in any hotel. Particularly one where a whole lot of soon-to-be single women will be floating about.

'Good to meet you,' Rob says, 'you certainly look busy.'

'Ah sure, all in a day's work, boy. You know yourself.'

Rob just nods and immediately strides past a fabulously relaxed seating area and throws open double doors that lead to a terrace outside with steps leading down to the garden below. It's my favourite part of the whole building actually, where I figure either a) smokers can knock themselves out or b) our soon-to-be-divorced guests can take a little breather to chill out in the enclosed, landscaped garden, far away from all talk about lawyers and problems and financial settlements.

At least, that's the *plan*. Once the garden is finished, that is. But right now, tiny and all as it is, it's more of a mud bath than actual garden and the landscapers are still working away on it, looking scarily like months and not weeks away from completion.

At that thought, my anxiety levels shoot upwards just as the landscaper calls cheekily up at me, as we step outside and look down at all the work that's going on. 'Howaya Chloe!' he waves. 'Any chance of a cuppa tea there, love?'

'Be with you shortly, Jack!' I smile back, then turn to where Rob is right behind me, arms folded, quick, grey eyes taking in absolutely everything. 'Well, you've got to look after your staff, don't you?' I shrug, trying to laugh it off.

'Certainly do,' he nods, eyes busily scanning every last little thing.

'Now okay, I know it's all looking ages away from being ready in time, but trust me, it will be. Jack's got it all in hand,' I say, trying to sound confident about it. 'Don't you, Jack?' I call down to him.

'Givvus a chance, will you love? Can't go any faster!' he yells cheerfully back. 'And where's me tea?'

'You know, I really think it'll be stunning out here,' I go on, talking to Rob's back now as he paces up and down the smoking terrace, as though he's testing it for length. 'I mean, we're in the dead centre of the city right now, and just listen, you can hardly even hear the traffic going by, can you? It'll be a lovely oasis of peace and tranquillity, wait and see. A place where . . .'

'Chloe,' he says. 'It's okay. I get it. Yes, it's gonna work.'

'Yes, but don't you want me to tell you how it's going to look when it's finished?'

'You're doing it again.'

He's stopped pacing now and is looking at me intently. 'Doing what?'

'Sounding like I'm only here to do a spot check so I can catch you all out and start firing people. Just because there's a bit of mud in the back garden and a few wires loose?'

'Emm . . . well . . .'

'You have to remember; I've been in this business a long time. I've seen countless hotels in the weeks before opening, in a far worse state, believe me. Sometime when I'm not rushing off, remind me to tell you the story of the Ferndale Beach Hotel in Dubai. It's the whole reason my hair's as grey as it is, you know.'

I smile at this and start to relax a little.

'And every hotel without exception was subsequently perfect when they needed to be, just as here will too. So don't worry. Because I'm certainly not.'

'Okay, then. If you say so.'

Am I wrong, or could there possibly have been a grain of praise buried in there? I think there might have been, but it's hard to tell with this guy. And if he only knew what I was thinking right now.

There you are looking at me now, judging me, assessing me, but do you even realize how badly I want this to be a success too? This job is the thing that picked me up off the floor, the whole reason why I didn't have to lie low in London any more. Believe me no one, not even you, Rob McFayden, wants this to work more than I do.

'Come on then,' he says briskly, snapping me out of my thoughts. 'Quick tour of the Games Room and then onto the top two floors.'

The Games Room, just a short flight of stairs down from Reception, thankfully meets with his approval, but then it's kind of been designed to be boy heaven. There's deep leather easy chairs dotted around the place, a full-size snooker table and a giant screen TV, which I'm guessing will be tuned to Sky Sports more often than not. Our lighting designer is planning on dim, low lights in here and I just know it's going to be something very special.

Rob nods his silent approval, so then I quickly lead him

onto the magnificent oak panelled library on the ground floor. It's utterly breathtaking in here with its high bookcases and comfy armchairs. The atmosphere is peaceful and calming and so quiet which I'm hoping will help ease some of the tension our guests are bound to be going through.

Just a curt, 'Okay, we're done here,' nod from Rob while I'm still waxing lyrical about leather wingback armchairs.

Right then, hint taken. So that much done, I lead him up the restored Georgian staircase (still in the process of being carpeted), which he takes impatiently, two at a time. Next thing, he's power walking through the bright, airy breakfast room, with its soft yellow wallpaper and rich, deep cashmere rugs in the most luxurious nude colours. So soft and so opulent under my feet, that I actually feel a bit shifty for having the cheek to walk on it with shoes on.

Rob doesn't seem to notice though, just takes it all in, then he's straight onto the gorgeous yellow drawing room just behind it and finally up onto another floor to where the relaxation room and bedrooms are. The relaxation room is one of my favourites, mainly because when I described the atmosphere of calm, soothing tranquillity I was after to our design team, they amazingly were able to create it exactly as it had been in my mind's eye. It's not all that big a space really, and unlike the rest of the building, it's quite modern in style, but it has the most gorgeous, massive floor-to-ceiling window, so is often completely bathed in sunlight and overlooks what will be the beautiful gardens.

My ultimate vision here is to have long comfy recliners dotted just in front of the window, where guests can stretch out, relax and just take in the panoramic views down onto the gardens below. God, but wouldn't I have loved somewhere like this to crawl away to and lock out the world, after Frank – well, you know the rest.

'Now of course, it's not quite finished yet,' I tell Rob, 'but when it is, just imagine this whole space almost like a health spa, with aromatherapy candles dotted around and . . .'

'. . . And I think we can safely assume it's a room where ladies will congregate, as opposed to blokes,' he says, finishing my sentence for me. Then adds with a hint of a smile, 'But then I suppose the lads will doubtless monopolize the Games Room, so fair's fair.'

And two minutes later, we're up another floor to the bedrooms, just a dozen in total. Wordlessly, he takes it all in, stopping only to check the flat screen TV's are all working or to make sure the sinks in the bathrooms are all in immaculate nick.

Finally, we're back downstairs at Reception again and now he's calling a taxi to take him back to the airport. Exactly forty-five minutes, I calculate. That's precisely how long he's spent in here. A lightning quick march around the kitchen downstairs, a brief hello to his HR woman, who sits bolt upright and smiles tersely when she sees him, and now he's ready to go.

'Good,' Rob says, as I walk, or more accurately race after him to the main door and we step outside together into the warm summer sunshine. 'Good work.'

'Well, we're getting there.'

'You know something, Chloe?' he says, turning to face me full-on now as, right on cue, a cab obediently pulls up outside.

'Yes?'

'I'm an intuitive kind of guy. Gut instinct. That's how I tend to operate. Have done so all my life. I knew from the minute I heard about the divorce hotel concept that it could work anywhere and I just know that this is going to fly for us.'

'I certainly hope you're right!' is all I can say back.

'Just remember, this is your big chance, Chloe,' he says, eyes really drilling into mine now. 'But I know you won't let me down.'

'I'll try not to,' I answer, thinking, jeez, no pressure. Next thing, he's clambering into the back of the cab, all long legs and angles. Then he rolls down the window and sticks his head out.

'Don't you worry though, I'm not leaving you high and dry. I'll be back. And sooner than you know.'

And he's gone, zipping off through the traffic and out of sight.

Two minutes later, I'm back downstairs in my office and Chris comes in, still ashen-faced and sounding breathy.

'Oh my God, Chloe, how did you get on? What did he say? Did he bawl you out of it for the state of the back garden?'

I fill her in as best I can.

'But then why was he in such a rush to leave?' she asks, puzzled. 'I thought he was here to stay, at least up until we open!'

'Ahh,' I smile knowingly at her. 'Not telling tales out of

school or anything, but it would seem there's a lady in the case. One he's very anxious to rush back to.'

Chris just rolls her eyes.

'Well, what else would you expect? With the Rob McFaydens of this world, isn't there always?'

TWO WEEKS LATER

Chapter Eight

Our Grand Opening. Actually happening. Here. Now. Tonight.

It's the very first day we've flung our doors open for business and every time I let nerves get the better of me, I come close to having to breathe into a paper bag, just to calm myself down. I've got twelve couples jetting in from four corners of Europe and even though my sane mind knows we're pretty much on track, every time I think of just how huge this is for me, I still have to resist the urge to slip off in a darkened room and wait for the panic attack to pass.

On the plus side though and with full credit to every designer, carpenter and builder who slaved so hard for us over the past weeks and months, the Hope Street Hotel is looking, dare I say it, so breathtakingly gorgeous, that I feel a chest swell of pride every time I trip down our magnificent *Gone With The Wind*-style staircase. Proud of the staff, the whole team and even, dare I say it, a tiny bit proud of myself.

If nothing else, Chloe girl, you made it this far!

All four floors are now carpeted in thick pale oyster cashmere carpet and look like they're nearly ready to appear in a design magazine. Every single fixture and fitting is utterly gleaming and our team of florists have really excelled themselves, with the most magnificent sprays of bouquets all in simple elegant shades of white and green adorning every room and spare surface, so the entire hotel smells fresh, fragrant and opulent.

Not only that, but each and every bedroom has been fully and personally vetted by me to make sure they've been kitted out with welcome baskets for each individual guest, plus toiletries in each en-suite bathroom especially sent over from Aspreys. Shower gels, make-up removers, toners, razors, even night creams; everything I could think of that a stressed-out guest might forget to pack, the whole works.

There's posh for you now, as my Mum would say.

Anyway, it's just past lunchtime and given that some of our guests can't arrive till after they finish work, our full programme doesn't really kick off properly till six this evening. I'm expecting a few early guests to arrive later this afternoon, and have made sure to have a full afternoon tea laid on for them, but for the moment at least, I've a short breather to myself to catch up on a few last minute details.

So I'm downstairs in my little rabbit warren of an office, frantically going over the programme of events for the weekend ahead and I'm not joking, you want to see the state of the place.

So many good luck cards are dotting the walls and covering my desk that you'd swear I was about to step onto the stage at Covent Garden to sing opera on an opening night. My family and pals have all been so amazing; it seems like every single one of them has thought of me and I'm genuinely touched to tears by their messages of support.

'We're so proud of you darling!' is staring back at me, on a gorgeous card from Mum and Dad and 'Good luck on your first weekend as GM,' from Gemma, with the tagged-on line, 'but just remember, the minute this is all over, you're jumping straight back into the dating pool . . . not taking no for an answer from you this time!'

Gemma, it has to be said, is on a perpetual quest to get me, as she puts it, 'back into the game again', now that I'm home. And only my constant pleas that I've barely time to brush my teeth these days, what with work being so all-consuming, has made her cut me a temporary bit of slack.

Of course I've been on a few dates over the past couple of years, but nothing of note. Goaded into it by all Gemma's encouragement while I was over in London, I did genuinely try my best to 'get back in the game again'. In fact at one stage, I'd been on more blind dates than a guide dog. Each and every one an unmitigated disaster.

First there was . . . what's his face . . . Eamonn, a 'free-lance TV director', who took me to dinner, then spent two excruciating hours explaining why we were all living through a golden age of TV, except that barely 30 per cent of audience share were gleaning it from telly these days; everyone else was watching online. He subsequently spent the rest of the date explaining in excruciating detail to an attractive blonde at the table beside ours exactly what the word troglodytic meant.

In desperation, I found myself telling him my favourite programme was *Britain's Got Talent*, just to get out of there that bit quicker.

Then there was Simon who I met online and who asked me out 'for Starbucks', like that was a noun these days. I honestly think the guy would have happily turned up in pyjamas, had it been an option. Anyway, I knew I was onto a loser when I asked what his plans for the weekend were and he proudly told me 'I'm going back to bed to try and beat my personal best at Angry Birds.'

I smile to myself, re-reading Gemma's card. But then right now, getting back into the dating pool seems like another bridge to be crossed at a later date, is all I can think.

Clicking on my computer and for about the thousandth time, I bring up our final guest list. And it's an interesting mix, to put it mildly, I think, scanning down through all the names. I've already met each guest individually, as of course, one of our hard and fast rules is that everyone's got to be personally vetted in advance of the weekend, just to make sure none of them are still at the stage of wanting to hurl furniture across rooms at each other and start calling each other lying, cheating bastards. But reading down through the guest list once again, I don't envisage that we'll have any problems. At least, I bloody hope not or let's face it, that's the end of me and the Hope Street Hotel.

Anyway, just like the original divorce hotel in the Netherlands, our guests really do seem to have come from all corners of the world. I've got couples from as far afield as Germany, Finland, Scotland, Sweden; I've even got a pair flying in directly from New York.

Lovely people too, the Fergusons, Larry and Jayne. By far the oldest couple I've got checking in, both in their late sixties, but with that sprightly energy and zest for life you see in retired people who take their fish oils regularly and have a golf handicap of approximately fifteen.

Course I was dying to know what brought them here in

the first place, when they've probably got the best divorce lawyers known to man right on their doorsteps at home. Kids or grandkids living in Ireland, I wondered? Or maybe some property investments here that they wanted to sell and divide between them?

Nah, the two of them laughed at me, when I spoke to them at the interview stage.

'Honey, we just wanted to get all the paperwork outta the way as fast as we could,' Larry said, then with a twinkle in his eye added, 'and give ourselves one helluva holiday, as soon as the legal bit is all over.'

'Sure, I mean, why not?' Jayne chimed in. ('Sure' pronounced Noo-Yawk style, so it sounded more like, 'Shu-waaah.') Jayne was one of those effervescent cruise ship blondes, with skin slightly too pulled back on her face and that New York sense of humour that always sees the gag in everything. I liked her on sight.

'Besides,' she grinned, 'I always love visiting Ireland.' (Pronounced, 'Ayre-laaand.') 'Can't stay away from the place!'

'Me too,' Larry nodded. 'Book of Kells, Trinity College, plus I hear you gotta lot of great golf courses here I wanna check out, while I'm at it.'

'And I wanna kiss the Blarney Stone,' Jayne giggled. 'Then go visit Knock, you know, at the grotto where our Lady appeared? Doncha get a miracle if you pray real hard there, like at Lourdes?'

'What do you wanna pray for?' Larry laughed. 'You're already gonna get half my money, thought that's what you wanted?'

'Well, there is that,' she said, poking him affectionately, 'but also I wanna pray for a new man to come into my life. Soon, before my knees give way!'

'She's just trying to make me jealous,' Larry grinned at me. 'But, just to be sure, we're still getting divorced, right?'

'Sure, honey. Just think of this as our fabulous divorce-y-moon. Kinda like the opposite of a honeymoon. Except better, because this way I walk outta here a helluva lot richer than I walked in!'

My easiest interview by far. I scrolled on down through my check-in list and my eye fell on another couple who'd really interested me. One Lucy Belton and Andrew Lowe. She's actually a really well-known model and has one of those faces you nearly feel you know as well as your own, she's in the papers that often. She's got – or certainly she used to have – the reputation as being a bit of a party girl and the press nearly always refer to her as 'Lucy Belter'. Or else 'Party Central', which is, if anything, possibly worse.

Back in her heyday, before she got married, I couldn't tell you the number of pap shots you'd see of Lucy in a skin-tight little dress (always a skin-tight little dress) falling out of some hotspot at 5 a.m., all long blonde tresses and killer heels.

Anyway, a few years ago, I remember there was a mass of publicity about the fact that the original party girl herself was suddenly about to settle down and get married. But not to some robust young soccer player with a monthly salary that ran into six figures, as you might expect.

It was just before I left Ireland – or rather, before I *had* to leave Ireland – and I remember being surprised that her groom-to-be was a much older, sober looking guy, a silver-haired, mustachioed businessman called Andrew Lowe. Of course no doubt disappointed that they were about to lose grade-A tabloid fodder, the papers had a field day with it, and I can still remember headline after headline

118

hinting that her sole interest in someone twenty-five years older than her most likely originated primarily in his bank account.

Mind you, I found it tough to even get a read on Andrew Lowe. On the day of his interview, he was super professional, answered all my questions, ticked all the boxes and was in and gone out of here in less than half an hour flat. Polite, businesslike and old-school gentlemanly. As for Lucy Belter herself? She arrived here a good forty minutes late the day of our 9 a.m. meeting, looking exactly like she'd come straight from a catwalk show and hadn't even bothered to change along the way.

Six feet tall with long, swishy blonde hair and immaculate 'camera ready' make-up, she was dressed in a tight little summery nude dress that on me would end up looking like bandages, but on her looked just . . . wow, traffic-stoppingly amazing. I couldn't help but pick up on the number of builders and workmen here at the hotel who made a point of hanging round Reception, just so they could get a good ogle at her as she swept by.

Funny thing was though, if you were to believe what you read in the papers, you'd have expected Lucy Belter to be some kind of gold-digger whose moment had now come. That's certainly what I'd primed myself for and yet that's not what I found at all. Once you got behind the fun, lively, Party Central image, I felt that underneath all the high octane glamour was just an ordinary, down-to-earth girl. Not only that, but someone who had genuinely married for love. As she kept telling me though, it was just 'circumstances' that broke them up.

I remember being utterly intrigued as we said our good-byes, thinking this is a girl who doesn't even want to be here in the first place. She's clearly coping with a lot of pain and I've nothing but admiration for how she's dealing with it so bravely, but what's baffling me is . . . what could have happened to bring a couple like her and Andrew to this?

I keep tapping a pencil off the list in front of me and my eye falls on the name of another couple that stopped me in my tracks. One Dawn Madden and her husband, who goes by the incredibly impressive name of Kirk Lennox-Coyningham.

A child, I thought, when I first interviewed Dawn a few weeks ago. My heart went out to the poor kid. If you saw her pale, frightened little face, you'd just want to take her home with you, give her a big feed of carbs and then allow her half an hour in front of the telly to watch cartoons, on account of she had to be up for school the following morning. I mean, come on, the girl got married at twenty-two. Who in their right mind gets married in their early twenties? Cousins and internet brides, that's who. For God's sake, I couldn't cross the street at that age, never mind get married. How, I find myself wondering, could her family and friends have stood by and just let it happen?

But then maybe they didn't. Sure, who am I to judge? Thing is, I've met her ex too, only last week. Kirk, who's only a few years older than she is. When he walked into his interview, I thought he was probably the most beautiful man I'd ever clapped eyes on, with jet black hair twice the length of my own, dressed head to toe in flowing white linen, and sitting cross-legged on the floor for our entire chat.

He was one of those guys that look right at you, deeply and evenly with soft brown eyes that seemed to bore into yours till it was nearly embarrassing. Casting agents, I thought would take one look at this fella and sign him up on the spot to play the lead in *Jesus Christ, Superstar*. And even leaving aside the fact that I'm a good ten years older than him, I can tell you t'was was a tough enough job to concentrate on the list of questions I had to go through, when all I wanted to do was gaze and admire all that gorgeousness.

The killer is that Kirk had seemed like such a sweetheart too. Kind and gentle. The type of guy, I thought, still gaping at him and trying to look professional, who'd give you a loving back rub if you had lady pains, then run out and buy you a slab-sized bar of Toblerone. So what could possibly have happened there?

Thing is, I've interviewed so many couples here over the past few weeks and I've listened to so many stories about marriages that have soured over the years, I thought I'd heard it all. I thought I was immune by now, that I'd even grown a bit detached, hearing the ins and outs of just what brings any married couple to our doors in the first place.

Then a young, vulnerable slip of a thing like Dawn walks in and just breaks my heart. Best and only hope I have to offer her is that she's so young. She'll move on in time. She'll rally again and find happiness with another. At least, I'd love to think so.

Next thing there's a rapping on my door and I look up to see Chris, barely visible under a massive bouquet she's carrying.

'Another good luck gift for you, Chloe,' she beams, plonking them square on my desk. 'So come on, tell me, do you have a secret admirer or what?'

'Doubt it very much,' I laugh back at her, ripping the card open and starting to read.

I hear tonight is the big opening of Hope Street Hotel. Will be thinking of you and wishing you well. Maybe we can meet sometime soon? Would love to talk.
Best, Frank.

'Well?' says Chris impatiently. 'Who are they from?'

I try to answer her, but somehow the words stick right in the back of my throat. And then a single thought that, once it takes hold in my brain, it just won't budge. In a parallel life, and if things had worked out differently, would any of these couples have been me? If I'd actually got to walk down the aisle that black day three long years ago, would Frank and I be checking into a hotel just like this too?

For a second I'm completely numb. Can't speak, can't answer Chris, can't even think straight.

So he did get in touch then. And he does know that I'm back here, barely a stone's throw from where he's working. And now he wants to talk.

'Chloe?' says Chris. 'You okay? You've gone all pale.'

Big weekend ahead. Do not let this get to you. Just file it back into the 'do not touch' part of your brain. Because you can't go there. Not now, maybe not ever.

'I'm fine,' I tell her, managing a wobbly smile.

And I'm yanked back into the present by an urgent text pinging directly into my phone.

I know you won't let me down this weekend. Will be there ASAP. Rob.

Absolutely no pressure, so.

*

122

Showtime. It's late afternoon and already, our first guests are streaming slowly but steadily through the front door. Tommy, our lovely barman is on hand in the marble-floored entrance hallway with a welcoming tray of champagne to greet all arrivals, before they head to Reception. Already the Webers, a fifty-something couple from Munich have just checked in, along with our couple from Finland and all are currently enjoying afternoon tea in the sun-drenched Lavender Room.

Next through the door are Jayne and Larry Ferguson and I instantly light up a little when I see them, but then they're kind of favourites round here already. Jayne dumps so much luggage with the doorman that you'd almost swear she was staying for a month instead of just a weekend.

'Oh honey, this is all looking so beee-utiful! You know, I could just break out into a tap dance routine on this awesome floor. Say, any chance I could just move in here after the divorce? I could be one of those resident guests who lives on the top floor and never leaves . . . whaddya say, Larry? You think my settlement will cover it?'

'Let's not jump the gun just yet, honey,' says Larry, grinning away and gulping back the freebie champagne. 'We've only just arrived . . . we're a long way off talking about hard, cold cash!'

I smile broadly, marvelling that they make it seem like such a breeze, and greet them warmly. Just as I'm inviting them to afternoon tea, I'm distracted by the sound of high heels clicking authoritatively through the door, followed by a bossy, abrasive voice wafting over from Reception. And instantly my stomach shrivels to the approximate size of a walnut.

'Jo Hargreaves and I'm here to check in. Now I called

in advance to request a southwesterly facing room, away from the lift and not under any circumstances to be on the same floor as Dave Evans. In fact, the further you can place us apart, the better I'll sleep.'

Ahh, Jo Hargreaves. What can I say about her? If the Fergusons are a firm favourite and if little Dawn is a pet that I want to keep a particular eye out for, then this one is one of those guests that I know from bitter experience will need to be handled in much the same way as you'd handle toxic waste.

Before we met briefly a few days ago, every iota of communication I had from her had been via email. One long, bossy list of edicts that she seemed to fire off from one corporate airline lounge, in some corner of the globe after another. Cancelling appointment after appointment on me, almost like she was cancelling a blow-dry and not the chance to sort out all her marital difficulties.

Now I know she's a big noise in some global company called Digitech, I know she's busy, but for God's sake, so are the rest of us! I met with her ex about a week ago, a chunky, slightly scruffy guy called Dave Evans; a jobbing actor, with a caustic sense of humour who asked if we could have our little talk in the garden outside, just so he could smoke. He just rolled his eyes to heaven when I mentioned in passing that his ex kept cancelling on me. I told him straight that I was worried whether she'd show up at all for the big weekend, given how much she seemed to travel and how many demands there were on her time.

'Oh, you don't need to worry,' he said dryly. 'Jo will be here if it bloody well kills her.'

Before we met for the first time, the mental image I'd formed of Jo Hargreaves was some kind of powerhouse of a human tornado in LK Bennett and heels, and yet she's absolutely nothing like that. She's tiny, round and pointy in the face, white as a ghost and with neat, bobbed hair, the kind that gets a three-week blow dry so it's less hassle and behaves itself at all times. Shellac nails, I notice too. The low-hassle kind.

As I trip across the hallway, I can clearly overhear her bossily dictating to poor Liliana, our lovely receptionist.

'And another thing,' she's saying, 'I want to see a full schedule of events for this weekend, so if you can have that sent to my room ASAP, I'd be grateful. I've got an important conference call to Chicago later tonight, so I'm absolutely *not* available to attend whatever's planned.'

'Well, actually . . .' Liliana tries her best to explain.

'Oh and just another point about my room,' says Jo, interrupting her, 'I want to be on a high floor, on no account at the front of the building, as there's far too much traffic. Also, if you have a pillow menu, can you forward it to me via email and I'll select my preference. A quiet room please, and it goes without saying, non-smoking.'

'We will, of course, do our best to meet with all of your requests, Madam,' I hear poor, patient Liliana finally getting to say. 'But I'm afraid that our events programme is obligatory for all guests.'

'Yes, well, you'll have to make an exception in my case,' Jo all but snaps at her, just as I step in to troubleshoot.

'Welcome to the Hope Street Hotel, Miss Hargreaves,' I smile at her. 'How may I be of assistance?'

'Ah, there you are, Chloe,' she says, shaking my hand briskly. 'Well, for starters, you can have my luggage sent up immediately and as I've some work to do, you can place a "do not disturb" on my room too.'

'Certainly Ma'am, and may I also offer you . . .'

'Oh and another thing, when Dave arrives?' she barrels over me, 'you can put him absolutely anywhere. Trust me, he'll barely even notice.'

Sweet Mother of all that's Divine, I think, smiling courteously back at her through gritted teeth.

What are we all in for?

Chapter Nine

Dawn.

Dawn was frightened, trembling and terrified. Sick and nauseous. And not sporadically either, this was all the time, round the clock, day and night. She'd become a complete nervous wreck to be around these days and knew only too well she was slowly starting to drive everyone around her up the walls.

But then that was the thing no one told you about marriage break-up. It was a bit like bereavement, because it was ongoing. Exact same symptoms: depression, listlessness, irritability and for some insane reason, round the clock exhaustion.

And to make matters worse, it was like everyone around her had colluded to get her to go to a divorce hotel. Seriously, she wasn't making that up, an actual *divorce* hotel. I mean, who wouldn't be freaked out just at hearing those two words in that particular order?

Of course it had all been her Mum's idea in the first place; she was the driving force behind this. Well, who else? She'd even offered to pay for the whole weekend, that's how strongly she felt about getting rid of a son-in-law she'd had serious doubts about, practically from the moment she'd first laid eyes on him.

'You need closure here, pet,' she kept firmly insisting. 'You need to put this chapter firmly behind you, so you can bring it to a civilized end and move on. You went sleepwalking into this marriage, as we all kept telling you at the time, if you'll remember? But you'd your head in the clouds and there was just no talking to you back then. And after all, you're still so young! You'll meet someone else in time, love, just wait and see.'

'But Mum!' Dawn had protested with the last few grams of energy she had in her. 'Suppose I don't care about meeting anyone else?'

'You may feel like that now,' was all her Mum would say, all but wagging the finger in Dawn's face. 'But that's only because you're still grieving this ridiculous marriage. Look at you, you're a complete mess! You're trailing round the place baggy eyed and a good stone underweight; we're all seriously concerned here. And who could blame you, after what that eejit put you through? Trust me though; life will be far, far easier once you're newly single again, love. After all, no man wants the messiness and baggage that a separated woman has to deal with, but once you're well and truly divorced, then it'll be an entirely different matter. You'll be free and ready to start over. Then wait till you see, you'll go on to meet a lovely fella. Someone who actually deserves you. For a change.'

Sweet Baby Jesus and the orphans, there were times when Dawn could have screamed. If she'd only had the energy.

'You know Mum's right, you've absolutely got to do this, hon,' her sister Eva drummed into her every chance she got. 'Because right now, you're stuck in a sort of limbo-land. Here you are, technically still married to that feck-head . . .'

'Please,' Dawn interrupted. 'It's Kirk.'

She was allowed to be disparaging about him, God knows, after what happened, she'd every right to be. But it wasn't okay when other people dumped on him. Just wasn't. Not yet, maybe not ever.

'Sorry,' Eva had said, rolling her eyes. 'Like I was saying, you're still officially married to – Kirk –'

Eva had a way of almost spitting his name and somehow managing to make it sound a bit like, 'prick'. 'And yet the two of you haven't been living together under the same roof, as man and wife for . . . what . . . over three months now?'

'Three and a half actually,' Dawn said quietly. Though in fact it was more: next Thursday, it would be exactly three months and three weeks since the day she'd first packed her bags and upped sticks. And she should know; she'd practically been measuring out the time in half-hour units. It was a coping mechanism and the only way she was somehow getting through this.

You'd think I'd have started to heal by now, she added to herself silently. *You'd reasonably assume that at least at this stage, I'd have come to terms with it, wouldn't you? After almost three months and three weeks? What the hell was wrong with her anyway? Why was she so leaden and dead on the inside? Why couldn't she just feel like everyone around her seemed to, angry and bitter and wanting nothing more than to pulverize Kirk's balls through a mincer for what had happened?*

'It's all over, there's absolutely no chance of

you reconciling after what he's done and yet, you're still officially tied to him!' Eva went on, taking a big glug of Pinot Grigio that Dawn had brought home as a special Friday night treat for the two of them.

'In fairness, we're separated,' Dawn corrected her. 'You could hardly still call us a married couple.'

'But sweetheart, it's ridiculous, that's what it is! Surely you can see that you can't just keep drifting on like this indefinitely? Sooner or later, you and Kirk will need to split all your joint assets, so there won't be any arguments about it down the line. Please understand, I've only got your best interests at heart here. You're in a kind of fug right now and, trust me, you need guidance.'

'And what joint assets would these be, exactly? We didn't even own our own home! We rented the flat and Kirk just took over the lease as soon as I left.'

Suddenly, Dawn was exhausted, way too tired to even entertain this conversation, no matter how well Eva meant. All she wanted to do was crawl back to bed and sleep for fourteen hours straight. Yet again. She stifled a yawn and hoped Eva might take the hint and drop it, but no such luck.

'You're way too modest, missy! Excuse me, but your little business importing spelt muesli is nicely profitable and growing every day, thank you.'

'Well, maybe, but that's only because at the moment, Kirk's taken over most of the day-to-day running of it. Fair's fair. He works just as hard as I do.'

And if the truth be told, these days he was working far harder. There was a time when Dawn had adored the whole challenge of building up the business and watching it grow, but somehow she just couldn't bring herself to it these days, even if she'd had the energy. Besides, seeing Kirk day in day out in a work situation when she'd have to be civil to him in front of other people was just too big an ask right now.

'Hmm. Well, it still needs to be divided fair and square,' Eva snapped. 'Ninety per cent in your favour, ten per cent in Kirk's. At least that's certainly what I'd consider fair and square, after everything that useless eejit – sorry, I mean, after everything *Kirk* put you through. Besides, I know this is the last thing on your mind right now, but it's only a matter of time before you'll meet someone else . . .'

'Oh please, not this again . . .' Dawn groaned, physically starting to feel ill just at the thought. Even after all this time, she still wasn't in a place where she could even contemplate looking twice at another fella.

Eva was having absolutely none of it though.

'Yes actually, this again. You know right well Mark in our IT department has a serious eye in your direction. He's always on at me to drag you down to the bar with the rest of us after work some night. And he's just one guy out of many who'd kill to date someone as lovely as you! Now I know you've got to go through the whole grieving process for your marriage, but believe me, in time you'll realize that you're far better off divorced, instead of being a separated woman with an ex who's clearly moved on –'

Honest to God, Dawn thought. Her family meant well, her sane mind knew they genuinely only wanted what was best for her, but left to herself, Dawn wanted nothing more than just to be left alone and in peace, not constantly encouraged to put her marriage out of its howling misery, once and for all.

*

Which was why late on a sunny Friday afternoon in July, a part of Dawn was almost surprised to find herself really here and about to check in. As usual, the good, docile girl, doing exactly what other people thought was best for her, yet far from certain that this was actually what she wanted herself.

But she had to admit her Mum and Eva were actually right. She had gone sleepwalking into marriage and now, shock and numbness were somehow making her sleepwalk her way out of it.

On auto-pilot, Dawn chained her bike neatly to the railings outside Dublin's newest boutique hotel on Hope Street, just off Fitzwilliam Square, took a deep breath and braced herself. She'd been here about two weeks ago for an initial interview with a lovely, caring woman called Chloe, so she knew what to expect, but seeing the hotel once again, it now struck her as weird.

Because from the outside, this place didn't look much like a hotel at all. It was one of those elegant old city-centre Georgian townhouses down a cobble-stoned street, ivy-clad and discreet. In fact, the only sign that betrayed that it was anything other than an upmarket lawyer's offices or a consultant's rooms, was a neat plaque on the wall outside, that read 'Ferndale Hotels, Hope St.'

Busy, professional looking people all bustled past Dawn, power walking their way into law offices or stockbroking firms or wherever the hell they worked, all yakking into mobiles or checking emails as they strode by her. No one took a blind bit of notice of this waif-like girl with the long straggly red hair down to her bum, almost trembling as she willed herself to walk up the steps and ring the front doorbell.

Climb the steps, just climb them. One at a time.

Can't do it can't do it can't do it can't do it can't do it

Just get up the steps and ring the bell, that's all you have to do. That's how easy it is.

It'stoomuchit'stoomuchit'stoomuchit'stoomuch

And now here it came, the fear. Shock, the cold sweats, the whole works. Was this really happening to her? And if she could barely even make it up the steps, then how was she ever supposed to face into what lay ahead?

A cold clutch of fear gripped her and she suddenly realized she was trembling. But then it had been so long since she'd even spoken to Kirk and the thought of having to go through this whole process side by side together was physically making her nauseous.

Right then. There was only so much arsing round with the lock on her bike she could pretend to be doing, to delay the inevitable.

Get it over with, Dawn, just get it over with. Remember, this isn't just what everyone around me wants, it's what Kirk wants too.

After all, Kirk had clearly moved on with his life. So wasn't it time she put the past behind her and did exactly that too?

A good, sobering thought that, and it got her all the way to the discreet buzzer at the side of the heavy, Georgian door. She buzzed and a young, smiley girl about her own age in a receptionist's uniform with a name badge that read, 'Liliana,' let her in. Funny, Dawn thought. I wonder if she realizes just how far a kind smile goes.

'Good afternoon! It's Miss Madden, isn't that right?'

'Emm . . . yes, I'm Dawn.'

'Come right on in,' came the smiling reply, in an accent that might have been Polish; it was hard to say. 'We've been expecting you.'

133

'Thanks.'

'And how are you today?' Liliana asked politely as she led the way into a stunning, black and white marble-tiled hallway.

'Terrific, thanks.'

Falling apart, that's how I am.

'Did you have any problems getting here?'

'No, none at all, thanks.'

Are you joking? When I was passing the canal, I almost wanted to throw myself in. Anything rather than have to face into this.

'May I offer you a glass of champagne?'

'No, thanks.'

It would physically choke me to drink it.

'If you don't mind waiting, our General Manager has asked to be told as soon as every guest arrives, so she can welcome you personally.'

Dawn traipsed after her and was led through the hallway and on into a gorgeous, quiet room, just to the right of Reception. She could hear voices drifting back from another room just next door, other early arrivals like herself, she figured. But given that she was in no kind of form to make polite chit-chat with total strangers, she was relieved when the room Liliana ushered her into was mercifully empty.

She found herself in a sort of cross between a library and a comfy sitting room, with high vaulted Georgian ceiling, leather wingback chairs and a chandelier you could possibly swing from if the mood took you. It was beautiful, comfy and welcoming, and yet to Dawn, the whole effect was just intimidating.

She was asked to sit down and did as she was told, just waiting on her 'fight or flight' hormones to kick in. The way she was feeling, it was only a matter of time.

Liliana made a polite bit of small talk about the general loveliness of the day, then offered afternoon tea. Dawn somehow found herself nodding yes, having barely registered a word she was saying.

'Please make yourself comfortable then,' came the reply, 'and I'll take care of your check-in and just let Chloe know you're here. She'll be with you straight away.'

Left on her own, Dawn took a moment to pace over to the window and gaze down at leafy Fitzwilliam Square, just across the street. Toddlers in strollers and a gang load of small kids were running amok down in the playground below, as the yummy mummy brigade sat on park benches looking proudly on, enjoying the late afternoon sunshine. Carefree, smiling women in skinny jeans and swingy tops with expensive looking handbags, who probably had loving husbands at home, to laugh with and row with and curl up to every night. Just like she'd signed up for. Just like she was supposed to have.

At that, sudden panic shot through her like an electric volt. *I shouldn't be here . . . I'm not sure I even want this! What am I even doing here in the first place?*

And what exactly would this whole process involve anyway? Oh God, even the thought of being in the same room as Kirk, with some total stranger asking them the most intimate details about their married life, was enough to make her stomach seize.

The palms of her hands were sweating now and her heart was palpitating, as her eyes filled up and her breath started to come in short, jagged bursts. A full-blown panic attack was imminent, no matter how much Dawn told herself just to get a good, firm grip.

Wonder if I could just make a run for it, she thought

frantically. Just get the hell out of here and tell Mum and Kirk and Eva that she'd just changed her mind?

I could easily do it, her mind raced. The coast is clear. I'll just tell everyone that I need the loo and then bolt for the hills. I can figure out what to do afterwards, can't I? But if nothing else, at least I won't have to go through with this . . .

Her thoughts were sharply interrupted as the heavy oak door behind her suddenly swung open. Next thing, in breezed Chloe, young and fresh and gorgeous just as Dawn remembered her, with her lovely shoulder-length blonde hair, bright blue eyes and that flawless 'Look! No make-up!' look, that Dawn knew right well took years to perfect.

Women like Chloe usually made Dawn feel a bit like a scruffy student, still smoking roll-ups and making the same pair of jeans last for a full week. And yet, Chloe was just so warm and friendly and down-to-earth, Dawn had taken to her on sight, the minute they'd met at their initial interview, just a few weeks ago.

Kirk was always going on about people's auras and hers was definitely yellow and blue. Colours of compassion and generosity. Might have sounded a bit mental, but somehow, for the first time since she'd crossed the threshold of this place, just being here with Chloe made her feel a bit less ick about being here in the first place.

'Well, hello there!' she smiled kindly, gripping Dawn's hand. 'It's so good to see you again, Miss Madden and huge apologies for keeping you waiting.'

'Dawn, please,' she said in a strangulated voice that she hardly recognized as her own.

'Ah, well then you'll have to call me Chloe. Please, sit down and can I just say that I'm here to personally make

136

your stay as comfortable and easy as possible. So if there's absolutely anything at all I can do for you . . .' She trailed off and there it was again, that warm, slow smile. Definitely a yellowy/blue aura. And Dawn would have put money on it that she was a Virgo. She had perfectionist written all over her.

Next thing, tea arrived and Chloe poured, politely asking her whether she'd had far to come? General, mannerly chit-chat. No doubt to relax you a bit, Dawn figured, before the shit really hit the fan, and she suddenly found herself having to tell some total stranger in this plush hotel all about the last time she'd had sex with Kirk.

And yet, so far, everything was . . . okay, she thought. For a start, Chloe actually seemed like a good listener. Would kind of put you in mind of an Aer Lingus hostess. You know, a giver, a people pleaser, one of those kindly souls who just couldn't do enough for you. The sort of woman who might just understand and unlike her well-intentioned family and friends, might even . . . shock horror . . . actually care about what Dawn had to say, for a change. Instead of dictating, 'This is the best thing for you right now!' and expecting her to just shut up and get on with it.

'I really should tell you,' Chloe chatted on, passing over a plateful of posh looking finger sandwiches. 'We've got a whole weekend packed full with a fairly exhausting schedule for you, which I have right here, if you'd like to have a look . . .'

Dawn drifted off and just nodded mutely, only half listening. Then after a bit more chit-chat, a silence fell and she was suddenly aware that Chloe was looking at her keenly, almost studying her.

'So, if it's okay with you, Dawn,' she went on gently, 'and before the whole process kicks off this evening, can I ask if you've any particular concerns that I can help you with?'

Well, this has to be it then, Dawn thought. The bowel-witheringly awkward bit. The part she'd dreaded. Her cue to sit here, and start dishing the dirt about her married life and why it had been so abruptly cut short. And why two souls who'd barely been married at all in the first place now needed out of it, fast. And just the very thought of the truth coming out, was now actually making Dawn feel like throwing up.

Suddenly it didn't matter how warm and trustworthy Chloe seemed. In spite of having come this far, now all Dawn desperately wanted to do was bottle out of it, say 'Sorry, I changed my mind,' and run away. Fast.

Chloe seemed to be onto her immediately though. Because in a flash, she'd got up out of the armchair where she'd been sitting and in one elegant move, was straight over to the sofa where Dawn was nervously perched right on the edge.

'You okay?' she asked, all concerned. 'If you don't mind my saying so, you don't seem to be.'

Dawn couldn't bring herself to answer though, just couldn't seem to piece together the right words to say in the right order.

'Because we don't have to do this, if you don't want. It's written all over you that you're petrified of what lies ahead. I know how awful this must be for you. Believe me, I know.'

Wow, Dawn thought. This is the first person in three months, three weeks and two days who actually seems to get how *I* feel about all this.

'And I'm sure it took nerves of steel to even bring yourself

138

this far,' Chloe went on. 'It's an awful, rotten situation for anyone to find themselves in and I can't promise you that the future will be all rosy and perfect once you check out of here, but I can at least tell you that what you're going through will all be over so, so soon. In a single weekend. Three short, little days out of your life and then that's it! You'll be free. For good. Free to start your life over, free to move on.'

'You don't understand,' Dawn said, suddenly finding her voice.

'Sorry?' Chloe was looking at her puzzled now.

'No one does. I'm barely able to take it in myself and I'm the one stuck in this whole nightmare.'

She broke off and was shocked to find that the fancy china teacup she'd been gripping onto was now actually rattling in her hands.

'I've been married for almost three years now, you see,' she went on. 'And I have to tell you, I don't want this. I don't want any of it. Kirk is – was – my best friend. My soulmate. I never thought I'd ever divorce him and I can't accept I'm even here in the first place. I can't accept what's happened.'

Chloe nodded understandingly.

'Of course, if you feel you're unsuitable for what we have to offer at the hotel,' she said gently, 'then I completely understand. You can just walk out of here and forget about the whole thing and that's absolutely fine. But if you don't mind, can I just say one thing?'

'Go ahead,' Dawn said dully, focused on the china teacup in front of her, studying the pattern on it, like she might have to take a test in it later on.

'Well, you've made it all the way here, haven't you?' Chloe

said softly. 'I know this must be hell for you, but you've come this far. So at least a part of you must have decided to go through with it. And your ex must want this too, surely.'

'Too right Kirk wants this. In fact, everyone around me wants this.'

And without even realizing it, suddenly Dawn's voice had choked up and the fat, salty tears that had been threatening ever since she first set foot in here were now starting to fall.

'Shh, shh, it's alright,' Chloe said, instantly producing a Kleenex from up her sleeve and slipping a comforting arm round her bony little shoulders. Then she looked at her full-on, eyes full of concern.

'It's going to be okay, Dawn. And you're going to be okay too. But you don't have to go through with this, not if you don't want to.'

'Oh, Kirk and I will be going through with this alright,' Dawn managed to get out through sobs muffled into the tissue. 'Whether we stick it out here or not, we're getting divorced. We have to, you see.'

'No, you don't! Not unless you both really feel it's the right thing for you . . .'

Dawn took a deep breath and braced herself. 'But you see, there's something about our marriage I need to tell you first. Something you don't know.'

Funny, Dawn thought. Wonder if my face went the exact same colour as hers, when I first found out the truth too.

Chapter Ten

Lucy.

Lucy was in foul, stinking humour and bloody hell, but did it show. All morning in work, it had showed, when a photographer she'd been shooting a commercial with bluntly told her, 'You look like complete dog shit today, love. You've got bags under your eyes I could carry luggage around in and your skin's like the surface of a pizza. Late one last night, was it then?'

Course, she'd told him where to shove it, but his words still bloody well stung.

Wasn't even her fault. Well, not entirely. Lucy had a rare day off yesterday and had insisted on dragging her pal Bianca into Carluccio's restaurant in town, 'just for the one!'

Ha! World's single greatest lie, she thought bitterly, popping yet another paracetamol from the plastic strip she'd rooted out from the bottom of her bag and knocking it back with a quick gulp of water. Anything to dull the crucifying, relentless hammering at her temples.

One glass of vino last night had quickly turned into one bottle of vino and blah-di-blah and on it went from there and before Lucy knew where she was, it was half one in the morning and she was drunkety drunk drunk. And of course, by then she felt on top of the world and in absolutely no mood to think about going back to Bianca's flat, which she'd been staying in ever since . . . well, ever since.

Are you joking? Go home? The newly single Lucy Belter? The girl once known as Party Central? On the same Thursday night when there'd been a big international rugby match on and when the town was only crawling with hot French blokes? Not a bleeding snowball's chance! So nothing would do for Bianca but to drag Lucy off to Lily's Bordello, the buzziest nightclub in town, to cheer her friend up a bit while they partied on into the wee small hours.

Not a bad plan, Lucy had thought. Why not drink on and get chatted up by properly wealthy guys who didn't necessarily have adult kids in the background, waiting to bleed him dry and piss all over her life in the process?

Anything to anaesthetize herself and keep her mind off the weekend to come and the whole ordeal that lay ahead of her.

She could barely remember what happened after Lily's Bordello. All she knew was that she woke up the following morning with a thumping head, parched with thirst and the very real sensation that she could puke. Hauling herself up onto her elbows, she groggily groped around the bedside table for her mobile to check what time it was. She was utterly disorientated, then with a slow, sickening feeling, it dawned on her that she wasn't even in her own bed.

Instead, she found herself in a strange hotel bedroom, with cheap nylon sheets that smelled like they hadn't been changed in weeks, an overriding stench of damp and lampshades a delightful, lurid shade of psychedelic 1970s orange.

Her breath stank like a brewery and – the cardinal sin for any model who happened to have a 9 a.m. photo shoot that day – still in full make-up from the night before. Even the pillow under her looked a bit like the Turin shroud, there was that much foundation and mascara caked onto it.

Worst of all though, she didn't seem to be alone. Through the gloomy half-light she could just about make out the lump of a giant silhouette in the bed beside her. And it was breathing.

Shit, shit, shit.

She hadn't, had she? Slowly, she slid her hand over to the other side of the bed and realized the lumpen shape beside her was bollock naked. Next thing, a stray hairy arm slid suggestively up her bare thigh and a French accent grunted, 'You want to slide over to my side of the bed, *chérie?* You ready for some more?'

It took Lucy all of approximately four seconds to haul herself out of the manky bed, somehow grab her clothes and shoes from last night and get the hell out of Dodge. Christ, could this really be happening to her, she wondered, head pounding and tottering uneasily in heels as she did the long, slow walk of shame out of the dingy, two-star hotel that was more like a glorified hostel in a rough end of town, and scoured round trying to find a taxi.

This was the kind of carry-on she got up to in her early – her very early twenties, for feck's sake! In a parallel life, she was supposed to be a happily married woman living in her beautiful home with a loving husband who adored her and maybe even a family of her own by now – not waking up in some kiphole of a hotel room with some bloke whose name she couldn't even remember! Was this really what her life had become?

143

Worst of all though, the morning ahead was due to be crazy busy for her; she was shooting a commercial for some highly overpriced tooth whitening gel stuff and needed to be absolutely on the ball, efficient and looking every inch the job. But one good look in her little compact mirror told her she wasn't near up for it.

She should have been more professional, she was someone who always prided herself on at least that. She should have known better. A lot better. But then last night, she hadn't given two shites, had she?

Needless to say, the whole shoot was an unmitigated disaster from start to finish. The clients weren't happy, the photographer was royally pissed off and as for the make-up artist? Lucy could have sworn he physically clutched his hand to his heart like a matron in an Ealing comedy, clad in twin-set-and-pearls circa 1950, when she'd eventually pitched up for work.

'Can you at least try and make me look human?' Lucy had pleaded with him groggily.

'Ehh . . . just so you know,' he'd said snippily, taking in how wiped-out and banjaxed she looked, with saggy, pimply skin and eyes more bloodshot red than blue. 'This is a make-up brush here. Not a magic wand.'

Lucy felt it in her waters that it was only a matter of time before a call was put into her booking agent, to complain about her. Who wouldn't? If she'd been the client, she'd have complained about herself too.

And to make matters worse, lo and behold, this was the very weekend she was scheduled to book in at that bloody divorce hotel. This evening was check-in. First time she'd have to be in the same room as Andrew since . . . well, she couldn't bring herself to think about that one. Not when she was still so completely woolly-headed and ropey, it physically hurt to even try to put two coherent thoughts together.

But thank God for Bianca, that was all she could say. After Lucy had crawled back home after work, her kind-hearted pal took one appalled up-and-down look at her and shook her head in despair.

'Oh Lucy, what have you done to yourself?' she said, horrified. 'I don't want to know what happened between you and that French guy last night, but Jesus, you pull one more stunt like that again and the agency will fire your ass so fast, you won't know what hit you.'

'Don't,' Lucy groaned, her body physically aching all over. 'Sorry, but I can't listen to this. Not now . . .'

'Into that shower immediately!' Bianca ordered, 'and I'll put on some coffee to pour down your throat. Over my dead body are you going in to face Andrew in that sorry state. You're about to head into the most intense weekend of your life and you need to be firing on all cylinders for this! Don't worry, I'll give you a lift into the hotel myself.'

'You really don't have to –'

'Yeah, right, like you're in any fit state to argue with me. If I put you in a taxi right now, you'd probably conk out in the back seat or else tell the driver to take you to the first bar you see. Jeez, the smell of stale booze off your breath! How many did you have last night anyway? And for God's sake, do something with your hair! You need to let Andrew see you looking like a million dollars, so he'll realize what he's been missing out on! Sorry for the tough love, but the state of you now, the man will take one look at you and think he had a lucky escape. So what are you standing there waiting on? Into the bathroom, now!'

145

In absolutely no condition to argue, Lucy did as she was told and half an hour later, was clambering into the passenger seat of Bianca's car, feeling if not exactly back to normal, then at least a tiny bit more human. Except of course now she was obliged to sit and listen to one of Bianca's well-intentioned 'little pep talks'.

'Now you just remember everything we talked about and you'll be absolutely fine,' Bianca told her from the driver's seat. 'Keep your head held high and don't forget the whole reason you're here in the first place. Andrew Lowe and that family of his as good as destroyed you. God, it makes my blood boil every time I think about it . . .'

Not in fact, what had happened at all, at least only the tip of the iceberg. There had been so much more to it than that. Still though, Lucy nodded along and made 'umm' noises when appropriate, barely listening to a single word of Bianca's advice, even though she only meant well. Couldn't. Not today, not now. Not when all she wanted to do was crawl back under the duvet, knock back a glass of Merlot and tell the rest of the world to feck off.

'And after all the misery his family made you suffer through, where did you end up?'

Pretty safe to say this was a rhetorical question.

'Heartbroken and living out of a suitcase, that's where! So this is it, love. You've got one single weekend to right a lot of wrongs and you can't under any circumstances mess it up. And of course, it's no harm to make sure you look utterly fabulous at all times and act like you're in a good place and moving on with your life. Remember what Ivana Trump so famously said?'

'Which was . . .?' said Lucy, not looking at her, instead,

desperately trying to freshen up her make-up in the tiny little passenger seat mirror.

'Well, when she divorced The Donald, her advice to all women was "don't get mad, get everything". Now I hate to sound mercenary, and it goes without saying that you're welcome to stay with me for as long as you like, but the hard cold fact is that you can't live the rest of your life with no home to call your own. It's not fair on you. You've got to give serious thoughts to splitting Andrew's assets.'

'Ehh, can I remind you that my soon-to-be-ex is about to be declared bankrupt? The man has nothing to split with me except debt and more debt!'

Even at that, Lucy shuddered to think how much worse things had got for Andrew since she last saw him. Sure, he'd once been wealthy, but he was a banker and a senior member of the Board at the Irish Banks Organization, which was basically how all their troubles had started. And it had been almost two months since they'd had contact of any kind. So how much further had his life free-fallen since then?

It broke her heart not being able to speak to him, but she'd been advised to communicate via her solicitor now, a Rottweiler of a woman who wanted to run all kinds of background searches on Andrew to see if he'd any hidden assets abroad. Big waste of your fecking time, Lucy had told her time and again, till she was blue in the face.

Firstly, even if he did, you can bet Alannah and Josh would have got their greedy paws on it by now and secondly, was it really worth all the bloody hassle? Anyway, Lucy had supported herself since the age of fifteen. And apart from a few recent blips, she hadn't done too shabbily, now had she? Yeah, sure she wasn't as young as she was, and maybe

147

she wasn't looking as fresh as she'd once done. But she was still well known and was still offered modelling gigs, even if they weren't coming in as thick and fast for her as they had done back in her heyday.

Lucy was smart though, streetwise in the way the business went, and knew it was only a matter of a few short years at most before the tabloids starting labelling her 'mutton dressed as lamb'. She'd had a good run, but snapping at her heels were another new crop of younger, hotter, fitter twenty-somethings wanting nothing more than to elbow her out of the way and move in on her turf.

Modelling was a piranha bowl of an industry like that and Lucy knew she was doing really well to still get offered work at all, at the grand old age of thirty-one. So, with grateful thanks to her booking agent, Lucy had lately started to diversify a bit.

She still had her regular slot on *Good Morning Ireland!* and now she'd been given her own newspaper column too, in the weekend pullout section of *The Chronicle*, advising anxious mothers of the bride about what upcoming Spring/ Summer trends were, or else giving seventeen-year-old debs a few tips on the best (read: cheapest) places to shop for their big night.

Not that there was huge money in any of it, but cash-wise at least, Lucy was somehow managing to keep her head above water. And she needed to earn, badly. Because of what had happened, she'd seen her entire world crumble right before her eyes and was frankly prepared to get a job stacking the shelves in Tesco rather than ever have to live through that humiliation again. Ever.

'Now you just hear me out, babes,' Bianca was still insisting, as they whizzed down the Stillorgan dual carriageway on their way into town. 'And try to keep a businesslike head on you. You've got to protect yourself money-wise and this is the weekend for you to do it. It's only fair and it's now or never. Remember, you poured all of your own savings into your beautiful home and you got absolutely nothing out of it, only grief and more of it!'

'Do we have to go over all this again? I swear, my head is actually walloping . . .'

'Are you honestly telling me that at his hour of life, the likes of Andrew Lowe doesn't have all kinds of overseas bank accounts and pension reserves, that you don't even know about?'

'But even if he did, you can be sure the banks would have swallowed it up pretty fast, to cover all his debts! Not to mention the fact that Alannah and Josh would have got their paws into it.'

'Stocks and shares you don't know about? Some hidden bank account buried away in the Cayman Islands?'

'That's a laugh! Besides, I've already been through this with my solicitor. She ran a full search on him and I'm telling you, there's nothing.'

'Excuse me,' Bianca said crisply, 'may I just remind you of something, Lucy Belton? When you first met Andrew, you were this gorgeous, outgoing, confident young thing with the whole town at your feet. And in the space of a few short years, he took you from being that fabulous girl to someone who's thin, miserable, effectively homeless, living in my spare room and grafting your arse off for every spare bean that comes your way. And what kills me is that none of it is even your fault!'

Lucy slumped back on the passenger seat and looked blankly out the car window as all the Friday evening rush hour traffic slowly inched past them. She was suddenly exhausted now, as the lack of sleep last night caught up with her.

'Are you even listening to a word I've been saying?' Bianca demanded. 'You've gone very quiet all of a sudden.'

'Yeah,' Lucy sighed. 'It's just that . . .'

'Just what exactly?'

'Well . . . I didn't marry Andrew for money, in spite of what everyone said about me at the time. At least, his first family certainly did. Do you remember how some of the scuzzier tabloids even made me out to be this gold-digger purely out for what she could get? But it was all complete horse shite. In spite of what they all said, I married Andrew because I was in love with him. End of. Absolutely nothing to do with what he had or what he didn't have.'

'So?'

'So after everything he and I went through, why has it suddenly become about nothing but money now?'

*

Soon, far too soon for Lucy's liking, here they were, pulling up outside the stately looking Georgian townhouse down Hope Street that looked absolutely nothing like a hotel from the outside. Hotels to Lucy meant flashy and gaudy, Vegas style, with valet parking, fountains in the front garden and usually a casino attached.

The kind of place she and Andrew used to stay in all the time, once upon a happier time. But this place was more like a posh lawyer's office, except one where you slept over till you'd thrashed out a separation deal, with minibars in the rooms and flat screen tellies. Lucy had been here once before; she'd already checked.

It took every last ounce of her resolve to haul herself out of the car, as she gave Bianca a warm hug and told her she'd be sure to stay in touch, every step of the way.

'Remember, I'm just on the other end of a phone if you need me!' Bianca yelled out the car window before tooting the horn and driving off.

Bracing herself, Lucy forced herself up the stone steps to the front door, wheelie bag clattering after her and rang the bell. And then, just on cue, a car she recognized all too well pulled up outside.

A Volkswagen Beetle, one of the Celtic Tiger-y ones with a soft top. The roof was down and she almost froze on the step when she clocked that Andrew was in the passenger seat with Alannah driving. The girl had sunglasses on, with her hair tied back in a Hermès scarf and a silk floral top Lucy instantly recognized as Stella McCartney.

Jesus, a Hermès silk scarf? Stella McCartney? After everything Alannah had put them through, she was still driving around in a flashy convertible, wearing designer gear that Lucy knew for a fact you could only buy in Brown Thomas for a minimum of seven hundred euro? (She could price it to the nearest penny; but then, she'd appeared in their last fashion magazine spread.)

Feck it, feck it, feck it, she thought, frantically buzzing on the door again and again. Would somebody inside ever open the door, quick, before Andrew caught up with her?

But she was a heartbeat too late. In a blink, Andrew was out of the car and standing right in front of her, first time she'd locked eyes with him in months.

A throbbing moment, where all Lucy could do was stare at him. He'd lost weight, she thought. And in that short space of time, he'd gone from slightly greying round the

151

temples, to almost completely silver-haired. He was always so handsome, tanned and distinguished looking, yet now he was pale and gaunt, a shadow of his old self.

'Hello Lucy,' was all he said, dark eyes focused on her and her alone. Then with a hurt and puzzled look, he added, 'Can you believe that we're really here? That we're actually doing this?'

The words caught in the back of Lucy's throat and she tried hard to think of something to say in reply, but instead all she could do was stare back at him like a mute eejit.

Just then, Alannah tripped up the steps after them, pointedly ignoring Lucy and handing Andrew a small weekend bag.

'You left this behind you in the car, Dad.'

'Hi Alannah,' Lucy managed to say, making a flash decision to try and be the bigger person here. Alannah turned to face her and for a split second, the two women locked eyes.

If it weren't for you, I wouldn't even be standing here in the first place, Lucy thought furiously, a hot flush of anger suddenly flooding through her.

But you're the one who's about to be divorced, Alannah glared icily back. *Which means one thing and one thing only.*

I win.

*

Finally, finally, finally, the door was answered. Well, it probably only took a bare moment in real time, but to Lucy it felt like an eternity. It was the General Manager herself, a lovely, bright girl called Chloe who she'd met just once before, when she'd first come here to see whether she was a suitable candidate for what the hotel had to offer.

Lucy had liked her instantly.

152

'Miss Belton and Mr Lowe, come in, you're so welcome,' Chloe smiled, and if she was surprised at them arriving together, her blank, professional face betrayed absolutely nothing. 'Let me have your luggage taken up to your rooms for you. And just before we get you checked in, may I offer you a glass of champagne at the bar?'

'Another time perhaps,' Andrew said politely, though more to Chloe than Lucy. 'And please forgive me, but I'm afraid I've got some emails I need to attend to urgently up in my room.'

Phew, Lucy thought, instantly perking up a bit. A drink was just what she needed right now and she'd relax and enjoy it all the more knowing Andrew wouldn't be around. In fact, she wasn't even sure how she'd get through the evening ahead without one.

Two minutes later, she was hopping up onto a barstool and gratefully accepting the champagne flute that an incredibly good-looking barman instantly poured out for her, with a wink and a warm smile.

Cheers, she said to herself, talking the fist delicious sip. *Here's to me. God knows what's ahead of me this weekend, but as long as there's a bar to hand, I'll get by.*

By the time she'd knocked back her first glass, she suddenly started to feel a whole lot better. The crippling embarrassment of this morning was fast fading into a dim, fuzzy memory.

But then mortification was a bit like a hangover, Lucy always found. The effects usually wore off as soon as you started drinking again.

Chapter Eleven

Jo.

Jo had been allocated a room plenty of losers would probably have given their eye teeth to stay in, but not her. Fortunately, she knew exactly what to do about it. Which was what she always did whenever room allocation wasn't up to her usual standards. In one expert, practised move, she flipped open her MacBook Air, logged straight into her browsing history and clicked on the webpage she was looking for. And then efficiently began to type.

Ferndale Hotel, Fitzwilliam Square, Dublin.
Reviewed by WellTravelledBusinesswoman_777
See my other TripAdvisor reviews.

It was with high hopes that I booked into the Ferndale group's latest addition to its firmament of stars earlier this evening. As a frequent traveller and indeed a member of the Leading Hotels of the World group, I've stayed in many other Ferndale hotels and can particularly recommend their Paris base; an oasis of calm in a bustling city, with five-star silver service and impeccable attention to detail throughout.

Sadly, the same cannot be said for its newest sister hotel here in Dublin. Firstly, like most well travelled members of the business community, when I check into a five-star hotel, it's with certain expectations. When I request a south facing room on a high floor, away from the elevator, I expect to be allocated one. Similarly, when I go to the bother and trouble of pre-requesting a pillow menu, I expect it to be supplied. And thirdly, the welcome fruit basket that was placed in my room, was thoughtlessly placed right in direct sunshine, with the result that two mangoes and one pear have now turned completely brown. (See attached photos.)

I have taken all of these issues up with management, and have yet to receive a satisfactory response.

A few moments later Jo looked sharply up as a gentle knocking on her bedroom door interrupted her. Instinctively she snapped her laptop shut and went to open it. It was the Head of Housekeeping, with two chambermaids directly behind her, one laden down with a selection of pillows, the other carrying a fresh fruit basket so huge, it almost dwarfed her.

'Apologies for disturbing you, Miss Hargreaves,' Jo was told. 'But we were told to bring these to your room right away. Also, just to say that you had requested a room on a high floor, and this is the highest there is. Sadly, though, the only south facing room available here is the laundry room, so we do hope this is alright for you. And the new fresh fruit basket is compliments of our General Manager Chloe Townsend, who hopes you'll very much enjoy your stay with us.'

Temporarily silenced, Jo managed to mouth a thank you as the ladies came into her room and started their fussing

155

around. Then, for no other reason than to get out of their way, she went into the en-suite bathroom and shut the door firmly behind her.

Why are you doing this? Why are you acting like such a complete bitch? she found herself asking her reflection, just like she did every single day, it seemed. *Look at yourself! Ever since you arrived, you've doing nothing but take it out on staff who are only doing their best. This is not you! This witch queen from hell surely can't be you!*

Should she go back out there and maybe apologize, explain? No, way too mortifying by far. Besides, where to even begin? So instead she settled for taking a good, long look at herself in the mirror before venturing outside again, tail firmly between her legs this time.

Reflection = not good news. Hollow, dark circles under her eyes? Check. Pale, saggy skin that plastering over with make-up somehow only made look even worse? Check. Lank, dark hair with a lovely crop of fresh grey roots coming up through it? Check.

Well, Jo shrugged, not that I'm particularly bothered what I look like. When have I time to get to a hairdressers these days? Besides, who in the name of arse would even be looking at her this weekend, only Dave? And he'd long ago forfeited the right to see her looking her best, that was for certain.

And then her eye fell on the neat cosmetic bag she'd put beside the double sinks earlier. Shit. Her pills. She'd almost forgotten. Two of the attractively named Gonal-F, one Follistim and all rounded off by the 200gms dose of Merional. Which by the way, was a state-of-the-art brand new wonder drug that her doctor swore was miraculous. Not that Jo had seen much evidence of that to date, but however. She lived in hope.

Over the last two years, she'd learned to.

When she went back out into her room, the chambermaids were just finishing up as the Head of Housekeeping gave her a big, bright smile and apologized once again for the mix-up over her pillow selection, pressing her to enjoy the fruit basket, 'with our compliments. And if there's anything else I can do to make your stay more comfortable, please call me directly and I'll attend to it personally.'

'Thank you,' Jo said, forcing herself to be polite and behave. She even generously over-tipped too, just because it felt right, then closed the door behind them as they finally left her in peace.

So what if she couldn't vent her anger on TripAdvisor or on innocent staff any more, the bitch troll that seemed to have taken up permanent residence inside her seemed to scream. There'd be plenty more for her to lash out on later.

Just wait until she was locked into the same room as Dave.

*

Dave, as it happened, was late. Nothing unusual there, Jo thought, Dave was always bloody late. In fact the man lived his whole life in a perpetual state of sending texts that read, *'running a bit behind, be there in 10 mins . . . sorry!'* She'd expected this. Been fully prepped for it, even.

But on check-in, Chloe had handed her a highly impressive tailor-made schedule which clearly stated they were booked in for an 'initial mediation meeting' with a solicitor called Sam Davenport. Naturally, Jo had Googled him to see exactly who this guy was beforehand, and was delighted to learn that he was actually one of the top, if not *the* top divorce lawyer in the country.

Even her own solicitor had been suitably impressed when she heard that Sam Davenport came as part and parcel of this whole weekend's package. 'Worth every penny,' she'd said to Jo at the time. 'And as it happens, for what you're paying, cheap at the price.'

Jo double-checked the neat printout she'd been handed and yes, there it was in neat black and white.

Friday 6pm: Meet and greet drinks in the downstairs bar.
7pm: Jo and Dave to hold an initial, private meeting with Mr Sam Davenport, specialist in divorce law.
8.30pm: Dinner in the Yellow Dining Room.

The 6 p.m. drinks thing, Jo just decided to skip altogether, which was why she'd just holed up in her room, opting instead to avail of the free Wi-Fi and catch up with work emails/arsing around on TripAdvisor. After all, what was the point in it? A meet and greet to say hi to all the other couples about to be ditched? Colossal waste of her time, even if she'd been physically up to it, which right now, she most definitely wasn't.

Or worse, were hotel management actually misguided enough to think that she'd want to spend any time socially with Dave, having a cocktail and a laugh and reminiscing about how great it had once been? Some chance. She was here to divorce him and divorce him fast, not to befriend the traitorous git all over again. She'd already acted out the whole pretence that they were a couple on completely friendly terms just to wangle a room here in the first place. Jesus, she'd given a performance worthy of Meryl Streep, hadn't she? Over and out. Enough.

As it happened though, her 7 p.m. meeting with Sam Davenport was the one single part of this entire process Jo had actually been looking forward to and she was bloody well prepped for it too. Thanks to her own solicitor's warnings, she'd arrived here ready for absolutely anything and had an entire wheelie bag full of her bank statements, household utility bills, affidavits from her own team to prove that she was the primary breadwinner – in fact, scratch that – the *sole* breadwinner. Moreover, that her beautiful apartment had been hers and hers only long before the unhappy day that Arsehole Evans had first waltzed into her life. You name it, she had all the necessary documents on hand, to back up everything she had to say.

And so promptly on the dot of 7 p.m., Jo turned up to the Library, wheelie bag in tow, all set to get this wrapped up and back to her room as quickly as possible. Sam Davenport was already there ahead of her; a youngish guy as it turned out. Dressed like the kind of man she was used to from work, in a tailored navy suit and a crisp blue shirt and tie.

The kind of man, Jo thought bitterly, that she should have ended up with. A successful professional, like herself. Someone who'd actually behave like a gentleman and stand by her, instead of that useless – she instantly dismissed the tail end of that sentence though and instead, took care to flash Sam Davenport her best 'professional, utterly in control' smile.

'Lovely to meet you, Miss Hargreaves,' he said, standing up to shake her hand as she barged in, wheelie bag clattering noisily over the parquet floor behind her. 'I'm Sam. Divorce law is my field and I'm just here to talk you and your ex through how we'll proceed over the course of the weekend. If that's agreeable to you, of course?' he added politely.

'Wonderful, yes, thank you,' Jo smiled back. First genuine smile she'd cracked all day. All month, in fact. 'And can I just say how lovely it is to meet you in person? You come very highly recommended.'

'We aim to please,' he replied graciously.

God, she thought, it feels wonderful to be in the hands of a real professional! Now all I need is for Sam to sit and listen to exactly what I have to say and it's all over bar the shouting. Wait and see, after ten minutes of hearing my side of the story, he'll probably end up hugging me and saying you poor woman, how anyone could have possibly put up with such a useless shit for so long is beyond me. In fact, Miss Hargreaves, not only do you deserve the fastest end to your marriage this side of Reno, but someone should give you a medal for putting up with everything you've had to endure at the hands of the medical profession. Not to worry though, I'm here to protect you and make sure Dave doesn't get his hands near a penny of your earnings and this will be all done and dusted in no time.

Easiest divorce I ever handled! That's what Sam Davenport will tell everyone, as soon as he's heard what I have to say, Jo thought confidently.

'Well, as you can see, I've arrived fully prepared, Sam,' she told him, indicating the stuffed bag she'd dragged along with her. 'I've got everything my own solicitor advised me to bring along, so that should significantly speed things up for us.'

'Excellent,' he nodded. 'I wish all my clients were as well organized as you.'

Jo nodded appreciatively and sat herself down on the sofa opposite him. Silence, while he looked down at his watch.

Still more silence.

'So . . . emm . . . where exactly do we start?' Jo couldn't help blurting out, anxious to cut to the chase. 'What do you need to know first? Because Dave and I have only been married for three years, but separated for nigh on five months now, so as you can appreciate, I'm anxious to close this unfortunate chapter of my life once and for all.'

Yet another pause as Sam took another quick glance down at his watch and out of habit, Jo found herself doing the very same. Exactly 7.10 p.m.

'Oh, I forgot to mention I may even be able to prove mental anguish, you know!' she tacked on brightly. 'I've got all the doctor's certs to back that all up. Because, when I tell you what I've been through – you just won't believe it!'

'That's all most interesting, Miss Hargreaves, but I'm afraid there's just one slight problem.'

'Well, I can't really see how there could be, actually. It's all here, everything you need. I just want to get a separation agreement that'll hold water in court, guaranteeing me I'll walk out of my marriage with absolutely everything I had walking into it, and then we can all go home. This,' she added with a smile, 'will be the single easiest case you ever had to deal with!'

'Yee-ess,' said Sam, 'and that's all good to hear. However, as you know, there's no such thing as a one-sided divorce.'

'Meaning?' Jo looked at him, puzzled.

'Meaning we can't proceed at all, certainly as of yet.'

'Excuse me?'

'I'm afraid it's going to prove something of a challenge to get you divorced, Ms Hargreaves. At least, not until your husband has the good grace to join us.'

Chapter Twelve

Dawn.

Two months, three weeks and five days. Dawn had counted. That was exactly how long it was since she and Kirk had even been alone together. Properly alone that is, in an actual room, where there was no escape from one another. Where they'd actually have to talk about the elephant standing between them.

She took a moment to glance down at the neatly printed, personalized schedule in her hands that Chloe gave her when she'd checked in earlier. Her eye darted down the page in front of her once more, just to be sure.

> *Friday 6pm: Meet and greet drinks in the downstairs bar.*
> *7pm: Dawn and Kirk to hold an initial, private meeting with Ms Kate Stephens, expert in conflict resolution services in the Lavender Room.*
> *8.30pm: Dinner in the Yellow Dining Room.*

There was no avoiding it any more. In just a few short minutes, she'd have to be in the same room as him. She'd have to somehow try to put on a brave face and act the part of someone calm, cool and reasonable. She'd have to remember at all times, that this was Kirk's doing, whether she liked it or not.

Of course she'd lost count of the number of times he'd tried to contact her during every day of the two months, three weeks and five days since Armageddon. But Dawn wouldn't, couldn't have the calm, civilized, 'I'm so sorry, please forgive me,' discussion that he so clearly needed to. Are you joking? It was out of the question.

Mainly because Kirk excelled at that kind of thing, he was like a living, Zen master class in getting people to spill everything out and openly express their emotions. Once they did, then of course, he was on home turf. It would be purely a matter of time before you ended up howling on his shoulder that you still loved him and of course, forgave him everything. Exactly the words that Dawn never would or could bring herself to say again.

So as a precaution, acting on her Mum's advice, when she first moved out, she'd changed her mobile number and made sure to give it to everyone bar him. Plus back at the flat, Eva was always there to call screen for her and God help Kirk if he called and was on the receiving end of one of Eva's tongue-lashings.

Their wedding anniversary had come and gone, he'd bombarded the flat with calls and somehow she managed to get through it all by just blanking him out. Or at least, by trying as best she could.

So predictably enough, Kirk's next step was calling into Earth's Garden, where she worked. Time and again, Dawn would look up from the till and there he'd be, standing at the door with the big brown eyes boring into hers, just willing her to drop everything and talk to him. That was all he wanted, it seemed, just to talk, just to try and get her back on his side again.

But she was a step ahead of him and had it all pre-choreographed with her pal Sheila, who worked alongside her in the shop. If and when Kirk did show up, then like clockwork and in a trembling quiver, Dawn would immediately leave the shop floor and head upstairs to her little office, while Sheila politely told him that either he could leave now or she could call the cops. Totally his call.

Then, in the past few weeks, he'd taken to writing to her, typical Kirk, via snail mail. So many letters, with her name neatly written in his copperplate handwriting on recycled, carbon neutral envelopes would land on her doormat, she'd lost count. But even though she was only itching to read what was inside and even though it took every last gram of strength she had not to rip open the envelope and have a good look, she'd disciplined herself just to return them unopened. And if nothing else did, then that would bloody well show him.

The man Dawn had married would have been cut to the quick to be deadheaded out of her life like this, but then that was his own tough shite, wasn't it? He'd hurt her first, he'd humiliated her and left her just this side of becoming a complete basket case and if he wanted someone to blame for the whole sorry mess, he only had himself.

Besides, having a conversation with him was completely pointless and a big waste of everyone's time. The only reason Kirk was so bloody anxious to talk to her was to make himself feel better. And once he'd wrangled the two magic words 'I understand,' out of her, then as far as he was concerned it would be slate wiped clean, the past forgotten and he'd be completely free to move on, while Dawn was supposed to sit happily on the sidelines with a smile plastered on her face.

God Almighty, did he really expect her to make it that easy for him? What kind of a pushover did he take her for anyway?

Worse, even his insane family, the Lennox-Coyninghams had started to move in on her lately.

'Now I know what's happened isn't necessarily the life path you would have chosen for yourself,' Dessie, Kirk's Dad had dropped into Earth's Garden to tell her, all Jesus sandals and stinking of dope. 'But you must remember, Kirk is like an overflowing vessel of love; always has been. He has so much love to give and this chapter of his new life is the natural expression of that. I really can't understand why you're not happy for him.'

'I'm afraid I don't have time for this,' Dawn had tried to interrupt, but now that he was here, there was no shutting Dessie up.

'Besides, what's so wrong with having an open marriage anyway? Think of the freedom it would give you, when the time comes when you move on and find another partner? It's the best of all worlds, for both of you! This way you and Kirk can still be together, and yet share all your sexual needs with another . . . what could be more perfect? Certainly works for Gaia and me.'

'Then the best of luck to Gaia and you, but I'm afraid I really have to ask you to leave please.'

'Dawn,' he said, stopping in his tracks. 'It may be the last thing you ever hear from me, but I only pray you'll listen! This is the healthiest and most natural way for any marriage to progress and flourish. You must trust me, I know what I'm talking about.'

It had taken every gram of strength Dawn had left in her not to fling the five-pound bag of lentils she was carrying into his face and only pray it would inflict lasting damage. An open marriage? What did these people take her for anyway?

'Believe me, it's the only way,' were Dessie's last words to her.

But no, it certainly wasn't the only way, she thought furiously. You know what was another highly effective route out of this, Dessie?

Divorce, that's what. So take that and shove it up one of your dope-clogged chakras.

*

Up in her hotel room, Dawn took a moment to glance at the TV, where Sky News was on in the background.

5.56 p.m. Which meant she had exactly four minutes and counting.

She was sitting catatonic on the bed, in a posh hotel room so impressively gorgeous that it was actually more of a suite really. It was super-luxurious with a flat screen telly and a bathroom big enough to throw a party in. Were you in the frame of mind for a party, Dawn thought wryly. If it had just been herself and her sister Eva checking in for a girlie weekend, then of course, somewhere this fancy would be utter bliss. But how was she ever really supposed to relax and enjoy it with a giant knot in her stomach, the size a sailor would use?

One good thing though; Kirk would surely hate, with every fibre of his being, having to stay somewhere like this. Particularly, as it was being entirely financed with the last few months' earnings from their little spelt import business. Which of course meant less money for all his precious goats out in Nairobi. No, Kirk would be far happier if they had to struggle through the misery of this weekend in a yurt, somewhere up a mountain, where you had to go to the loo behind a tree and walk two miles to find the nearest tap that had running water.

Dawn, on the other hand, could get very used to all of this luxury, thanks very much. This was the kind of room where even the cushions had cushions and she could swear the carpet under her bare feet alone was deeper and softer than any bed she'd ever slept in.

I work bloody hard, she figured. So when there's a few quid there, why not enjoy it? And after all, what was so wrong with flat screen tellies, Jacuzzis and room service anyway? Just because you happened to enjoy padding round in thick, oversized hotel dressing gowns enjoying the complimentary fruit basket didn't exactly make you public enemy number one, now did it? Though while she was married, she'd certainly felt that way.

Kirk you see, had a major thing about luxury and how guilty it made him feel, while children starved in Africa and twelve-year-olds worked in sweatshops in Bangladesh. And corporate hotels were a particular bugbear of his, on account of the strain they put on the earth's resources; something to do with all the linen he reckoned they had to launder day in, day out.

But then Kirk had issues with anyone who had the bare-faced cheek to wash towels and bed linen every *single* day. In fact, Ferndale Hotels would probably be the kind of place you'd find him outside on a Saturday morning, chained to the railings with a placard that said, 'Sheets used here made by eight-year-olds in Hizlapara! Boycott this hotel!'

It'll *kill* him being here, she thought.

Good. Serves him right. After all, he was the one who wanted the quickie divorce in the first place, so let him just bloody well deal with the consequences. And the best of luck to him.

Her phone on the bedside table beeped beside her, for about the twentieth time since she'd checked in. Pointless, she thought listlessly, even bothering to check it. It was either Eva, with one of the regular little cheerleading messages she'd been sending all day, along the lines of, 'Stay strong sweetie!' or 'Just think, in a few short days, you'll be one step closer to being young, free and single again!'

Or worse, it was her mother to say, 'Now love, don't forget everything I told you. Whatever you do, you make sure to give that useless eejit hell!' All well-intentioned, sound advice. No question, her family had nothing but her best interests at heart. Just the last thing Dawn wanted to hear right now, that's all.

She glanced at the TV, where Sky News finally told her it was just coming up to 6 p.m. Almost showtime. She gave herself a quick once over in the full-length mirror by the wardrobe one last and final time. Hard call, knowing exactly what to wear to meet the man who shattered your whole life apart and somehow try and look like you were holding it together.

Easy option; her black dress, but then Kirk was an expert in what he called 'colour deciphering', and you could bet he'd interpret that as a sign she was still mourning the loss of him. Which wouldn't do at all. She had a pair of jeans and a bright red top from Zara, but somehow jeans didn't seem like the right fit in a hotel this snazzy and red seemed far too celebratory. So in the end, she'd put on a simple white sundress with her long red hair flowing loose and a comfy pair of sandals. The good old reliable, 'couldn't particularly be arsed' look.

Just as the 6 p.m. news came on, Dawn steeled herself one last time. Be brave, she thought. Be strong. You've come this far. And remember, this is all *his* doing, not yours. You're not in any way responsible. He's the one who wants out, so this is the price he's got to pay.

You can do it, you can do it, you can do it.

Then feeling exactly like she was about to face the guillotine, she forced herself out of the room and slowly made her way downstairs.

*

The bar was already filling up as Dawn stood nervously in the doorway, fidgeting with her hands and glancing all round her to see if there was any sign of him yet. Weird thing, though. If she'd imagined that the mood in the hotel this evening would be all morose and miserable, then she couldn't have been more mistaken.

Instead, it was filling up nicely in here and waiters were expertly weaving their way in and out of guests, laden down with trays of fancy looking cocktails and champagne. Accents from all corners of Europe and beyond drifted towards Dawn and she found herself doing a double take. Here she was, a total nervous wreck at the thought of having to face Kirk, and yet plenty of other guests seemed not only delighted to see their exes, but were acting like this whole weekend was some sort of celebratory knees up.

Mother of God, they were even drinking champagne!

Who in their right minds would possibly want to celebrate being in a place like this? But one quick glance over at the bar told Dawn exactly who was doing most of the laughing and more than her fair share of boozing.

Sitting perched up on a barstool, looking fabulously blonde and glamorous with legs that seemed to go all the way up to her armpits, was Lucy Belton, the famous model. Dawn recognized her instantly, but then it was hard not to. The girl was never out of the papers and was on telly a lot these days too, as a sort of 'fashion and trend commentator'.

Sure enough, Dawn could remember reading that her marriage was on the rocks around the same time her own had so spectacularly imploded. Then something came back to her about her husband being a much older guy; there'd been a lot of quite bitchy Catherine Zeta Jones/Michael Douglas comments about the two of them when they'd first tied the knot. Some ancient looking businessman, Dawn seemed to vaguely remember from photos of them appearing in the gossip columns. Newly divorced, filthy rich; pretty much the type of fella you'd nearly expect to see with a gorgeous leggy model hanging off his arm.

Surely though, the guy sitting up on a barstool beside Lucy now couldn't be her ex? He seemed way too young for starters, late thirties at the most. Short-ish and over-weight with jet black scruffy hair, wearing a t-shirt and shorts, a bit like one of the hairy bikers. And yet by the intimate way Lucy was leaning into him, deep in lively chat, and judging by how he was hanging on her every word, the pair of them actually looked a bit couple-y. Like they were here for the night. Like they were imminently about to score, in fact.

'Well! Isn't this just the best, sweetie?' Dawn jumped,

suddenly hearing an American accent from right behind her. 'I mean, can you believe it? Come Monday morning, we'll be all single and ready to mingle again!'

She turned round to see a much older lady, sixty-something, with platinum blonde hair in one of those helmet-y 'dos', dressed like she was here for no other purpose than to party, in a glittery black dress with expensive looking jewellery only dripping off her.

'I'm Jayne Ferguson, by the way,' platinum-head went on, smiling brightly. 'And sitting right over in the corner there is my soon-to-be-ex, Larry.'

'Emm . . . hi. I'm Dawn Madden,' she answered, remembering her manners and politely shaking the proffered hand.

'You look a little lost, honey, you okay?'

You have no idea. I'm standing here, crumbling inside and you have absolutely no idea.

'Absolutely fine, thanks.'

'It's natural to feel a little apprehensive. But hey, that's what the champers and cocktails are for! To loosen us all up a little. You sure you're okay, sweetie? Hope you don't mind my saying, but you're white as a sheet.'

No, I'm absolutely not okay. I'm about as far from okay as it's possible to be.

'Yes, everything's great. Just lovely.'

'Well, I gotta say,' Jayne said cheerily, 'aren't you a little young to be getting divorced, honey? You must have been just a baby going down the aisle.'

Dawn managed to force a nervy smile, but said nothing. Just cast her eyes round the bar once more, to see if she could see him anywhere. Tall, long hair, more than likely wearing white like he usually did . . . in fact, it was hard

172

to miss someone who looked like Kirk in any room. But still no sign.

'Starter marriage, right?' Jayne asked her straight out, to stony silence. 'Happens all the time back in the States, sweetie. You marry young, because you think you know it all, then you both just grow up and grow apart. It's no one's fault, sweetheart.'

For the love of God, stop, Dawn silently willed her. *Please, just stop. You haven't the first clue what you're talking about.*

'Now I'm Larry's second,' Jayne happily chattered on, 'though for me, he's just my starter marriage, even though we've been together for over thirty years. Can you believe it? Two kids, both grown up and married themselves. So I guess you could say, I'm officially on the lookout now for my number two! So how about you, honey?'

But Jayne had just lost her audience. Because suddenly, there he was. All six feet of him, sure enough, dressed in a white linen shirt and jeans, standing over by the terrace door that seemed to lead out towards a very pretty garden area. The brown eyes locked into Dawn's and suddenly it was like the whole room shrank down to just the two of them.

'Well, hold me back! I'm gonna go out on a limb and guess that's your ex, standing right over by the garden door,' Jayne kept babbling away. 'Such a cutie too! Sure you want to get rid of him, sweetheart? Cos I'll trade you for my Larry anytime you like! Just say the word. I'm in the market for a younger model!'

'Would you excuse me?' Dawn half stammered as Kirk slowly wove his way through the crowd over to where she was standing, rooted.

173

For what seemed like an age, neither of them spoke. He just looked softly down at her, then gently went to take her hand.

'Come out to the garden, Dawn. We can talk there. There's so much I want to say to you.'

'But I'm not here to talk to you,' she managed to get out coherently, instinctively pulling her hand away, almost like she'd been electrocuted.

'I'm here to get divorced.'

Chapter Thirteen

Jo.

At exactly the same time, Jo went clattering on her high heels into the bar to try and find that git-face Dave himself. She didn't even waste time looking in any of the other reception rooms on any other floor for him, so rock certain was she this is where she'd find him.

And lo and behold, there he was. Sitting up on a barstool, nursing a pint of Guinness and – the bold, barefaced cheek of him – actually looking like he was enjoying the party and settled in here for the night.

Incandescent with rage, Jo wove her way through the other guests and strode over. Weird though; Dave must have sensed she was right behind him because her heels made such an almighty clatter on the wooden floor, yet still he made her poke him sharply in the back before he'd even turn around.

In other words, playing games with her, the rude bastard.

'Excuse me, Dave?' Jo snapped, trying her best to stay cool. 'You are aware that you've an appointment right NOW and that you're –'

'Well, well, well. If it isn't the old trouble and strife!' he slurred, grinned broadly, reached out to give her one of his bear hugs, which she immediately swatted away. 'How are you, dearest wifelet? Come here and give your old man a kiss!'

Oh God, he was drunk. One of the country's top divorce lawyers was patiently waiting for them both at a conservative cost of about seven hundred and fifty euro an hour, while this moron just sat here drinking? And what's more, after their meeting, there was to be a formal dinner in the hotel's restaurant. Yet here was Dave, looking like something a dog had vomited up on the side of the road. He hadn't even bothered wearing a suit, Jo thought disgustedly. He hadn't even shaved. Instead, he'd just rolled up here in a t-shirt, shorts and socks, with his head of thick black hair standing on end, as though to feign maximum disinterest and disrespect in all this.

'Come with me this instant, you idiot!' Jo hissed at him, only hoping that the barman and other guests behind her couldn't overhear. 'You're keeping one of the country's top divorce lawyers waiting, you know. While you just sit here drunk off your head, knocking back pints all alone, like the complete saddo you are. Now get off that barstool this minute and move!'

'Ha! There you're incorrect, my darling,' Dave beamed triumphantly back at her. 'That is, I may have had a few, but I'm most certainly not alone. Ah! Here she is now, the beauteous Ms Belter's back from powdering her nose . . . oops, sorry, Belton, I meant to say. Sorry, Lucy, that's what happens when you read one too many tabloids! Monikers tend to stick.'

Jo heard heels behind her and turned round to see what can only be described as a Glamazon weaving her way towards them. Christ Almighty, this one must easily be six feet tall, Jo thought, with long swishy blonde hair and dressed in the tightest little dress Jo had ever seen this side of an Egyptian mummy. Skyscraper high heels that she didn't even need, and make-up so heavy, it could only be described as nightclubby. In short, the kind of woman that usually ended up married to Rod Stewart.

'Hi there,' Glamazon smiled cheerily, 'I'm Lucy. S'good to meet you. You must be Jo, right?'

Hang on a sec, I know this one, Jo suddenly remembered. She's a model and a well-known one too. Never out of the papers and on just about every second TV chat show and magazine ad going. Married too . . . Jo racked her brains to think, and then it came to her. Of course, Andrew Lowe. He sat on the Board of the Irish Banks Organization at senior level. She'd met him before in fact; Digitech had sponsored one of their awards dos a few years back. In the days when corporations still used to shell out for awards dos, that is.

Bloody hell, she thought. And I thought Dave and I were a mismatch.

'Very nice to meet you,' Jo nodded curtly back at the Glamazon. 'But if you'll excuse us, Dave and I really have to get going –'

'Now whaddya want to go divorcing a complete sweetie like this for?' Lucy grinned, perching an impossibly tight little arse on the barstool beside Dave and, to Jo's annoyance, draping a possessive arm round his shoulder.

'He's just so adorable! Hey, Tommy?' she broke off, banging on the counter and calling over the barman. 'Another pint for my lovely friend Dave here and keep the champagne flowing . . . look!' she added, waving an empty glass over to him. 'We need refills! Urgently!'

Give me strength, Jo thought furiously. This one is fluthered off her head too. Not that it was any of her concern. Did she care what Lucy Belter, or whatever it was the papers called her, got up to? Party Central, Jo remembered was her nickname and doubtless, she'd end up leading conga lines of separated couples out through Fitzwilliam Square before the night was over. But frankly, let her; that was entirely her own concern.

'Dave, please,' Jo said as threateningly as she could, but all Dave could do was grin sardonically right into her face.

'And so the drama unfolds. You see Lucy? You beginning to get a glimmer what I've had to endure all this time? You have perhaps picked up on the bossy air of absolute authoritarianism about my beloved other half? That single-mindedness is what's propelled us here in the first place! I mean, a shagging divorce hotel, did you ever? A hotel where no one in their sane mind even wants to be in the first place.'

'Now you just listen to me, Dave,' Jo pleaded with him. 'I'm giving you exactly two seconds to peel your arse off that barstool and get into this meeting. Can you at least do that much for me? May I remind you that you promised!'

'Tommy!' Lucy interrupted her, banging loudly on the bar. 'Over here! Look, we need more drinkies!'

'Chill out and have a bevvie with us,' Dave grinned, patting Jo on the shoulder, like she was his best mate Bash, or one of his blokey pals. 'Might loosen you up a bit. For God's sake, look at yourself, you're about as tightly wound as a guitar string. It's Friday night, have a drink with us. Do you good, love.'

'Another drink!' Lucy chirruped beside him. 'Now that is a faaaaabulous idea! Join us Jo, come on, we're having a laugh! What can I get you? Glass of champoo maybe?'

'No thank you.'

'Suit yourself,' Lucy shrugged. 'But you know, it's gonna be a long, tough weekend, so the least we can all do is try to anaesthetize the pain. I know I certainly could do with a few more before I've to face into scary meetings with my ex!'

She and Dave burst into fits of drunk, stupid giggles at that, till Jo honestly didn't think she could take much more.

'Excuse me, do you mind staying out of this?' she all but barked at Lucy, glaring thunderously up at her.

'O-kay,' Lucy shrugged, before stage whispering at Dave, 'Maybe now I'm starting to see what you were talking about.'

'Oh, I could tell you stories,' Dave said dryly, 'that would make your hair stand up at the back of your neck.'

'Please!' Jo insisted, unable to take much more. 'This is your last chance, Dave –'

'Oh come on now, just one little drinkie,' Lucy insisted, pulling at Jo's jacket sleeve. 'Trust me, you'll feel faaaabulous! Dave here has been telling me so much about you, that I really feel like I know you already.'

'That I doubt very much,' Jo said irritably. 'Now would you kindly mind staying out of this?'

'That's a good man, you just keep 'em coming, Tommy boy,' Lucy said stoutly, patting the barman's hand as he topped up her champagne glass. And of course, no sooner was it served than half her drink was gone in just a few gulps.

'Dave. Move it. Now. This is your final warning,' said Jo, fully prepared to turn on her heel.

And yet still Lucy wouldn't butt out and mind her own business.

'You know something?' she said, head starting to loll slightly to one side. 'I think you're one veeeeery lucky lady, Jo.'

'Please, can you just stay out of this! You haven't the first iota what's going on here.'

'Ah, but that's where you're wrong! Jo, you have to listen to me. Because Dave here – my new best friend Dave –'

'New best friends! Well, I'll certainly drink to that!' Dave beamed, clinking glasses with her as Jo just stood there, seemingly powerless to break up this cosy boozing session.

'. . . Anyway if you ask me, I think our Dave here,' Lucy slurred, 'still loves you! Very much, too. Don't you, Davey-wavey! He no more wants to be in a place like this than I do!' Then dropping her voice down to an exaggerated stage whisper, she grabbed Jo's arm and added conspiratorially, 'And just between you and me, Jo? My sister-in-law went through the exact same thing as you, you know . . .'

'Dave,' Jo interrupted, beyond caring if she was being rude, 'don't make me go and get a manager to drag you out of here. Because if I have to, I will.'

'. . . The whole IVF thing, I mean,' Lucy stage-whispered kindly. 'And it messed her round no end too. Totally changed her entire personality! Just like you! I was just telling Davey here that she went from being this lovely, kind-hearted person to this unrecognizable BITCH in the space of just a few short months . . . you've never seen a transformation like it . . . And you can be sure that's all that's wrong with you too!'

A white-hot silence now as her words just hung in the ether.

Afterwards, Jo remembered thinking it had felt a bit like being slapped. The exact same sensation of shock mixed with swift, sharp pain.

Had she been hearing things? Could Dave really have

done that to her? After everything that had passed between them, had he really just betrayed her to some total stranger, in public?

Jo had said nothing though, couldn't if she tried. Instead she just stood rooted to the spot, looking from Lucy to Dave and back again, jaw dangling somewhere round her collarbone.

'Perhaps it would be timely to change the subject?' Dave had said to Lucy, at least having the good grace to redden and look mortified at this.

'No, no, hear me out!' Lucy insisted, totally unaware of the full import of her words. 'Jo, you gotta hear this! Anyway, after two bloody years of all these fertility drugs and clinics and treatments and sis-in-law biting the face off anything that moved, well . . . my poor brother was about to pack his bags and get the feck out of the line of fire. But then, on their very last round of it, whaddya know? Lo and behold, it worked! Sister-in-law was suddenly up the duff and nine months later, my gorgeous little nephew came along.'

There was a pulsing silence while Jo fought hard to stay calm. But try as she might she couldn't do it. A moment later, she and Dave locked eyes with each other as inconvenient tears, the kind she never allowed herself, started to well at the corners of her eyes. Next thing Dave drunkenly tried to haul himself onto his feet.

'Jo . . .' he said, sounding instantly sobered when he clocked exactly how upset she was, but it was too late.

Shaking, barely in control, Jo had turned on her heel and head held high, walked out of the bar so fast, she was almost a blur.

'Oh, shit,' she could hear Lucy saying, clamping her hand

over her mouth and looking apologetically over at Dave. 'Did I land you in trouble just now?'

'Well, what do you think?' said Dave, staring after his wife.

'I'm so sorry! I meant it to be a hopeful story!'

*

Jo could hear footsteps behind her as she raced for the lift and urgently pressed the call button. It arrived just in time for her to see Dave standing uselessly behind her.

'Jo please, I'm so sorry. She didn't mean a thing, it was just a stupid, throwaway comment, that's all . . .'

Thankfully though, the lift door slid over, so Jo didn't have to listen to another word. She even managed to make it all the way back to the privacy of her room, before collapsing behind the door, into a fit of hysterical sobs.

Chapter Fourteen

Dawn.

7 p.m. on the dot. Time for their initial, private conflict resolution with Ms Kate Stephens, as their schedule had so clearly spelt out.

Dawn was perched quietly on a sofa in the Lavender Room downstairs, about as far away as she could possibly sit from Kirk, who as ever, just sat cross-legged on the floor, eyes closed, like he was meditating and completely miles away.

Jeez, how could he do that, she thought, fresh anger suddenly flooding through her. Just tune out of the whole situation? A situation, she reminded herself, that they were only in because of him in the first place?

Kate Stephens, expert in mediation services, turned out to be absolutely lovely and so easy to talk to, just like everyone else round here. Late forties, Dawn guessed, small, blonde, red-faced, round and so welcoming, you almost felt like she'd start passing round mugs of tea and clotted cream scones next.

Or else telling fortunes, she just had that kind of aura.

'So Kirk and Dawn,' Kate smiled warmly at them both.

'The reason I'm here is to help resolve any outstanding areas of conflict and to identify any possibly contentious issues. This is just so when you both meet with our legal team to discuss division of assets which I understand is happening . . . emm . . .' she broke off to briefly refer down to her notes. 'Yes, you're both booked in for that tomorrow morning and again in the afternoon. So, this is just to help us iron out any possible areas of potential difficulty before we take you through to that stage.'

Well, that all sounds okay, Dawn thought. Nothing too scary. So far.

'In fact the way I like to describe my job,' Kate adds serenely, 'is as a sort of mirror to reflect the relationship's difficulties. Then together I can help you make all the vital decisions that you need to, so you can both freely move forward.'

Must look hysterical on passport application forms, Dawn thought. Occupation: 'A mirror to reflect divorcing couples' relationship difficulties.'

'Right then,' Kate said, sounding a bit like a kindly primary schoolteacher now. 'So who'd like to go first? Who's going to be brave and kick things off for us?'

Having avoided all eye contact since they set foot in here, Dawn now chanced a lightning quick glance over at Kirk, but still absolutely nothing doing from him. Instead, he was just focused dead ahead, still in a calm little chilled-out bubble of Zen.

Right, she thought. If he won't step up to the plate, then fine, I may as well get it over with. And he can bloody well sit there and listen. And just let him try to charm his way out of what I've got to say. Him with all his shite-talk about being an overflowing vessel of love and how it wasn't his fault if he was put on earth to spread the love in every direction he could.

If he even could.

'Okay, I guess I'll go first,' she heard her own voice saying, as she focused on Kate and only Kate. Easier that way.

'Excellent,' said Kate, all smiles. 'Whenever you're ready, then.'

'Well, you see . . . Kirk and I have been married for nearly three years now,' she began, a bit shakily. 'And for most of that time, everything was fine. In fact, more than fine, it was wonderful, we were happy. At least I stupidly thought so, until just a few months ago. When . . .'

Come on Dawn, she prompted herself. *You've got a captive audience here. Let him just sit there and hear it said out loud. Let's hear him try to defend the indefensible.*

Let's just see him try.

'Yes?' Kate prompted.

'Well, when I first discovered Kirk was being unfaithful to me.'

She let the sentence hang in the air for a minute. And oh God, but it felt good. Just saying it out loud to an impartial observer, while Kirk himself had no choice but to sit there and take it on the chin. She almost enjoyed it. In fact, she could almost get used to this.

Kate nodded, but crucially avoided saying all the things Dawn so desperately had hoped to hear from a detached stranger. Like, 'You poor girl. And Kirk, you utter arsehole! No wonder you're getting divorced, Dawn love, and as for you Kirk, I only hope you go on to have a miserable life with your new fancy woman, whoever she is. And may you

185

have an even worse break-up than this one and may you subsequently go on to be utterly miserable and end up broke and alone, living in sheltered housing and worrying about all your alimony payments.'

'Tell me more, Dawn,' was all Kate did actually say to her, sounding annoyingly impartial though and not taking sides.

'You see . . . I guessed something was up,' Dawn told her evenly. 'I'd sensed it for a while. For a long time, in fact.'

At that, she chanced a quick, surreptitious glance down to where Kirk was sitting on the floor, but still he was giving absolutely nothing away. Just staring out the window as late evening sunlight streamed in, utterly focused on a sycamore tree outside.

'And is there anything you'd like to say at this point, Kirk?' Kate asked.

Yeah. Because I'm all ears, Dawn thought coldly.

'Just let her speak, let her finish, she deserves to have her say,' was all Kirk said though, softly and barely audibly, almost under his breath.

'Please go on then, Dawn.'

'Well, I felt . . . that is I *knew* something wasn't right and it had been worrying me sick. I'd done everything I could to try and get us back on track again because . . . well . . .'

And here it came, the icky part. The bit Dawn had bloody dreaded, where you had to tell a total stranger that your husband who once couldn't keep his hands off you, had over time started to make you feel like you'd about as much sex appeal as a potted geranium.

'Keep going. You're doing really well.'

'Well . . . we'd been living under the same roof more

186

like brother and sister really, than anything else. For months on end. It was starting to drive me mental.'

Again no reaction from Kirk. No attempt to deny it. Not even the merest eyelid flicker, nothing.

'And how did this make you feel?'

How do you bloody well think? How would you feel? Like a sack of potatoes prancing round him in highly uncomfortable dental floss knickers and see-through bras, that's how. When I might as well have gone round our flat with a t-shirt on that said, 'Unsexiest woman in the world.'

'At first, I was worried sick,' was what she actually answered though. 'So then – well, I started to dig a little deeper. Because all the signs were there, I'd just chosen to ignore them. And when I finally discovered what was going on behind my back . . . under my own roof, a lot of the time . . . I mean, can you just imagine?'

Kirk, she noticed out of the corner of her eye, had finally started to focus on her now, calm and serene and cross-legged on the floor. Making absolutely no attempt to defend himself, just letting her have her say.

So on Dawn went, growing bolder by the second, it felt.

'You ask me how I felt,' she went on, 'and the answer is . . . just so worthless. Valueless. Like the past three years of my life counted for absolutely nothing. Like I'd been a complete eejit for not guessing sooner. Because when it came down to it, the blindingly obvious had been staring me in the face for so long.'

Only the truth. Flashing back, Dawn rewound back to just a few short months ago, when she'd first gone to Kirk's computer to check something. (In actual fact, her bank balance and what a lampshade she'd put on eBay was now bidding for.)

187

And there it fecking well was. Her first tiny clue. A whole series of emails in glorious Technicolor, right on his computer screen. Gobshite hadn't even the sense or the good taste to delete them, just in case she chanced on it. Almost, she clearly remembered thinking at the time, as though he actually wanted her to see. Worse, as though he felt he had absolutely nothing to hide.

And now she saw that Kirk was still calmly listening, making absolutely no attempt to contradict her or to jump in till she'd had her say.

They hadn't been living together for so long now that Dawn had almost forgotten he was like that. A listener. Even if someone was calling him a lying, cheating bastard of a husband, he'd just sit there and take it and continue to take it till they eventually ran out of expletives and were left with steam coming out their ears. And that was usually when he'd launch into one of his 'love and peace' speeches. Or else the one Dawn had nicknamed the John Lennon memorial speech because it went something along the lines of, sorry for making you bawl crying.

'Hmm, I see,' Kate nodded sagely. 'And again Kirk, can I ask if you've got anything you'd like to say at this point?'

But Kirk was now single-mindedly concentrating on Dawn and Dawn only, worry and sadness etched all over his beautiful, tanned face.

'We don't have to do this,' he said softly, just to her, acting like Kate wasn't even in the room. 'You and I are bigger than this, don't you see? This negativity, all these accusations, you and I don't need it. We can rise above this. This isn't who we are.'

And next thing, in one of his fluent yoga moves that Dawn could never master on account of the way her knees cracked, Kirk was up off the floor and right over beside her, gently cupping his hand over hers.

'Don't touch me,' she said stiffly, instinctively sliding up the sofa from him. 'Don't you ever touch me.'

He looked hurt, she noticed. Bloody good enough for him.

'You must know how sorry I am. I never meant for any of this to –'

'Leave it, Kirk. I'm sick of it. I'm tired of your excuses and all your ridiculous speeches about how you've so much love to give and how you don't want to lose me. Because you know what it amounts to? A big pile of shite-ology! Just like reiki healing, Kirk, which by the way, I also happen to think is a load of dog poo. And while we're on the subject, the astro-chart reading you gave me for my birthday? Eva and I laughed ourselves silly over it and she even suggested we use it as loo roll.'

'But I thought –'

'I thought we were husband and wife and that meant something to me! I'd have said anything! I'd have said mass if I thought it would make me fit into your world that bit better. But then, you'd know all about lying, wouldn't you? You and your double life!'

'It's okay,' he said, putting his hand in the small of her back and immediately going to massage it. She baulked though, and he instantly stopped. 'Just let it out, Dawn. All the anger, the harshness and acrimony. Let it all go. Verbalize it, then visually imagine it all inside a pink balloon, that's just floating away from you . . .'

'Oh, will you shut up about bloody pink balloons! Because you want to know something? Getting married to you was a horrible, awful mistake and everyone is right,

189

my mother and Eva and everyone. All I can do now is try to extricate myself from it as quickly as I can!'

And having held it together for so long, the tears were finally threatening.

'We don't have to do this,' Kirk said, looking like a hurt little boy. 'Not here, not like this, not now. You know I never stopped loving you . . . not once . . . and I never will either. Nothing has changed between us, not a thing. I still love you as much as I did the day I first committed to you. Loving someone else doesn't mean I love you any less. I love all women, you know that. And there's no reason why you and I can't continue on, just as we were . . .'

'How could you, Kirk!' Dawn yelled at him for all she was worth. 'In our flat, in our bed! How could you have done that to me? You lied to me, you deliberately misled me and all I can do is sit here and hope to God you suffer for it. You're the one who's always banging on about karma, aren't you? So why don't you try shoving that in one of your pink balloons?'

'Please, both of you!' Kate tried her best to interrupt the pair of them. 'Let's just try to stay cool and detached. Remember, there's never any need for raised voices!'

Too late though. Now that the two of them were physically locked in a room together and had actually started to communicate, after months of enforced silence, there was suddenly no shutting them up.

'I never lied to you,' Kirk said, still so annoyingly serene that Dawn wanted to screech and fling a vase at him. 'I never led you on . . . it was never my intention to . . .'

'To what? To do what exactly, Kirk? To have an affair right under my nose? Why can't you for once in your life, accept that you can't just do whatever you want, whenever

190

you feel like it? Your actions have consequences for other people around you . . . in this case, me!'

'You have to understand that . . .'

'That what? That you and your lover just accidentally fell into bed together and things went from there? Is that what you want me to believe? Just how stupid do you think I am! What kind of an eejit do you take me for anyway?'

'You know that isn't what I think at all –'

'Oldest cliché in the book, isn't it? The wife is the last to know! So just how long had things been going on between the pair of you before I walked in on you? Care to tell Kate all about that?'

Kate, meanwhile, was up on her feet now, like a school-teacher in a classroom she could no longer control.

'Please, I really must ask you both to lower your voices and to stay nice and calm for me. All of this is getting us absolutely nowhere!'

Dawn completely ignored her though.

'So will you tell her or will I, Kirk?'

'You're not even attempting to listen to me –'

'I asked you a question!'

'And I need to talk to you. But not here and not like this!'

'Fine, if you won't, then I will.'

A pause while Kirk just looked at her. And suddenly, feeling scarily in control of the whole situation, Dawn turned back to where Kate looked like she was practically about to call security.

'You'll notice Kirk won't fill you in on my replacement,' she said quietly. 'Someone he's seeing still, as it happens. So it's up to me. But you'd better prepare yourself for this though. It's quite a shocker.'

191

'Then let's all discuss that, but nice and sensibly,' Kate said, sounding relieved that at least things seemed to be cooling down between them a little.

'Fine by me. But I think you may want to sit back down for what's coming next. I certainly know I had to.'

Chapter Fifteen

Chloe.

So I'm barely out of one meeting when I'm striding through Reception heading straight into another (banqueting manager, tomorrow night's scheduled shindig, don't ask) just as our guests are drifting into dinner.

And so far so good, I'm thinking. All our guests seem to have settled in well and are busy with initial meetings, just before the showstopper of a dinner our head chef's laid on for later this evening. I allow myself a tiny sigh of relief and am just touching wood that everything continues to run this smoothly, when suddenly my mobile rings.

One quick glance down at the screen is all it takes and my heart rate has instantly shot up into the high nineties. Him. Rob. One of his 'hi, just checking in with you!' phone calls which as he and I both know by now, are actually anything but. They're spot checks, just under a slightly friendlier name, that's all.

Which is fine and which I completely understand; after all, it's his money at stake here, isn't it? It's just that all this constant micromanaging is making me feel like the guy still doesn't quite trust me to do the gig and do it right.

What in God's name, I wonder, will it take for him to see that I've got everything under control?

I slip into the entrance hallway, where it's that bit more private, so I can really hear him properly.

'Chloe, talk to me, how's it all shaping up?' is his cut-straight-to-the-chase opener.

'Rob, hi!' As always, I somehow manage to over-compensate for how nervy these calls never fail to make me with slightly OTT cheeriness. 'How's everything?'

'More to the point,' he says, 'how is your first evening going so far?'

Sounds incredibly busy, whatever corner of the globe he's calling me from this time. And trust me, with this guy he could literally be anywhere. Zimbabwe, the top of Mount Olympus, you name it. There's roaring in the background, like engine noise. Way too noisy for a regular car, barring it was a Ferrari Formula One model. We both have to shout to even hear each other.

'Everything is absolutely perfect!' I yell over the noise. 'All of our guests have checked in and everyone seems to be absolutely delighted with their room arrangements. Oh and by the way, the mini flat screen TV's in the bathrooms went down a bomb too, let me tell you.'

'They always do in my experience. So no complaints so far?'

'Are you joking? Absolutely not!'

Only a tiny little white lie, as there was that Jo Hargreaves. But then from the first time I laid eyes on the woman, I just had her down as the kind of guest who absolutely nothing is right for, no matter how well you looked after them. There's always one, isn't there? In any hotel I've ever worked in, you can take it as read that there'll be a guest that needs to be handled, and the big challenge for me as GM is to turn their whole experience completely around and send them home a happy camper.

Besides, I remind myself. Jo Hargreaves is here to get divorced. Hardly surprising if she's not exactly dancing on the ceilings, now is it?

'Everyone about to have dinner round now, I'm guessing?' Rob asks, again almost having to shout over the noise around him to be heard.

'Eh . . . yeah, yeah, that's right!' I tell him. 'We'll be serving dinner shortly and then first thing tomorrow morning . . .'

'Speak up a bit, will you? The racket going on in the background here is something else.'

Too right, it's almost deafening me.

'Rob? Whereabouts are you?' I have to really shout this time, just so he can hear me.

'Long, long story. Tell you when I see you. So everything's okay and our first evening went well? You're happy with the progress?'

'Absolutely,' I tell him confidently. 'I think I can safely say we're off to a great start. All of our guests have settled in well, they seem relaxed, comfortable and happy to take the first steps towards getting divorced now. So do you plan on coming over to see how things are running here for yourself?'

No offence, but please say no. We're all under quite enough pressure here without Rob McFayden breathing down everyone's back.

'You know neither the day nor the hour,' is all he gives me to go on, though. Which let's face it, could fecking well mean anything.

'Anyway Chloe, I really have to go. Just checking that no soon-to-be-exes were overturning tables and stabbing each other in the eyeballs. At least, not to date.'

'Don't you worry a bit,' I laugh a bit pitchily. 'Things couldn't be running more smoothly really! Each one of our couples was carefully screened before they got here and it goes without saying, they're all on the absolute best of terms with each other . . .'

Suddenly, I'm interrupted by the sound of screeching, coming from right behind the closed Lavender Room door.

'YOU COMPLETE AND UTTER *BASTARD!!!* YOU LIED TO ME JUST LIKE YOU LIED TO EVERYONE ELSE, PRACTICALLY FROM DAY ONE!'

'Dawn, please, I really need you to calm down and listen to me . . .'

'NO I BLOODY WELL WILL NOT CALM DOWN! I'M FED UP WITH EVERYONE TELLING ME WHAT I SHOULD AND SHOULDN'T DO! WHY DID YOU DO IT, KIRK? YOU WERE THE ONE WHO INSISTED THAT WE GET MARRIED IN THE FIRST PLACE! WHY PUT ME THROUGH ALL THAT WHEN YOU KNEW ALL ALONG IT WAS NEVER GOING TO MEAN ANYTHING AT ALL TO YOU?'

Oh, holy shit. I recognize both voices instantly. Dawn and Kirk. Missing dinner, still in their mediation session and by the sounds of it, only a heartbeat away from properly gouging each other's eyes out.

'Chloe? You still there?' Rob asks worriedly, dragging me back to the call.

'Emm . . . yes . . .'

'Marrying you wasn't just what I wanted then,' Kirk's insisting, and not in his usual deep, sonorous, calm voice at all. Right now he sounds heated and intense, which catches me off guard, bearing in mind, this is probably the last man on earth you could ever imagine losing his cool. 'It's *still* what I want, Dawn. The last thing on my mind is to just cut you out of my life. Do you think for one second that I could ever contemplate that?'

'NO! YOU CAN'T SAY THINGS LIKE THAT TO ME KIRK! YOU DON'T GET TO HAVE THE BEST OF BOTH WORLDS!'

Sweet Jesus. They're actually killing each other. And right now, from the sounds of it, poor Dawn is only a degree away from setting fire to Kirk's long, swishy ponytail and flinging all his white, flowing *Jesus Christ Superstar* gear onto a bonfire.

'Chloe?' The urgency in Rob's voice pulls me back to the phone. 'What was that in the background? Is everything okay there?'

''Yes! Perfect! Couldn't be better. Well, thanks so much for the call, but I'd better get back to work here . . .'

'Because that sounded like shouting to me. A whole lot of it.'

'Nothing to worry about, all under control.'

Next thing, a very flustered looking Chris comes racing down the stairs.

'Chloe,' she hisses urgently, 'you'd better come up here as soon as you can. Room two eleven. We've got a problem.'

'Now what?' Rob insists down the phone.

'Absolutely nothing! Few minor emm . . . teething problems, that's all! Well, thanks again for phoning and . . .'

'. . . And I'll see you very soon,' are his last words to me, before hanging up.

'SO WHY EVEN BOTHER MARRYING ME IN THE

FIRST PLACE KIRK? THAT'S WHAT I'D LIKE TO KNOW!
AS WOULD MY WHOLE FAMILY!'

Oh God, now it's like the entire hallway can hear Dawn
Madden's shrieking voice, reverberating round the marble
floors at Reception.

'Don't tell me that's Dawn and Kirk?' Chris asks
worriedly.

I nod gravely. 'And what's worse is that there's precious
little we can do about it either, remember. No matter how
much I'd like to. They're in a mediation session. You can't
interrupt that, no matter how much you might want to.'

That was drummed into me ad nauseam during orientation for this job. Apparently interrupting a one on one
session with any of our counsellors or advisors is akin to
barging into a confession box with a video camera, then
uploading it onto YouTube.

'Why do you *think* I married you, Dawn?' Kirk is
insisting, and for the first time starting to sound heightened
and upset, so unlike the usual chilled-out state he's been
wafting round in ever since he first arrived. 'Because I loved
you then, as now! Just because my circumstances have
changed, doesn't mean that's any different. You know I still
worship the sacred feminine!'

'OH PISS OFF KIRK AND STOP PATRONIZING ME!
DO YOU KNOW WHAT A GOBSHITE YOU SOUND
LIKE WHEN YOU START SPOUTING CRAP ABOUT
THE SACRED FEMININE?'

'I do not believe this,' I hiss over to Chris, shaking my
head. 'I thought of all the couples staying with us, this pair
would be the last to cause trouble. The husband, Kirk? Big
gentle giant of a fella, wouldn't hurt a fly!'

And as for Dawn, right from our very first meeting, she

198

was kind of my secret favourite round here. So young and frail and frightened, all I wanted to do was hold her hand and tell her it would all somehow work itself out. Though now I'm not so sure.

He's had an affair, she'd told me earlier. An ongoing one and now he'd someone special in his life that he'd absolutely no intention of giving up, married or not. So to be perfectly honest, were I in poor Dawn's shoes, I think right now I'd be yelling far worse at him.

'You think that's bad?' says Chris. 'Wait till you see what's waiting for you upstairs.'

There's damn all I can do for Dawn and Kirk now, so I make a mental note to try and get a private chat in with Dawn whenever I can get her alone, as Chris and I grab the lift and shoot up to the second floor. And this time it's a man's voice doing most of the roaring; I can hear him loud and clear the minute the lift doors slide open. Jeez, we should give serious consideration to re-naming this place 'Screechy Towers'.

Together, Chris and I race down a corridor, turn it at the bottom and there he is. Dave Evans, husband of Miss High and Mighty Jo Hargreaves, hammering at her bedroom door so violently that he's threatening to do himself an injury.

'FOR FECK'S SAKE JO!! WILL YOU JUST LISTEN TO ME!!!'

'Piss off! Just leave me alone,' comes her voice from behind the door, thankfully sounding a bit calmer than him, and at least not turning this into another full-on screaming match.

'It was just a stupid, throwaway remark, Jo, that was all! Lucy didn't mean it, she didn't set out to hurt you,' Dave yells at the locked door, and as he's so chubby and stocky, the wallop he gives the door almost makes it shake. He looks sharply up as he hears us approach. And I'm not messing, I swear I can smell the stench of booze off him from approximately ten paces away.

'Evening Mr Evans,' I smile as brightly as I can. 'Everything alright here? Can I possibly help you with anything?'

We're trained to deal with potential situations like this and let's just say in my experience, belligerent guests tend to cool the head a bit when treated with firm politeness.

'Oh shit,' he says, ignoring the question and going back to thumping on the door. 'JO? FOR GOD'S SAKE, OPEN UP! SECURITY ARE HERE AND THEY LOOK LIKE THEY'RE ABOUT TO CART ME OUTTA HERE!'

'Good!' comes her muffled reply. 'The sooner the better.'

'Except,' he says, suddenly speaking conversationally in that dry way he has, 'naturally, with this being the five-star establishment that it is, security in question is actually an extremely hot blonde and her trusty sidekick.'

And with that Dave turns to face Chris and I full on, speaking nice and calmly now. Only the fact that he's swaying slightly on his feet betrays that he's blind drunk.

'Evening, ladies,' he slurs at us. 'As you can see, I'm doing nothing more than trying to have a private conversation with my beautiful, soon-to-be-ex wife. Was I making a bit of a rumpus? Other guests unable to hear their in-room tellies over my banging? Mortified apologies.'

He throws a fake, flourish-y theatrical bow and a rush of relief washes over me. If nothing else, at least the guy seems to be making it easy for us. When a guest has let's just say, over-indulged, you never know what way things could go.

'That's quite all right, Mr Evans,' I tell him firmly, 'but just to say you're both missing dinner. May we escort you back downstairs to the dining room?'

There's a long drawn out, weary sigh while Dave slumps down on the ground with his back against the door and stretches two hairy legs out on the carpet, looking utterly defeated.

'No, no I don't think so,' he eventually says. 'And there won't be any need for the handcuffs or the armed escort either, ladies. I'll come quietly. Wasting my time here and frankly, the thought of dinner would only choke me. I doubt very much that fancy truffles and posh petit fours would do me much good this evening, the way I'm feeling. But thanks for asking all the same.'

'In that case, may we offer you something from our room service menu?' I ask politely, bending down on my hunkers to look him in the eye. Something to eat, is my reasoning, is by far the best way to sober him up a bit.

'Most kind of you,' he smiles at me sardonically, running his fingers through thick, unruly hair, so now it stands on end, a bit like he's just been electrocuted. 'But if it's all the same, I'll pass. I'll be far happier spending the rest of this miserable night staring at the four walls and who knows? Maybe dreaming up ingenious new ways to try and get my wife to actually listen to me for a fecking change.'

He hammers his fist into the door one more time and instantly we all hear Jo's voice loud and clear, 'Do that one more time, Evans, and I'm calling security! You have been warned!'

201

Chris and I shoot a look at each other and in a flash, we both know exactly what to do.

'Let's get you back on your feet again,' I say, linking his arm and helping to haul him back up. Chris grabs the other and we eventually manage to hoist his dead weight up into a vertical position.

'I think I may just . . . emm . . . have a little lie down now,' Dave slurs, head lolling a little.

'Great idea.'

'Or at least it would be, if I could only remember where my room was.'

'I'd be delighted to show you, it's not that far,' Chris says obligingly as she leads him down the corridor and round a corner, him ambling alongside her, unsteady on his feet.

'Gimme two secs,' I mouth silently at her, 'I'll be right after you.'

I wait till they're both well out of the way, then tap gently on Jo's bedroom door.

'Miss Hargreaves? It's Chloe here. Could I have a quick word?'

Long pause. Then her slightly muffled reply, 'One second, please.'

A minute later Jo opens the door and I almost get a fright when I see the state the woman's in. She's in her dressing gown, blotchy-faced and with eyes roaring red, like she's been up here crying for the longest time. Looking a million miles from the neatly groomed, be-suited power ball that landed in on top of us a few hours ago, and who's done nothing but moan and gripe at staff ever since.

Because Jo looks so small and defeated right now, for the first time since she got here, I'm actually starting to feel a bit sorry for her.

'Oh, it's you Chloe. Good, I'm glad you're here,' she says, motioning for me to come inside. 'I wanted to speak to you anyway.' I follow after her and spot her laptop open on the bed, surrounded by snotty Kleenex, almost as though she's been reading something online and having a good bawl about it at the same time. She notices me seeing it though, and instantly snaps it shut.

'Just making sure you were alright,' I smile. 'And of course, if there's anything at all that I can do for you –'

'There is,' she says, in a wobbly little voice. 'The thing is . . . I know I can rely on you to disregard Dave's little performance just now. Because believe me, that's all it was. A performance. He's quite good at that. In fact,' she adds bitterly, 'it was how he got me to marry him in the first place. Just kept on mortifying and haranguing me in public, until I eventually said yes.'

I say nothing. But I can so well imagine the scene playing out.

'And there's something else,' she goes on. 'We had an appointment with a divorce lawyer earlier, Sam Davenport. And Dave never showed up for it.'

'That's not a problem. I can reschedule that for you, if you'd like?'

'If you would, thanks. Though not for this evening. Right now, I'm just not in a place where I can . . .' she breaks off here and suddenly looks so wounded, that I almost want to give the woman a hug and tell her it'll all be okay.

'I'm so sorry,' she says, voice cracking just the smallest bit. 'I'm just . . . well, I'm not really feeling myself this weather.'

'Don't worry,' I tell her gently. 'Believe me, we've all been there. And it'll all be over soon and everything will be just fine. Please trust me.'

'Bless you for that,' she says, looking at me with eyes starting to tear up again. 'I just wish it – this – wasn't so bloody difficult. I had no idea. I thought he'd make it easy for me. I thought it was the least he could do, all things given.'

'How do you mean?'

'Because,' she sighs, slumping down defeatedly onto the edge of the bed now. 'I know right well what everyone thinks when they look at Dave and me. They all assume that I'm only trying to shove him out of my life, because I'm not . . . well, let's just say because I'm not quite myself at the moment. And everyone jumps to the conclusion that Dave is the wronged party here and that none of this is his doing, it's all just one hundred per cent me, as usual. The big bad she-wolf.'

I say nothing, though to be perfectly honest, that was exactly what I'd assumed myself.

'But they're quite wrong, you know,' she goes on. 'There are two sides to everything you hear. Two sides to every story. Just remember that, Chloe.'

'Of course,' I tell her gently. 'And if you ever want to talk about it, well, here I am.'

'Thank you,' she mouths, like her voice is choking back tears she's too proud to shed in front of anyone else. 'But I'm afraid now just isn't the best time for me. So if you'll excuse me . . .'

As I take my cue to leave, it's only heartbreaking. And I think the sight of her determined chin stuck out, like she's too proud to crack in front of me, goes straight to my heart quicker than anything she could possibly say.

Chapter Sixteen

Jo.

I didn't used to be like this, Jo thought now that Chloe had just left her in peace. And it was kind of the girl to check up on her, way above and beyond the call of duty. She'd kept on saying 'Am I disturbing you?' and Jo had instantly snapped her laptop shut, like she'd been busily working away. But the truth was, she hadn't been working at all.

She'd in fact, been re-reading emails. From just a couple of weeks before she and Dave had first got married, oh what felt like an eternity ago now. Hard to explain, and given that Jo was a complete emotional yoyo at the minute, even harder to put into words, but the unclouded part of her brain needed at least this much.

She desperately wanted to remind herself that she wasn't slowly going mad and there was once a time when she and Dave had been happy. When she'd actually been in love with him, and was genuinely looking forward to getting married.

Might have sounded mental, but it was just something she needed to do right now, and badly. Because her acting like such a thundering cow towards him, as she had been for so long now, not to mention all his incessant barbs and put-downs couldn't have been the way things used to be, could they? There surely was a time when the pair of them weren't at each other's throats, wasn't there? Were even, dare she say it, happy?

And then, scanning down through a pile of ancient emails, dated from three years ago, just a few weeks before they'd married, she began to read.

From: Jo_Marketing_Director@digitech.com
To: davesblog@hotmail.com
Re: Outstanding pre-wedding tasks that need to be done today and please Dave, I really do MEAN today!!!
January 31st, 9.17 a.m.

DAVE!!!! Are you still asleep??!!! No apology if this email wakes you, feck you anyway, you should be up and about by now. Come on love, remember you've that massively big job interview this morning and by the way, I left out what I think you should wear for it on the spare bed. But please, please will you listen to me on this one Dave? NO TRAINERS. If someone walked into my office for an interview wearing trainers, I'd call security.

Anyway, much, much, much to do and as you know, I'm en route to New York, then Chicago till the end of the week, so here's a few outstanding jobs that I really, seriously need you to take care of by the time I get home.

Firstly, can you confirm with the florist that the groom and best man's buttonholes are the correct colour match? I know you think this kind of thing

206

doesn't matter, but trust me, every single woman who's going to the wedding will notice. Mood board is on my bedside table; all colour schemes are clearly laid out there.

Secondly, you've this afternoon completely free, so do me a huge favour and collect my dry-cleaning, would you? There's at least two outfits there I need for the Digitech conference the day after I get back. Really BEGGING you not to forget this Dave, unlike last time I asked you and you forgot on account of you had to watch the Monaco Grand Prix live on Sky.

Lastly, any chance you'd call into Brown Thomas re: the wedding list and tell them to strike off the Vera Wang teapot and to replace it with the one by Villeroy and Boch in the Grey Pearl pattern? This may seem trivial but it's actually of EXTREME importance. Tom from Accounts very kindly offered to get us the Vera Wang, but when I look at the pattern closely, it looks less like 'aquatic scene' and more like killer scorpions are coming to get you.

Think that's everything for now, but I left you a copy of my pre-wedding to-do list on the kitchen table. Can you go through it with a fine toothcomb and make sure there's absolutely nothing I'm overlooking? And don't do what you did with the last schedule I gave you, and use it as liner for the cat's litter tray.

Funny the first time, not so funny now.

Right, I've just arrived at airport security, gotta sign off. Be back to you soon as I board.

Kisses and a big warm hug,

Jo xxx

From: davesblog@hotmail.com
To: Jo_Marketing_Director@digitech.com
Outstanding pre-wedding tasks that need to be done today and Dave, I really do MEAN today!!!
January 31st, 9.47 a.m.

Jaysus woman, I'm out of bed now. Happy? And as it happens, darling wifey-to-be, I'm actually not around this afternoon to jump through hoops and do your bidding. I'm working on an audition piece for a part in a Noel Coward show that's going into the Gate. Then I'm meeting a bloke I know from the Equity for a few scoops; he needs advice on getting a new agent.

But before you have a heart seizure up there in the business class lounge, relax, rest of the jobs outlined will all be done by the time you get home Thursday. Even if it does involve me having a conversation with some total stranger, about shagging china teapots.

You are a complete control freak, you know that?

Lucky for you though, I happen to love you, very much.

Dxx

PS. your dry cleaning? Get a grip.
PPS. I lost my key to your flat. Caretaker have a spare by any chance?
PPPS. re: this whole wedding of the century; I personally couldn't give a shite if we cancelled the whole three-ring circus it's turned into and just pitched up at the registry office instead. Told you we should have just gone to Barbados and got married on a beach, with two strangers for witnesses. HA! Starting to regret not listening to me now, aren't you, my pet?

From: Jo_Marketing_Director@digitech.com
To: davesblog@hotmail.com
Re: Outstanding pre-wedding tasks that need to be done today and please Dave, I really do MEAN today!!!
January 31st, 10.42 a.m.

Jesus Dave, are you kidding me about losing your key? This is the third spare key I gave you that's gone AWOL. Angie on the second floor (apartment no. 7) has a spare; you can take hers and get it copied.

Now you do realize that it's now well past ten thirty and if you're still in the flat, then that means you'll be late for the job interview . . . so step away from your bloody iPhone and MOVE!! Let's not forget the trouble I had even getting you this interview in the first place. And I know you don't give a shite about the theatre critic's job and think it beneath you, but trust me, you need to find something worthwhile to do with your time while you're 'resting between engagements'.

But be warned, do not, repeat; DO NOT describe yourself as a 'blogger'. Trust me, the minute you say that, all any potential employer hears is 'lies in bed all day playing Angry Birds on Facebook'. Remember what I was saying about going in there and cutting a professional dash.

Air hostess now blatantly glaring at me for emailing during the safety announcements; better sign off.

Jo x

PS. on no account are you to wear your black jacket to the interview, it makes you look like a Goodfella. Navy one I left out for you far more suitable.

From: davesblog@hotmail.com
To: Jo_Marketing_Director@digitech.com
Re: Outstanding pre-wedding tasks that need to be done today and please Dave, I really do MEAN today!!!
January 31st, 10.44 a.m.

Sorry Jo, got emails crossed there with Jane Austen who actually came out with the phrase, 'cut a professional dash.' Relax, chillax, you're up in there on a Business Class flight, so for feck's sake just knock back a glass of champagne and switch off your bloody phone, like a normal person.

FYI, you'll be delighted to know I'm wearing the gear you laid out, even if the shirt and tie are f**king killing me. If I happen to run into Bash or any of the lads while I'm in town, I'll never hear the bleeding end of it.

Kindly remember, dearest love, you're the one who wanted this job for me, not the other way around.

Travel safe,

Dave x

PS. Where's the Cheerios?

From: Jo_Marketing_Director@digitech.com
To: davesblog@hotmail.com
Re: Outstanding pre-wedding tasks that need to be done today and please Dave, I really do MEAN today!!!
January 31st, 10.50 a.m.

Me again love,

I know I'm driving you insane with all my emails plus there's an air hostess now threatening to confiscate my phone and I'm being glared at by a highly overwrought looking businessman sitting right beside me.

But I forgot to say I love you and I can't wait to marry you,

Jo x

PS. Best of luck with the interview, but then I know you'll ace it.
PPS. Cheerios are the top cupboard, the one to the left of the fridge. Jesus Dave, where they always are.

From: davesblog@hotmail.com
To: Jo_Marketing_Director@digitech.com
Re: Outstanding pre-wedding tasks that need to be done today and please Dave, I really do MEAN today!!!
January 31st, 10.53 a.m.

And very fortunately for you, I happen to be in love with you too, in spite of all the complete control-freakery.

Dave x

Funny thing, but sitting in her Hope Street Hotel room right now, Jo even knew where she'd been when she'd first written those emails. She vividly remembered sitting on that transatlantic flight all those years ago, kicking off her neat LK Bennett court shoes, sitting back and for the first time in weeks, allowing herself to relax and just concentrate on breathing deeply.

She remembered closing her eyes and repeating her mantra: all is well and my wedding WILL be wonderful. Everything that could possibly be organized had been, and the only thing over which she had no control was the weather on the day. (Long range forecast was good though; at that stage, she'd been Googling it twice daily.)

Then, just as the plane started thundering down the runway for take off, she remembered thinking about Dave. And okay, so even though he needed looking after pretty much as you would a ten-year-old, how lucky was she to even have him in the first place?

Three short years ago, she'd reminded herself, you were a thirty-six-year-old single woman who hadn't even had a date, never mind a serious relationship since turning thirty. There had been three popes since the last man she'd even kissed, never mind dated seriously. Hadn't the time.

Besides, by then, Jo had been promoted to marketing director of Digitech and was now working with the world's top ten agencies and advertisers. She was on a flight twice a week, every week; it had got to the stage where she was on first name terms with a lot of the cabin crew.

And yet something had shifted inside of her. God knows, she loved work and loved her career but couldn't stop herself from asking, was this really what she wanted for herself at the grand old age of forty? Living out of a suitcase, shuttling from hotel room to hotel room and from one conference centre to another? With no time to socialize, no time to do anything in her downtime, bar catch up on laundry and then last thing at night, to go to bed alone and lonely.

So Jo made an executive decision and did what she always

did – took complete control. She made an appointment with a good, old-fashioned matchmaking agency called Two's Company and briefed them thoroughly on precisely what she was looking for.

Then after an agonizingly long wait, the agency eventually came up with Dave. Their first date had been a lunch at her request, just in case she took one look at her blind date and needed to make a hasty exit. And sure enough, when Dave first strolled in to meet her, a full ten minutes late, her heart had sunk like a stone.

This bedraggled, overweight, hairy, out-of-work actor, dressed in a t-shirt and shorts who smelt like he hadn't even bothered to shower that morning, was about as far removed from what Jo was looking for as you could imagine. Yet the very fact he'd come to her via a dating agency at least showed he was serious about getting serious with someone too.

So she forced herself to stick it out. It's just lunch, she told herself. It's only an hour. And okay, so Dave mightn't have exactly been the alpha male she'd always imagined she'd end up with, but to her surprise, she found he was warm and kind and funny. And just somehow got her and poked gentle fun at her and made her laugh at herself. And he was generous and thoughtful in small ways too, which meant an awful lot to her.

Yes, he wasn't without his flaws, but there was a downside to just about every man on this planet, wasn't there, Jo reminded herself. Dave had fantastic points, that was for certain. Just a few rough edges that needed sanding down and working on, like any other man. Yet she remained utterly convinced that with just a bit of gentle prodding, he'd ultimately make a great husband for her. Maybe not perfect, but was there any such thing? And after all, wasn't this better than being single and married to her career?

Her flight was airborne by then, Jo remembered, and as she looked at the city receding away from her climbing skywards, she finally started to breathe a little easier.

Okay, so Dave could try the patience of a saint, but he also made her laugh at her own absurdities. Yes, he was stubborn and there were times when she honestly thought having a toddler under her roof would be less hassle than Dave wandering around in his underpants with a piece of toast in one hand, going mental because he'd lost his iPhone. Yet again.

But back then, she was a thirty-eight-year-old woman with a ticking biological clock and a wedding planned for less than two weeks away and counting. One hundred and eighty guests were flying in for the big day from all round the world, including most of the board of directors at Digitech. The reception alone was costing Jo the bulk of eighteen thousand and her dress was a Vera Wang special import from New York.

This was not the time for last minute doubts or worries about whether someone like her actually needed a wife, rather than a husband.

Come two weeks that Saturday, she was getting married.

*

No, Jo thought back at Hope Street, as she snapped her laptop shut and headed to the bathroom to take her night-time dose of pills.

You're not losing your grip on reality.

The wedding really was one of the best days of your life.

And there really was a time when you and Dave were happy.

214

Chapter Seventeen

Chloe.

Just after 8.30 p.m. and I'm frantically trying to do a discreet check on all guests. Low level panic driving me, mainly because my worry is if Dave managed to get that ossified drunk, chances are high he had a boozing buddy with him. I've worked in the hotel business a long time and trust me, I know the way these things play out.

I check the bar first, but it's empty. Which is good, means they're all still at dinner. Odd that Tommy's not around, but then he could be downstairs in the wine cellar restocking, while it's quiet round here.

So I slip into the back of our Yellow Dining Room just to check everyone else is all-present and correct, which by the way, is a hugely impressive room off the first floor, meticulously restored with a stunning Farrow & Ball paint job and sweeping views all the way down onto the gardens below.

We've laid on a set menu for tonight and it's no exaggeration to say there really is something for everyone in the audience. Well, given everything our guests will be facing into this weekend, it's my mission to see at the very least that everything else around them, the food particularly, is world class and completely fabulous. Our maître d' and I pre-approved the whole menu together and to be honest, I thought everyone would turn up for dinner, just so they could salivate over it. You wanna see it! Hand dived scallops in garlic butter, lamb rump with homemade ricotta, fillet of pork with black pudding rosti. 'Worthy of a bloody Michelin star,' as Nick, our head chef had proudly – and not unjustifiably – boasted to me. To be perfectly honest, if it were me, I'd want photos of each finished mini-masterpiece dish, just so I could post them up on Facebook and Twitter.

And while it's fairly full in here and most couples at least seem to be enjoying the banquet laid out for them, a second glance round the tables and somehow I don't exactly get the feeling that all's well.

For starters, two absent couples stick out like sore thumbs. Dawn, Kirk, Jo and Dave. Some chance of any of them wandering in here late and looking to be fed and watered now, I think ruefully.

Another lightning quick scan of the room and to my surprise, tucked into a discreet corner I see Andrew Lowe, eating alone. Polite, polished Andrew Lowe, who looks so handsome, greying and distinguished that I almost feel there should be a portrait of him hanging up on one of our walls somewhere. He just has that kind of face, that carries fifty plus years of authority with him. He looks up and catches my eye, so I weave my way through the tables over to him.

'Good evening, Mr Lowe,' I smile politely. 'Just making sure everything is alright for you so far?'

He raises an eyebrow and pushes aside the *Financial Times* he'd been reading.

'I'm afraid, my dear Miss Townsend,' he says with a gracious nod, 'that I can only answer that particular question in relation to your fine service and menu. Which, as you'd expect, are completely flawless.'

'Glad you're enjoying it,' I smile back warmly. But then, I really *like* Andrew Lowe. If all of my other guests were like him, I'd have absolutely no bother round here.

'And I hope your initial mediation session before dinner wasn't too exhausting for you or Miss Belton?'

'It certainly wasn't.'

'Oh, well that's good to hear.'

'Mainly because I'm afraid we didn't go.'

'Excuse me?'

'Which, naturally I apologize for, but, well I'm afraid Lucy didn't turn up for it and the last thing I wanted to do was go looking for her and force her into something she may not have been entirely comfortable with. In fact, as soon as I arrived and checked in, I had some business to catch up on in my room, so I'm afraid I haven't seen her all evening, as of yet. I was hoping she might join me for dinner, but as you can see –'

I do not fecking well *believe* this. That's two no-shows on our very first evening. First Jo and Dave, now this pair. Not good. Not by a long shot. Then a sudden alarm bell shoots through me. Come to think of it, I haven't set eyes on Lucy since she first checked in either.

Oh, Christ no. Don't tell me I've another guest about to cause trouble on my hands? Don't tell me she was down in the bar boozing the night away with Dave earlier, while I was stuck in a bloody meeting?

Andrew Lowe seems to be a sensitive man though, and correctly reads my thoughts.

217

'Miss Townsend?'

'Please, it's Chloe.'

'I'm afraid I must ask you to make allowances for my wife right now,' he tells me calmly. 'You must remember, as I'm trying so very hard to, that she's in fact the blameless party and not at all responsible for why we're staying at your delightful hotel in the first place. So may I suggest relaxing the schedule just a tad as far as she's concerned?'

He must cop the puzzled look on my face, but he's far too well mannered to say any more. So the professional half of me knows now is the time to offer him a drink on the house, then beat a hasty retreat and leave him alone to his thoughts.

But then a part of me won't let up. Because Andrew seems lovely and kind and genuinely concerned for Lucy. And he still refers to her as 'his wife'. So what are they doing here in the first place? What in God's name could have gone wrong there?

And then we both hear her, right before we see her. A woman's voice, loud and clear, wafting all the way up from Reception, just downstairs.

'Get your fucking hands pawsh off me, you human gorilla! SHHTOP IT! YOURE MAN . . . hic . . . MANHANDLING ME!!'

I do not be-fecking-lieve this. Not more trouble. Please dear God, not more –

But it's her alright. It's Lucy. With every head in the restaurant turned to look at us, Andrew is up on his feet in one fast move and the two of us are out the door, following the sound of the racket.

Which isn't all that hard, really. We follow the noise down the short flight of stairs to Reception, where Lucy's being half led, half lifted by poor Tommy the barman, clearly trying to guide her into the lift. Chris is right beside them, making soothing noises and every now and then saying useless things like, 'Wait till you see, you'll feel a whole lot better after a little lie down, Miss Belton!'

'I was just relaxing and having a few harmless shrinks . . . sorry . . . I mean drinkies out the back garden!' Lucy practically spits into poor Tommy's face. 'What kind of a pissing hotel do you call yourselves anyway? Can't a guesht even have a harmlesh little drink without being hauled off like this?'

'I'll take it from here,' I hiss at both Chris and Tommy as I step into the lift beside her, pressing for the third floor and just praying she doesn't start having a go at me once we're left alone.

As the lift door slides shut, I see Andrew standing right in front of us. And just the look on his face alone tells me everything I need to know.

Chapter Eighteen

10.45 p.m.

Andrew Lowe was an even-tempered man, one slow to anger and quick to forgive. Or so he liked to think. Difficult though, to keep a cool head when your wife – or rather, the woman you'd separated from – had clearly spent the entire evening acting like some kind of a vapid, air-headed good-time girl. The kind of girl the gutter press had insisted on labelling, 'Lucy Belter,' a moniker Andrew had always hated.

It was unfair, it did her absolutely no justice. If they knew the real Lucy, no one would paint her to be 'Party Central'. Yet another crude nickname that made him wince with embarrassment.

Because this most definitely was not Lucy. The woman who caused that mortifying scene just now, the woman who practically had to be dragged into a lift by Chloe and an obliging barman, was most definitely not the girl he'd married. Yes, Lucy had always been vibrant and full of energy and fizz, it was one of the many things he'd adored about her, but never falling down drunk and making a complete sideshow of herself, as she had been this evening. Why did she insist on conforming to stereotype like this?

It stabbed at Andrew, physically hurt to think that he was the root cause of that pain and unhappiness. This had been the girl he'd loved, in spite of everything and everyone that had conspired to come between them. What had become of her? What had she turned into since they separated?

But worst of all was the one accusation that kept running round his addled mind on a loop. No denying that he himself was to blame. Or more accurately, he and his family, with Alannah playing significantly more than a minor supporting role in all this.

It was just coming up to 11 p.m., still too early for bed yet, so, with his mind racing, Andrew stepped out into the cool of the garden outside and found himself a quiet bench under an apple blossom tree, to sit quietly with his thoughts. He lit up a cigar, sat back and exhaled deeply. Under normal circumstances, a quiet cigar in a tranquil setting never failed to relax him, and God knows he'd certainly needed more than his fair share of calming down over the past eighteen months.

But for some reason, the old charm didn't seem to work. In fact, Andrew was hard pressed to remember the last time he'd been utterly at peace with himself. He'd been living with worry and stress for so long now, it was tough to remember back to a time when things were otherwise. The few friends he still had remaining on the Board of Directors had all variously said to him that the pressure he was operating under would have felled a lesser man.

Worse, his GP was taking things a helluva lot more seriously, but Andrew brushed that aside for the moment. Bloody man, always fussing. If it wasn't over his high cholesterol, it was some blood pressure issue. Utterly ridiculous! Andrew still had the strength and energy of someone ten years younger and after all, given that people he knew were actually taking their own lives because they'd lost everything in the recession, he figured all in all, he was holding up astonishingly well.

Until this came along. Left to him, the last thing on earth Andrew would ever have wanted was a divorce. It was the last thing that had entered his shattered mind when his whole world spectacularly combusted, just under two years ago. Not all that long after he and Lucy were first married, in fact.

He felt a sharp pang, just thinking back to Lucy and the woman she'd been back then. How breathtaking she'd looked at their wedding. He'd made a solemn vow to her that day, standing toe-to-toe, barefoot on that sandy white Caribbean beach . . . was it really only three years ago now? For richer for poorer, for better and for worse. Till death us do part. He'd sworn that promise to her and now look at where it had brought them. The hurt he'd caused her. All that unnecessary pain.

These days, Andrew was renting a small flat, laughingly referred to as a 'bachelor pad' by the estate agent, but to this day, with digital clarity, he still had recurring nightmares about the removals van pulling up outside their home, to clear away the remains of their whole life together. He could handle the loss of status, all the trappings of a life of wealth and privilege being stripped from him, bit by bit. His statement home, his Bentley, his pension reserves, all his stocks and shares, even his club membership had to go. In fact, he could school himself to bear far worse. But the loss of Lucy was something very different.

Had she been wrong to act as she subsequently did? To bring them both to this? *For richer for poorer, for better and for worse.* There was no question that she got a raw deal, being plunged into the 'for worse' part of their marriage almost from the word go.

And yet, with a niggling conscience, he couldn't help thinking back to something Alannah had pointed out. Lucy had made exactly the same vow on that tropical beach, hadn't she? So why had she bailed out on him at the first sign of trouble?

He inhaled deeply, feeling a familiar pang at the fact that their marriage was even denied a brief honeymoon period before real life intervened. He didn't blame her, if anything he blamed himself. And Alannah and Josh, he sadly had to acknowledge, had certainly played their part in what had subsequently transpired. Although he was quick to absolve them; after all, a great deal of pain and unhappiness had been caused to his first family when he and Lucy got together. So really, was it any wonder his children had acted the way they did?

Andrew thought back to Lucy, who right now was probably lying up in bed, surely with the mother of all hangovers just hovering over her. What to do?

'She's just tired and emotional at the moment, I believe is the phrase,' he'd calmly explained to Chloe, who seemed like such a sweet-natured, understanding woman. 'I'm anxious that she's allowed to rest and isn't disturbed.'

'Of course,' she'd reassured him.

He'd made a point of seeking Chloe out after she'd safely seen Lucy to her room and telling her that his wife – or rather, his estranged wife – had been working herself to the bone as of late and that they'd just have to reschedule their meeting till sometime tomorrow instead. With of course, his sincerest apologies.

Chloe had been incredibly diplomatic about it though and even offered to have dinner sent up on a tray to Lucy's room later on, if she was feeling up to it. Sensitive of her, Andrew had thought, to unquestioningly accept his excuse and act as though there was nothing wrong with Lucy other than tiredness, when it had been glaringly obvious to anyone who saw her what was really the matter with her.

But then Chloe seemed considerate and discreet in small ways; the hallmark of a good manager. The sort of woman who should have been working on the board of his bank, Andrew thought, and then maybe they could have neatly side-stepped a lot of the mess they were in now.

In fact, it was taking bloody calls from work and fending off urgent emails while holed up in his room after he'd first checked in that had caused all this trouble in the first place. Had Andrew actually put his wife first, as he right-fully should have done, had he sought her out considerably earlier this evening, he'd have been aware that she was overdoing it at the bar and could have dealt with it himself there and then. But no, instead he'd stupidly stayed in his room/office, trying to put out urgent fires at the Board. For all the good that did him.

He took a deep, soothing puff on the cigar, just as yet another email pinged into his iPhone, shattering the stillness.

Damn. This late on a Friday evening? Hardly the office he figured, or yet another panicky message from a fellow board member. Not this late at night, surely?

That could only mean family trouble in that case. Josh onto him from Berlin, maybe? Or something up with Alannah, yet again? And yet what could possibly be the problem with either of them? Between them and with particular credit to Alannah, they both had to share equal responsibility for he and Lucy being here in the first place.

His phone beeped again, momentarily distracting him and pulling him back to the unread, urgent email. Ha, he thought ruefully, weren't they all urgent these days?

And sure enough, when he glanced down and read it, his instincts had been on the money. The very second Andrew read the email, from his Chief Financial Officer at the Board, as it happened, he'd regretted it.

When sorrows come, he thought bitterly, they come not as single spies, but in battalions.

*

The letter had been handwritten and shoved under the bedroom door.

My darling.

Remember the first time we met? Remember the trainee waitress who got our order all wrong and kept texting on her mobile while we were trying to attract her attention? And how you'd probably have dealt with her in lightning quick time if it had been any ordinary day, but so anxious were we to impress each other that we just decided to find the whole thing hilarious?

Well I remember, vividly. In fact, I carry the image with me to this day. Walking into that restaurant you'd chosen, one I was unfamiliar with. Feeling rough after a late night, not being in the mood for a date at all. Silently checking the time on my watch. An hour tops, I'd given myself. So as not to appear rude. Then I'd make some perfectly polite excuse and exit pronto stage left.

And then I saw you. So much better looking in the

225

flesh than in that horrific photo you'd sent. Did you no justice whatsoever. But you seemed to me like this tightly coiled little ball of tension, sitting bolt upright, checking your phone every three minutes, visibly jumping each and every time an email or text pinged through for you.

Well this is never going to work, was my first thought. Sod all chemistry for starters. We were just too different, too unsuited, from different worlds; in a million years, I never thought you and I would have a single thing in common. You seemed far too distracted to even focus; there was an air about you of someone in a mad rush to be somewhere else. Anywhere else.

It was only when I got to know the real you that I really began to understand. It wasn't general antsiness on your part, just nerves. It became one of the traits I slowly grew to love about you. How you mask insecurity in a social situation with toughness, whereas actually my darling, scratch the surface and underneath it all, you're just a marshmallow. Same as the rest of us.

Our date got steadily worse. Food arrived and I made the mistake of ordering spaghetti with meatballs, thinking the carb-hit might wake me up a bit. Now I defy anyone alive to try to impress, while trying to suck up spaghetti and with bolognaise sauce dribbling down their chin. But you were polite enough to pretend not to notice and I of course, tried to lighten things up a bit with a few gags.

Remember my asking you about the worst date you'd ever been on? You rolled your eyes and we started swapping tales from the ugly coalface of internet dating. The married men actively trawling websites, making it perfectly plain that they weren't available evenings or weekends. 'Daytimes only.' One eejit had even posted a profile photo clearly taken on his wedding day, with the bride cut out, but her bouquet still visible in her severed right hand.

And so we started to laugh. Do you remember? You finally began to relax and really open up to me. I told you that when someone said in their online profile 'fond of a drink,' it could loosely be translated as 'would basically suck the alcohol out of a deodorant bottle'. You said that 'chubby' was a euphemism for 'overweight' and that 'sociable', meant someone who'd happily spend five nights a week sitting in a bar till 4 a.m., or until the place was raided, whichever came first.

And we both agreed that 'seeks friendship' was the saddest of all. That meant someone who lived alone in a bedsit the size of a converted wardrobe, who'd absolutely no friends and only the odd stray cat for company.

Before we knew it, we were both laughing. Genuine laughter too, not just doing it out of politeness. What should have been a lunch that lasted a bare hour suddenly stretched out to past five in the evening.

I think I knew right there and then. Just knew. Just because you and I weren't a likely match, didn't mean it couldn't work.

And now here we are.

My darling, if I could turn back time, believe me I gladly would.

Yours now, yours always.

Whatever the outcome of the next few days.

Xxxxxxxxxxxxxxx

Chapter Nineteen

Lucy.

Thrashing about in her bed, dizzy and nauseous with sleep refusing to come, Lucy found her thoughts wandering. Maybe it was seeing Andrew again after so long, or maybe it was just the lorry-load of drink she'd been laying into, but try as she might, she still couldn't hold back the memory. Pin-sharp, like it had all only happened yesterday.

*

It had been a baking hot, gloriously sunny day too, not all that long ago really. And awful things like this weren't supposed to happen while the entire world felt like it had just gone on holiday. She was standing on the front lawn outside their beautiful house in leafy Rathgar. Her home, their family home. Where she and Andrew had lived so happily before they got married, and for the brief tiny interlude of what you might call a normal married life they were allowed immediately afterwards.

Their primary asset, as the banks kept describing their home. That she and Andrew had bought jointly. That she'd scrimped and saved for. That she'd put so much of herself into, that she'd done countless photo shoots for magazines in. She'd worked so bloody hard to maintain it . . . and now this.

Her white-hot fury directed not only at Andrew, but primarily at Josh and Alannah. How could they have done this? How could they have colluded to bring this about? Leaving aside the fact that they were the single most manipulative siblings on the face of the earth, how in God's name did they manage to pull this one off? Lucy wasn't stupid, she knew right well they'd both wanted her out of the picture from day one. But that they'd somehow schemed their way to bringing this about?

Then image after image started to crowd in on top of her. And dream or no dream, it still felt just as raw now as it had done back then. Solicitor's letters and registered bank letters suddenly turning into final demands. Endless months of gruelling meeting after meeting with their bank manager, their mortgage advisor, their solicitor, everyone. She and Andrew had started out battling them and ultimately ended up pleading with them. If they could just hang on to the family home, they argued. Not possible, they were curtly told. And the only option you have is to go quickly and quietly, so as not to make this any harder on yourselves.

Then finally, the utter humiliation of a removal van pulling up outside their home – her home – and having to load up every single thing she and Andrew had ever owned. In full view of the neighbours, some of whom where kind enough to come over and sympathize, but most of whom just kept a polite distance. Like repossession was something contagious.

But one kind neighbour, an elderly widow who lived alone, came striding up the path to hug her and say goodbye.

'Never you mind, love,' she'd told Lucy. 'You and Andrew still have each other. And that's what really matters, isn't it? Sure, this is only bricks and mortar at the end of the day!'

Lucy had smiled and hugged her fondly back. Kind-hearted old Mrs Walsh. Bless her, she only meant well.

Even if she didn't know the half of it.

*

Still sleep wouldn't come and then thirst got the better of Lucy. Horrible, rasping thirst, like her mouth was lined with carpet underlay. Suddenly she became aware of a dull throbbing at her temples and realized the hangover to end all hangovers had already set in.

Oh God, she wondered, had the whole evening been just some kind of a rotten hallucination? She hauled herself out of bed and checked the time on the alarm clock beside her bed. Early-ish. Well, for her, anyway. Just coming up to eleven. She padded across to the minibar and helped herself to the largest, coldest bottle of water she could find. Then she rooted out two paracetamol from the bottom of her handbag, gulped them back and lay back down on the bed, while she waited on them to work their magic.

Bits of the evening started to float back to her, in horrible, fragmented shards. She remembered sitting up on a barstool downstairs and hammering loudly – probably that bit too loudly for a posh place like this – for Tommy the barman to keep the champers coming. Fuck it, she figured. If she couldn't get a few drinks into her at a time like this, then when could she?

Something else came back to her too. There'd been a guy with her, chunky, thick-set, late thirties. Dave something or other. They'd fallen into one of those easy, drunken chats about the misery of their respective love lives and what exactly had brought them both to this pass.

And although Lucy mightn't have exactly been anyone's idea of an agony aunt, she thought she'd done a pretty good job of convincing this Dave bloke that his situation wasn't quite as bleak as hers. He had told her all about his wife and all the problems she'd been having trying to get pregnant. All the expensive fertility clinics they'd been going to, not to mention the countless cocktails of hormones and steroids they'd been pumping through her body. The gruelling rounds of treatment and the horrible effect they'd had on his wife, both emotional as well as physical.

With a jolt, yet another memory shattered through her fuzzy, unfocused mind. His wife striding into the bar and in one single, sharp glance taking in herself and Dave cosily drinking together, as they had been all night. Jo, was that her name? A slim, petite woman in a Reiss suit and neat, dark, bobbed hair that Lucy could tell at first glance was at the winding down stage of a three-week blow dry. Scarily white skin, absolutely no make-up at all, arms folded, coldly furious.

She could remember this Jo hissing at Dave to get out of there, something about a divorce lawyer who was standing waiting on both of them.

Oh Jesus, Lucy thought with a sudden jolt back into reality. Had the next five minutes really happened? Had she really been cheeky and invasive enough to tell Jo all about her sister-in-law who'd been through IVF too?

Lucy was sweating now, palpitating to think back on what else she might have said to that poor woman. She couldn't remember exactly, but it must have been bad, because no sooner had she opened her big mouth than

231

Dave had rightly abandoned her. And would you blame the guy? She must have made a holy mortifying show of herself! For God's sake, why did she have to go and interfere in the first place? Even if all she'd been trying to do was cheer Jo up a bit.

Still more memories started to flood back. An American couple, the Fergusons, they might have been called, joining her after Dave disappeared. Sixty-somethings, Jayne and Larry. Great fun, so much so that Lucy remembered thumping the bar and demanding to know why the hell they felt the need to bother getting divorced in the first place. 'Look at the two of you, you get on like a house on fire!' she'd drunkenly told them.

Then someone – and she'd a horrible feeling it might have been her – decided it would be a great idea to start a sing-song. 'Because you both need to start learning a few Irish come-all-yas while you're here!' she'd bossily told Jayne and Larry, who seemed all on for it. At least, at first.

There was definitely singing but the evening started to blur a bit from then on in. 'If you're Irish, come into the parlour!' Lucy remembered trying to teach them. And then – oh dear God no – had she really got up in her too-high heels and started trying to teach the pair of them a few steps of *Riverdance*?

She remembered falling. Then laying face down sprawled out on the floor, with a crowd gathered around her. Concerned voices.

'Who's she with?'

'Someone get Chloe.'

'Someone get the husband, whoever the poor eejit is.'

Then Jayne's worried voice in her ear.

'Honey, I think you've had enough for one night. Don't

you think you'd feel a whole lot better if you came outside for some nice fresh air?'

Then Tommy, that lovely barman, physically lifting her back onto her feet, half carrying her out to the garden and then a woman's voice. Hers. Yelling all sorts of unprintable obscenities, just because he wouldn't go back to get her another drink. Followed by several kindly, well-intentioned voices saying that maybe she'd feel so much better after a little lie down. Tommy trying to steer her back inside and towards the lift.

Then seeing Chloe come over to her and insist on escorting her all the way to her room, 'just so you can rest up a bit. It's been a long day for you.' Tactfully brushing over the fact that Lucy had just made a roaring disgrace of herself.

And then the worst memory of all. The one she'd gladly have herself lobotomized just to suppress, were it only possible.

The lift door gracefully gliding shut, just in time for her to see Andrew looking back at her, having taken in the whole scene. And the pained expression on that worried, handsome face was somehow worse than anything.

Chapter Twenty

At about the same time as Lucy suffered out her hangover, Kirk realized that absolutely zilch was working for him. He thought his usual nighttime transcendental meditation session might help, but no, nothing doing. Neither did listening to his beloved 'Homage to Mother Earth' CD. Not even when he tried to realign his chakras using rose quartz – which he'd always found so effective when it came to healing. And even the smell of incense that he'd been burning in his hotel room wasn't having its usual effect.

There were two things on this mortal plane that Kirk didn't believe in: the first was lies and second was deceit. And yet, with Dawn, his beloved girl, his best friend, he'd practised both. And now, trapped in this ridiculously extravagant hotel room, he had nothing to do for the whole night ahead but to dwell on it. Learn to live with it, if that were even remotely possible.

But try as he might, he couldn't. Kirk just wasn't hardwired like that, none of his family were. They were freethinking and free loving and took life just as they found it. And after all, the last thing Kirk had ever gone looking for was love. Not after Dawn came along. His princess, his goddess; he'd been with countless other women before he met her, but never felt for any of the others what he'd felt for her and surely never would.

He could still remember the look on Dawn's worried, pale little face, when she'd first started to suspect all wasn't well. But I'm here, he'd told her at the time, constantly trying to reassure her. There never was any other woman for me and there never will be, he said. And I'm never going to leave. Why would I? Why would anyone who had a cherished soul like you in their life, ever want to walk away from that? How insane would you have to be?

Those had been his exact words.

The thing was, Kirk meant it as sincerely then as he did now. He wasn't going anywhere and it cut him to the quick to think that Dawn had dragged him to this awful place, this hotel he'd hated and felt so uncomfortable in from the word go, just so she could 'perform a Kirk-ectomy on her life', as his Dad, Dessie had so succinctly put it.

Times like this, Kirk envied his Dad and Gaia, his step-mother. They'd never had to deal with anything like this. Kirk had lost count of the number of lovers his father had taken over the years and Gaia seemed to have absolutely no problem with a single one of them.

Ditto when Gaia herself had fallen in love, and subsequently had a seven-month-long fling with a bloke who installed water features at her local garden centre. And what had Dessie done when she first confessed all to him? Laughed and wished her well and immediately invited Mr Water Features round to hang out and smoke some weed. In Kirk's world, this was how civilized, evolved beings behaved.

Had either of them reacted with hate and negativity? Had they insisted on dragging one another to a ridiculous divorce hotel like this? The kind of place that ordinarily, Kirk and his friends at the Yoga Rooms would have shaken their heads at and wondered how bitter and unloving a soul you'd have to be to cross the threshold of in the first place? Of course not. Dessie and Gaia had worked it out between them so everyone was happy, everyone was sexually fulfilled in every way and no one was left out. That was what you did when you had a life partner. You made it work, no matter what.

Which was why Kirk was genuinely at a complete loss right now. He'd thought he and Dawn were able to read each other like pages from a book. He thought she'd understand, as he himself would have, if the shoe had been on the other foot. He thought she knew exactly what she was signing up for, that far distant day when they'd had their commitment ceremony in Mount Druid at Midsummer, what seemed like another lifetime ago now.

And yet there it was, the telltale guilt, that no matter how hard he tried, Kirk just somehow couldn't seem to shift. Fact was, for all his deep love for Dawn, he'd betrayed her. He'd duped her and under the pathetically thin veneer of 'anything goes', and then even had the barefaced cheek to try to defend the indefensible. And now someone like him, who'd lived his whole life battling lies and deceit, had to somehow try to come to terms with it.

He'd been sitting cross-legged on the floor, but at that uncomfortable thought, suddenly got up and started to pace round a bit. Anything to try and shift the negative ions rattling through him. Yet he couldn't, try as he might.

So his frustration quickly shifted to this ridiculous hotel room instead. It was irritating him now and Kirk was rarely irritated, unless you were talking about the plight of the Tibetan people or something along those lines. Seriously though, he thought. All the unnecessary waste and expense that a hotel like this incurred, not to mention the toll it took on the environment? And still they never even bothered to have the place feng-shuied?

In fact, Kirk thought, maybe a bit of feng-shui might just help. Maybe he'd have some outside chance of easing his mind if he just rearranged the furniture a bit. So with considerable effort, he managed to haul the heavy oak bed over to the southwest corner (so it ended up exactly blocking the bathroom door, as it happened), and tried that out.

But no. Sleep still wouldn't come. And now all Kirk could do was lie there and listen to the air conditioning thingy hum away in the background. He'd been trying to switch the thing off ever since he arrived, and couldn't. Air conditioning! Didn't Ferndale Hotels realize the strain that even one air-conditioner put on the earth's resources?

That was when he sat bolt upright on the bed, with its ludicrously soft mattress, that a whole family of geese had probably sacrificed feathers for. He had a wedge of grass here with him somewhere, he was sure of it. Dessie had given it to him a while back, 'to help ease the pain of the journey you and Dawn have to face'. It was stuffed in the pocket of the backpack that went everywhere with him. Three ounces of his Dad's best homegrown. Who could ask for more?

Just what he needed right now. Perfect antidote to all the negativity hovering in the ethos round here. Nothing else would tune out Dawn's voice earlier, harsh and bitter, her accusations, tears, anger and the unavoidable fact that he was the root cause of it.

In one fluid move, Kirk was out of bed and rummaging round the bottom of his bag.

Two minutes later, he'd blazed up and suddenly started to feel a whole lot better for it.

Chapter Twenty-One

At about the same time, Andrew had finished up his cigar and was just about to leave the garden and head back inside, when a tiny, muffled noise suddenly distracted him. Strange, he thought. He could almost have sworn it sounded like sobbing. A woman's voice too. The light from the hotel bar spilled out onto the garden as he got up and strolled deeper into the garden.

Turned out he'd been right. Not far from where he'd been sitting all this time, he suddenly saw a young girl, mid-twenties at most and dressed head to toe in white, curled up on a bench, twisting a Kleenex nervously round and round her finger.

She jumped when she sensed someone approaching and immediately sat up straight.

'I'm so sorry if I startled you,' Andrew said politely, 'but I just wondered . . . are you alright?'

'Fine, just fine,' she said in a tiny, strangulated little voice, but one look at the girl told you she was far from it.

A waif, Andrew thought, looking down at her and almost feeling fatherly and protective towards her. Tiny and slim with long, straggly red hair and big soulful eyes that somehow only made her face look even smaller still.

Someone who worked here maybe? Or a fellow guest? Surely not. She looked far too young, not only to have got married in the first place, but for that marriage to have subsequently ground to a halt.

'Andrew Lowe,' he said, reaching down to shake her hand. 'I don't think we were introduced earlier.'

'I'm Dawn,' she sniffed, dabbing at her nose with the Kleenex.

'May I sit down for a moment?' He didn't like to intrude, but it just didn't seem right to turn his heel on her and walk away. This slip of a thing seemed upset and maybe talking would help a little.

'Sure,' she said, sliding over on the bench to make room for him. He stubbed out the dregs of his cigar and joined her.

A silence fell as she shifted uncomfortably beside him.

'And, may I ask,' Andrew eventually said, 'if you're staying here too?'

'Unfortunately, yes.'

'Have to say,' he added, 'I never thought I'd end up here.'

'Well, that certainly makes two of us,' Dawn replied, with a weak little smile.

'And might I have met your husband earlier?'

'I'm not sure. Kirk is – well, he's tall and has long hair down well past his shoulders. White shirt and jeans? You'd know him if you saw him.'

Bingo, Andrew thought. Yes, he'd walked past someone who fitted that description on one of the upstairs corridors. Rather a strange looking individual, he'd thought. The sort of man just two steps away from shaving his head, and banging on a tambourine on Grafton Street.

'I needn't ask you who you're here with,' Dawn said. 'You were married to Lucy Belter, the model, weren't you?'

'Technically, I'm still married to her,' Andrew gently corrected her. 'And it's Belton, actually.'

'Sorry. It's just the papers always –'

'Never believe a word you read in the papers, my dear,' Andrew smiled. 'They have a habit of stereotyping, particularly when it comes to women like my wife, sadly.'

Another silence, but somehow, now that they'd broken the ice a bit, it was that bit less tense and awkward now.

'Of course it's absolutely none of my business,' he ventured tentatively, 'but you seemed a little upset just now. May I ask if everything's alright?'

Dawn looked across at him, with big watery eyes.

'What do you think? I'm twenty-five years old and I'm sitting in the garden of a posh hotel about to wind up the last three years of my life. Other girls my age are out on the town tonight, enjoying themselves, having a laugh, young, free and without a care in the world. And look where I ended up. No, everything is not okay. Everything is so far from okay, I can't tell you.'

'And nor does it get any easier with age, let me tell you,' he said wryly. 'Just try being at my hour of life and about to be divorced for the second time.'

'Can I ask you something?' Dawn said, looking directly at him now.

'Fire away.'

'Well . . . how did you know Lucy was the one? I mean, the one for you? If it's not too personal, that is.'

'I've a feeling I'll be asked questions a lot more personal than that over the course of the next few days, my dear.'

'So how did you know for certain?'

Andrew sat back, remembering. And it was funny, but in a weird way, given everything he'd been so overloaded with of late, it was almost soothing to think back to happier times.

'It was – close to four years ago,' he smiled. 'The bank I work for was sponsoring an awards do. In the Four Seasons hotel,' he added. 'Although it's hard to imagine that we'd shell out for anything so lavish in the present economic climate.'

'And she was there?'

'Presenting an award. She bounced out onto the stage and in a matter of moments, had the whole room guffawing with laughter. It had been quite a formal night up until then and Lucy just broke the ice completely.'

'Thank Christ I get this over with now,' was what she'd actually said into the microphone. 'I've been hanging round backstage for the last two hours waiting to do this and my shoes are only killing me. Besides, the quicker the awards bit of the night is over with, the quicker the dancing starts!'

The room chortled along and Andrew vividly remembered sitting there utterly transfixed. He was newly separated, and for the first time in twenty-five years, found himself if not exactly young, then certainly free and single. The wives of various board members at the table had all been dressed in sombre black, whereas Lucy was in vivid scarlet, a colour she seemed to dominate. As only she could.

He'd sat there as she addressed the room and almost felt cartoon-like, so sure was he that steam was beginning to come out of his ears. That body, that face, those endless legs . . .

'You're drooling, stop it,' he remembered the CEO's wife had teased him, but Andrew had barely registered her. He made a point of seeking out Lucy afterwards and inviting her to join their table. And she seemed just to light up his whole evening from then on, like she never failed to do. Till she'd bounced along, conversation round the table had been about golf handicaps, the shocking price of maintenance fees on your average villa in Marbella and who was on a waiting list for a hip operation.

But with Lucy, suddenly everything changed. She was funny, fearless and fabulous, she lived life on her own terms and didn't care what anyone thought. There and then, Andrew was a man completely smitten. In work the next day, he'd made a point of tracking her down and managed to get hold of her booking agent's number. And the rest was history.

'And that was when you knew for certain?' Dawn interrupted his train of thought.

'It was like my whole life suddenly went from black and white to glorious Technicolor,' he said. 'If that makes any sense.'

'Yeah,' she nodded, focused on a rockery straight ahead of them. 'Yes, it does.'

'How about you?'

'Seems like another lifetime ago,' she said. 'Kirk is a yoga instructor and one fine day, he just called into the store where I work.'

'Don't tell me,' Andrew smiled. 'Your eyes locked across a crowded shop floor and that was it?'

'Not quite. He was giving out flyers for the Yoga Rooms where he works and he asked if he could put one in our window. So I said yeah and . . . and that pretty much would have been the end of that, only the thing was . . . I just . . . had to see him again. So myself and my pal from work signed up for one of his yoga classes and I made sure to turn up in my tightest leggings and skinniest crop top.'

'I'm sure he was very taken with you.'

'Funny, not at first. He was lovely and sweet to me but then he's lovely and sweet to everyone. But then we were doing this weird position where you have to lie prostrate on your tummy with one arm and one leg stuck up in the air. Everyone else in the class was doing it no bother, but when I tried, all you could hear was this awful cracking noise and it turned out I'd broken one of my floating ribs.'

'What? I thought yoga was supposed to be good for you?'

'You'd think, wouldn't you? But not if your name is Dawn Madden, it seems. Anyway, Kirk insisted on taking me to the A & E for an X-ray. Waited round for me and everything. Sat with me for hours while I had to hang around to be seen by a doctor. Kept running to get me bottles of water and even gave me a reiki healing while we were sitting there.'

'I'm sorry, he gave you a what?' said Andrew, puzzled.

'Reiki. You know, it's the laying on of hands, to transfer energy.'

'Does it actually work?'

'Not really, no. But I liked Kirk so much I pretended it did. And then when I was all bandaged up and ready to leave, he insisted on walking me home. So I asked him up for coffee, and . . . well, that was it really. I just knew there and then. Just like you did.'

'And now here we are.'

'And now here we are,' Dawn smiled. For the first time, Andrew noticed, since he'd sat down. 'We sound like two prisoners, don't we? Swapping "what are you in for?" stories. Wonder if we could just stage a mass breakout? Like they do in movies? Just climb over the back wall there and make a run for it?'

'Doubtless searchlights would instantly start beaming at us, an alarm would go off and the hotel would release teams of trained Alsatians after us.'

And now Dawn gave a light, girlish little giggle. Good, Andrew thought. If nothing else, then at least I've brightened up someone's day.

'I take it this wouldn't be your preferred course of action, then,' he said, though it wasn't really a question. Blatantly obvious that this poor girl was the divorcee here, and not the prime instigator of all this. Not unlike himself, really.

'No, it's not that,' Dawn said thoughtfully. 'I've got no other choice but to be here. Believe me when I tell you, if I could change things I would, but I can't.'

'Would it help to talk about it? I'm a good listener, or so I've been told.'

'You're kind but . . . no. At least not now. I just can't. It's already been a grueller of an evening, you see . . . and well . . . I'm afraid I really let Kirk have it earlier. Don't even know what came over me, except that we haven't had any contact in so long, that once I got into the same room as him, there was suddenly no shutting me up.'

'Clearing the air can only be a good thing,' Andrew said, only wishing that he and Lucy could do the same. 'Did it make you feel any better?'

'Don't ask.'

'Not if you don't want me to,' Andrew said, tactfully dismissing the subject.

'What about you though?' Dawn asked, suddenly turning the tables. 'You and Lucy Belter – sorry, Belton – well, it's none of my business, but the two of you were always in the papers being photographed at all these glamorous dos and you just looked like you were having such a good time together. How did you end up here?'

'It's not all that easy to describe how things first began to unravel.'

'Who are you telling?' Dawn groaned, throwing her eyes to heaven.

'I know Lucy firmly puts the blame on my two children. From my first marriage, that is.'

'Your children? But why? What did they have to do with it?'

'Let's just say they may not have been as welcoming towards a new stepmother as I would have hoped.'

'But why would they be like that? Surely they were happy to see you happy?'

And now it was Andrew's turn to stare straight ahead in stony silence. God bless Dawn's innocence for even asking. Though it was a question he'd asked himself many times over in the past few miserable months and one he certainly wasn't proud to answer.

'You see my children – who are both several years older than you, my dear – could never bring themselves to forgive either of us for what we'd done. Or rather for what I'd done. For what I'd put my family through. For falling in love so quickly after I'd separated from my first wife and then as soon as my divorce had come through, for remarrying. The way they saw it, there was a price to be paid, and by God, did they make sure we paid it. With interest.'

'But what did you do that was so awful? After all, you were separated when you and Lucy first met, weren't you?'

Andrew gave a long, weary sigh. And yet somehow, it felt easy to open up to this complete stranger, this non-judgmental young girl who clearly had been through worse herself.

'Technically yes, though that's not how my children saw it. To my eternal shame, I have to say that any family breaking up, no matter what age the kids happen to be at, even if they're grown adults, is one of the most painful things a parent can inflict on them. My ex-wife had hoped that in time she and I might reconcile, but when Lucy and I fell for each other so fast . . . well . . . you can just imagine.'

'So what happened with your children?'

After a lengthy pause, Andrew just said, 'Let's not go there. Some other time, maybe. So, what about you? You and your ex sounded so happy and well-suited. What can possibly have gone wrong there?'

A pause, while Dawn pulled her knees up to her chest and hugged them tight.

'Kirk had an affair,' Dawn told him simply.

'Then Kirk is clearly an idiot.'

'And it's ongoing.'

'I see,' Andrew said thoughtfully. 'And may I ask if you know the other woman involved?'

'Who said anything about it being another woman?'

247

Chapter Twenty-Two

Chloe.

'You look like you could do with this,' says Chris, handing me over a warm and welcome mug of tea. 'Though after the evening we've had around here, I'm guessing a vodka and tonic would probably be far more in order.'

'Bless you, sweetheart,' I say, gratefully taking the mug from her, slumping exhaustedly back on my office chair and rubbing tired, red eyes. It's coming up to a quarter to twelve at night and I still have all my nighttime rounds to do before I can hand over to the duty manager, clock off for the night and finally get home and catch up on some sleep.

'But if it's all the same with you,' I smile back at her, 'let's save that drink till the very last guest has checked out of here first thing Monday morning. God knows, I'll probably need it then. Certainly if this evening's shenanigans were anything to go by.'

'Oh come on now, it wasn't all that bad,' Chris reassures me, trying her best to sound positive. Bless her, she has the loveliest habit of being able to completely tune out the negative. In fact, everyone should have a Chris in their office to cheer them up, particularly after a day like the one I've had. She's kind of like a long, blonde Pollyanna round here.

'After all, the majority of our couples are settling in well and getting on with each other brilliantly –'

'Chris, I've two couples who I almost had to call security to deal with earlier and another guest who more or less passed out in the back garden and had to be strong-armed all the way to her room.'

'Okay, so we've got three couples that might be causing us a little bit of trouble . . .'

'Did you just say a *little*?' I groan back at her, slumping forward on my desk, head in hands. 'How did I let them in here in the first place? I should have been held back, someone should have physically held me back . . .'

'Can I remind you you're talking about three couples out of twenty-four guests in total? Not bad going, if you ask me.'

She's being way too lovely but the truth – and I know it – is that the buck rests solely with me and only me as to how this inaugural weekend pans out.

Mother of God, I shudder as yet another memory from this evening comes back to haunt me. Me, having to undress poor Lucy Belton and ease her into bed, pretty much the way you would with a small child. Even saw all her lady bits while I was struggling to help her out of that tight little bandage of a dress she was wearing, including body parts you'd normally only see if you were giving someone a very intimate bikini wax.

Times like this, I honestly don't think I get paid enough. Anyway, I make a mental note to have a private little chat with her first thing in the morning. The girl is going to feel like hell on earth after she's slept it off and I'm guessing she'll need a sympathetic ear to tell her she didn't behave as badly as she might have remembered. That's part of a hotel manager's job sometimes: lying to guests to make them feel slightly less bad than they already do.

'Let's be honest, the whole evening was a bloody, out-and-out disaster!' I moan at Chris. 'So what are we going to do now? If tonight was anything to go by, this time tomorrow someone could end up with blood on their hands.'

My head is slumped exhaustedly in my hands now as one nightmarish image after another starts to crowd in on me. Things are bad enough, but suppose they get worse? Suppose little Dawn Madden maybe smashes a bottle into Kirk's face over brekkie? While he probably spouts some crap like 'She's only acting like this because her chakras are out of alignment.' Jeez, I'd probably be tempted to whack him one myself.

Or maybe Dave will decide to lock himself into Jo's room and threaten to jump out the top floor window if she doesn't reconsider giving him another chance? I take a brief, shuddering moment to digest the image. To be perfectly honest, given his carry-on tonight, I wouldn't put anything past the guy with a few drinks in him.

As for Lucy? If she was this bad tonight, God only knows what she'll get up to tomorrow. Then there's Andrew, that stoic, gentlemanly husband of hers. The hurt, pained look on his face as I carted her off in the lift will be imprinted on the back of my eyeballs for a long, long time to come.

'Anyway, leaving all that aside for now,' I tell Chris, as I catch the poor girl trying to stifle a yawn. 'You should scoot off and get some rest, if you can. Today was bad enough, but believe me, tomorrow things are going to heat up round here even more.'

She's halfway out the door, when my mobile rings.

The minute I glance down at the caller ID, I'm suddenly sitting up straight and back on high alert. Him, yet again. Rob. Sure, who else would be calling me at this hour? And of course, it's another spot check phone call.

Which of course is absolutely fine and I'd expect no less from the boss. It's just that this is approximately the fifteenth of these calls so far today, not counting emails, faxes, Skype calls, etc. And it's just so bloody late at night. And still he won't let on what corner of the globe he's in or more importantly, when we can expect him to land in on us. Mother of God, is it any wonder my brains are like mince?

'Rob, hi, how are you?' I say, trying my best to snap myself awake and instantly sound alert.

The minute she hears who I'm onto, Chris stands frozen, half in and half out the door. Which looks almost comical, were I in the mood to laugh.

'So? I hope you're going to tell me our first evening was a roaring success?' Rob asks, cutting straight to the chase as always. And as ever, I have to strain to hear him. Sounds like he's calling me from a car that keeps moving in and out of a crappy signal.

'Emm . . . yes, I think overall everything went pretty well,' I tell him as Chris gives me two big thumbs up, before disappearing out the door.

No, things did not go well. We could well have a homicide on the premises before this weekend is out.

'No problems you need to raise with me? It's just there were a few raised voices in the background last time we spoke and I was concerned.'

Oh please. Where do I bleeding start?

251

'Chloe? You there?' And there's just the slightest hint of concern in the tone of his voice.

'Em . . . no, nothing for now. And that row you over-heard? It was a couple in a mediation session, but . . . well, it's not really anything that I can tell you over the phone,' I say worriedly.

'That sounds ominous. Anything I can do to help?'

Ehh . . . maybe start looking round for a new General Manager? Because after this weekend, I could end up getting propelled to the back of a dole queue so fast, it actually makes my head spin. Because three couples causing trouble for us means three couples that I didn't screen properly, which all in all, doesn't exactly add up to good news if your name is Chloe Townsend.

'Absolutely nothing, thanks. So if you'll excuse me, I'm just off to do my nighttime rounds before . . .'

Suddenly, an alarm goes off in the background. And there's no mistaking that ear-piercing racket.

Oh, sweet holy shit no. Please, please, for the love of all that's holy, don't let this be happening . . .

But it *is* happening. The fire alarm. No mistaking it. In all its ear-piercing, deafening glory. And it's even louder than when we did a few trial runs with it a few weeks ago. Head-splittingly so.

'Sorry about this Rob, I have to go, I'll call you back,' I have to shout at him abruptly, yet again trying to keep the hysteria out of my voice and doing a pretty crap job of it. I don't even say goodbye, just race out of the office and upstairs and instantly, automatically begin fire drill and evacuations, panic driving me.

Supposing this is serious is all I can think, worry working like yeast on my mind. After all, if anyone is injured – or

252

worse – then this could potentially close us. Could finish this Ferndale Hotel off, before it's barely opened. We'd end up being the hospitality industry's equivalent of the *Titanic*, sunk on our maiden weekend. And suppose a guest or a member of staff is seriously hurt? Or even worse?

Tommy comes racing out of the bar and Chris is already bolting upstairs, just like we're all trained to do. We've rehearsed this, we've drilled it time and time again, never for a second thinking we'd need to put the plan into action on our very first weekend. We all know exactly where we're supposed to be and when. Even if – please God – this is just a hoax or turns out to be absolutely nothing, it still doesn't matter. All fire alarms must be taken seriously. Particularly in a listed Georgian building like this one, where a fire could break out literally *anywhere*.

And suddenly it's a case of all hands on deck, as any and all staff still on the premises leap to it. All around me I can see uniforms flying here, there and everywhere, opening all exit doors to marshal guests safely outside.

The fire brigade are automatically alerted the minute an emergency like this breaks out, and they even call me back to tell me they're on the way. Trouble is, in all of the chaos and with the racket of the alarm blaring away in the background, I can hardly hear a word they're trying to tell me.

'Evacuate all guests out of the hotel immediately,' a man's voice is barking down the phone at me, sergeant-major style as I race up to the top floor to start doing exactly that. 'And once they're outside, don't let anyone back in again . . .'

'I'M SORRY,' I have to yell back over the alarm. 'CAN YOU SPEAK UP PLEASE?'

'Remember the lift is completely out of bounds –'

'IT'S OKAY, IT'S AUTOMATICALLY DEACTIVATED WHENEVER THE ALARM GOES OFF . . .'

'Also, make sure you feel all door handles before opening them. If they're hot to touch, don't open them. If there's a guest trapped inside a room, we'll get them out through a window.'

'WINDOW. OKAY. GOT IT,' I shout breathlessly, thinking, please for the love of God don't let it come to that.

'Also, you need to instruct staff to close all doors and tell guests to keep their heads down low if there's smoke . . .'

'YES, WE'RE ALREADY ONTO IT –'

'And make sure to check the kitchen area, closing all doors there behind you. Most hotel fires start in the kitchen. We'll be with you in five.'

The rest of what he says to me is totally drowned out by the roar of a fire brigade siren, so I click off and finally get to my station on the top floor, just like we drilled.

I bump into Liliana from Reception already knocking on bedroom doors as I immediately start helping to evacuate guests from their bedrooms. 'Kitchens are cleared, Chloe,' she has to shout at me to be heard. 'And there's definitely no fire there. My guess is it has to have started upstairs, probably in one of the bedrooms.'

As you'd expect, a lot of guests have already been disturbed and are sticking anxious heads round bedroom doors, wanting to know exactly what's going on. But this is all part of our training and all around me, I can see the whole team quickly and efficiently dealing with this. Urging everyone to remain nice and calm, to leave all personal belongings behind and to follow staff outside to our assembly point. Big, calm smiles everywhere you look, notwithstanding the blaring that would make you wish for a pair of earplugs.

'Oh my lord, this is such an adventure!' I can hear Jayne drawl in the Noo-Yawk accent. I catch a quick glimpse of her on the landing in her dressing gown, the head of platinum hair covered in a net and clutching an old-fashioned vanity case, as one of the lounge staff guides her towards the emergency stairwell.

'But if you think for one minute I'm leaving this little beauty behind,' she says, patting the case and circling a protective arm around it, 'then you've got another thing coming. Every single piece of jewellery that I own is in here. Everything Larry ever gave me. And you'll have to prise it outta my cold, dead hands to get it off me!'

All of my couples from Germany and Finland are already out of bed and leading the way downstairs and from all corners of every corridor, guests are streaming out of their rooms and following them. And aside from the din the alarm is making, everyone's being reasonably calm, thankfully. So far.

I knock on Andrew Lowe's door, but no sooner do I rap against it, than he steps out, wearing a paisley dressing gown so expensive looking that the only other person who might possibly wear it is Noel Coward.

'Fire alarm?' he asks, looking pale-faced and exhausted. 'Do you know where it's broken out?'

'I'm afraid not yet, Mr Lowe, but there's absolutely nothing to worry about, it's just standard procedure that we evacuate all guests downstairs.'

'Is there anything I can do to help?'

'If you'll just make your way to the fire exit, that would be terrific, thanks . . .'

255

'But Lucy – my wife –'

'Don't worry sir, I'll personally see to her.'

The next door I hammer on is Dave's and there's a quick, 'gimme a minute!' before he opens up and comes out barefoot, dressed in a pair of boxer shorts and a Bruce Springsteen t-shirt, hair glued to the side of his head and standing up on end, like he's just stuck two fingers in a plug socket.

'I'm so sorry to disturb you . . .' I begin to say, but he interrupts, practically sleepwalking past me in a somnambulant state. 'S'alright,' he groans. 'But if this turns out to be a hoax, then Ferndale Hotels can send me on an all expenses paid hollier to Vegas. At the very least.'

Then a white-faced Dawn comes racing out of her room, looking like a waif from a Victorian melodrama in a long white nightie.

'I heard the racket; is it the fire alarm?' she asks worriedly.

'Absolutely nothing to be concerned about, everything's under control,' I tell her. 'Now all you need to do is follow me to the emergency stairwell and make your way outside. Don't worry, staff will be there to guide you and this will all be over within no time.'

Jeez, it's astonishing how much more blasé and confident I sound, than I actually feel.

I guide Dawn to the stairs, where big, burly Tommy, bless him, is waiting to show her the rest of the way and it's Jo's door next. I rap briskly against it, but she's a step ahead of me and has it opened instantly, the only person to come out fully dressed and trailing a wheelie bag efficiently behind her. Suit, tights, the whole works, looking like she's on her way to a corporate takeover meeting, unlike everyone else, drifting around in various states of undress and low-level panic.

'I wasn't asleep anyway,' she says a bit waspishly, 'but if this doesn't turn out to be a hoax, I'm sorry, but I'm afraid Ferndale Hotels will be hearing a lot more from me.'

And not for one second do I doubt it.

'Standard procedure,' I smile at her and guide her safely on her way. 'But it would be best if you leave your bag behind.'

'Sorry, but it's out of the question. No, not even for you, Chloe. Everything I need to get divorced is in here and if it goes up in flames –'

She doesn't even finish the sentence. Like the very thought propels her to get the hell out of here as fast as is humanly possible.

Lucy's next. Takes a few goes, but she eventually answers, without my having to resort to using my passkey. She's groggy and a little red-eyed, but still looks a helluva lot more presentable than I would, given the state the woman was in a few short hours ago.

'Feck this anyway. What's up now?' she asks me, blunt as ever.

'Nothing to worry about, but the thing is I just need you to . . .'

'Fire alarm?'

'I'm afraid so, but this is just a precaution –'

'Shite.'

'I know, but I really have to insist –'

'Ahh come on Chloe, do I have to go too? It's just my head is pounding.'

'I'm afraid all guests must be evacuated immediately, so if you wouldn't mind just –'

257

'Bugger it anyway. And when I get to the evacuation point, I suppose HE'LL be there?'

Fire drill in progression or not, there's no denying the full import of what she's asking me.

'All guests are required to be outside at this point, yes.'

'Fair enough,' she groans, then goes back inside to change. I knock on the door beside her and a heartbeat later she reappears, dressed in the most immaculate nightie, long, silky and flowing, that honestly makes her look all tall and gorgeous, like a Helen of Troy about to grace Fitzwilliam Square with her presence.

'Right then. Which way?' she asks, betraying absolutely no sign that she must currently be nursing the hangover from hell. I point her in the right direction and she's on her way.

Last and final room on this floor. Kirk. Who knowing him, probably could answer the door stark naked on account of he's doing nude yoga or something. I brace myself and knock.

No answer. Knock again. Still no answer.

Right then. Sorry, but this is what happens in an emergency and I've no choice in the matter. I whip my passkey out of my jacket pocket, swipe it and barge my way inside.

And lo and behold there he is, with his iPod headphones glued to his ears, completely tuned out and utterly oblivious to all the racket and panic. He's perched on the windowsill, with the window thrust wide open, smoking out of it and blissfully unaware that the whole room is thick with smoke by now. In a flash, the smell alone tells me what it is he's been puffing away on.

Dope. I'd know it a mile off and not just from a couple

of misguided puffs at college either. And now suddenly, it all makes sense. The smoke detector in his room is blaring away and of course, this automatically would have triggered off the main smoke alarm.

It all started in here, I think, instant fury flooding through me. There is no shagging fire and there never was. It's just Kirk and his bloody spliff.

And right at this moment as I look at him, all calm and cool, peacefully looking out the window with his earphones plugged in, I happily think I could shove him out the window and just be done with it. Dawn would probably hand me a medal and it would serve him right for jeopardizing my entire career.

Kirk clocks me instantly, but instead of stubbing out the joint and looking guilty, like any normal person would, he just nods at me benignly, gesturing at me to join him.

'You gotta try some of this grass,' he half whispers, his eyes all blurry as he attempts to focus on me. 'It's seriously good stuff.'

Not a bother on him that the hotel manager is hovering over him, arms folded, with a thunderous expression that might as well say, 'Start packing your bags now, hippie boy.'

He can't hear a word I'm saying, of course, with the headphones stuck in his ears, so I'm forced to lean into him and physically click off his iPod. In a split second, he registers the blaring alarm, but instead of hopping to, like a normal person, instead he just shrugs and says, 'That me who set it off, huh?'

'Yes, sir,' I say as politely as I can, given that my teeth are clenched tight. 'I'm afraid it was, and now I'm going

259

to have to ask you to evacuate the hotel. Along with the rest of our guests who are all making their way to the outdoor assembly point, right now.'

'Bummer. Sorry if I caused you any hassle.'

If? I want to yell at him, as I follow him out of the bedroom and guide him downstairs. *If* you caused me any hassle? Because of you, on our very first night, every single guest and member of staff are currently shivering in their night attire out in Fitzwilliam Square and you're asking if you *might* have caused hassle?

I don't though. Instead I stay tight-lipped and quietly furious as I escort him off the premises. We're the very last out of the hotel, so I guide Kirk towards where everyone else is standing at the assembly point, just in front of Fitzwilliam Square, directly adjacent to Hope Street.

Staff are efficiently buzzing around everyone, assuring them that they should be able to re-enter the hotel shortly, while guests stand around looking a) the way anyone would look after a broken night's rest and b) extraordinarily pissed off.

'All present and correct,' Chris tells me breathlessly. 'I've just done a full headcount.'

I'm just about to thank her and all the team for a job so well executed, when two things happen simultaneously. The fire brigade swoops round the corner and lands outside the hotel, all sirens blaring.

Then a taxi pulls up right alongside it.

Red-eyed and a little bleary, like he's been travelling all day and still hasn't come up for air, out steps Rob McFayden.

*

The second handwritten letter had been shoved under her door just before dawn.

My darling.

   Do you remember our very first holiday together? We rowed about it, I'm pretty confident from the whole idea's first inception. I was, ahem, let's just say a tad limited when it came to matters monetary, whereas you didn't particularly give a rat's arse where we went as long as it was in a five-star hotel somewhere on the Upper East Side of Manhattan. They were your conditions.

   My humble suggestion was that we should head to Edinburgh for festival week and catch a few shows. Scotland, I thought. You'd love that, I figured. Who wouldn't? Theatre and romance and a few boozy nights all combined with a bit of culture. I thought that would surely appeal to my highbrow amour? After all, it was our very first holiday together. Vital to get it right.

   Row one was when you point blank refused to consider it, claiming that the only shows actually worth seeing would have been booked out way in advance, which meant we'd be left sitting in damp cellars watching would be stand-up comedians recycling stale gags, in the hopes they might end up winning a coveted slot on Mock The Week.

   But you wanted to go to Manhattan, you insisted. So what part of 'I'm stony broke,' don't you understand, was my counter argument. Hence row two. Which if memory serves, lasted right up until I came up with a plan that I thought was the answer to our prayers. Unknown to you, I'd trooped to a letting agency and managed to get a short lease on a tiny holiday cottage down in the wilds of

Wexford. Why not give this a whirl? I asked you, presenting you with a fait accompli. Romantic log fires, I pitched. Long, lazy strolls down winding country lanes through the mist, I told you. We'll be like a couple in an ad for Bord Na Móna peat briquettes.

You reluctantly agreed, and even though I could tell you weren't all that keen, I knew you did it for me. God, I loved you for it. For not making me feel in any way embarrassed just because I didn't exactly have the same financial clout as you did. For not judging me, just because New York was out of the question.

I think row three broke out by the time we got to the far side of the M50 and you lost all signal on your phone. Be patient, I kept telling you from behind the wheel, do you remember? I got the smile back on your face by painting you this bucolic picture of the two of us sitting in quiet country pubs, drinking hot port and dining out on organic local produce and fish freshly brought in off a trawler only that morning.

But it wasn't to be. You will perhaps recall things decelerating even further when we actually arrived at the cottage. 'Bijou and artisan,' was how the letting agent had described it. 'A perfect romantic bolthole,' he'd told me.

Lying fecker. No sooner had we crossed the threshold when I saw that dark, troubled look crossing your face and I instantly knew I'd backed a loser. 'Bijou and artisan' turned out to be estate agent-speak for 'filthy and freezing'. And 'romantic bolthole' turned out to mean, 'in the middle of a deserted ghost estate of long abandoned holiday cottages in even worse nick than this one, with the nearest Centra a good five mile drive away.'

Stout heart that you are though, you put a brave face on it and claimed it was perfect, even though you've got a slight 'tell' when you lie, as you're unable to make direct eye contact. But how long did you last before eventually cracking? My darling, I could almost have timed you. I'm certain it was after we drove for miles trying to find a gastropub where we'd visualized having that cosy, romantic dinner together. However, the only 'gastropub' we could find turned out to be a spit-on-the-floor old man bar, pitch dark, with diddly-aye bodhran music in the background, with a choice of either Tayto cheese and onion crisps or else smoky bacon for dinner. The look of the owner's face when you politely inquired about his à la carte menu is to this day, still etched in the 'all-time great comic moments' quadrant of my brain.

Do you remember what happened next? You snapped, abandoned me in the bar, took off in the car and were gone for so long, I honestly thought you'd hightailed it back home, with a catalogue of holiday disaster stories to entertain all your colleagues with at work. But come back for me you did, all of about two hours later, wreathed in smiles so wide it gladdened my heart to see.

You'd driven all the way into Wexford town, you told me. And found an internet café for yourself. Not only that, but with a few clicks of a mouse and a quick flash of your credit card, you'd gone and booked us two seats on the following day's flight to New York JFK. Airmiles upgrades, the whole works.

My darling, how could I possibly argue with that beam on your face? I grandstanded a little about how I'd insist on paying you back next time a gig came in for me and you were sensitive enough to act like that could possibly happen any day soon. And so the following morning, there we both were, 'turning to the left' as we boarded our flight from Dublin to NYC, sipping chilled champagne and toasting our lucky escape from the holiday from hell.

I thought I'd use a discount card I had to treat you to a few Broadway shows that I thought you'd like, but it wasn't to be. Because the minute we checked into that extravagant suite you'd booked at the Waldorf, that was the end of it. Did we even come up for air for the first three days? Not in my memory. Day four and a chambermaid politely knocked on the door, wanting to change the sheets.

'Are you and the pretty lady enjoying your honeymoon?' she asked in a Czech accent.

And we laughed. Surely you must remember. And you've got to give me at least this much. We were happy then. Weren't we? I really do think so, my love. You've got to be Meryl Streep to carry off fake happy and sadly you, my darling, are no Meryl.

My darling, please forgive me. If I could turn back time, believe me I gladly would.

Yours now, yours always.

Whatever the outcome of the next few days.

SATURDAY

Chapter Twenty-Three

Jo.

Of course, as Jo could have predicted, the whole thing had all turned out to be nothing more than a false alarm. Something to do with that weirdo hippy-dippy looking fella, the guy who'd been streeling around the hotel the evening before in his bare feet, with hair far longer than her own.

Oddball. Didn't quite fit in. He looked all wrong here, she clearly remembered thinking when she bumped into him earlier in the lift. And it seemed his ex, or rather his ex-to-be was that slip of a thing in the room right next to hers, a kid who looked like she'd barely done her Leaving Cert. Dawn something or other.

She and Jo had nodded brief hellos at each other as they'd met on the upstairs corridor and Jo remembered feeling the hugest pang of sympathy for her. After all, she herself was a grown woman scarily late into her thirties, and having a failed marriage behind you at that hour of life was fairly acceptable, if unfortunate.

Whereas poor Dawn just looked far too young to cope with all this. The girl was mid-twenties at most, at a time of life when she should be all happy and in the first flush of love. There was just something about her being a guest here that seemed wrong on every level.

Anyway, it turned out that Dawn's ex was the root cause of all this malarkey, though God alone knows what he'd been getting up to. Having some kind of New Age ritual in his room that involved burning things? By the look of him, you certainly wouldn't put it past him. In fact, maybe now it wasn't so hard to see why Dawn was divorcing him in the first place.

As Jo stood on the street outside the previous night, slightly apart from where the rest of the guests had congregated, she'd stayed quiet and just listened to the never-ending rumours that were circulating all round her. An electrical fault up in one of the bedrooms, that American woman with the white blonde head of hair had insisted. No, apparently it was nothing more than a chip pan down in the kitchen that had got out of control, someone else swore blind.

And then Hemp Boy himself came out of the hotel, with Chloe hot on his heels, looking even more stressed than Jo herself usually did. Next thing Kirk – if you could indeed believe that there was anyone outside of *Star Trek* who actually went by that name – bowed his head to his fellow guests and in a deep, low voice made a brief apology, saying that it was all his fault, as apparently he'd been smoking up in his room.

Cue a few exasperated groans, filthy looks and a lot of tsk tsking, but most guests seemed fairly understanding and just glad that they could get back to the warmth of their rooms. Even though it was July, it was a cool evening and the vast majority were in flimsy nighties and slippers.

'Could have happened to any one of us, man,' Jo distinctly heard Dave telling him, patting him on the back. She could only hope he caught her glaring icily into the back of his head, dark and all as it was. Cheek of him, acting all nice to Kirk when he'd just gone and disrupted a night's sleep for everyone.

As for Jo herself, the minute the fire brigade had checked the place over and given the all clear, she was the first back up the steps and into the hotel, clattering her wheelie bag alongside her and with a 'whatever any of you do, don't dare approach me' vibe practically pinging off her.

She'd had quite enough drama for one night, tomorrow was another day and scheduled to be a busy one at that. Much to do, much to get through and not one bit of it was going to be easy. Certainly not if Dave's carry-on to date was anything to go by.

*

First thing on Saturday morning, Jo ordered breakfast to her room. She was just stepping out of the shower, when there was a low, discreet knocking on her door.

Excellent, she thought. Room service and bang on time too. It had been well past 2 a.m. before she'd even got back to her room last night and she'd slept badly after all that unnecessary drama, no thanks to that git with his stray fag end, not to mention all of Dave's antics earlier in the evening.

But a good strong Americano and some fresh fruit (all the calories she ever allowed herself at this time of day), would surely revive her a bit. These days, she couldn't even risk taking a sleeping pill, not with the whole other cocktail of medications flooding through her system.

She wrapped a towel round wet hair, slipped into an

269

oversized hotel dressing gown and flung the door wide open.

But it wasn't room service at all.

Instead there was a very sheepish looking Lucy Belton. At least she might have looked sheepish; it was a bit difficult to tell underneath all of that make-up.

'Can I come in?' she asked Jo in a quiet little voice.

'Bad time, as you can see,' Jo replied briskly. 'I'm afraid I'm just about to get dressed.'

'It's just . . . there's something I really need to say to you.'

'To be perfectly honest, I think you said quite enough to me last night. Don't you?'

'Won't take two seconds,' Lucy pleaded, looking at Jo with such desperation in her wide blue eyes, that she found herself wavering. Immaculately made-up eyes too, Jo thought from out of nowhere. God Almighty, how early did this one have to get up in the morning to get herself looking like this? And quite apart from anything else, where did she find the time?

'Two seconds then,' she sighed, stepping aside to let Lucy in and folding her arms as much as to say, 'Just tell me whatever it is and get the hell out ASAP.'

'I just wanted to tell you how very sorry I am,' Lucy began tentatively, 'for being so out of order down in the bar last night.'

'Fine. You've said your piece,' Jo told her curtly. 'Can you leave now please? I still have to get dressed and organized, as you can see.'

She sounded rude and knew it, but she couldn't bring herself to care. When she thought of what Lucy had drunkenly said to her last night, actually talking – in public – about

270

IVF and the strain all the synthetic hormones can have on a woman's personality . . . well, to Jo, it had felt the exact same as being slapped across the face.

And now here she was, standing in front of her, all healthy looking and young and probably blooming with fertility. Wait till you see, Lucy would turn out to be one of those women who'd go on to have a whole clatter of effortless pregnancies and for some reason, this made Jo irrationally angry and jealous.

Suddenly she knew she couldn't listen to another word. She put one hand on the door as though about to show her out, but it seemed Lucy wasn't finished.

'Jo . . . I couldn't sleep a wink for thinking about all the awful things I said to you –'

'Well, that certainly makes two of us.'

'There's no excuse for how I behaved or for sticking my nose into your private business and believe me, I'm utterly mortified, but . . .'

'I'm afraid I really must ask you to leave. Now. Please.'

'If that's what you want,' Lucy sighed dejectedly, as though she sensed she was only wasting her time here. 'But just before I go –'

Jo didn't answer her though. Just stood, arms folded, foot tapping impatiently, waiting on her to leave. Another quick rapping on her door and this time it actually was room service with her breakfast order for real.

Good, she thought, a distraction and with any luck, Glamazon here would take this as her cue to go. But as she busied herself with tipping the waiter and telling him where to leave the breakfast tray, still Lucy stood there, like she absolutely wasn't budging.

Silence as Jo swished about the room saying absolutely

nothing, just whipping the towel off the top of her head, turning to face the mirror and starting to roughly dry her hair with it. But the two women's eyes locked in the mirror and Jo felt a sudden flash of frustration. What was this one still doing here anyway, standing like a deaf mute? She'd already made her apologies, couldn't she see she was in the way now?

'Was there anything else?' Jo asked, a bit rudely, but not really caring. It was after all, no worse than this one deserved after some of the home truths she'd dished up to Jo last night; the brazen neck of her.

'Well . . . I guess I probably should leave you in peace,' Lucy eventually said, shrugging her shoulders and finally making to go.

Jo did absolutely nothing to stop her, just stayed focused on drying off the ends of her hair.

'But look . . . can I just say one last thing before I go?'

Christ, what now? Jo thought.

'Well . . . there's at least one aspect of all this that I really do envy you.'

And suddenly out of nowhere Jo wanted to laugh right in her face. The idea that anyone could look at her life from the outside and find something to envy, was beyond a joke at this stage.

'If you don't mind, I'm afraid I'd far rather not hear it.'

But Lucy moved a step closer to her, towering over her now and twisting her hands nervously, like she wasn't quite sure how to put this.

'The thing is Jo . . . I know I'm always getting in trouble for sticking my nose into other people's business, but there's something I really have to tell you. I think Dave still loves you, you know. So much, far more than you

272

know. You were all he talked about down at the bar last night. He'd do anything for you. He's only here in the first place because he genuinely thinks this is what you want. There's a man down there that would do anything to make you happy. And I for one would kill to be in that position, believe you me.'

And suddenly Jo was flushing, with her face raw red.

'I'm afraid I have to ask you to stop right there –' she interrupted, but Lucy still wasn't done.

'Do you know how rare it is to find someone like that? Who loves you through thick and thin? Because after what I've just been through, I can tell you that I certainly don't have that luxury. So please Jo, take a look at what you've got here. Someone who adores you and wants to be with you no matter what! It's easy to be happily married when everything's going great. It's only when the tide goes out that you really see what your relationship is made of.'

Jo shook her head wearily.

'I appreciate your concern,' she said tightly, 'but please bear in mind you've only heard one side of the story. Dave's. Did he tell you the primary reason why we're here in the first place? What happened between us not so long ago?'

Lucy shook her head, starting to look a bit puzzled now.

'No, I didn't think so,' Jo went on, pouring herself a large, strong coffee. 'Dave's an actor, you know. Highly persuasive at getting his side of things across, not so hot on cold, hard facts, I think you'll find.'

'It's not my place to say this, of course,' said Lucy, 'but he genuinely seems gutted about losing you.'

'Then I suggest you go and ask him about what came out in the wash just a few short months ago. And then you can barge in here and start telling me how much my husband loves me.'

'Jo . . . please . . . I'm so sorry if I offended you . . . I only meant well . . .'

'Or maybe you'd like to save all the bother and let me tell you here and now?'

*

Ten minutes later, Lucy said goodbye, too shell-shocked even to apologize any more.

Sweet baby Jesus and the orphans, she thought. And I thought Andrew and I had problems?

Chapter Twenty-Four

Chloe.

'Chloe, could I have a quick word?'

Barely eight thirty in the morning and if I had a euro for every time someone has said that to me so far today, etc, etc.

I'm in the Yellow Dining Room on the first floor, which is one of my favourites at the hotel; all sun-drenched and airy with the most breathtaking view down onto the Square below. I'm mucking in and generally helping out with service here, plus smoothing over ruffled feathers and making sure no one wants to lodge a complaint after, ahem, the events of the last twelve hours.

Luckily though, most guests are fairly understanding about the fiasco that was last night, with Jayne Ferguson even managing to have a good old giggle about it.

'You know, I was certain that was my Larry who set off the fire alarm,' she laughed as I chatted to her over breakfast earlier. 'Just so he could get to see me in my night attire for the last and final time!'

So far, so good, but you never can tell. Given the fact that everyone under this roof is currently operating on about five hours' sleep thanks to last night's mini-drama, would it hardly be any wonder if guests felt like having a good old gripe at me?

'Chloe?'

And now it's Dawn who's caught me this time, my little pet and favourite guest, so I instantly beam down at her and give her my full attention.

'I just wanted to talk to you . . . well, about . . . you know,' Dawn says, shoving aside a plateful of half-eaten eggs Benedict.

'I hope you weren't disturbed too much,' I smile warmly back down at her, resisting the urge to act like an Irish Mammy and tell her to eat up the rest of her brekkie, like a good girl. 'But I'm afraid it's standard procedure though. Once a smoke alarm is sounded, we don't have any choice but to evacuate the entire building.'

'No . . . it was actually *you* I was worried about,' Dawn says simply, twisting a stray stand of red hair round her fingertips. 'Such a shitty thing to happen on everyone's first night – oops! Sorry, didn't mean to use bad language in a posh place like this.'

'Don't you worry,' I whisper, bending down to her. 'I said far worse myself last night, believe me.'

'Can I ask you something?' she says, in that unflinchingly direct way the girl has. 'Exactly how much trouble is Kirk in right now?'

And I could be mistaken, but it's almost like she's hopeful that the answer will be 'So much trouble, you wouldn't believe it.' And that I'll tack on for good measure, 'Don't you worry, we'll be packing Kirk's bags for him, fining him two hundred euro and I'll personally see to it that he gets a police escort off the premises, just as soon as I'm done in here.'

'Well, I'm afraid this is a non-smoking hotel,' is what I actually tell her though, discreetly omitting to mention what it was that he was puffing away on, though I'd say Dawn could hazard a guess. 'But of course, accidents will happen.'

Subtext: it's highly unlikely any five-star hotel would ever throw out a paying guest, just because of one slip-up. Providing, of course, he doesn't try it on again. For a split second, I swear the girl looks a bit disappointed.

'What a roaring eejit, to go and do something like that,' she says, twisting a coil of her long red hair round her finger. 'I mean, how thick do you have to be to realize that a non-smoking hotel means exactly that? And that dope is considered a bit of a no-no in any fancy hotel? Barring you play lead guitar with the E Street Band, that is.'

I don't answer, mainly because I one hundred per cent agree with her.

'But . . . how about you?' Dawn persists knowingly. 'Will Kirk's antics land you in it?'

Actually a very good question. When Rob the Bossman unexpectedly landed in on us last night, there was barely time for he and I to exchange two syllables. Instead he seemed to guess at a glance exactly what was happening and just started to help me and the rest of the staff to escort guests safely back to their rooms. Not a word passed between us otherwise, apart from him briefly grabbing my elbow, steering me towards a taxi and saying, 'We'll talk properly tomorrow. Too late right now. Go home and try to get some rest.'

Rest? Yeah, right. Instead I just lay awake in my old bedroom back at my parents' house thinking, when this weekend is all over, my arse is so fired. Let's face it, your boss unexpectedly landing in on top of you in the middle of a fire evacuation is never good news. The mental image of twenty-four guests, shivering in nighties and PJ's in Fitzwilliam Square in the middle of the night, just as a taxi pulls up and Rob McFayden hops out, is going to take a long, long time to dislodge.

For the moment though, here I am in the dining room, coffee pot frozen in my hand while Dawn is still looking expectantly up at me, so I make an effort to act all relaxed and just smile back. 'Never mind about me,' I say. 'You've got a busy day ahead, don't you?'

'Don't start,' she groans, rolling her eyes. Not that I blame the poor kid either. Apart from a conflict resolution session this morning, the bulk of today is all about division of property and joint assets. We've booked estate agents, property valuation experts and even an expert on pensions to liaise with each of our couples throughout the day. And it's gonna be a long 'un.

There's a brief, fleeting moment where Dawn and I each look at each other, each silently thinking 'good luck with yours, love. But I don't think I'd swap places with you for a million quid.'

And then suddenly I'm called away. Rob's waiting at Reception, one of the wait staff whispers discreetly in my ear, he asked for you the very second he arrived. Was he brandishing a P45 'welcome to dole-land' form with him, I can't help but wonder?

I take a deep breath and keep repeating the one thing that's been running through my head all morning. Smoke alarms have a habit of going off and after all, how much trouble would I be in if I *hadn't* chosen to follow procedure and evacuate? Palms still sweating a fair bit though, I have to say.

Rob is standing by the door by the time I get to Reception, as ever, dressed down in chinos and a light blue shirt. He sees me coming, holds open the main entrance door for me and immediately says, 'Hi there. You okay?'

'Yes, Rob. Thanks,' I answer tersely.

Shite. Am I to be shown the door this fast? I mean . . . isn't that illegal, for starters?

'Good. Come on then. Let's go. After you.'

'*Leave?* You want me to leave the hotel?' I ask him, dumfounded. 'Because I just can't! I've a meeting in like, half an hour and then it's all hands on deck for the early lunch sitting –'

'Oh now, surely you can spare me a few minutes,' Rob says, looking me straight in the eye, really taking me in, head to toe. 'By the look of you, I'd say a bit of fresh air wouldn't go amiss.'

Why does he want me out of the building, I think, my blood pressure suddenly rocketing. To haul me over the coals? Away from the hotel, where I might cause a scene in front of all our guests?

We're standing right at the bottom of the steps in front of the hotel now and I'm just wondering exactly where he was planning to go anyway, when he suddenly takes a sharp left and says, 'This way.'

'Where to?'

'Well, to get some breakfast, for a start. I'm starving and I'd hazard a guess you haven't eaten either.'

I don't argue. I've been at the hotel since first light and even then, I only managed to grab a coffee on the run. No time. Throw that in with the fact I'm operating on about four hours' sleep and I suddenly realize I'm ravenous.

Next thing, Rob and I are power walking side by side to

Café Sol on Baggot Street, just around the corner. He politely asks me what I'd like, takes care of all the ordering and two minutes later, we're back out in the warm sunshine, laden down with takeout cappuccinos, a cream cheese bagel for him and a passion fruit granola for me.

Wordlessly, Rob leads the way back up to Fitzwilliam Square, but then surprises me by steering clear of Hope Street and heading into the square itself. Next thing he plonks down on a secluded park bench, just inside the gates, which faces out over an immaculately maintained rose garden.

'Here okay for you?' he asks, stretching long legs out in front of him.

'Emm . . . yeah, if you like.'

'I just figured we'd have a bit more privacy,' he goes on, clocking the puzzled look on my face as I ease down onto the bench beside him. 'Thing is Chloe, at the hotel, you're being pulled in about fifty different directions all at once. At least here, I get to talk to you. I mean, talk properly. Hope you don't mind?'

'Emm, no, not at all,' I say, handing over his bagel and cappuccino. 'But just so you know, we've kitchen staff not twenty feet from us who could have rustled you up a brekkie worthy of a Michelin star. For free.'

'I'm sure they would. But then we wouldn't really get to chat without interruption, would we?'

Subtle way of bringing up last night. So I jump in at the deep end and go for it. What the feck, nothing to lose.

'Thing is Rob . . . well, you know I really can't apologize enough for . . .'

'For what?' He's looking right at me now, like I'm a few sandwiches short of a picnic.

280

'Put it this way. There's never a good time for the hotel owner to arrive unexpectedly. Particularly when you've lined up most of your guests shivering in pyjamas in the middle of the street, when it's well past midnight.'

'I guess I timed my arrival pretty badly, huh?' he says, mouth twisted down into just the hint of a grin.

I do a quick double take, but no, I wasn't mistaken, there was definite grinning action going on here. Which has to be a good thing, I think, my mind accelerating. Doesn't it?

'It's never good news when your boss witnesses a fire evacuation, no,' I say, looking right back at him, trying to gauge exactly what he's thinking. He's tanned, I notice for the first time. And a bit stubbly, like he just hauled himself out of bed and came straight here. Smells nice though. Citrusy. Makes me suddenly aware that I'm probably stinking of bacon and sausage from overseeing breakfast earlier.

'Come on, Chloe,' Rob says, smiling properly now. And this time, there's no mistaking it. That's a proper, ear-to-ear grin. Takes years off him too, almost making him look boyish.

'Do you honestly think in all my years I've never seen a fire drill before?' he goes on. 'Rotten luck that it happened on our first night, of all nights, but when some tosser decides to light up in his room, then that's what we gotta deal with.'

'You mean . . . you didn't bring me out here to bawl me out of it, then?'

'Why would I do that? Just for doing your job? For prioritizing safety?'

'Well, you know . . .'

'Believe me,' he says, whipping the bagel out of its bag

and hungrily wolfing down a mouthful. 'I'm long enough in this game to know a well-functioning hotel when I see one. And I genuinely think you're doing a terrific job here. Don't you worry, you'd know all about it if that weren't the case.'

'Then . . . why did you want to talk to me in private?'

'Ah yes,' he says, pausing for a bit because his mouth's completely full. 'Remember when I spoke to you yesterday evening?'

Ehh, exactly which phone call would that be, I want to ask him, mainly because the guy rang me about a dozen times yesterday. But instead I just nod and take a tiny sip of the cappuccino that's starting to burn my hand off by now.

'As it happens, when I called you last night, I'd just got back to London from our site in Milan,' he goes on in between mouthfuls. Italy; explains the tan, I think. 'Anyway, I was worried. I could clearly hear a lot of raised voices in the background. It was always my intention to get over here this weekend anyway, so I jumped on a flight and hightailed it here as fast as I could.'

Ahh, that. A pause while Rob just looks at me coolly, calmly awaiting further elaboration.

'Yee-ess,' I tell him straight up. 'Well, let me put it this way: out of a dozen couples staying here, the vast majority seem to get on perfectly well. They're all here to get this done and dusted as quickly as they can. They're being perfectly civilized and mannerly towards each other about the whole thing, and they're making my life so easy. But . . . the thing is . . .'

'Go on,' he says. He's stopped eating now, I notice, and the grey eyes are looking over at me expectantly.

Tell him the truth, Chloe. He's going to find out anyway and after all, it's better coming from you.

'Well . . . I've got three couples here that are maybe not dealing with the whole process quite as well as I would have hoped.'

'Tell me more.'

So I do. I tell him all about Dawn and Kirk and how I thought I'd almost have to throw a bucket of cold water over the pair of them yesterday evening, they were bickering that much. Weirdly though, instead of asking me why I hadn't pre-screened them a bit more carefully, he seems far more interested in the ins and outs of their relationship.

'The young girl with the long red hair and Arson Boy?' he asks, catching me completely off guard.

'That's them.'

'So what do you think went wrong there?' he asks, looking at me keenly.

'Well, they married far too young for a start. But . . . without breaking a confidence, there's a helluva lot more to it than that.'

'When it comes to relationships, there always is, at least in my experience. So come on, fill me in.' Then with a wry smile, he adds, 'After all, if they're about to start ripping up furniture under my roof, I think I've a right to know.'

'You mean . . . you're not annoyed, because I should have spotted long before they even checked in here that they possibly weren't suitable?'

'You think I'm here to haul you over the coals for not being a mind-reader?'

'Emm . . . well . . .'

And suddenly he's grinning again.

'What's so funny?'

'Chloe, come on. If there's a human being alive who has the ability to X-ray the exact state of any couple's relationship at any given time, then I'd really love to meet them. So come on then, back to Dawn and Arson Boy. Tell me more.'

I have to take a second for a quick sigh of relief, before answering.

'Well,' I think, choosing my words carefully on account of I gave Dawn my word I'd keep the real truth of it to myself. 'She did tell me Kirk's been having an ongoing affair and apparently it's not one he's any intention of giving up anytime soon.'

Rob shakes his head.

'But if that's the case, then rough and all as that is for her, surely she'd at least be glad to get rid of him? Better all round in the long run, wouldn't you say?'

I just nod, but say nothing. Because there's much more to it than that, considerably more. But I gave my word to say no more, so I won't, simple as that. To be brutally honest though and particularly in light of last night's shenanigans, I'm not all that bothered about what'll become of Kirk, but I do so badly want a happy ending for Dawn. The girl deserves no less, after the horrors she's been through.

Then I fill Rob in about Jo and Dave too and how Dave was almost battering her door down, the minute he'd got a lorry load of drinks into him.

'So why do you think that one went belly-up, then?' Rob asks me directly, all interested.

'Well, that's a bit of a mystery, to be honest. Jo hinted to me that she's having a lot of medical issues at the minute, but she stopped short of saying any more. She just said everyone assumed she was to blame but that there was a whole other side to her story.'

'Always is,' he says, nodding. 'Certainly in my experience.' Then, bagel finished, he sits right back against the bench and faces the sun, like a man with all the time in the world to sit here and lap up every UV ray going. 'Though you said you'd three couples giving you a headache? Come on, tell me more. Who's the third?'

So I fill him in about Lucy's antics the previous evening and he just nods.

'The tall blonde?'

'That's her.' But then in all fairness, Lucy's hard to miss. 'And to be honest, they're the one couple staying with us who I figured would find the whole process relatively straightforward. Andrew, that's her ex, is so protective of her, you just wouldn't believe it. His only concern after I'd finally got her to bed last night was that she'd be okay.'

But again though, some instinct tells me that there's an awful lot more to Lucy and Andrew's break-up than meets the eye. What though? Try as I might, I just can't fathom it. When we first met, Lucy mentioned it was something to do with his adult kids having a lot to do with it, and yet what could they have done to bring this about?

A pause, while Rob stretches out on the bench a bit more, luxuriating in the morning sunshine.

'Exes,' he eventually says, shaking his head a bit. 'We all have them, don't we? And as the saying goes, there's always three sides to every story. Your side, the other person's side and then usually somewhere in the middle, there's the truth. So I've always found at least.'

I take a sip of coffee, while he just stares off into the middle distance, miles away.

'And were you ever married?' I ask him eventually. I don't even know why, the moment just sort of feels right. He doesn't wear a wedding ring and even with all the press his work generates, I don't ever remember reading any mention of a wife.

'No,' he says. 'At least, not yet.'

I nod and turn away to disguise a smile, remembering back to when he was here a few weeks ago. Rob taking a very personal phone call and littering the chat with 'love' and 'darling' and 'can't wait to see you!'

Stands to reason really, I figure. A catch like this fella? Rich, successful and attractive? I mean, as long as you could handle all the constant globe-hopping and the mobile ringing day and night, you'd be well and truly laughing. Whoever his mystery lady is though, I'd safely hazard a guess that now she has her claws in him, she ain't about to quit anytime soon.

'Course I don't need to ask whether you've ever been married or not,' he says, turning his head towards me and looking at me keenly now, the grey eyes focused directly on me.

'Why's that?' I say defensively, caught completely off guard.

'Chloe, it's okay,' he says simply. 'I know.'

And after the relaxed, easy chat we'd been having, suddenly it's like no air moves between us.

'You do?' I say, sounding a lot more staccato than I'd have liked.

'When I interviewed you first, remember? It struck me as odd that you'd left the Merrion Hotel as abruptly as you did, two years ago. You'd impressed me and I was pretty certain I wanted to hire you, but I needed to run a background check on you first, just to make sure you weren't the type to leave me high and dry. So I made a few phone calls over to the Merrion . . .'

He doesn't need to say another word though. I can see it written all over his face. No doubt my manager there told him everything. About my aborted fiasco of a wedding day. The whole reason why I hightailed it to London in the first place and only called my old boss to explain once I'd safely got there. And yet how understanding they'd all been. Particularly when I explained that there was just no way on earth I could ever show my face in this town again. Not after what I'd been through, and certainly not after the ultimate humiliation.

And now, here I am, back again, surrounded by broken hearts that make what I went through almost pale into insignificance.

'Oh,' is all I can manage to get out though, suddenly aware that I'm flushing to my roots. 'That.'

'Of course your personal life is absolutely none of my business,' Rob says, 'but back when I first interviewed you, you told me that if anyone was qualified to run a hotel where broken-hearted people came to fix themselves, to put their lives back together and move on, then you were the girl.'

'I remember.'

'I really saw something in you that day, Chloe,' he goes on, surprising me by actually sounding quite gentle now. A million miles from his usual brisk, businesslike self. 'I knew that if I was looking for the kind of woman well qualified to try and fix other couples, then you were certainly the perfect person for the job. And for what it's worth, I think you're doing fine work here and I know you won't let me down.'

Our eyes lock for a moment and somehow I don't know what to say to him. I'm touched and staggered and overwhelmed all at the same time.

'I'll certainly give it a try,' I manage to say, wrapped in thought at just how wrongly pegged I had this guy. And how the public Rob and the actual guy himself seem so completely different.

'Do you mind my asking you something personal?' he goes on.

'Of course not.' Jeez, I think, we're chatting about so many personal things right now, sure what's left?

'That ex of yours. Now that you're back on your home turf, ever hear from him?'

Frank. And suddenly I think back. The flowers. That ludicrously overpriced bouquet that landed in here yesterday to wish me luck. Frank's suggestion that he and I 'might meet up soon'.

What with all last night's shenanigans, I'd managed to completely blank it out, but now it's back fresh and uppermost in my mind. And the killer is, it still has the power to stab a little. Even after all this time. Unbe-fecking-lievable.

'Yes, as it happens,' I tell Rob, looking straight ahead of me. There's a father in the distance who's teaching his son how to ride a bike without stabilizers. Poor kid keeps falling off, but his Dad is encouraging him to persist, saying he's almost there and it'll be well worth it in the end.

'Yes, just yesterday, would you believe. Frank got in touch to wish me luck.'

'That's his name? Frank?'

'Yup.'

'I see,' and suddenly Rob's face is back to being all blank and unreadable.

288

Another lengthy pause and after such an unexpected heart to heart between us, all of a sudden, it seems not much else needs to be said, so I stand up and busy myself clearing away wrappers and paper coffee cups. He jumps to his feet and helps me, but then, just as we're both heading back towards Hope Street, he stops me in my tracks.

'But just for what it's worth, Chloe?' he says, looking right at me now.

'Yeah?'

'What that Frank guy did to you on your wedding day? No offence, but what a total arse.'

Chapter Twenty-Five

Lucy.

A 'conflict resolution' meeting, that was where Lucy now found herself, if you could even believe it. Nine in the morning, and here she was, hung-over as a dog and feeling as though she'd rather have hurled herself out the window rather than have to face into this right now, this morning. Alongside Andrew, to make matters even worse.

He was sitting in an armchair just opposite her, but the few sneaky glances Lucy had stolen over in his direction had frankly made her worry a bit. Because he didn't look one bit well, not his usual tanned, vigorous looking self at all. He was wearing a green cashmere jumper she'd given him a few years ago, one she usually loved on him; it brought out the colour of his eyes so perfectly. But today, he just looked pale and strained, which was so unlike him. Did he hate this just as much as she did, she wondered?

Bloody hard to imagine otherwise.

'Now, here's what I'd like you both to do for me,' a lovely, smiley women with a sweet face called Kate said, crossing her legs and putting aside a very authoritative looking notepad for the moment. 'As an exercise, I'd like you to tell me all of the things that you still love and respect about each other. Each other's best qualities. The things that made you both fall in love and marry in the first place. Just tell me, stream of consciousness. Let's start from there and then we can move forward. So, who'd like to kick things off?'

'Ladies first,' said Andrew politely, giving Lucy a tiny nod.

'Each other's *good* qualities?' Lucy blurted out. 'Did I just hear you right? Because believe me, that's not what I thought we were here to talk about. Andrew's good qualities aren't and never were the issue here!'

'Trust me Lucy,' Kate persisted. 'Remember, conflict resolution is a process. Not just a Band-Aid temporary measure.'

'Oh. Well . . . okay then, if you insist,' she said reluctantly, aware that Andrew's eyes were full on her. So she forced herself to sit back against the plush leather couch, stare out the window and take a nice deep, soothing breath.

Shite anyway. She'd have been so much more comfortable talking about what his bloody family had put them through. Why couldn't they have started off with that? You wouldn't have been able to shut her up on that particular topic. Each other's good qualities, my arse, she sighed.

'And try to relax,' Kate added encouragingly.

Relax? That was a right laugh. Lucy had never felt like such a ball of tension in her life. And having to go through all this conflict resolution malarkey wasn't made easier by the fact she'd been on the bender to end all benders down in the bar the previous night. So now of course, she just felt muggy-headed, tired and in absolutely no bloody humour for any kind of deep probing. The bright lights overhead were actually stinging her eyes and half of her wondered if it would be rude to go through this whole session with her sunglasses on. Would that make her look a bit like a Soprano?

'Anytime you're ready, Lucy,' Kate smiled patiently.

'Well . . . up until . . . what happened recently . . .' she began tentatively, trying to pick her words. But no sooner had she started than she'd had to break off to reach for the glass of water that was thoughtfully placed in front of her when they'd first arrived.

No choice. This was a lot harder than she could ever have imagined.

'Sorry, Kate,' she suddenly broke off. 'But do you mind if I take a few paracetamol?'

'Of course not. Are you feeling okay?'

'Migraine,' she lied, whipping a strip of painkillers out of her handbag and gulping back two.

She caught Andrew's eye and because he knew right well what was really wrong with her, she felt a flush of gratitude towards him for not saying anything.

'Ready now?' Kate gently prompted.

'Yeah. Well . . . Andrew is . . . that is . . . well, he certainly was – at least back in our early days –'

But she had to struggle a bit, to find the right words here. Tough sentence that particular one, to have to finish without choking up. Mainly because when Andrew had been good, God, but he'd been amazing.

All kinds of memories started to resurface. How thoughtful he was in small ways. How kind he'd always been to her mother and all her family. Even insisted on whisking her Mum off to Marbella on holiday with them twice a year, knowing the poor woman would never have been able to afford it otherwise.

292

But then, Lucy's family were what his side would snobbishly have called blue collar, compared with someone as classy as Andrew. Yet it was touching how hard he'd worked to try and fit in with them all. He was forever inviting the whole lot of them round for dinner, or else hosting her entire extended family – seventeen of them in total, in-laws included – at expensive restaurants in town. Then he'd discreetly take care of the bill when no one was watching, so as not to embarrass anyone.

In spite of herself, Lucy thought back to the way he'd gamely pitch up at countless of her nieces' and nephews' First Communions and Confirmations. These past few years, the way he'd muck in with the rest of them, even though it was so glaringly obvious he'd little in common with any of Lucy's brothers or the rest of her male in-laws, most of whom just wanted to sit round the telly, drinking beer from the tin and talking about the soccer results.

Andrew on the other hand, was more of an opera and fine wine type of guy, yet never once did he complain. Never once did he groan at Lucy and say, 'Not another night out with your relations again!' Like so many of her ex-boyfriends had in the past. Not even when one of Lucy's five-year-old nieces clambered up to him and said, 'Are you really married to Auntie Lucy? You're so old! You're like, the same age as my Grandad!'

Not even when Lucy's boisterous godson accidentally spilt tomato ketchup all over his favourite Italian silk shirt.

Then there was the way he'd bring her a mug of tea and toast in bed every single morning without fail, even though he'd a far more gruelling day ahead of him than she had. How he'd tease her about reading *HELLO!* and *OK!* magazine, tell her that they'd melt her brain, yet still go out and buy them for her, without her ever once having to ask.

'Lucy?' Kate interrupted her thoughts.

'Sorry,' she said and for the first time, she turned to face Andrew, who was now looking over at her intently. 'Look, the thing is, to be perfectly fair, you tried your best to be a fantastic husband.'

'And you were never anything less than a wonderful wife,' he smiled gamely back at her. 'Please know that whatever the outcome of the next few days, I'll cherish the memories of our married life together for always.'

'Thank you . . .' Lucy struggled to get out, 'and for my part . . . well, you and I were compatible on just about every level you could think of. We've exactly the same sense of humour, and . . . well, and . . .' but she abruptly broke off here. Because the tail end of that sentence was 'sexually, I always had a fantastic time with you. In bed, it was incredible.'

But she couldn't, not here, not now. Fine to talk about your overactive sex life to Bianca over a few mojitos in a late night bar, but somehow in this posh library, with a stranger staring down at her over a clipboard, it just didn't seem appropriate somehow.

'You see, Andrew is – that is, or at least he *was* . . . in many ways – my ideal man, really,' she told Kate, trailing off a bit. But then that was easy enough to say, because Andrew wasn't exactly the problem here, was he?

'Thank you,' he said simply in return. 'And you know for my part . . . well, it goes without saying, I feel the same.'

'Oh well now, isn't that just lovely?' Kate beamed delightedly. '*Very* good. Well done, you two. For the moment, let's keep focusing on all the positives about your relationship before we move on. So when would you both say conflict began to creep into the marriage?'

And now here it is. Here we fecking well go, Lucy thought, steeling herself. Don't jump in feet first, though. Don't let your first sentence be, 'He and I were happy, shame about the spawn of the devil that he and his ex-wife managed to produce, who drove us to this sorry end.'

'I should point out here that I've got two grown-up kids from my first marriage, Alannah and Josh,' Andrew said, smoothly taking over. 'Adult twins, as it happens. And then of course, there's my ex-wife Greta too. And naturally, they need to be looked after as best I can.'

'Which I totally agreed with,' Lucy interrupted, addressing Andrew directly now. 'And if nothing else, I've always respected the fact that you're so good to your children.'

Well done, she told herself. You sound like a reasonable, balanced woman here. So far, so good.

'Let's talk about your other family then, Andrew,' said Kate, still looking pleased that they were being so civilized towards each other.

'Well, to be perfectly honest, it's Alannah and Josh that first started this whole bloody nightmare we're stuck in . . .' Lucy blurted out.

'Lucy, please,' said Andrew warningly.

'But they're the whole reason we're sitting here in the first place. That pair are the root of everything, surely you can see that!'

'We've been through this and you already know that I freely take full responsibility for what's happened,' Andrew interrupted her, reddening slightly the way he did when his blood pressure was at him.

'Do you think it's possible,' Kate interrupted, 'that

295

because Josh and Alannah felt you were responsible for the break-up of your first marriage, Andrew, that they were subsequently acting out? Because as we know, adults can do that just as effectively and indeed sometimes far more deviously, than children. It's almost like we rehearse our worst selves in front of family, purely and simply because we can. So tell me when the cracks first began to show. Why don't you both tell me from the very start.'

Tell you? I could put a fecking date on it for you, Lucy thought bitterly, playing with the tassels on a cushion beside her and trying to get this out as rationally as she could. If at all possible, without a) bad-mouthing Josh for the bone-idle sponge he was and b) cursing Alannah for being so vicious towards her and calling her every name she could think of.

No, wrong approach. A cool head and a bit of rationality were what was called for here, she had to remind herself, biting her tongue and trying to somehow untangle the hellish mess the last couple of years had been. Try to sound like a reasonable, levelheaded woman, she told herself.

And failing that, just tell the truth.

'Well, I think things started to go under just about two years ago,' Lucy began. 'Not long after we were first married. When Alannah was first made redundant from work.'

'Go on. Tell me more about Alannah.'

'Well, with no job, she couldn't pay her rent any more,' Andrew said smoothly, taking up the story from her. 'Which of course meant she had to move out of the flat she'd been living in. Now, ordinarily, she'd have moved back with her Mum, my ex, Greta. But for some reason, she insisted on moving in with Lucy and I instead.'

'I see. And how did you feel about this, Lucy?'

296

'It was unexpected, but of course, I didn't mind, thinking this was going to be a temporary measure, just until Alannah found work again. Except it didn't quite turn out that way.'

Understatement of the century.

'How do you mean?'

Lucy let out an exhausted sigh so deep, it felt like it might have been coming from the soles of her feet.

'Lucy?' prompted Kate, one eye on the clock.

And so Lucy thought back. Those godawful days and weeks, which quickly turned into months, when she and Andrew were just newly married and essentially living with a flatmate from hell. Charming to Andrew's face of course, and a thundering bitch to Lucy the very second his back was turned. Someone who, as she quickly copped on, had absolutely no intentions of moving out anytime soon. After all, why should she when she could live in comfort and luxury courtesy of the free Bank of Dad and new Stepmum?

'Can I just point out that Alannah was twenty-eight years old at the time?' Lucy suddenly blurted out. 'And yet all she wanted to do was live off her Dad and me and by the way, live a pretty flashy lifestyle at that. One neither of us could afford to sustain.'

'It goes without saying that I'll do anything to support my children,' said Andrew with just a note of warning in his voice.

'Which I totally get,' Lucy countered, 'but if I were Alannah's age and unemployed, I think I'd have got a job sweeping the streets rather than sponge off my father and stepmother! I'd have gone out and scrubbed toilets rather than be a burden. And yet she'd absolutely no problems with it. It was all, "Dad, I've been invited to go skiing, can

297

you cover the cost of my trip?" Which of course, would frequently run into thousands.'

'So, we're agreed there were issues around Alannah moving in with you when you were first married?' prompted Kate.

'Well,' Lucy said reluctantly. 'Yes and no. It wasn't a black and white thing to start with. I mean, Alannah is Andrew's daughter and of course we were hardly going to turn her away.'

'Naturally.'

'But I have to say, it was a huge strain having her under my roof twenty-four hours a day. Especially when Andrew and I were both working full-time. And working incredibly hard too, may I add.'

'You said you were supporting her. So how are you both fixed financially?'

A bloody good question. Especially seeing as how Andrew had money to burn at one stage, but certainly not now.

'We're what you might call the squeezed middle,' Andrew answered smoothly. 'I'm afraid things aren't what they once were at the bank, where I serve on the Board of Directors.'

'Understatement of the year,' Lucy couldn't stop herself from chipping in.

'Go on,' said Kate.

'Well,' she went on, with just a sideways glance over to Andrew to see how he was reacting. 'The fact is, Andrew's investments have mostly dwindled down to nothing; all his stocks and shares at the bank are practically valueless, his pension's completely gone and really . . . well . . .'

'I think what Lucy is trying to say,' said Andrew, taking the reins up for her and reddening still more, 'is that when

298

everything else depreciated so dramatically, all we really had left was the family home.'

'Plus both our salaries,' Lucy added helpfully. 'But after tax, that still didn't leave a huge whack of cash. Certainly not compared with the kind of money Andrew was used to pulling in, back in the day.'

'Did this make you feel pressurized in any way?'

'Of course it did,' Lucy said, trying hard to keep her voice even. 'Can I just point out that Andrew's nearing retirement age and should be slowing down, yet still had to work to capacity, just to finance his two adult children? Out of a joint savings account, with all my hard-earned wages going into it as well, by the way?'

'You and I discussed this openly at the time,' Andrew said coolly, for him. 'And after all, Alannah is my daughter. So if she needed help, then it was our duty to give it.'

'Which I had absolutely no problem doing,' replied Lucy, 'same as I would for anyone. All I asked in return was for a little bit of politeness that never came. And while we're on the subject, can I just point out that there's a helluva difference between helping someone out and just shelling out guilt money?'

'Lucy, that's most unfair and you know it,' Andrew said crossly, but there was no shutting Lucy up now.

'And let's not forget that Alannah wasn't even bothering to go out and find any other work at all!'

'Was she interviewing?' Kate interrupted. 'Updating her CV? Going to recruitment agencies?'

'In this economy, I'm afraid she found it very difficult,' said Andrew.

'There you go, making excuses for her yet again!' Lucy heard herself saying. 'But deep down though, you have to know the truth. Which was that for the first two years we were married, Alannah was perfectly happy to just loll around our house all day long, sitting pretty, watching TV, doing her nails and rifling through my wardrobe!'

'Lucy, she had nowhere else to go!'

'The girl never once lifted a finger and not only that, but when I'd come home, bone tired after a day's shoot, she'd rarely fail to complain about whatever was served up to her. "This food is cold," that kind of crap.'

'Okay, okay, we don't need to go any further,' Kate interjected before things really got heated. 'I think I have the picture here. So you felt that the tension really started to ratchet up and that things only went downhill from there?'

'That's not quite the whole story though,' said Andrew, scarlet in the face now.

'I certainly won't argue with you there,' Lucy had almost snapped back at him. Because there was so much more. God, she could sit here for a week straight telling step-daughter from hell stories that would turn the air blue.

There was Alannah and Josh's constant, unrelenting rudeness, not just to her, but to all her extended family too. Lucy's relations were far from posh and by Christ, this pair weren't ever going to let them forget their Finglas roots anytime soon. She'd snapped sharply at them both, when she'd caught them sniggering at her mother over dinner one night, because she'd thought they were calling Lucy a crusty tartlet, when in fact, they'd only been referring to the starter.

'We really must remember to make allowances for step-monster's rellies,' Lucy had overheard Alannah saying to Josh in the kitchen.

'Too right!' Josh had snorted disparagingly. 'But then,

you have to bear in mind that where her lot come from, a batter burger and an onion ring are considered a delicacy.'

'Instead of bringing a bottle of wine next time you come over for dinner,' Alannah quipped, 'why not bring a six-pack of cider that they can drink from the tin instead? Let's face it, Heather Mills and her lot would certainly appreciate it far more.'

There'd been blue murder over that particular episode and it was fast getting to the stage where Lucy was beginning to wonder how much longer before she cracked. It was like the more she allowed them to goad her, the more of a kick they got out of it whenever she'd rise to the bait. And running to Andrew with it was no use; he'd invariably revert back to the upset he'd caused when he and Greta first separated and how incredibly tough it had been on his kids. 'We found our happiness so quickly afterwards, darling,' he'd tell Lucy time and again. 'But at what cost to others? Let's just tread carefully and make every allowance here.'

Like it or not, Lucy was stuck in a no-win situation.

One which was about to get spectacularly worse.

'Naturally, this must have put a huge strain on you both,' Kate said sympathetically.

'We only did what any parents, even step-parents would do,' said Andrew tightly.

'But that's only the warm-up,' said Lucy. 'And you know it.'

'Yet, I think we've had enough on the subject of Alannah as a housemate, don't you?' said Andrew, slightly clamming up now, the way he always did, every single time she even tried to have this conversation with him.

301

'What about last Halloween for instance?' Lucy countered, taking advantage of the fact that Kate was here and for once, he couldn't shimmy out of it with an evasive answer. 'I haven't forgotten that particular debacle, even if you've decided to airbrush it.'

'Alannah apologized, and you know that!'

'It would still help me to talk about it,' Lucy pleaded with Kate, who nodded and waved at her to keep going.

'Well, you see, over Halloween last year, Andrew had taken me down to Wexford for a little weekend mini-break,' she went on, wondering if she'd manage to get to the end of the tale without losing the rag altogether.

'And?'

'It was supposed to have been just the two of us, a break from all the tensions at home but then Andrew invited Alannah along too . . .'

'. . . Because I didn't want her to feel excluded or unwelcome, that's all,' Andrew interrupted.

'. . . As it happened though,' said Lucy, picking up the thread, 'she said she'd prefer to spend the long weekend at the house instead, "just to hang out with a few friends", as she'd told us.'

Which alone should have alerted my suspicions, Lucy thought to herself. But to be honest, she was just so anxious by then to get away from the little madam, even just for a short break, that she was fully prepared to hand over the run of the house to her while they were gone.

'Keep going,' said Kate, listening intently.

'And . . . and sure enough, three days later, we came home to complete mayhem. A squad car in our front driveway, the whole works.'

'Go on.'

'It seemed Alannah had decided to throw an impromptu Halloween party and it unfortunately spiralled out of all control,' Andrew explained. 'A bit like one of those horror stories that you see on Sky News; you know, one of those Facebook parties where word about it goes viral and whole streets get smashed up.'

'Our entire house was totally destroyed,' said Lucy, getting angrier and angrier the more she thought about it. 'Red wine had been sloshed all over our lovely cream carpets, furniture had been knocked; two windows had even been smashed in. I even found a total stranger dressed as Batman puking in the sink of my en-suite.'

Days, that particular row had lasted. Even from a safe distance of eighteen months, it still had the power to make her break into a cold, clammy sweat.

'How did you react this time, Andrew?'

'I'm afraid I lost it when I discovered the entire contents of my vintage wine collection had been glugged back by a crowd of boozers . . .'

'. . . who probably couldn't differentiate between Châteauneuf-du-Pape and Jeyes cleaning fluid,' said Lucy, finishing the sentence for him.

'But really, it was unfair to dump all the blame squarely on Alannah,' Andrew said defensively. 'Because in actual fact, none of it was her doing. She'd just invited a few close pals, who dragged a gang load with them back from the pub and things had spiralled out of control. She was a victim and not the prime organizer.'

'You see? There you go again, making excuses and letting her off the hook. Yet again!' Lucy said, suddenly feeling her anger levels start to shoot skywards. 'Did it ever occur to you that the girl might just be doing her level best to drive a wedge between you and me?'

'A great deal of pain and hurt was caused when you and I first got together, you know that,' Andrew said, looking Lucy square in the face now. 'You must understand how difficult it was for my family seeing you and I together.'

'But I *did* understand and I made every possible allowance for that! Surely to God no one can accuse me of acting any differently . . .'

'You have to remember that they went through a lot . . .'

'Five years ago! And yet you spent our entire marriage paying the price for that?' Lucy yelled at him, unable to help herself. Now the barriers were really down. Even if she did regret the words the second she saw a familiar look of pain cross his face.

'Greta was hugely upset at the way you and I moved on,' said Andrew, red-faced. 'And of course, the kids took her side. All I asked of you was that you remembered to treat them sensitively and to tread softy. It was hugely difficult for them.'

'So why can't you for once accept that it was bloody difficult for me too?'

'You have to appreciate I may have divorced their mother, but I certainly didn't divorce my children too! After all, family is family.'

'I know that and I tried to build a good relationship with them! Tried till I was blue in the face! And in return, all I got was either downright rudeness or else they patently ignored me! I know it was hard for them, but when are you going to realize that it was fecking well tough for me too?'

'Please don't swear . . .' Andrew said loudly, which

worried Lucy, but then he never raised his voice, on any pretext, ever.

'Just once, Andrew, just bloody once, I wish I had a husband who was actually on my side!'

'Excuse me for interrupting,' said Kate. 'But given that this is how you both feel, then I have to ask . . . why did you ever get married in the first place?

Dawn.

Division of property and joint assets. If you could possibly believe that a couple like herself and Kirk could have even found two minutes, never mind a full morning, to spend time discussing that. Division of what exactly, Dawn had wanted to laugh. Our rented flat? The telly my Mum gave us as a wedding gift?

Their little spelt import business, which Dawn was so proud of, Kirk had wanted to hand entirely over to her, but she'd insisted on splitting the proceeds fifty-fifty. After all, they'd set it up together and he did an equal share of work. It was the fair thing to do, the right thing to do. Even if she was still so angry that she could barely make eye contact with him, she at least knew that much.

And now here she was, with an hour-long breather to herself, until whatever their next session was; Dawn hadn't even bothered to check. Instead, she wandered off to the relaxation room and finding it empty, headed over to a soft cushy recliner over by the window to pass the time there.

Beautiful spot too, she thought, kicking off the flat ballet pumps she was wearing and curling up. She was right by a floor to ceiling window that overlooked the stunningly manicured garden below and wasn't sure whether it was the lack of sleep from last night, the fact that all the tension between her and Kirk was taking so much out of her, or just the warm, sundrenched room, but pretty soon, drowsiness got the better of her.

Not long afterwards, Dawn woke to the sensation of someone gently tucking a warm blanket over her and slowly opened her eyes. There, silhouetted against the sunlight, was Chloe's pretty face looking right down on her, like a kind of lovely, gentle guardian angel.

'Shhh, go back to sleep, sweetheart,' Chloe said softly, 'you looked like you were deep in dreamland.'

'I was . . . and thank you.'

'Everything okay, I hope?'

'Maybe not just yet,' Dawn smiled drowsily, 'but you know what? I'm really starting to feel like I'm finally getting there.'

'Oh you'll get there alright. Trust me. You'll definitely get there.'

Chapter Twenty-Six

Chris was busily heading downstairs towards Chloe's office, clutching a rough draft of that evening's menu, which their head chef needed Chloe to sign off on. She never seemed to have a minute to herself round here, it was all go, go, go, and yet, somehow Chris didn't mind the tiredness and emotional intensity. All down to Chloe really, she thought, and how amazingly easy she was to work for.

She was one of those rare General Managers for whom nothing was a problem and who just mucked in and got on with it, same as everyone else. So unlike other GM's Chris had worked for in the past. No doubt about it, she loved working here and really wanted to support Chloe every way she could. This opening weekend just meant so much to them all, particularly with the added pressure of Rob McFayden in situ and watching everything unfold live.

Anyway, Chris was just skipping down the last few stairs and heading for the main entrance hall, when she noticed a short-ish, bald guy standing over by Reception, wearing a neat navy suit and tie, looking like he'd just come from work. Not a guest either, which immediately alerted her.

'I'm here to see Chloe Townsend,' he was telling Liliana at Reception.

'I'm afraid Ms Townsend is in meetings all morning and can't be disturbed,' Liliana patiently explained. 'But if you'd care to leave your name, I'll be sure to tell her you called.'

'I'd much rather see her actually,' baldy-headed guy insisted. 'Can you at least let her know I'm here? I promise, she'll want to see me too. Just tell her Frank is waiting at Reception for her.'

Bloody hell, Chris thought, stopping dead in her tracks. That's the guy who sent her that massive bouquet for our opening. Immediately, she stepped over to him, smiled and shook his hand.

'Hi there, I'm Chloe's assistant,' she explained. 'And don't worry a bit, I'll be sure to let her know you're waiting here to see her.'

*

About half an hour later and Chris was busy working away down at her desk, when suddenly Rob McFayden stuck his head around the door. Chris normally tensed up just at the sight of him and yet not this time. It was strange, she thought, but he seemed so much more mellow and chilled-out this weekend, not a bit like the Rob McFayden she knew of by reputation.

'Any sign of Chloe?' he asked. 'I'm been looking all over for her.'

'Oh, she's just taking a short break right now. An old friend of hers called to see her and I think they went out to the garden.'

'An old friend?' Rob asked, with a raised eyebrow.

'Yes,' Chris smiled helpfully. 'Actually, the same guy who sent her that enormous bouquet on her desk. Someone called Frank?'

Chloe.

Jesus. He's here, actually here, in the hotel. Just turned up like a bad penny. As soon as Chris alerts me, the jittery shakes start, so I bolt to the staff loos to take a minute to compose myself. A tiny splash of cold water on my temples, a dab of lip gloss so as not to look like I'm trying too hard and next thing, I'm clickety-clacking up the back staircase to meet him.

Stay cool, Chloe girl. Just remember he's now on your territory, so just cling tight to that advantage.

'Frank.'

Ridiculous opener, but somehow, now that the moment had come, it was all I could think of to say. Funny, but I'd rehearsed and rehearsed this moment in my head so many times, and yet now that it's actually come to pass, the power of speech seems to have deserted me.

'Hi,' he says, giving me this quick up and down glance, a mannerism of his that I'd completely forgotten about. 'You look well, Chloe. And you're doing really well here too. I mean, General Manager at a new Ferndale Hotel. Pretty good going.' He breaks off here to whistle, as he glances round the hallway, sharp eyes taking everything in.

Little piglet-y eyes, I suddenly find myself thinking. Too close together for their own good. Always thought so, but it's only now I'm somehow able to properly articulate the thought without feeling any disloyalty. Without feeling anything in fact, which takes me by surprise.

'It's good to see you, Frank,' I tell him as briskly as I can, arms folded, heel tapping nervily. 'But I'm afraid I don't have time to talk just now. You've called at a rotten time . . .'

'Yeah, yeah, sorry about that,' he says, eyeing up the ornate furniture so closely, you'd swear he was about to bid for it at auction. 'Wow, this stuff must have cost Rob McFayden a fortune! And those carpets too . . . cashmere! Not cheap.'

'Frank, I really can't do this now. You have to understand that it's . . .'

'. . . That it's your opening weekend. Don't worry, I won't stay, I know you're probably run off your feet. Just wondered if you and I could have a quick word?'

Part of me wants to say, 'Did you even hear me? Do you know how busy we are in here?' and yet part of me is completely intrigued. So I give a quick, curt nod and barely before I know what I'm at, I'm ushering him through the bar and out to the terrace.

Quieter out here, is my reasoning. More privacy. After all, I've waited eons to play this out, a bit of discretion is no harm. Frank follows me, taking everything in, as ever missing absolutely nothing. We step outside to the terrace and into the warm sunshine as I turn to face him full on, determined not to blink first. Pride, etc.

Meanwhile he shuffles about for a bit and plays nervously with the bald pate at the back of his head. So he's nervy too. Good. And that's yet another mannerism of his I'd totally blanked out. Nothing wrong with it, I'd just . . . forgotten, that's all.

'So, did you get the flowers I sent?' he asks out of nowhere, piglet-y eyes on me as I'm suddenly jolted back into the world of manners.

310

'Oh, ehh . . . yeah. Yes, I did. They certainly came as a surprise, to be perfectly honest –'

I'm about to tack on, 'plus given what you put me through, it'll take more than a bunch of roses to make amends,' but he interrupts.

'Got them in that posh florist on Dawson Street. You know, that really flashy, expensive one.'

And then, unbidden, another whole set of memories start to resurface. The really irritating way Frank would splurge out on you and then spend the next month reminding you of just how much it cost him in the first place, thereby taking all the good out of it.

'Look Frank,' I tell him, foot still tapping away like a jazz dancer's. 'Just calling in like this . . . it's . . . well, I have to ask you straight out. Why are you here? Why did you come?'

'Well, there is something actually,' he says, shuffling awkwardly and avoiding my direct gaze. 'I mean, you know how tiny our industry is, Chloe. I hear things. And the word on the street is that you're doing brilliantly here.'

'Oh . . . well, thanks, I suppose,' I say uselessly.

'And in fact, that's part of the reason I'm here.'

'*Part* of the reason, Frank?'

He shuffles around the terrace a bit, checking out the patio heaters and ostensibly taking in the view over the gardens below. Though I know by now there's something else on his mind. The fidgetiness alone is a dead giveaway.

'Well, actually it's the Merrion,' he eventually says. 'Things aren't so good there right now, you see. We're way down on guest numbers and they're making staff cutbacks right, left and centre. So the thing is . . .'

'Yes?'

311

'You see, I'm keeping my eye out for other managerial jobs pretty much anywhere I can. And then when I heard the Ferndale group were opening up here, I thought now was as good a time as any for me to come forward. So maybe, if you ever hear of anything going, you'd put in a good word for me? I'd really appreciate it.'

I just stare back at him, open mouthed, utterly shocked. But it seems he's still not finished.

'Oh and by the way,' he goes on, 'rumour in the business has it that Rob McFayden himself is actually spending the weekend here in Dublin. Is it true?'

'Yes, actually.'

A pause and I swear I'm actually dreading what's going to come out of his mouth next.

'So . . . is there any chance you could possibly introduce me? And maybe let him know that I'm now Assistant General Manager over at the Merrion? But of course, that I'm happy to consider other offers, if the right one ever came along. You know yourself. I'm well qualified to work as General Manager; I just need the right break, that's all.'

I look at him, speechless. So it's not just *a* job he's after, more specifically, it seems to be *my* job. Should things not work out for me here at Hope Street, he's most likely thinking.

What do you say to that? What do you say when the man who dumped you on your wedding day, the man you thought you were going to spend the rest of your life with, suddenly bounces back into your world again, not to say sorry, or even just to wish you luck, but chasing after your job?

'And . . . is that really all you have to say to me, Frank?' I eventually manage to get out, not even caring if it sounds a bit rude.

312

'Well . . . yeah. Apart from, it's good to see you again. So if you ever fancied a drink, or maybe dinner . . .'

I cut him short. Hard to explain. Just have to. Can't really listen to much more.

'You know something, Frank?' I say, stopping to face him square-on. 'I could do the polite thing here. I could choose to be the bigger person and forgive and forget and agree to meet you for a drink and even offer to introduce you to my boss. But I'm not going to. Because you know why? You don't deserve it, none of it. You didn't deserve me three years ago and you certainly don't get to saunter back into my life right now, just because things have turned around for me, and hope to ride on my coattails into the sunset. You weren't sure of me three years ago, but I'm pretty certain about you right now. And I wish you every success for the future, Frank, I sincerely do. But I can tell you right now that I'll certainly have no part in it. Now if you'll excuse me, some of us have work to do.'

He's scarlet in the face now, but for the first time all I can think is, feck you anyway. Then in total silence, as I briskly show him to the terrace door, a thought lodges in my head that somehow won't leave once it's taken hold.

Had he and I actually gone ahead and got married that dim, distant day long ago, would we be checking into a hotel like this right now? Would I be a guest here and not managing instead?

A no-brainer, really.

*

Five minutes later, I'm standing at the main entrance door watching Frank walk away – stomach churning, but feeling

313

strong and somehow vindicated and an awful lot better than I ever imagined I would – when I hear the sound of quick footsteps behind me.

Rob.

He stands right beside me wordlessly, towering over me as usual, as we both watch Frank recede into the distance.

'You okay?' he asks softly, with his eyes on me, scanning my face, as though he's worried I might burst into tears at any minute.

So I turn to face him full on.

'In a funny way . . . yeah. I'm fine. Better than fine, in fact. Didn't think I would be and yet somehow . . . I am.'

And then he smiles down at me. A warm crinkly smile that reaches all the way up to his eyes.

'So you needn't worry,' I add. 'You don't have a General Manager who's suddenly about to go AWOL on you.'

'I wasn't worried about my General Manager,' he says gently. 'Actually, I was concerned about you.'

I feel a tiny flick of surprise, so I give him a reassuring grin as he steers me back inside.

'I heard that git was here and was sort of on standby, just in case you wanted his arse kicked for him.'

'Well . . . emm . . . thanks . . .'

'. . . But I took it as a very good sign that he didn't stay.'

'It was,' I tell him.

A pause as Rob looks down at me, bit puzzled now.

'So, that's him then. The runaway groom.'

'Yup.'

'Chloe, if I ask you a straight question, will you give me a straight answer?'

'Depends,' I say, feeling evasive and not even knowing

why, other than it feels like he and I are about to cross a line here or something.

'Why did he do it?'

'What?'

'I mean, why would any guy in his right mind, put someone like you through something so awful? And on your wedding day? I just don't get it.'

And now I find I'm suddenly stammering uselessly.

'It's well . . . look, it's not that I don't appreciate you asking or anything . . . but . . . well . . . I can't . . . I just . . .'

Another pause and this time he looks wrong-footed.

'Hey, I'm sorry if I went too far; I was just concerned, that's all. Forgive me?'

And then Liliana interrupts, to say there's a call for me at Reception.

'Maybe I'll tell you sometime,' I tell him, slipping away to take the call.

'And maybe I'll hold you to that.'

Chapter Twenty-Seven

Jo was back up in her room, completely stuck. The day had gone reasonably well for her so far, given that Dave had actually decided to behave himself and stop acting the maggot. In fact, he'd been pretty quiet all day for him, muttering an apology to her before their first session and not giving her a single ounce of hassle since. Meek and mild, like he was ashamed of what happened last night and . . . well, like he was just about ready to finally accept that this was happening, whether he liked it or not.

But right now Jo was rightly flummoxed. One of the 'assignments' that Kate, their marital relations counsellor, had given each of them earlier was to write down all the positive qualities that they loved and respected about each other and that was the whole problem. She could still accurately list off what she'd initially liked – loved – about Dave.

The way he put up with her, for instance. Which by the way, most other fellas in their sane minds wouldn't. At least, not for very long. Then there was the way he made her laugh. Even at herself. With a pang, Jo suddenly found herself missing that. *I haven't laughed in so long*, she thought, I'm actually starting to forget what my teeth look like.

But her worry now was . . . would Dave be able to do the same for her? Given the way she'd been treating him of late?

Re-reading a pile of emails from just a few days before they'd checked into the Hope Street Hotel certainly didn't throw her any crumbs of comfort either.

From: Jo_Marketing_Director@digitech.com
To: davesblog@hotmail.com
Subject: My fabulous divorce.
July 9th, 10.27 a.m.

You up yet, arsehole?

Doubtless you won't even see this email until long after you've stirred from the alcoholic coma you and your delightful chum Bash drank yourselves into last night. Same as the pair of you do every other night after you collect your dole. Bit like a twenty-first century version of that movie about the drunks that Richard E. Grant was in.

But when you do finally surface to the gourmet meal of eggs on toast that Mammy will lovingly serve up to you, would you kindly have the goodness to confirm that you actually got it together to keep your appointment with Chloe Townsend at the hotel yesterday? And that you didn't manage to make a holy, mortifying show of yourself? I've just met with her now and can confidently say that I think we're in.

As long as you did absolutely nothing to f**k this up on me.

As you can appreciate, I'm anxious to put the sad spectre of what could be laughingly called our marriage out of its misery once and for all.

Jo.

PS. Am on my way to Berlin. Kindly get back to me before I take off, to confirm.

Even reading it made Jo wince now. And his reply was, if possible, even worse.

From: davesblog@hotmail.com
To: Jo_Marketing_Director@digitech.com
Subject: My fabulous divorce.
July 9th, 10.37 a.m.

Dearest soon-to-be-ex,

Dole? *Dole?!!!* You think I'm still on the scratch???!!!

I am aware that in Jo-world, the phrase 'I'm sorry,' is an acute sign of weakness, but prepare, dearest one, to swallow your words. Had you taken the time/ trouble over the past eight weeks to do your wifely duty and inquire as to what was happening in my life, you'd know that I've actually gone and landed a part in a telly gig. Ha! So take that and swallow it!

Enjoying the bittersweet taste of your own words, my lovely? Anyway, said gig involves many, many long hours shooting late into the night, so as it happens I'm currently enjoying a typical actor's breakfast and preparing for a busy day ahead in front of the cameras.

And no, before heading off on your broomstick to go and terrorize your minions in some far-flung corner of the globe as yet uncolonized by Digitech, allow me to reassure you that brekkie for me these days doesn't actually involve Irish coffee and vodka on cornflakes, as it once might have done. Or, more correctly, as you once drove me to.

Cue shock horror in Jo-land! I can just picture you now, dearest heart, sitting up in your air-conditioned corporate lounge at the airport, espresso coffee frozen mid-air in manicured claw as your jaw freezes somewhere around your collarbone whilst reading this. But then my angel, you never did like having to recalibrate your bad opinion of anyone, did you? Least of all me.

So sorry to disappoint your preferred assumption that your husband is an out-of-work washed-up alcoholic, with the liver of Richard Burton and the work ethic of Withnail from that Richard E Grant movie, that you so lovingly – and inaccurately refer to.

And just as an aside, how can any human alive not know every immortal line of dialogue ever uttered in that movie? For the love of Uncle Monty, *how*?!! What did you spend all your years in college doing, anyway? Studying? When you could have been far more gainfully employed learning Withnail and Monty Python off by heart?

shakes head sadly in disbelief.

So excuse me if you will, my love. Taxi will be here shortly and to quote yourself back at you, some of us have actual work to do.

Kisses, hugs, arsenic. What you will.

Dave x

PS. Hardly know why I even bother telling you all of the above. Goes without saying, not that you're remotely interested in anything that's going on in your husband's life. Despite the fact that it's actually considered quite polite in the real world to at least occasionally show some kind of interest in one's spouse, dearest one.

From: Jo_Marketing_Director@digitech.com
To: davesblog@hotmail.com
Subject: My fabulous divorce.
July 9th, 10.52 a.m.

Dave,

Wonders will never cease. You in an actual job! And what exactly is the nature of this telly gig anyway? Playing the rear end of a panto horse on some kid's TV channel with all of three viewers, including your mother?

You still haven't answered my question. Did you get to your interview with Chloe at Ferndale Hotels yesterday? And if so, would you kindly fill me in on what happened? As you'll perhaps recall my telling you (I only sent you about thirty emails on the subject), they insist all couples be on friendly, amicable terms before they let you through the front door.

So I bloody well hope for your sake that you remembered to keep your end up and act the part of my best friend who's sorry his marriage is over, but who'll continue to be friends with me once we come out the other side. Look on it as the most challenging role you've probably ever played in your sad little career.

I mean it Dave. We are checking in and out of that hotel next weekend if it kills us. Under no circumstances am I prepared to drag this out for years and years through family law courts. Not when I can be rid of you in just a few short days.

Arse this one, last thing up on me, and I will swing for you. Gladly.

Flight's boarding shortly. A prompt answer would be appreciated.

Jo.

From: davesblog@hotmail.com
To: Jo_Marketing_Director@digitech.com
Subject: My fabulous divorce.
July 9th, 11.11 a.m.

My my, we are in a nark today! Something awful happen to you? Champagne not sufficiently chilled for you up in business class? On-board massage facility booked out? Poor baby. Never mind though, you'll soon cheer up once you've fired off a few more of your by now legendarily vitriolic emails. And of course, you always have good old Dave, aka your emotional punch bag, to act out on. At least, while we're still this side of a divorce, you do.

To clarify. As it happens, no, I'm not playing the rear end of a panto horse on some kid's TV channel, though thank you for your faith in my acting prowess. I'm inclined to forget what a loving and supportive spouse you've always been to me.

Once again though, with apologies for disappointing

321

you, you're quite wrong. In this business that we call show, my new gig is actually a highly sought after one, in a cop-opera where I play the part of a drug baron who's under investigation. It's a recurring role, it's good and meaty, there's loads of close-ups and I get my own dressing room and everything. With an actual fruit basket and freebie bottles of water.

So how do you like that, my beauty? Absolutely certain that you still want to go through with this divorce lark now? Care to think again? Think of the scores of women out there who'll be queuing up to date a bona fide TV star and B-list celebrity after we're officially divorced!

So if you change your mind, you can get back to me. There's still time.

Your soon-to-be-bigger than Ross Kemp hubbie,

Dxxx

PS. When are you going to stop blaming me for everything? Just out of curiosity?

From: Jo_Marketing_Director@digitech.com
To: davesblog@hotmail.com
Subject: My fabulous divorce.
July 9th, 11.22 a.m.

Christ Almighty Dave! I had thought that trying to have an adult conversation face-to-face with you was bad enough, but emailing you is if anything, even worse. Like trying to pick up mercury with a fork.

For the last and final time, what exactly happened at the hotel yesterday? Bear in mind that if you tell me you slept it out or forgot all about it, then I'll fly all the way to Reno if I have to and divorce you there and then, with or without you.

You would be well advised not to strain my already-stretched patience any further.

Jo.

PS. I don't entirely blame you. I blame myself for being idiotic enough to marry you in the first place. What was I thinking?

From: davesblog@hotmail.com
To: Jo_Marketing_Director@digitech.com
Subject: My fabulous divorce.
July 9th, 11.44 a.m.

Jo, calm down, take a Zanax, take a shot of whatever tranquillizers vets give horses to knock them out, whatever it takes. Just relax, breathe and stop acting out like this.

Yes, as it happens I did remember to keep that bloody appointment at that bloody hotel yesterday. A lovely, pretty, smiley girl called Chloe chatted to me for ages and showed me over the place. Very posh, very friendly, very fanciable.

Chloe, that is, not the actual hotel.

JOKE!!!

And no, I didn't let the side down.

Just asked Chloe for a double shot of bourbon from

the bar, then flung myself round her ankles like a kid having a tantrum and screamed, 'I don't want this! My wife threw me out and I don't want a divorce!'

As you see, I'm prepared to do absolutely anything to avert this. Threats, anything. I've no shame anymore. If necessary I'll chain myself to the outside of the hotel like a suffragette, with a sign round my neck saying, 'Getting divorced against my will.'

I'll do anything.

My pride was the first casualty in this.

Yours,

Dx

From: Jo_Marketing_Director@digitech.com
To: davesblog@hotmail.com
Subject: My fabulous divorce.
July 9th, 11.57 a.m.

Thank God you turned up yesterday and I only hope you're messing about the rest.

Now piss off and stop being so bloody childish.

Have to go. Flight taxiing, snotty looks from very camp airline steward, blah-di-blah.

I'll see you on Friday week at the hotel.

Don't mess this up on me, Dave.

Till then,

Jo.

God Almighty, Jo thought, sitting back against the chair by the desk in her room. She'd been vicious bordering on cruel. How did Dave manage to put up with her? And how would any man in his sane mind?

Dave's reply to that particular tirade didn't make for easy reading either.

From: davesblog@hotmail.com
To: Jo_Marketing_Director@digitech.com
Subject: My fabulous divorce.
July 9th, 12.14 a.m.

Right then wifey,

I've done my yoga, eaten the lumps of mouldy old cardboard that passes for healthy fare these days and drunk as much as I could of this vomity stuff called wheatgrass juice that apparently will take ten years off me and make me live to be 101. All the longer to torture you, darling girl.

Anyway, in the shower, I had a good think. And I'm now taking full advantage of the fact that you'll be airborne for at least the next three hours and therefore won't be able to fire one of your snotty emails back at me with a dismissive 'oh just piss off, Dave!' Or similar.

You won't meet up with me face-to-face anymore, barring it's at this effing hotel, which I no more want to go to. When I call you, you won't pick up. Last time I pitched up at Digitech HQ in Dublin, you almost had a coronary and had to be restrained from calling security to escort me off the premises.

All I've got left is email. So here goes.

Jo, you're rushing headlong into this, like you rush headlong into every major decision you've made about your personal life ever since I first met you. You know how I feel; God knows, I've told you enough times at this stage. You know I don't want this, never wanted it. But as I've told you, if getting rid of me is the price I have to pay to get you back to being the girl that I once knew, then I'm prepared to do it.

I mightn't like it, but I will.

And now to the elephant in the room. Jo, you know what your poor body has been through of late. You know how you're still suffering. I can speak with some authority here, as I can claim at least 50% of that grief for myself. Sorry dearest, but you don't get the monopoly on that particular avenue of pain.

Doctor after doctor and specialist after consultant have all told us the same thing. With each round of IVF, our chances are diminishing each time. And I know you're doing all this via the fertility clinic and that I've practically no hand, act or part in the whole process, but remember that you and I have a deal. And I'll stick to my part of it if you stick to yours. The main thing is though, that whatever the outcome, it'll take as long as it takes for you to heal and get back to the Jo of old. They've been saying it'll take at least a year. So why won't you allow yourself that relatively small chink of time?

Since . . . well, you know since what . . . all you've done is bury your head in work and more work and travel and more of it again. Sometimes I feel it's like you can't bear to share the same land mass as me and will do anything to get the feck off it as often as you can.

And now you've come to this snap decision that we're checking into this flashy, snazzy hotel so you can be rid of me in a single weekend.

Fine, if that's what you want, if that's what makes you happy, I'll learn to live with it. But Jo, think. I know you hold me fully responsible and there's only so many times I can apologize to you for what's gone on between us. Or rather, for my part in it.

But when are you going to stop dumping all the blame on me? I'll happily take 50% of the blame, but draw the line at any more.

You don't need me to reiterate how I feel. You know, in spite of you and even more laughingly, in spite of myself and my own better judgment, that I do in fact, still love you. Very much.

I'll be there for you on Friday week.

Though you'll probably find me in the bar. Or alternatively, under it.

Yours,

Dx.

Roughly, Jo shoved away her computer and it was only when she went to the bathroom and took a good look at herself in the mirror that she even realized she'd been crying.

Chapter Twenty-Eight

Lucy.

Between the rest of the meetings all day Saturday about boring money (which she and Andrew just didn't have) and even more boring property (which they no longer owned), it was just coming up to five in the afternoon before Lucy even managed to get a breather.

She slipped up to the privacy of her room and made two quick calls. The first was to room service, to order something to perk her up a bit and the second was down to Chloe's office. A woman called Chris with an efficient voice told her Chloe was busy in the dining room at the moment, but that she'd be sure to pass on the message.

'I know she's up to her tonsils, but could you tell her I just wanted a quick word with her?' Lucy asked.

And exactly ten minutes later, with a discreet knock at her door, there was Chloe herself, laden down with the tray from room service that Lucy had ordered.

'Wow, now that's what I call above and beyond the call of duty!' Lucy beamed, genuinely delighted to see her. 'Thanks so much for coming.'

'You're more than welcome,' Chloe said warmly, carefully

placing the tray on an empty desk. 'I heard you wanted to speak to me. Would you like me to pour some mint tea for you?'

'Nah, I'll take care of that. This, you'll notice, is the new me. No more boozing and making a holy mortifying show of myself from now on. Herbal teas and fitness and well-being, that's the brand new, reinvented Lucy Belton for you.'

And she meant it too. She was fed up waking up with a pounding head, a rasping throat and a hangover to beat the band. Last night had been bloody mortifying and today had been hell because of it.

Enough was enough.

'I'm well impressed,' Chloe laughed, 'and I only wish I had your self-restraint!'

Bless the woman, Lucy thought fondly to herself, pouring out the tea into a china cup. Only someone as sensitive and diplomatic as Chloe could possibly use the word 'self-restraint' in connection with her. Given the way she'd been carrying on lately, anyway.

'Thing is . . .' Lucy said, uncertain of where to bloody well start. 'Well, first things first. I was dying to talk to you about . . . well, about what happened last night. God, I made such a complete fool out of myself. How someone didn't end up smacking me, I'll never know.'

Chloe said nothing though, just politely stood there, listening. It was one of the things Lucy really liked about her. Not just the girl's discretion, but the fact that she was a listener. God knows, they were a very rare breed.

'I can't tell you how sorry I am,' she went on. 'On your very first night and everything – to start acting the maggot like that –'

'Please, you really don't have to –'

'Trust me, it's more of a penance if I do. But the truth is . . .' Lucy sighed, easing herself wearily down onto the bed now, kicking her shoes off and stretching her long legs out. 'That's just not the kind of person I am. It's like – ever since Andrew and I separated, I've reverted back to making the same dopey mistakes I did as a teenager and of course then I end up hating myself for it. Drinking like a fish and acting like a stupid, drunk idiot who should know better. I genuinely don't know what's come over me. I didn't used to be like this not so long ago. Back when I was still –'

She broke off here though. Because the end of that sentence was, 'when I was still with Andrew,' and that was something she just couldn't bring herself to articulate.

'Look, I know you're going through the most unimaginable trauma right now,' Chloe said gently, perching on the edge of the bed beside her. 'But there is light at the end of the tunnel, you know.'

'Yeah. Knowing my luck, the oncoming train to finish me off.'

'No, I was actually talking about Andrew,' Chloe persisted. 'Course, it's not my place to say this, but he was really concerned about you last night. So anxious you wouldn't be disturbed after you went to bed.'

Lucy shrugged and lay back, staring up at the ceiling for a bit and stretching toned, tanned legs out in front of her.

'Well, I have to say that's Andrew alright,' she eventually said. 'I don't think he wants to be here any more than I do myself. But then we don't have a choice. Neither of us.'

'Oh now, come on, everyone has a choice.'

'Not me. And certainly not Andrew. Not unless the pair of us fancy a life of complete misery ahead of us. And I really do mean misery, by the way. The meeting we had this morning was awful, just bloody awful.'

A long silence, but still Chloe showed no inclination to move away. Good of her, Lucy thought. There was some big fancy dinner scheduled for later that evening and she was probably up to her tonsils in it, but she still stayed, devoting her time solely to Lucy and her woes.

'You miss him, don't you?' Chloe eventually asked. Lucy didn't answer. Instead she just looked away, and started fiddling absently with the phone cord by the bed beside her. Then realizing that Chloe was patiently waiting on an answer, she rolled her eyes and just said, 'It's not that simple.'

'When it comes to relationships, is it ever? But just so you know, I'm here if you ever need to talk,' Chloe offered, almost as though she sensed that was the real reason why Lucy had asked to see her in the first place. 'All part and parcel of the service.'

'Mother of God, where to even start?' Lucy groaned.

A long pause, then eventually Lucy said, 'Can I ask you something a bit personal?'

'Fire away.'

'Were you ever married? Or I mean, in a relationship as intense as a marriage?'

Chloe looked thoughtful and it took her a while to find the right words to answer.

'Almost married once, yes.'

'Idiot for letting you slip through his fingers. If you don't mind my saying so.'

'To be honest,' Chloe smiled, 'in my case, I think I had a lucky escape.'

'I'm starting to wish I'd had a lucky escape too.'

'Oh now, come on! You seem so certain that whatever went wrong between you and Andrew is unfixable. But in my experience, nothing is ever irrevocable.'

'Trust me, this is.'

'He really cares about you. And I think you care about him too, more than you know.'

'Yup,' Lucy nodded, staring up at the elaborate fabric canopy over her bed. 'Course I do. He was The One, you see. No one thought so when we first met, but they were all wrong. And I don't give a shite that all his money is gone, that was the last thing I married him for, even though everyone else thought otherwise. But I do mind very much about the fact that I can never trust him again. Him or his family.'

'If you don't mind my asking . . .' Chloe asked, intrigued, 'what does his family have to do with it?'

'Ha! Where to even start?'

And then, Lucy began to open up. To really get it off her chest, in a way she hadn't been able to ever since she first arrived here. Funny, but after an endless afternoon talking to one divorce law specialist after another, not one of them had bothered to ask what had even driven her here in the first place. All they seemed concerned about was money and the lack of it and a whole load of other stuff involving periods of separation and a decree nisi. Chloe was the first person to actually look like she cared.

So Lucy filled her in. On absolutely everything this time. About Alannah and Josh and how bitchy bordering on vicious they'd been towards her practically from day one.

'You see Andrew was newly separated when we first met,' she said, staying firmly focused on the ceiling, while Chloe said nothing, just nodded understandingly.

'But of course, when he and I met and got together so quickly, well in the eyes of his family, I was entirely out to snag him and was basically the whole reason why he and Greta, his ex, could never reconcile. Even though we'd done absolutely nothing wrong. Technically. But as far as they were concerned, I destroyed their family and they weren't ever going to forget it. For Andrew and I, our timing in getting together couldn't have been much worse if we'd tried. I know that and believe me, we've both crucified ourselves over it often enough over the past few years. And did his children make us pay for it or what?'

'But what did they do exactly?'

'I'd have to go back almost three years to answer that,' Lucy went on in a faltering voice she hardly recognized as her own. So she filled Chloe in, going right back to when she and Andrew were first married and when Alannah moved in with them. With all the tensions and back-stabbing that ensued.

'Sounds so stressful,' Chloe nodded sympathetically, 'and under your own roof too.'

'That's only the warm-up act. Believe me, it gets much worse. Alannah eventually decided she was going to start up an internet company; something to do with recruitment. So she moved back in with Greta, and set up her office from her townhouse in the city centre. The idea was that she'd live there and work from her new base and at first Andrew and I were so relieved. Him because Alannah was actually doing something with her life, and me because I was finally getting her out of my home. God forgive me.'

'But surely things improved a little once she'd gone?'

'You'd think, wouldn't you? But a few months went by

and after a while, I just knew something was wrong. I could sense it.'

'Women usually can.'

'I think it was all down to the way Andrew was behaving. That had been what first alerted me that something was up. Something very serious.'

'How was he acting?'

'He wasn't like himself, far from it. Andrew was usually so affectionate and attentive, so physical with me, but around then, he'd started acting all remote and detached. He complained of tiredness a lot, which wasn't like him at all.'

It was about the same time they'd stopped having sex too, though Lucy was way too mortified to come out with that.

'Always a warning sign that something's up. But go on.'

'Then a whole pile of registered letters began to arrive at our house, all addressed to him and when I'd ask what they were all about, he'd just dismiss it as, "just boring old bank stuff. You know what the banks are like these days."

'Absolutely nothing for me to worry about, that's what he told me and kept on telling me. And I think that's what's got me so angry right now. That he kept so much to himself, "not to worry me". God, the irony of that!'

'If he was keeping things from you, then of course, you'd a perfect right to be annoyed. What happened afterwards?'

'Well, after months of this carry-on, I was starting to get seriously worried about him and had asked him straight out what was up. I told him I knew right well he was hiding something from me and to just tell me whatever it was. But when he did, it was . . . God . . . just so . . .'

334

Lucy broke off here and had to sit up and take a gulpful of tea from the cup on the bedside table beside her.

'Take your time,' Chloe said patiently.

'You see, Andrew had bought Greta the townhouse as part of their separation agreement and she owned it outright. But Alannah needed massive capital for her start-up, so she persuaded Greta to mortgage the house and lend her the money. That would have been fine, except what Andrew didn't tell me was that to help Alannah out, he'd agreed to be guarantor on the loan. Which he was absolutely entitled to do. My only problem was that he never told me, but then he never imagined that what happened would actually come to pass. Neither of us could. But the fact is that what subsequently transpired affected me, as well as him. Affected me every bit as much. So you don't have to be Einstein to figure out what happened next.'

Just get it out, she told herself. *Almost there. Chloe will understand.*

'I'm listening.'

'Well, pretty soon, it was obvious that Alannah's internet company just wasn't going to work out. Creditors were really hounding her and she ran out of funding so Andrew started to lend her more and more – from our joint bank account this time – and that's when the trouble really started.'

'So . . . did she stop paying her mortgage on Greta's home?'

And now the hard part. The bit Lucy had dreaded.

Deep breath. Just say it. Then it's done.

'And slid into huge arrears, yes. So of course when the bank started chasing after her, she dumped it right on her

Dad. Said he was guarantor on the loan as well and that he'd just have to honour the debt. Not to mention all the creditors her company owed. Which was a bloody long list, I can tell you.'

Chloe shook her head in shock. 'What a mess,' she said. 'You certainly have my sympathy.'

'Which was why the banks started to close in on Andrew. And boy, did they really hound him. We had to make sure Greta kept the roof over her head at all costs, so to do that, the banks chased after Andrew's primary asset. Our home, our beautiful family home. It wasn't entirely his fault . . .' but again Lucy had to stop and compose herself before she could go on.

Because this was like sticking your finger into a wound that hadn't even begun to callous over yet. Sharp, unrelenting agony. Chloe said nothing, just wordlessly leaned over to give her hand a supportive squeeze, bless her.

Normally, with the exception of these last few weeks, Lucy felt she was pretty good at holding it together, good at being tough when she needed to be. But dredging it all back up was just too much to bear, even in the safe environment of a hotel bedroom, with a kind and impartial listener who wouldn't judge. And then the one question that had been dogging her ever since the shit hit the fan. *Why was I punished for something I didn't even do?*

'Take a tissue, Lucy,' Chloe prompted, thrusting forward a big box of man-size Kleenex.

'Sorry for sounding like such a basket case,' was all Lucy could manage to get out. 'It's just all been such total hell. You've no idea. I'm someone who's always worked hard and grafted to get by, but for the first time in my life, I don't know what to do or where to turn.'

'And you really think there's no hope for you and Andrew?'

'How could I? How could I ever have trusted him again after that? He went guarantor on a huge loan that involved my home and never even told me! I completely accept that he had to take care of Greta and the kids, but he let us go under as a result, and there was damn all I could do about it, only stand on the sidelines and watch. So you see, I'm in a place where I can barely look at him, never mind live under the same roof as him.'

'But surely . . .'

'I can handle that our fabulous lifestyle is gone, I can handle that the days of five-star beach holidays and shopping trips to New York are long over, but I can't handle that he kept things from me. He says I'm blaming him unfairly, but who else is responsible? My whole life has just spiralled off into this . . . this free-fall and I want it to stop and now it just won't.'

'And are you really prepared to go through with this? To go the whole hog and get divorced?'

'Have I a choice?' Lucy laughed bitterly. 'The man kept things he shouldn't have from me and in the process, lost not only me, but the home we loved as well. And I'm not materialistic and I know it was only bricks and mortar, but you asked about my marriage, and the honest answer is that I can't be around Andrew or his bloody family. Not now, not ever. How could I possibly trust him or any of them again after this? What kind of moron would that make me? I can't do it. I can't and I won't. They made my life hell once before and given the chance, they'll do it over and over again. Because if Andrew and I get back together, you can be sure his family will find some other way to break us. Mark my words. They'd see it as their life's mission.'

She couldn't go on, so instead Lucy sat back and angrily twisted a teary, soggy Kleenex round her finger.

The silence hung there as she thought, dear God, the irony. Earlier that morning, she'd been the one gently trying to persuade Jo to give Dave a second chance. Love is a rare and precious thing, she remembered trying to convince Jo. And if you're lucky enough to find it, then you need to cling tight. And yet that was something she herself could never do. Alannah and Josh would ruin her if she did. Ruin her and destroy Andrew, for a second time.

She was almost afraid to say it and yet, this was it, it was real, it was actually happening.

She was already separated from the man she'd loved.

And before she knew what day of the week it was, she'd be divorced.

Chapter Twenty-Nine

Dawn.

Dawn had just left her room and was skipping down the main staircase, already late for a champagne reception to be held in the bar. Apparently a goodwill gesture on the part of the hotel to make up to guests for last night's fiasco and everyone was invited.

And that's when Dawn first overheard him. Kirk, clear as crystal, deep in conversation on his phone. Downstairs in the main hall and unaware that even though he was speaking low, his voice was still drifting up the staircase for all to hear. The gobshite.

'I miss you too, you know that . . . yeah, tomorrow evening . . . no, I'm not just looking forward to it, I'm absolutely *living* for it . . . yeah . . . absolutely . . . I only wish you were here too . . . you'd find a way of making it all the more bearable for me. Somehow you always do.'

Instinctively, Dawn froze and half wondered if she should turn on her heel and just get the lift downstairs instead.

Then some inner voice made her change her mind and keep on walking. To hell with him anyway, she thought. If Kirk was eejit enough to be on the phone to his lover somewhere public like this, then he deserved to know he had an audience. So instead, she strode down the staircase with her nose in the air like Scarlett O'Hara, his voice growing louder with every step closer she took.

'Oh God . . . it's been such a downer . . . but you know, it's Dawn I worry about most, really. Her anger levels yesterday were so frightening . . . like a huge ball of negativity . . . she's finding it impossible to accept us and to move on . . . to let go . . . and I want that for her so badly . . .'

Ball of negativity? Did he really just come out with that? What a patronizing eejit, Dawn found herself thinking. So typical of Kirk; now that he'd found happiness, he thought nothing could be easier than for the whole world to follow suit, so he could just glide over the mess he'd created and act like everyone got their Hollywood ending.

'And yeah . . . Saturday's protest march against fracking sounds good to me . . . count on me, man . . . you know I won't let you down . . .'

Oh, spare me, Dawn thought, getting even closer now. That was the kind of thing he used to say to her, way back when. In fact, a day out at some anti-fracking rally was more or less Kirk's idea of the ideal date. Being brutally honest though, she suddenly found herself wondering if there ever really was a time when she thought that spending her Saturday afternoon with a placard clamped to her, while she marched around in circles trying to look impassioned, was actually fun? But then Kirk's idea of a good time and hers were so very different, it was actually scary.

Turning a corner onto the very last set of stairs, this time she saw him, with his back to her, long jet black hair scraped back into a ponytail. She could just so easily picture the other side of the phone call too. Her rival, calling to check in of course, doubtless to make sure that Kirk had in no way changed his mind.

He heard her footsteps on the marble floor and turned sharply around. And after a full day of one interminable session after another, where Dawn had studiously ignored him as lawyers discussed dividing their little business up, now she found herself able to look him dead in the face.

'Be sure to give Shane all my love, won't you?' she said sarcastically, then just kept on walking, head held high.

*

By the time she got to the bar, it was already packed out. The champagne reception was in full swing and it looked like most other guests were already here and in high good humour too. From the corner of her eye, Dawn could see Chloe calmly topping up glasses, smiling and engaging in chat all round her.

Such a warm soul, Dawn thought. She'd certainly made this weekend an awful lot more bearable for her. She spotted one new face too, a tall, lean guy, late forties at a guess, who was dressed casually like a guest, but was mucking in behind the bar. Good-looking guy too in that older man way, lean with a Richard Gere, salt and pepper hair thing going on.

Odd Dawn hadn't seen him before now, she knew pretty much all the guests and staff to see by now, but she thought no more about it and found herself drifting through the melee and out into the cool of the terrace outside. Bit of alone time, she figured, would do her no harm before she had to face Kirk yet again over dinner and pretend to be polite. She had the whole terrace to herself so she found a bench close to the door and sat down, hugging her knees tight to her chest.

341

Three months, three weeks and five days. That's how long you've lived with all this.

Every now and then she kept reminding herself. And with perfect recall, she could still bring herself back to that godawful night, like it had only happened yesterday. Of course the irony of it was that she wasn't even meant to be home in the first place; that particular evening she was supposedly meeting Eva after work to go to a movie.

'No worries,' Kirk had said, when she told him she'd be out for the night. 'I'll probably be late home myself anyway, I'm teaching at the Yoga Rooms till well past ten. So you just enjoy your night out and I'll see you when I see you.' All delivered casually, almost like a throwaway remark, so of course she thought absolutely no more about it.

But Eva had been forced to cancel their plans, something about a late evening meeting her project manager had called at the last minute. So Dawn found herself home unexpectedly early. God, had there been one single detail she hadn't relived over and over again in her mind's eye, in the three months, three weeks and five days since?

She remembered slipping her key into the lock, hearing music and smelling dope. So Kirk wasn't working then? Bit strange, she could still remember thinking. His yoga class must have been cancelled. And that in itself was weird, because he never, ever cancelled classes.

Their tiny sitting room was empty, so following the music, she made her way to their bedroom, flung the door open and there they were. Like something out of a third-rate soap opera.

Kirk and Shane, naked and tangled up together. In bed. In *her* bed. Pair of bastards didn't even have the good grace to look embarrassed about it.

342

Afterwards, even trying to explain why her marriage had so spectacularly imploded to other people had been mortifying. She'd tried her best to explain to Eva that what Kirk had done was a betrayal not just of her, but of her whole sexuality as well. Because if it had been the old cliché of him having an affair with another woman, in many ways it might have been easier to deal with. If that even made sense.

'If that roaring eejit is now claiming to be bisexual,' Eva thundered time and again, 'then he's even more delusional than I took him for. Because as far as I'm concerned, bisexuality is just a halfway house until you're officially out loud and proud. So why put you through that? Why even bother getting married in the first place?'

A very good question and one Kirk had been expert at side-stepping. He was 'exploring his sexuality', was one particular gem he'd come out with. And 'he didn't feel comfortable being boxed into a corner, like straight or gay'. No, only the best of both worlds was good enough for him. While he just expected Dawn to accept all this and stay in what's laughingly known as a 'lavender marriage'.

Yet, sitting alone here on the terrace this balmy summer evening, the more Dawn dwelt on it, the more she seemed to realize that something funny was finally beginning to shift inside her.

Normally dragging up such an acutely painful memory never failed to reduce her to a complete and utter basket case. But yet this evening, looking down over the beautiful gardens with the sun just setting, it didn't. Instead, for some astonishing reason, she surprised herself by feeling cooler, even calmer about it.

After so long apart, suddenly spending all this time with

Kirk under the one roof this weekend was turning out, in a funny way, to be eye opening for her. Being able to let rip at him last night had somehow cleared the air for her, like the way a thunderstorm clears humidity. Finally getting to tell him to his face what she thought of him and what he'd put her through was liberating and cathartic. Healing even.

There was something more to it too. Slowly, Dawn was beginning to see that there was only so much she was just settling for with Kirk. And so much more about him that was actually starting to drive her completely mental. The incessant dope smoking for a start, till Kirk ended up spending approximately ninety per cent of his time going round glassy eyed and slurred and talking complete shite about Shamanism or something equally rubbishy. Then there was his firm belief that for anything to be good for the planet, it had to involve extreme discomfort, a vegan diet and more hemp than you'd normally see at Glastonbury.

But I hate hemp, Dawn suddenly thought. And so what if I fancy a lovely juicy fillet steak every now and again? Just because I don't visit the compost heap with bagful of kitchen waste as often as I should, doesn't make me the spawn of the devil either, now does it? And don't even get me started on yurts, because frankly I've sat on Ryanair flights that were considerably more comfortable.

Another thought surfaced: she'd compromised so much for Kirk over the years and yet, had he ever done as much for her? She loved going to the movies and maybe eating out the odd time, nowhere flashy or expensive, but Kirk would have absolutely none of it. Not when they could sit in that poky little flat eating brown rice and tofu and listening to crap Ravi Shankar sitar music night after night.

All I put up with to make it work with him, she thought.

344

While he barely lifted a finger for me. Just expected me to slot into his lifestyle and automatically assumed because he was happy, that I'd be too.

She remembered back to her wedding day, three long years ago. And for the first time since, actually surprised herself by saying aloud, 'Mother of God, what was I even *thinking?*'

'I thought I heard someone out here,' a man's voice suddenly came from right behind her.

Startled, Dawn instinctively jumped, then saw that it was the barman, standing just at the door that led out onto the terrace. Tall, broad guy about her own age, with an unmistakable Kerry accent. She remembered him from the fire evacuation, when he'd guided her downstairs and calmly told her everything was going to be okay.

'Can I get you something to drink . . . ehh . . . Miss . . . Miss Madden, isn't it? Isn't that right?'

'Yeah, sure is,' Dawn smiled, 'but please, I'm Dawn.'

'And I'm Tommy,' he grinned back. Nice crinkly blue eyes, she thought. And a warm smile.

'We actually met,' Dawn said. 'During the fire evacuation last night, remember? You were good enough to take me down the emergency stairwell.'

'Course I remember the lovely lady in the white nightie,' Tommy smiled back. 'Hope you didn't get a fright or anything? Terrible bad luck for that to happen on our very first night.'

'No harm done,' said Dawn.

'Anyway, sure I saw you out here all by yourself and just wondered if I could get you anything? Maybe a drink?'

'Emm . . .' Dawn dithered for a bit, as she normally wasn't much of a drinker, but Tommy here seemed to be having absolutely none of it.

'Go on,' he said, twinkling down at her. 'Just a wee nip of champagne. Sure, it's on the house.'

'Just the one then. And thank you.'

She smiled to herself as Tommy disappeared back inside. What the hell.

It had been three months, three weeks and five days. Now maybe it was finally time for her to let go.

*

The very last letter of all had been shoved under the door, just before dinner.

My darling,

I needn't even ask if you remember events of last Christmas. Or more specifically, just a couple of days before Christmas Eve. You know what I did, you know how badly I messed up and I think you must, on some level, know how much it killed me when I finally 'fessed up and came clean to you. And yet I had to. I couldn't live with your not knowing. We needed to be honest with each other if we were to move on as I'd hoped. As I still hope. And if it were the other way round, I'd like to think that you'd tell me too.

But my timing, as ever, was a disaster. You weren't long out of hospital, you were at your lowest ebb and you needed me.

And what did I do? I big, fat went and blew it. There was no excuse for what happened and I've none to offer you, my love. I've asked for your forgiveness so often now, I'm starting to feel like a broken record.

But believe me when I say if I could only turn the clock back, I would.

If you'd only give me a second chance, I'd spend every hour of every day for the rest of my tomorrows trying to make you happy.

Yours always. Yours forever,

Xxxxxxxxx

Chloe.

Just past seven thirty and I swear, I haven't felt this strong and confident about myself in I can't remember how long. Closure really is a wonderful, magical thing. In fact they should make an elixir drug that gives you that same sensation of pride in yourself, mixed with hope for the future.

Because if I thought I'd be a weak-kneed basket case after I saw Frank earlier, I really couldn't have been more wrong. I called my pal Gemma to fill her in and her whoops of joy when I told her about practically escorting him off the premises nearly deafened me.

And I know just how she feels too.

Anyway, I'm down in the bar and there honestly isn't room for a cat in here. The entire bar is packed out, the champagne is flowing (no surprises there, it's on the house tonight) and there's a definite air of celebration, now that things are drawing to a close. Well, that is among the majority of our couples, but sadly not all.

It's all hands to the pump and like the rest of the staff here, I'm whizzing about topping up glasses, overseeing things and clipping in and out to the dining room every spare second I get, to make sure everything's all set up for dinner at eight.

But the person who's astonishing me most of all is Rob, who saw that we were a bit understaffed, so he just rolled up his sleeves and started to muck in with the rest of us. He's standing behind the bar now, knee deep in orders and proving to be a more than capable mixologist.

'Fair dues, you're a dab hand with the aul' cocktails,' I laugh over at him at one point, as I go to grab fresh champagne flutes.

'Remind me to tell you about the time I worked behind the bar in Raffles, Singapore,' he grins back, winking at me. 'And if you fancy a Singapore Sling after work, I'll make you the best one this side of the Pacific.'

'Ha, I might just need one after tonight!'

'You won't regret it. My Singapore Sling is the stuff of legend.'

By now, guests are spilling out onto the terrace and drifting into the Library next door, so I do a quick whizz around taking fresh orders and topping up champagne glasses wherever I can.

As I head out to the terrace to see if anyone needs refills, I'm greeted by the sound of happy, giggly laughter and when I step outside, I'm surprised to see Tommy deep in chat with Dawn.

'No,' Dawn is saying to him. 'I never even knew it existed!'

'Ah, where have you been, anyway?' Tommy's laughing back at her, arms folded, completely relaxed and not looking a bit like someone who's meant to be working. 'Now, if you're a genuine movie lover, then the Mezzanine in Dundrum is your only man. It's the nearest thing to a private screening room I've certainly ever been to, and sure they get all the new releases in there first. Course the tickets are that bit pricier, but they do include free wine and popcorn. And did I mention the nachos with cheese?'

'Well, now you're speaking my language,' Dawn giggles. 'But then I never could sit through a movie without a bucket of nachos beside me!'

'I'm actually going there after work on Monday. They're showing that new Robert Downey Junior movie . . . big summer blockbuster . . .'

'Oh, I LOVE him . . .'

'Yeah, and it's had some really great reviews too . . .'

Tommy breaks off here though and immediately stands up as he clocks me for the first time. God love him, he even looks a bit guilty, like I'm here to haul him over the coals for skiving off.

'Sorry Chloe,' he says a bit sheepishly. 'Just coming back inside now.'

But Dawn is smiling, so I smile too. I think it's the first time I've seen her do that since she got here, and you wouldn't believe what a sight for sore eyes it is.

'Stay where you are,' I tell Tommy firmly, waving at him to sit back down again. 'We're fine inside. Don't worry, I'll give you a shout if I need you.'

We're not actually, it's crazy busy inside . . . but then the matchmaker inside me has suddenly shot into overdrive. I slip behind the bar and start clearing away empty glasses, when next thing Rob is right by my shoulder. Towering over me as usual, sleeves rolled up, grey eyes looking right at me.

'You're looking very pleased with yourself, Ms Townsend,' he grins.

'Tell you later,' I tell him teasingly.

'Something going on out there that I need to know about?'

I don't get the chance to answer him though, because

next thing Dave is standing at the bar in front of us, first time I've seen him all evening.

'Dave! Lovely to see you,' I tell him. 'What can I get you?'

'Nothing, thanks,' he says flatly.

He hasn't bothered changing for dinner either, I notice, like most other guests. Instead, he's just wearing his usual hairy biker gear of jeans and a t-shirt with a pair of trainers and looking like he hasn't shaved since he got here.

'Emm . . . is Jo down yet?' I ask tentatively.

'That I can't answer you,' Dave says in that dry, laconic way he has. Then he just slumps forward on the bar, burying his head in his hands and cradling his head.

'Dave? What's up?'

He sighs, hauls his head up and looks right at me, glassy eyed and with the thick black hair standing up in tufts now. For a second, it's actually like the poor guy is going to bolt out of here in a minute.

'Emm . . . is everything okay?' I say, leaning across the bar to him.

''Fraid not. In fact, everything is about as far from being okay as is possible,' he sighs wearily.

'Anything I can do to help?'

There's a moment where he just looks at me, as though weighing up whether I can be trusted or not.

'Can you keep a secret?'

I just nod.

'Then maybe you and I could go somewhere to talk. If you can spare me five minutes, that is.'

I glance over at Rob, who seems to have overheard everything. He just mouths a silent 'Go,' at me, so I do. Discreetly, I lead Dave through the packed bar, across the entrance hall and into the empty office just behind Reception.

And for the first time since he got here, he *really* tells me everything.

*

Jo was sitting in a quiet little booth at the very back of the bar area, away from the melee where she wouldn't be disturbed. Laptop propped up in front of her as she just stared uselessly at the blank screen.

'Emm . . . okay if I join you?'

She looked up and was surprised to see Lucy standing there, actually looking quite dressed down tonight, at least, for her. Instead of wearing one of her usual bandage dresses with legs on full show, tonight she was in a simple floor length white maxi and flat sandals with her long, fair hair tied up in a ponytail, Grecian style. Overall effect? Utterly stunning.

She was carrying a champagne flute along with a glass of fizzy water and immediately thrust the champagne out towards Jo.

'A little peace offering,' she said sheepishly. 'To say sorry for being such an arse last night. Not to mention barging in on top of you this morning and . . . well, I'm sorry for everything, really.'

'Thanks, but the thing is, I'm not really supposed to with all the bloody drugs I'm on –' said Jo, but Lucy was having none of it.

'Ah, go on, just the one won't do you any harm.'

'Alright then, if you insist,' Jo said, gratefully taking the offered glass and taking a tiny sip. The champagne was cool and delicious, just what she needed, in fact.

'Am I disturbing you?' Lucy asked, with a nod towards the laptop. 'It's just . . . well, you kind of look like you're in the middle of something.'

351

'Not at all,' Jo said politely. 'Sit down please, join me.'

She actually meant it too. Unburdening herself to Lucy this morning had, in a way, been a big relief and the girl had surprised her by being a sensitive listener. In spite of all her first impressions, Jo found herself slowly beginning to thaw towards Lucy. Something she'd barely have thought possible not twenty-four hours ago.

'Thanks,' Lucy smiled warmly and slid down into the booth beside her. 'But please don't tell me you're still working? Seriously? On a Saturday night?'

Jo said nothing, just gave her a wry glance and showed her the blank computer screen.

'Dave and I have to compile a list of each other's best qualities. To quote Kate from conflict resolution, "everything that made you fall in love in the first place".'

'Oh, don't remind me!' Lucy laughed good-naturedly. 'I had to do that earlier too. So how are you getting on?'

Jo took another sip of champagne and sat back against the leather booth.

'I'm doing okay, in that I'm well able to list off all the things that I loved about him. My worry is, can he do as much for me? Thing is, he and I have been at each other's throats for so long now, that it's hard to remember back to a time when things were any different between us, really. You should have seen some of the email exchanges we've had; you'd die. They're actually toxic. We've both been so vicious to each other . . .'

But Lucy was having absolutely none of it.

'Are you kidding? Of course Dave won't have a problem with this!' she insisted. 'Just go back into that meeting and remind him about, say for instance, your wedding day? How he felt when he looked into your eyes and a priest declared you man and wife.'

Jo took a second to think back. Her wedding day seemed like such an age ago now. And yet she could still remember Dave leaning over to kiss her as soon as she arrived beside him at the altar. Beaming with pride as he told her she was beautiful, which she wasn't, by the way. Jo was no beauty and knew it, but it was amazing what a bit of professional make-up and a good up-style did for her. But the fact that he thought so just meant such a lot to her.

She remembered he made her snigger during the most inappropriate bits throughout the whole service, when the priest's back was turned. And how he still had the price tag stuck to the soles of his shoes, so when he was kneeling down everyone could clearly see.

Jo was certain he'd have happy memories of their honeymoon too, but then that had been hard to forget. Besides, who didn't have fond memories of their honeymoon? But then another memory resurfaced; their first big row, not long after they were first married. Dave had stormed out of the apartment in a huff, and then in the middle of the night, decided that what was called for was a Big Romantic Gesture. So he climbed up the fire escape clinging to a bunch of garage flowers, but then got stuck two floors below her room and had to yell to be rescued.

In spite of herself, Jo had found it hard not to laugh at the sight of a bedraggled Dave being rescued by the fire brigade and in no time the row was all but forgotten.

'I took it as a good sign,' he'd told her later on, 'that you called the emergency services and didn't just leave me dangling off a ledge on the second floor.'

The making-up part that night was pretty hard to forget too. Surely he'd remember that there was a time when she hadn't been such a nightmare to be around all the time?

'See?' Lucy interrupted her thoughts. 'You're smiling. Must be a lot of good stuff whirling round your head.'

'Yeah, there's certainly some happy memories in there,' Jo sighed.

'Always are,' said Lucy sagely.

'You see, I'd been on my own for so long before Dave bounced into my life, that when we first got together . . . I'd actually forgotten what it was like to even be in a relationship. Does that make any sense?'

Lucy just nodded and smiled knowingly.

'But for so long now, I've been such a complete bitch to the guy.'

'It's nothing more than those bloody IVF hormones, Jo. That's all. Trust me, Dave understands.'

'You really think so?'

'Absolutely. And if you don't mind my saying so, there's something else you're forgetting. Something even more obvious than that.'

'There is?'

'Come on. Do I have to spell it out to someone as smart as you?'

Jo just looked at her, genuinely baffled.

'Can I also remind you that he wanted to have a child with you? And still does? And you must want it too, because after all, you're still pumping all those drugs into you.'

'I know, I know,' Jo sighed, sitting back and staring ahead. 'You see, I was fully prepared to be a single parent and to raise the child alone. I'd told Dave as much too and he said as long as he had visitation rights, then he was okay with it. We even made a deal. So after we broke up, I was facing into IVF all alone. But right now, I can't help feeling that . . .'

'You want to know something, Jo?' Lucy interrupted softly.

'What?'

'It's never too late to change your mind.'

*

Andrew still wasn't even properly dressed for dinner yet. Ever since he'd come back up to his room after a gruelling day thrashing everything out with Lucy, he'd made the mistake of checking in on his emails and getting back to the pile of missed calls on his phone.

And immediately wished he hadn't. Christ, today had been bad enough, but now this? On top of everything else he had to deal with, apart from all the other stresses and pressures in his personal life, now he had to deal with yet more trouble and strife at the Board. He'd spent the entire day with Lucy at his side barely even able to be civilized to each other and that had been bad enough. And now it seemed Armageddon had just broken out in work. Yet another pension fund had just crumbled and stocks were plummeting fast and furious.

To cap it all off though, he hadn't been feeling particularly well all evening. He was sweaty and clammy, most unlike himself. And if he stood up too quickly, the dizziness was almost nauseating. Must have been the chicken he'd eaten at lunchtime, he figured. That was most likely causing the sick feeling he had and the walloping sensation in his chest. Slight bit of a tingling sensation in his arms too.

But it's nothing to worry about, he thought dismissively. Sure, he was fit as a fiddle from all the golf he played and had the stamina of an ox. *This is nothing more than a perfectly natural reaction to pressure,* he told himself. A marriage breaking up has to be one of the most traumatizing things any man can possibly go through.

Of course it hadn't felt the same when he and Greta had split up, but he'd had Lucy by his side to ease him through it all back then, didn't he? Somehow nothing felt like a problem with her beside him. Once she was around, he was indomitable.

All very different now though.

A lie down, he thought, stretching out on the bed and laying his head on the cool pillows. Just for a moment. That would put him to rights. The dizziness would surely pass then. And this shooting pain up and down his arm.

Course it would. Probably.

*

'Dinner is served,' Chris smiled politely at both Jo and Lucy, still tucked away in their little booth, chatting away companionably.

'Great,' said Lucy, draining back the rest of the fizzy water in front of her. All she'd allow herself to drink tonight. Maybe even all she'd allow herself from now on. 'Don't know about you, but I could eat a horse.'

'God knows where you put it,' Jo smiled. 'With the teeny little doll's figure you have.'

'Ha! What you can't see is the giant pair of Spanx knickers I'm wearing underneath this to yank me in!'

By now, guests had started to drift from the bar towards the main dining room on the ground floor and Jo and Lucy walked companionably side by side, continuing on with the conversation they'd been having.

'So, the same question back to you,' said Jo.

'How do you mean?' said Lucy.

'Andrew's good qualities. Come on then, list them off for me.'

They were just filing through Reception and at the mention of Andrew's name, Lucy automatically started to look around for him. Come to think of it, she hadn't seen him since that bloody meeting with that boring family law expert earlier that afternoon.

'He's late,' she said distractedly. 'And it's not like him to be late.'

'Stop dodging the question,' Jo insisted.

But as it happened, Lucy didn't even need to think about the answer though.

'His heart,' she shrugged. 'I think Andrew's got the biggest heart of any man I've ever met before in my whole life.'

*

Andrew often thought he'd lost so much, that all he had left to give Lucy was his heart. And at that exact moment, it was just about to give out on him.

Chapter Thirty

Chloe.

Rob came to the hospital with us and thank God that he did. He's been only amazing ever since. Constantly asking Lucy if she was okay, time and again reassuring her that there was nothing to worry about. Reiterating over and over that he was sure Andrew would be absolutely fine in no time.

Even though that could be so far from the truth that it's actually terrifying.

Rob's over at the vending machine now in the tiny corridor outside the ICU unit where they took Andrew, the minute the ambulance got here. Lucy waited here with us throughout the whole procedure, white-faced and anxious, but then just a moment ago, a consultant who looked so young it was almost scary, came out of the room where they'd brought him.

Lucy gripped onto my hand and I was full sure the girl would pass out.

'Who's Mr Lowe's next of kin?' the consultant wanted to know.

'Emm . . . that would be me,' she told him in a wobbly voice. 'I'm . . . well, I'm his wife.'

'Would you like to step inside, please? We've still got a lot more to do, but you can at least wait with him now, if you like.'

So here I am, sick to my stomach with worry, thinking please dear God, don't let this be happening.

Rob has his back to me and is watching lukewarm coffee gush from the vending machine into a white plastic cup. He brings it over to me, but even the smell instantly turns my stomach.

'Come on, Chloe. Stay strong. You can do it.'

He grips my hand tight so I grip it back. Grateful.

*

Cardiac stents, the consultant was warbling on about. Something about cardiac stents that they'd just inserted and valves to relieve the pressure and how lucky Andrew was to have survived this. And that tests would show whether he needed bypass surgery, and then a whole lot of questions to Lucy about what kind of stress levels he'd been operating under lately.

And all the while Lucy could barely even take it all in. She just focused on Andrew, grey in the face and looking waxy as he lay on the ICU hospital bed beside her, not a bit his usual handsome self at all. Did I do this to you, was all she could think. Was it separation and divorce that pushed you over the edge?

Then finally, after what seemed like an age, the consultant left her alone with him. But Andrew had been heavily sedated after the whole procedure and she'd been told he'd be out for possibly hours more.

'That's fine,' she'd told the ICU nurse. 'If it's okay, I'll wait.'

And now she was really properly alone with him.

She took his hand and wondered if some part of him could register the sensation of her touch.

'Darling, I'm here,' she told him, hoping that even though he was out cold, maybe a tiny part of him could hear. 'And don't you worry. Because this time I'm not going anywhere.'

*

Back at the hotel, there was an understandably muted atmosphere throughout the whole dining room over dinner. Word had spread like wildfire about what had happened to Andrew Lowe and of course now it was all anyone could talk about.

'You know the exact same thing happened to good friends of ours back in New York,' Jayne was happily telling anyone who'd listen to her. 'Jack and Shayla Lowenstein. They were going through a really messy divorce and bickering over just about everything. Then whaddya know, one fine day Jack goes for a jog in the park and has a massive heart attack right there. Dead before he even hit the ground. Found by a lady out walking her dog. Total shocker.'

'Mind you, Shayla did say it saved her a fortune in lawyer's bills,' Larry chipped in over her shoulder. 'Plus, because they hadn't actually finalized the divorce, she ended up getting everything!'

'Larry! Time and a place!' Jayne instantly pulled him up.

Dawn had been there when the ambulance first arrived and her heart had gone out to Lucy. The poor woman looked ashen faced as she walked behind the stretcher, with Chloe supporting one side of her and that tall, lean guy with the greyish hair at the other.

Please don't let this be happening, Dawn had thought. Not to Andrew. Not to that kind, lovely gentleman who'd she'd chatted to only the previous night. Who'd been so sensitive and lovely and who'd made her laugh and cheered her up after possibly the shittiest day known to man.

If anyone up there can hear me, she found herself silently praying to a God she didn't know if she believed in, then please let Andrew be okay. Please let that gorgeous, warm soul get through this somehow. Please.

So of course, what was meant to have been a fancy celebratory dinner that evening turned out to be anything but. The dining room was still full, but the atmosphere was far more subdued and low-key. Dawn hovered uncertainly over by the door, not even sure where she'd like to be seated. The last few meals she'd either sat alone or else at a group table with Jayne and Larry and some lovely people from Finland with perfect English and who promised they'd definitely call into Earth's Garden to try out some of her spelt muesli.

And that's when she saw him. Kirk, sitting all alone. Tucked away in a quiet corner of the room, looking morose and with a book propped up in front of him. Typical him, reading *The Seven Spiritual Laws of Success* by Deepak Chopra. But it was the first time he'd shown up for any meals at all and until now, Dawn just assumed he was eating up in his room.

His eyes must have sensed hers on him because as soon as he spotted her, he was up on his feet and over to her side, smelling of incense and lavender, like he always did.

'Join me,' he said softly. 'Please. Just this once. It would be so good to talk like we used to.'

Well why not, Dawn thought? Why not have this last

and final supper together? After this weekend, he'd pretty much be out of her hair for good, so this was probably the last time they'd ever be able to do this. Besides, she thought, for all that Kirk had almost driven her to the brink, how would she have felt if that had been him led out of here on a stretcher and whisked off to an ICU? She shuddered just at the thought.

So Dawn followed him to the table, a waitress came over, they ordered drinks and she sat back, for the moment enjoying the silence. 'Letting the angel pass,' as Kirk always said.

'It's so painful to think about that poor soul,' he began, 'Andrew something, isn't it?'

'Andrew Lowe, yeah.'

'You know I did offer him a reiki massage in the ambulance, but his wife said no.'

'Kirk,' Dawn told him gently, 'the man just had a massive heart attack. You really think you holding your hands over him and doing a bit of deep breathing would help? You don't think a fully prepped medical team with oxygen masks in an ICU might possibly do the job a bit better for him?'

'The life force energy flows through us all, and is what causes us to be alive –' but Kirk broke off here, realizing he'd just lost his audience. 'I'm sorry, Dawn,' he added softly. 'And I'm guessing that coming out with that kind of thing is yet another reason why you and I are even here in the first place.'

'You could say that, yeah,' she said wryly.

'I always knew you thought my reiki healings didn't work . . .'

'Ehh . . . no offence, but that's because they *don't* . . .'

'And what you said yesterday about chakra realignment –'

362

'Nothing against it, but it's just not really me.'

'And I suppose the same with aura reading?'

'Kirk, I'm sorry, but it's just fortune telling with a fancier name. You might as well just read your horoscope in the back of a magazine. Same difference.'

But instead of that well-known wounded look he'd worn ever since they arrived here on Friday, now Kirk surprised her by actually grinning.

'Bless you,' he said simply. 'For the kindness of trying so hard back in our early days.'

'Well, you certainly have to admit, I did make an effort,' she smiled back.

'Remember the time I took you off to the Energy and Wellness retreat up in the Wicklow mountains?'

'Oh Kirk, don't remind me! Thought I'd need therapy to get over that one . . .'

'We were supposed to fast from sunrise to sunset and in the meantime, explore our deepest emotions through the freedom of dance . . .'

'. . . And everyone else was amazing at it, but the subtext of my dance drama was "I'm bloody starving. And smelly. Where can I shower? And where's the nearest bus stop so I can get the hell out of here?"'

'I can't believe how much you put up with, just for me,' Kirk said, looking at her fondly. There was a candle lit on the table between them, and he just looked so *beautiful* in the flickering light, Dawn thought. There was a time when just the sight of him would have melted her. And yet, not now. Something had most definitely shifted inside of her. Maybe even healed, as Kirk might say.

'I was twenty-two years of age,' she told him simply. 'I'd have said or done anything to make it work between us. You know that. But now, it all just seems so different. Aside from you and Shane and the horrible way I found out, and the humiliation of it all. Even leaving all that aside . . . we're two very different people, Kirk. Don't you see?'

'Yes,' he nodded calmly. 'You know I do.'

'Thing is, I'm just an ordinary, normal girl. I enjoy my job and I love doing things like going out for dinner every so often or . . .' she broke off here, thinking back to that lovely barman from Kerry and the great aul' chat they'd had earlier. 'And I like going to the movies and maybe even the odd play. Simple things really, but all things you've no interest in. I mean, I'm only twenty-five and I just want to enjoy my life a bit more. And I'm sorry, but sitting round the flat smoking dope and listening to sitar music while eating brown rice and tofu just isn't me really.'

Kirk just smiled and shook his head. 'All you put up with for me. And I did so little for you in return, when I think of it. In fact, I've been meditating a lot about something you said to me on our first night here. Something that really hit home.'

'Don't remind me,' Dawn said, rolling her eyes. 'I bombarded you with so many insults that night, which one do you mean?'

'You said I needed to realize that my actions had consequences for others around me. And I suppose pure, mute selfishness on my part made me block that out. So what I'm really trying to ask is . . .'

They were interrupted just as the waitress arrived with their drinks orders. Then Kirk leaned forward, the big, soulful brown eyes brimming up with concern now.

'Do you think you'll ever be able to forgive me? Because words can't describe how eaten up with guilt I am ever since I came to this place and the full reality of what I'd put you through really hit home. You know that.'

Dawn took a sip of white wine and had a good think before answering.

'You were my best friend and lover,' she eventually said, 'and I lost both in one fell swoop. The lover bit I can get over, but losing my best friend wasn't easy, I can tell you. But then ever since we came here, there's a big part of me thinking, does it really matter *why* we were so wrong for each other? The fact is that we were just wrong.'

'Dawn . . . I'm so sorry. I really am. I know it's naïve and cheeky to even think you'd want me as your friend after what I put you through, I know that. But if there was any way forward for you and me as true pals –'

'Hey . . . now, let's not run before we can walk,' she laughed.

'You always were a far wiser soul than me,' Kirk smiled back warmly, that gorgeous dimply smile that once used to make her liquefy. 'And certainly a far more generous one. You know, I think in a past life, you definitely must have been a Shaman . . . I've always said it.'

'Ehh . . . let's not get into shamanism right now, Kirk,' she said firmly.

Just then the waitress came back to take their order.

'After you,' he said.

'Alright then,' said Dawn. 'And now I'm going to do something in front of you that I've wanted to for the longest time.' Then turning to the waitress, she said, 'I'd like to order the duck liver pâté to start and for the main course, I'll have the fillet steak, medium rare, please.'

She looked over her menu, caught Kirk's eye and for one lovely moment, they both laughed.

*

Jo had been really looking forward to dinner, but after what had happened to that unfortunate Andrew Lowe, her appetite had instantly evaporated. She'd been texting Chloe to see if there was news, but so far, no answer. But then, she guessed if they were all in an ICU, all phones would have to be switched off, wouldn't they? So she'd skip dinner and just go up to her room, she decided. And continue to do the homework on Dave's good qualities that had to be done in time for her first session the following morning.

But then, speaking of Dave, it suddenly struck her that she hadn't set eyes on him all evening. So passing by Reception she paused for a moment and casually asked Liliana whether he was up in his room too?

'Mr Evans?' Liliana smiled prettily back at her. 'No Ma'am, I'm afraid not.'

Instantly, the hackles on Jo's back were raised.

'Well, do you know where he is?'

'I'm afraid not, ma'am. But I can tell you that he's not here.'

'Excuse me?'

'You see, Mr Evans left the hotel about an hour ago.'

SUNDAY

Chapter Thirty-One

Chloe.

It was the smallest part of the wee, small hours. Just past midnight now and Rob and I are still here, still outside the ICU, still waiting on news. I can't believe the guy's waited with me this long. And not only that, but he keeps trying to jolly me along and stop all my incessant stressing and fretting. Not that anything will stop me worrying, but still, I'm appreciating his efforts.

In fact, ever since we got here, I've lost count of the number of times he's gone to the vending machine for coffee that actually tastes like a lukewarm puddle on the side of the road, then forced it down my throat, telling me that it'll do me good. Or how often he's said, 'Okay, so I know you think this is high drama, but believe me, this is nothing. Remind me to tell you about the night I had three ambulances outside my hotel in Paris.'

And I'm smiling at him and appreciating the gesture, but then reverting back to my natural factory default setting of 'worry'. Anyway, after what feels like an eternity of this carry-on, Rob eventually slips his arm around me and gives me an awkward sort of sideways hug.

'Come on, Chloe,' he says encouragingly. 'We can't blame ourselves. When you're in a business where you deal with the public, anything can and will happen. I've seen it all before and I've still lived to tell the tale.'

Then not long after midnight, this attractive looking young woman arrives. Late twenties, dark shoulder length hair, dressed in boyfriend jeans and a fabulously expensive looking top; very Harvey Nichols, if you get me. As if she was out somewhere fancy and had to drop everything to rush here. She comes in, looking pale and shocked and makes straight for an ICU nurse.

'Hi,' she says in a small, frightened little voice. 'I'm here to see my Dad, Andrew Lowe. I'm his daughter, Alannah.'

'Oh, yes,' an exhausted looking ICU nurse tells her, 'I'm afraid Mr Lowe is under observation right now. But don't worry, his wife is with him and we're doing everything we can.'

Alannah nods but says nothing, so taking the lead, I introduce myself.

'Hi there,' I tell her, 'I just wanted to say that I'm Chloe, General Manager at the Hope Street Hotel, where your Dad was staying . . .'

'Good to meet you,' Rob says, sliding up beside me, all tall and confident. 'Rob from Ferndale Hotels. I just want to say that we're here for you and if there's anything we can do –'

'Thanks, that's good of you,' Alannah says and for a split second, behind the immaculately dressed surface, I can see a worried, frightened little girl underneath.

Just at that moment, Lucy steps out of the ICU, looking ghostly white and washed out, bless her, and practically swaying on her feet with tiredness.

Immediately, Rob and I are on our feet and straight over to her.

'I can't believe you both waited with me all this time!' she says gratefully, as I give her hand a tight squeeze. Then she spots Alannah and immediately says 'Hi,' addressing her directly.

'Lucy,' says Alannah, stiffening just a little. But Lucy heads over to where she's standing and puts a supportive arm on her shoulder.

'It's good of you to come,' she began, a bit nervously.

'Of course I'm here, I came the minute you called . . . and thanks, by the way.'

'For what?'

'For letting Josh and me know.'

'Alannah, of course I wanted you both to know! And your Dad will be so pleased you're here.'

'How is he?'

'Honest answer? I don't know yet.'

'They've put in a stent, I overheard that young consultant saying,' Rob says helpfully. 'That's surely good news.'

'Yeah,' Lucy nods. 'And they've just run a pile of tests too, but they're keeping him in to do a few more tomorrow, just to make sure there aren't any further blockages . . .'

She sounds a bit wobbly, the combination of anxiety and exhaustion really hitting her, so I go to give her a big, warm hug and hold the girl tight.

'Come on now. The main thing is that he's getting the best care possible,' I tell her comfortingly.

'Of course, yeah . . .' is all she can keep repeating, like it's still all sinking in. 'I've asked the nurse if I can stay with him tonight and she said it would be fine. I'm not leaving him here alone, I just couldn't . . .'

And then the most astonishing thing of all. A small step for man, a giant leap for mankind. Walking over to Lucy and linking her arm supportively, Alannah steers her back towards the ICU and says, 'Don't worry. I'm here now. So what do you say we wait with him together.'

*

Back inside the ICU, Lucy sat tensely by Andrew's bedside and gripped his hand tight.

'I'm right here, sweetheart,' she told him gently, far from certain that he could even hear her. 'And if I had any part in driving you to this, I'm so, so sorry. Just pull through this, Andrew. And I'll be right here waiting for you. Because from now on, I'm never leaving your side again. And that's a promise.'

She didn't have a tissue, so she dabbed her eyes with the edge of her sleeve and then caught Alannah looking over at her, with just the weirdest expression on her face.

'You okay?' Lucy asked, genuinely concerned.

'Be a lot more okay if Dad wasn't in an intensive care unit.'

'Well, wouldn't we all?'

A long pause while both women just looked across Andrew's bed at each other.

'Alannah . . . I hope you know how sorry I am,' Lucy eventually said to her, barely knowing why. It just somehow felt that the moment was right. 'Well . . . for everything. For all the pain that your Dad and I caused your family. For absolutely everything. I really do mean that, so sincerely. Because, God forbid, if anything happens to your Dad . . . well . . . I know the one thing he'd want is for us to get along.'

She had to dab her eyes again, so this time, Alannah spoke.

'That's . . . well, I suppose . . . if nothing else, I appreciate you saying it. And for my part . . . emm, if I ever gave you a hard time, then I'm sorry too.'

A tiny, minuscule breakthrough, and yet somehow it gave Lucy a small bit of comfort. Maybe there was hope for her and Andrew after all. Another pause before Alannah spoke again.

'You really do love him, don't you?' she said, studying Lucy's expression closely from across the bed.

'Course I do. I mean . . . what did you all think?'

Chloe.

There's nothing more we can do tonight, only wait and pray, so not long after 1 a.m., Lucy steps out of the ICU to thank Rob and I for waiting and to tell us to get home and sleep.

'Don't worry,' she says, as I give her a warm hug goodbye. 'I'll be in touch the minute there's any news.'

So wall-falling with tiredness, Rob offers a cab to take me home, then him back to his hotel and I gratefully accept. He steps outside to order the taxi and I follow him a few minutes later. It's pitch dark outside and I walk to the far side of the car park looking right, left and centre for Rob. As it turns out though, I hear him before I actually see him.

'Hi sweetheart, I know you're fast asleep by now, so this is just a quick voicemail,' he's saying in a low voice down into his phone. 'But I just wanted to say I'm so sorry for not calling you this evening. I'll explain all when we're talking tomorrow. And I can't wait to see you next week. Love you, my angel.'

He's onto the girlfriend. Funny, but he and I have been working together so intensively over the past few days that I'd actually put that whole side of his life entirely out of my mind.

Shame though, I find myself smiling, thinking back to when he and I first met and how intimidated I was by Rob. Because now . . . well, we've been working together side by side this whole weekend so closely and intensively, that . . . well, I suppose I'll just miss him when this is all over and he whisks himself off to Dubai or Milan or whatever five-star hotel in whatever exotic corner of the globe that's screaming out for him to troubleshoot in. Kind of like Superman, except with money.

Bloody typical, I think. First interesting, funny, warm-hearted man that I've met since, well since my one-time fiancé and wouldn't you know it, he's a) my boss so therefore off limits and b) clearly in a deeply committed relationship with a woman he can't wait to get back to. But then what did I expect? It's a truth universally acknowledged that the Rob McFaydens of this world are never single, isn't it?

I freeze in my tracks a few steps behind him, not wanting him to think I was eavesdropping, and yet there's no way round it. Rob spots me, waves then clicks off his phone, just as our cab arrives and he holds the door open for me.

'Well that's certainly one night I won't forget in a hurry,' he says dryly, as I give the driver the address of my parents' house.

'Are you joking me? I'll be having therapy about this for years to come!'

'Don't be too hard on yourself, Chloe,' he says, looking at me keenly through the darkness. 'These things do happen. Believe me, when you've been in the hotel business as long as I have, you grow a thick skin. Births, marriages, deaths, I've seen the lot. When this weekend is over and when the last guest has safely checked out on Sunday night, I'll take you out and tell you a few choice stories. I promise you, they'll make you think this weekend was a gentle stroll in the park.'

'I'll tell you one thing though,' I say, looking absently out onto the empty streets we zoom past. 'Please God, if Andrew pulls through this, then I certainly don't think he and Lucy will be heading for the divorce courts now, do you? They just couldn't, they're still mad about each other. Did you see that poor girl's face in the ambulance? I thought she'd pass out, I really did.'

'I sensed a bit of ice breaking between Lucy and that daughter of his too,' he says perceptively. 'Which can only be a good thing, I imagine.'

'I know, and . . .' I break off here, because it's hard to put into words. And yet somehow I've got a feeling that Andrew will pull through and that he and Lucy will come out the other side so much stronger.

And then I find myself yawning. Hardly surprising, given that I can barely remember the last time my head hit a pillow.

Rob cops it instantly.

'Look at you, you're exhausted, Chloe. No need to come in for breakfast serving tomorrow, get some rest. You've earned it.'

'That's kind, but I couldn't. We've all invested far too much not just in the hotel but in our guests too. And I

375

have to be there every step of the way. Besides, I just have to know how each of their stories will play out in the final reel. Don't you?'

*

At about the same time, Jo was up in her hotel room wearing her nightie, stretched out on the bed, sleepless with worry and working herself up into a right lather by now. Why had Dave left the hotel so late in the evening anyway? He wouldn't . . . just have checked out, would he? Just given up, like that? Just packed up that manbag that went everywhere with him and walked out the door without a second glance? Would he?

And then a fresh anxiety. If he did – was she herself to blame? After all, she forced herself to admit, she'd been nothing but abrasive and horrible to him ever since they first checked in.

Then she remembered the awful sight of poor Lucy following her husband out of here on a stretcher and being led into an ambulance, with God knows what lying ahead of her. How would she herself have felt had that been Dave, for all their bickering and with all the bitterness that lay between them?

Jo lay there, cursing her insomnia and tossing and turning till the sheets were twisted around her legs. Then, suddenly a sharp pinging noise through the silence made her sit up. Shit. She'd left her iPhone switched on and it must be a text coming through, she figured. So she switched on the bedside light and grabbed the phone, which was sitting there recharging.

God, was it really half twelve already? Must be someone from Digitech screaming for me, she thought. Made sod all difference that it was the wee small hours here, this kind of thing happened all the time. Particularly with the US office, who expected you to be on the tightest of electronic leashes at all times, weekends, public holidays, the works.

Jo squinted at the tiny screen in front of her as her eyes adjusted to the light. Just three short little sentences, that was all.

GUESSING YOU'RE STILL AWAKE.
ROOM 377 NOW.
JUST TRUST ME.

So, exactly five minutes later here she was. Clad in an oversized hotel dressing gown and not having the first clue what this could be about. She knocked gingerly on the door and he opened it immediately, surprising her by being smartly dressed, in a blue shirt and chinos she'd bought him ages ago that she loved on him, but he professed to hate. He'd shaved too and smelt lovely. Made a real effort, just like she was always nagging at him to do.

'Thank Christ you opened the door when you did,' she whispered, so as not to disturb anyone else. 'I was afraid one of the staff would walk past and assume I was here on a booty call.'

'You know, somehow I doubt they'd object,' Dave grinned down at her, lighting up to see she'd actually come. 'Bearing in mind that you and I are still married. At least, technically.' He stepped aside to let her in and Jo actually found herself gasping – for a split second thinking she was seeing things.

There were red rose petals scattered all the way from the door to a table for two, set up in the dead centre of the room.

Three Diptyque mini-candles – in that rose fragrance that she loved so much – were flickering away as a centrepiece, and the entire room was filled with vase after vase of long stemmed stargazer lilies, her all time favourite flowers. Not only that, but tiny tea lights were dotted about on just about every surface going and all the room lights had been dimmed, giving the whole place a magical, almost fairyland feel.

'Dave!' she exclaimed. 'It's like walking onto the set of a Disney movie!'

'But in a non-ironic way, I hope,' he said, slipping behind the table and whipping a chilled bottle of champagne out of an ice bucket, then trying to uncork it, but making a right pig's ear of it, like he always did. Which of course never failed to make Jo smile.

'Give that to the expert here,' she laughed, taking the bottle from him and opening it expertly in one wrist movement herself. It was Dom Perignon too. Her all time favourite. No doubt about it, he'd really pushed the boat out.

'Ehh yeah,' said Dave. 'I probably should just stick to opening tins of beer, like I'm used to.'

There was more too. The table was laid out with a whole picnic consisting solely of absolutely everything she loved. Duck liver pâté, smoked salmon, even the Neufchâtel cheese that she adored so much and hardly ever allowed herself, on account of the fact it had approximately the same amount of calories as a Big Mac Meal.

'I don't get it,' Jo kept saying, genuinely baffled. 'You went to all this bother? For me?' No one ever made thoughtful gestures like this for her. No one.

'No bother at all,' he said dismissively. 'I just jumped into a cab, did a bit of late night shopping here in town, then went and found the nearest twenty-four-hour Tesco, that was all. Mind you, the hall porter here had to give me a hand lugging all this up here. The guy must have thought I just held up a supermarket at gunpoint. Fear not though, I tipped him handsomely and all was well.'

'But . . . why, Dave?' Jo asked, taking the champagne glass he offered her and easing into the seat he held out for her. 'I just don't get it!'

He slid down into the chair opposite her.

'Because if this is it, if this is the end for you and me, then I so badly wanted it to be special. I figured it was the least I could do, given what I put you through.'

'But you didn't have to . . .'

'No,' he said, raising his hand, 'hear me out. If I may just refer momentarily to the elephant in the room that we so rarely discuss . . .'

'Dave . . .'

'. . . What I did was callous and thoughtless and cruel and stupid . . .'

'. . . Well, I certainly won't argue with that,' she said, wincing a bit at what he was referring to.

'. . . And although nothing would make me happier than if you were to forgive me and let us start over, I've long since accepted that particular miracle just isn't going to happen.'

Then he broke off and leaned forward on the table to really face her and even though there was only candlelight, she could still see his face flickering with sincerity.

'But Jo, believe me, it was nothing more than a pathetic, misguided, misjudged, drunk-off-my-face one night stand. She meant absolutely zilch to me and I haven't spoken two words to her since.'

379

'You don't have to say any more, please . . .'

Now that he'd started though, there was no shutting him up.

'. . . It was Christmas Eve and you and I had rowed about God knows what. In fact that whole miserable Christmas, the pair of us had been acting just like George and Martha from *Who's Afraid of Virginia Woolf* and I . . . well. Wanted to lash out, I suppose.'

Jo felt a sudden flush of anger just at the memory, but she bit her tongue as Dave went on.

'. . . And I had to tell you. Nothing would have been easier for me than to shut up about it and say nothing and act the innocent, but I couldn't keep it from you. If nothing else, we've always been brutally honest with each other . . .'

'. . . To the point of viciousness at times,' she said sardonically.

'. . . And I felt like such a shit, I can't tell you. You were just heading into your final round of treatment and were weak and vulnerable, not to mention ill. And what did I do? I went and betrayed you. And even though I hate being here with every fibre in me, there's a big part of me that can't blame you for wanting rid of me. But Jo, I really am so sorry. You'll never know how sorry. Through my own stupidity, I lost you and I deserved to. So that's what this is about really. If this is the final act for you and me, then I thought the least you deserved was a worthy and fitting curtain call. I felt the very least I could do was to give our marriage a decent burial.'

A long pause as Jo sat back and really tried to digest all this. Which was weird, because she wasn't used to silence around Dave. Normally, each of them rarely let the other get a word in edgeways.

'Thank you for your letters,' was all she could bring herself to eventually say.

'Well, we always seem to be emailing each other, I often think the written word is our main artery of communication. So in a way, it sort of seemed fitting.'

'And thank you for tonight. I'm going to need time, Dave. An awful lot of time. But for what it's worth, I do mean this sincerely. Thank you.'

'Anytime,' he said simply, and for one lovely moment, they both smiled.

Chapter Thirty-Two

Chloe.

The final furlong. Our very last day and there's already an atmosphere of finality about the hotel. It's well past five on Sunday evening and each of our guests completed their last sessions (all about division of assets and pensions) earlier on this afternoon, Hallelujah be praised.

Anyway, the main news to report is that Lucy called me first thing this morning from the hospital, with the wonderful news that Andrew is far more stable today and has been moved out of the ICU to a private room instead. I swear, I could hear the relief in the girl's voice as she told me, and boy, did it do my heart good. So I told her to stay put and that I'd see to getting all of her and Andrew's things packed up and sent off to whatever address she thought best. And I've got the strongest feeling that both sets of luggage will be going to the same address too.

Anyway, I've got twelve couples here in total and thankfully the vast majority seem to have sailed through the whole weekend with ne'er a cross word between them. In fact if anything, they were all full of thanks and praise for the staff and for the whole team who'd eased them as far as this point.

We had a late lunch scheduled for guests before this evening's check-out, but it's such a gloriously sunny day that our head chef decided to hold an impromptu barbecue out on the terrace, to really send everyone home in style. Which I have to say was an inspired idea and the perfect send-off too.

It's still beautifully warm and sunny outside and guests are dressed down, mostly in jeans and casual gear, all congregating round the barbecue where the most fabulous, mouth-watering smells are emanating from. People are sitting anywhere and everywhere in the garden, chatting and yakking amongst themselves, happily soaking up the last of the evening rays.

'Hey honey, you come sit by me!' Jayne from Noo Yawk is calling over to Kirk, who's wandering around in bare feet with a plateful of couscous, scanning the crowd as though he's looking for someone. Kirk obligingly does as he's told and ambles over as Jayne pats the empty seat beside her.

'You're just far too cute to be straying around here all alone!' she says fondly, then nudges him and winks. 'So tell me this much. You ever considered dating an older woman? Maybe a cougar like me? 'Cause I gotta tell ya, honey, my Larry's been very generous to me this weekend! You're looking at a pretty wealthy lady now!'

To his credit, Kirk just smiles and bats it aside.

Meanwhile I'm as ever, torn between trying to be in five places at once, as plenty of guests need to check out early to make it to the airport for flights home and it's important I'm there to wish them goodbye and wave them off. So I'm busy circulating around the terrace and keeping drinks topped up along with the rest of the staff, scanning around

383

the garden either for Dawn or else Jo and Dave, but so far, no sign.

And I'm also wondering where Rob has got to, when Liliana suddenly appears at my shoulder.

'You're needed at Reception right now,' she tells me discreetly.

'Our Finnish couple ready to check out?' I ask her anxiously. They'd an early evening flight and I know they were concerned about getting to the airport in plenty of time.

'Just go,' Liliana smiles mysteriously. 'You'll see.'

I head back through the bar and into Reception and there's the biggest, most ludicrously overblown bunch of flowers waiting there, oddly enough looking like they're being held up by a man's legs. Hairy legs, in a pair of Bermuda shorts. And there's only one guest round here who goes round in shorts day and night.

'It's me here, under this miniature garden!' says Dave and I immediately burst out laughing.

'Dave, are these for Jo? Because I think she's still upstairs packing . . .'

'No, lovely girl,' he says, leaving the bouquet on the reception desk. 'These are for you. I came to say thank you.'

'Dave! There was absolutely no need!'

'Excuse me, but there very much was a need,' he grins cheekily, shoving a clumpful of his hair out of his eyes, so as usual, it ends up standing at a really weird angle to his head. 'You helped me so much yesterday evening. You listened, you advised me what to do and so, I did it.'

'Hey, that's fantastic!'

'You told me to woo her. To make one, big, grand romantic gesture. So I did. I arranged this sort of late night

384

midnight picnic, with all the fancy grub she likes and I hate. And we talked, like grown adults having the first civilized conversation we've had in months. No rows, no recriminations, just two people trying to figure out where to go from here.'

'I'm so proud of you! And do you think maybe it worked?'

'A little early to say yet, but let's just say you can watch this space with great interest.'

As if on cue, the lift door glides open and out comes Jo, followed by the hall porter with her luggage. Dave strides over to her, takes the wheelie bag she's dragging behind her and helps the porter to carry it all outside and into a taxi for her. Jo thanks him, then immediately smiles when she sees me.

'I'm so glad you're here, Chloe,' she says, sounding different to her usual brisk, efficient self. Warmer, somehow. 'I didn't want to leave without saying goodbye. And thank you. So much. For everything.'

'You're so welcome. And I'm delighted that things are all finalized.'

'Well, we've certainly worked out our divorce agreement, and between us we've settled everything that we possibly could. But I think we both know I'm not just talking about division of property and bloody assets and pension reserves here either.'

I say nothing, just smile.

'Thank you, Chloe. You've been my sanity these last few days. I mean it,' she says sincerely.

'Anytime. Are you sure you need to leave right now though? We've got a gorgeous barbecue on the go outside. Won't you stay and have something to eat before you go?'

'Can't,' she says, shaking her head firmly. 'I've got a mountain of work to catch up on after this weekend and I'm on a flight to Chicago first thing tomorrow, so I'm afraid this really is it. This is goodbye.'

She'd already checked out earlier, so there's nothing for me to do but to hug her goodbye and wish her a safe trip. I walk her out the front door in time to see Dave and the porter loading up a cab for her, but then, sensing that the two of them would rather have a little moment alone, I wave her goodbye and step back inside to give them a bit of privacy.

My mind is wandering as I head back outside to the garden. Because Jo and Dave may well have finalized their divorce agreement alright, but if you ask me, they're still a very long way from –

I'm suddenly interrupted by a burst of giggles coming from the terrace. And to my delight I see that it's my little pet Dawn deep in chat with lovely Tommy, who's clearly just cracked her up about something.

'I swear to God, that's a totally true story!' Tommy is telling her while Dawn, I notice, is blushing very prettily. She looks absolutely gorgeous this evening too, in a pretty floral summery dress with the long red hair tied up in a ponytail.

'And did I tell you about the time I was working in a bar in London and who walks in only yer man, Robert Pattinson . . .'

'. . . Oh God, I LOVE him!'

'. . . At least I thought it was Robert Pattinson, all the bar staff did, so we started giving not just him, but all his entourage free drink for the night. And then it turned out he was only an aul' lookalike! Nearly got the sack over that one, I can tell you.'

'You big eejit!'

She roars laughing again and pucks him playfully, just as Larry calls Tommy over and orders a whisky chaser for himself. The minute Dawn's all by herself, I give her a little wave and walk over to her.

'Having fun?' I ask her, faux innocent.

'Just, you know . . . enjoying the chat, that's all,' she starts off coyly, then seeing the glint in my eyes, immediately drops the act. 'Oh Chloe, he's such a pet. And he makes me laugh too. And believe me, I can't remember the last time that happened.'

Suddenly I get a flashback to the very first time Dawn and I ever met. And how nervous and vulnerable and fragile she'd seemed way back then. And I look at her now and I swear to God, it's a bit like looking at a different person. Gladdens your heart, that's all I'm saying.

'Well, I have to say how good it is to see you having fun,' I tell her.

'And I can't tell you how good it feels! Especially after the last few days and . . . well you know, the crap we went through before we even got here. Seriously though, it's hard to believe it's all over now. And that Kirk and I will be divorced in no time.'

'But you'll move on. I know you will,' I tell her knowingly.

There's a tiny pause and she leans in closer to me, the big blue eyes sparkling. 'Tommy's asked for my phone number. Just last night. And he's talking about going to the movies this week. And so I thought, sure feck it. What have I got to lose? Aren't I young, free and single now? And why not? After all, there's plenty more fish in the sea, aren't there?'

Certainly are, I think, silently blessing Tommy for being

in the right place at exactly the right time. Then our German couple call me away and I'm just making my way to them, when finally I spot him.

Rob. Right at the very bottom of the garden and deep in chat with my lovely Finnish guests, all chatting and laughing happily together.

For a moment, I stand there, just taking him in. He really is attractive, I find myself thinking, though one of those guys who seems blissfully unaware of it. Tall and lean, in a light blue shirt and jeans today, standing there chatting away in the evening light, he looks, no other words for it, highly fanciable. Gorgeous even. He catches my eye and winks, so I give a tiny wave back. Then he ambles over to where I am and stands by my side, as ever towering over me as we survey the crowd together.

'All in all, not a bad weekend's work, Ms Townsend. Wouldn't you say?'

'Not one without its fair share of drama, I'd say.'

'I'm looking at a lot of happy guests here this evening. A lot of satisfied customers. I told you a while ago, standing right on this very spot if memory serves, that I always know when I'm onto a winner. Do you remember?'

'Course I do,' I laugh. 'It was just a few weeks before we opened and we were up to our tonsils with builders here. Then you just landed in on top of us without a word of warning . . . I was terrified!'

'Remember me telling you this hotel was going to do me proud? Well, I knew it then and know it now. I can just feel it.'

'Always good to know that the owner is happy.'

'More than happy. And you must know that a large part of that is down to you.'

And then he turns to face me full on. 'So come on then, Ms Townsend. You've worked like a dog all weekend long and I don't think I've seen you come up for air once. Now that our work is almost done here, tell me this much. What are your immediate plans?'

'Well,' I tell him, racking my brains through the fug of near exhaustion I'm working under, 'we've got a meeting in the morning about our next batch of guests, but seeing as everyone has worked so hard, I was going to give all the staff a bit of a lie in and . . .'

'Chloe, you're not listening to me. I meant your immediate plans for tonight?'

'Are you kidding me? Sleep and lots of it.'

'You know, you'll always sleep better on a full stomach . . .'

'True . . .'

'So before you leave, is there any chance I can take you out to dinner?'

*

Well, this is a work dinner. Course it is. I mean, obviously it is. Because what else would it be? And okay, so maybe I did change out of my uniform and back into what I'd worn into work that day (pink shift dress with a pair of summery sandals. Not very dressy, but somehow I'm just more comfy like this). But it's absolutely not a date, that much I'm sure of. And yes, I may have lashed on a *little* bit more make-up than normal, but still. I'm well aware of what this is. Or rather what it isn't. Just saying, that's all.

Anyway, it's coming up to eight as Rob and I are strolling in the still-warm evening out of the hotel and down Leeson Street, though I haven't the first iota of where he's taking me. But to be honest, after the weekend I've had, it feels good to sit back and let someone else make decisions, for a change. Our very last guest has just checked out and I can't describe the sheer feeling of weightlessness that – for the most part at least – the whole weekend seems to have gone well.

'Hope you're hungry, Ms Townsend,' Rob says, looking across at me with just a glint in the grey eyes.

'Are you kidding me? I actually can't remember the last time I sat down to a proper meal, actually served up to me, as opposed to just grabbing sandwiches on the run.'

'Atta girl. I've booked somewhere very special, as it happens . . . and by the way,' he adds appreciatively, 'I'm loving that dress on you. The colour really suits you. You look terrific.'

'Emm . . . thanks.'

But he breaks off here, as his mobile starts ringing.

'Sorry,' he says, 'but I've got to take this. Do you mind?'

'Course not,' I say, noticing that his whole face completely lit up the second he saw who it was on the caller ID.

Work call, my arse I think. On a Sunday evening? It's her, whoever she is. And really would you blame her? If I'd a fella like this on the go, I'd find it hard to stop myself checking in on him myself. In fact, I'd be tempted to have him chipped with a tracking device, so I could monitor his movements at all times.

'Sweetheart!' Rob beams down the phone. 'You're such an angel to call. How was your day today? Good, great in fact. But tell me about you, what did you do?'

He chats on easily and I deliberately look away as we stroll out onto Stephen's Green.

'. . . Yeah . . . perfect, sounds good to me. Well, how about next Friday then? I'll be back in London then and

390

can't wait to see you . . . fantastic. Look I can't really chat now, but I'll call you first thing tomorrow. Love you too!'

Then, to my surprise, Rob steers me towards Shanahan's on the Green, one of the poshest, not to mention the most expensive restaurants in the whole city. The maître d' already seems to know him, as he rushes out to greet Rob effusively and escorts us to a gorgeous table, right in the dead centre of the restaurant. We're given menus and wine lists and a silence falls while we each study them. Then a waiter takes our order and comes back with a very expensive bottle of wine, which he pours, while Rob leans forward and grins over at me.

'Here's to you,' he says, clinking glasses with me.

'Well, thank you,' is all I can say, delighted. 'And thanks for taking me here . . . talk about swishy!'

'I wanted somewhere special, somewhere memorable. So I could really thank you properly. Because you really did a terrific job,' he says sincerely, eyes twinkling in the dim candlelight. 'I knew I made the right call the day I hired you.'

'You do?'

'Absolutely. You were the perfect woman for the job. No one could have done it better.'

'But, well . . .'

'You've a problem with my complimenting you, Ms Townsend?'

'No,' I laugh, 'it's just that . . . well, what about all those phone calls to me? Day and night. The constant micro-managing. I had the feeling that you didn't quite trust me. Am I right?'

He says nothing for a bit, just thoughtfully glances down at the menu.

'Well . . . there might just have been other reasons for checking in with you as often as I did,' he says lightly, almost deliberately not looking at me now.

He leaves it hanging there and I'm completely intrigued and dying to probe him a bit, but just as abruptly he changes the subject.

'Oh and by the way, I've got the strongest feeling that you were doing more than your fair share of relationship counselling behind the scenes over the weekend. Am I right?'

I take a sip of the crisp, white wine he ordered and sit back a little.

'Well . . . maybe just a little . . .'

'Come on, you can't pull the wool over my eyes,' he grins, laughing over at me now. 'It's all over anyway now, so you've nothing to lose by telling me. What about Dawn Madden then? And that long-haired guy who tried to set fire to the whole place our first night?'

'Ah, you mean my little pet, Dawn . . .'

'I'm listening,' he says, sitting forward, looking at me keenly.

'Well, it's just that . . .' I break off here, thinking back to my very first interview with Dawn and how terrified she'd been, like the poor kid was on the verge of an anxiety attack. Kirk had so clearly moved on and while I wasn't particularly bothered about the intricacies of his love life, it was Dawn I worried about. And how happy it makes me to see her finally about ready to move on.

'The truth please, Ms Townsend. Were you doing a little matchmaking for her over the weekend?'

'Ah now, would you blame me? And I've absolutely no idea if things will work out between Dawn and Tommy, but that's almost beside the point, really, isn't it? After what that poor girl had been through, she just needed the confidence boost of a good-looking man chatting her up and asking her out, that's all. Just to know that life does, somehow, go on.'

'So what about Jo Hargreaves and Dave? I couldn't help noticing you had a good long private chat with him last night . . . so tell me, what was that over?'

So I fill him in, blushing a bit to think of how little I'd warmed to Jo, way back when I'd first interviewed her. Or more correctly, when she first interviewed me. Then how my heart had gone out to her, that night she told me that everyone assumed she was to blame for the marriage falling apart, and yet . . . there were two sides to every story.

'You see, Dave still loves her,' I say. 'Adores her, in fact, in spite of everything. And I think she's a lot more dependent on him than she thinks. He messed up though, big time and yet something tells me that they'll find a way to work through this.'

'You think they'll still divorce?'

'I can't say. But I think whatever happens, you can be sure they'll work through it together now, side by side. In fact, Dave's last words to me were, "You just watch this space."'

'Listen to you,' he grins easily. 'You sound just like Aunt Sally in the *Sunday Times*. Fixing everyone all around you. So come on then, while you're on a roll, tell me about Lucy and poor Andrew Lowe.'

I shake my head firmly.

'I'll pan-fry my own liver if that pair get divorced. Couldn't you see it for yourself last night? She adores him and I'm certain he feels the same. All weekend long, he was so concerned about her, constantly kept referring to her as his wife . . .' I break off here a bit, then just shake my head. 'No. It was just circumstances that broke them up, nothing more. But you know what? You could just sense a bit of a thawing between Lucy and Andrew's daughter last night. And I really think once he's well again, the pair of them will be able to get through anything, no matter what the future throws at them. Maybe even as a family this time. I just feel it.'

'Chloe Townsend,' says Rob, leaning forward now and giving me that intense look he has. Very, very sexy, I now find myself thinking from out of nowhere. 'You know the more I listen to you, the more I think what a loss you were to the relationship counselling profession.'

'It's not me,' I tell him, 'it's Hope Street. If you ask me, there's healing in the bricks and mortar of the place.'

'Maybe you're right.'

'Besides,' I go on, smiling wryly, 'we've all been there, haven't we? We've all been in bad relationships that went belly-up and we've all known heartache. And I suppose I'm living, breathing proof that life does go on. And that tomorrow is always another day.'

'Which neatly brings us to Frank,' Rob says, all interested.

'Oh, yeah. Frank.'

'Chloe,' he says, more softly now, 'now it's absolutely none of my concern, but when he just showed up at the hotel like that . . . I really thought I'd inflict lasting damage on the guy. After what he did to you? Talk about having a brass neck!'

I don't argue. Mainly because, after the initial shock of seeing him had worn off me, I'd pretty much felt that way myself for the rest of the day too.

'Can I ask you something?' Rob goes on, seemingly unwilling to drop the subject.

'Of course.'

'Something a bit personal?'

I take a deep breath and nod, almost sensing what's coming next.

'Why did he do it? Because that's what I can't get my head around. Why any man would put someone like you through something so bloody indescribable. And on your wedding day too? When I brought it up yesterday,' he adds, 'you did promise you might tell me over dinner sometime. So here we are.'

I have to take a moment before I can gather my thoughts enough to answer him. So I take another tiny sip of the crisp Pinot Grigio in front of me and sit back, somehow trying to piece it all together in my head.

Jagged memories start to surface. I remember locking myself into the bathroom of my hotel suite at the Merrion all that time ago, with lovely, loyal Gemma right beside me, heated rollers still in her hair and wobbling danger-ously, so she looked a bit like a Dalek.

'Chloe sweetheart, would you please just tell me what happened between you and Frank in here, not ten minutes ago?' she kept on asking me. 'Otherwise how are we going to be able to fix it and get you to the church on time?'

I was perched on a ledge over by the bathroom window, that much I can still remember too. My room looked directly down onto the hotel's immaculate gardens below and I had a bird's eye view of the catering staff bustling around, as outdoor chairs were being set up for the Merrion's famous afternoon tea on the terrace, after the church/boring bit of the day. As I'd done myself for so many other brides on countless other wedding days.

How can they all just continue on with their lives as normal, like nothing just happened? I found myself thinking from out of nowhere. *Don't they realize the whole world has just suddenly stopped spinning round on its axis?*

My job there was all about management and containment and reducing dramas down to their proper proportions, but somehow the normal rules just didn't seem to apply at times like that. I mean outside of Hollywood movies, who did you ever hear of that ended up in a situation like mine?

'Chloe love,' Gemma insisted, patting me gently on the back like a colicky baby. 'You've got to tell me.'

Right then, I thought, staring dully down two floors below. You asked for it, so here you go. Head aching, I somehow tried to piece it all together in my head, so I could at least get to articulate it right. So I slumped back against Gemma and somehow forced myself to try and find the words.

'Chloe?' says Rob, who's still looking over at me all concerned, waiting on an answer.

So I take a deep breath and then just plunge straight in.

'In the end, it was a classic case of cold feet,' I tell him out straight. 'It only happened just about an hour before we were due to leave the hotel for the church, in fact. Frank came into my hotel room to tell me . . .'

'Yeah . . .?' Rob says, alert, utterly focused on what I'm going to say next.

'Well, that he'd been having second thoughts and . . . that he didn't think he could go through with it.'

'He said *what*?' He actually looks flushed now. First time I've ever seen Rob looking angry.

'Don't get me wrong, he was very apologetic and everything, I mean, I'll give him that much, Frank's always very polite . . .'

396

'And did he give you any reason why?' he asks, face tight, instantly back to being unreadable.

'Well, he said that it wasn't me, it was him.'

'I'll bet the bastard did. But go on.'

'He said . . . well . . . that he'd been feeling completely overwhelmed by the whole marriage thing for the past few weeks . . .'

'And he thought right then was the appropriate day to tell you? One hour before you were due to walk down the aisle?'

'Then I remember him saying . . . well, which was worse? To have a miserable few years together and ultimately end up divorced, or else to do the brave thing and call it off right there and then. He actually used those words: "A few miserable years." He said he didn't want to end up divorced like his parents, and that in the long run, this was avoiding us both all of that unnecessary pain.'

In fact, that's the astonishing thing about the whole nightmare. The way Frank put it back then, you'd have sworn he was nearly doing me a favour.

A pause, and it's a while before Rob eventually speaks.

'I'm sorry, Chloe. Painful memories for you and I shouldn't have asked you something so personal. I'd absolutely no right to. I just had to know, that's all.'

'It's okay,' I tell him and surprise myself by really meaning it. 'I mean, yes, for a long time afterwards I was a complete mess. After all, I was the girl who got stood up on her own wedding day. I thought I was tarred for life and that the epitaph would follow me everywhere. Thing is,' I go on, breaking off to take another sip of wine, 'I'm an invisible-type person, an in-the-background type who you take absolutely no notice of, but who's ultimately there to fix things, to smooth everything over for you, to make your life easier. That's my job, it's what I do.'

'And you do it beautifully. Though I don't think I'd quite describe you as invisible,' he says, with a tiny smile.

'But after that, my fear was that I'd take front centre stage for as long as I was alive. I felt like a living, walking, breathing, twenty-first-century Miss Havisham.'

Not to mention the fact that I thought I'd never trust another man with my heart as long as I was alive.

'And do you ever think about, well, what might have been?' Rob asks, leaning forward, eyes burning now.

'You mean . . . if we'd gone ahead and . . .'

'Well, yeah.'

No polite pussyfooting around what he's referring to, so there's nothing for it but try to root around for the right words.

'The truth is, I never thought I'd get over what happened to me. And it took a long, long time to get over, that's for sure. And yet . . . it's hard to put into words . . .'

'Go on,' he says, all ears.

'But there's just been something very soothing and grounding about working with all these couples. And like I said, the Hope Street Hotel really does seem to be like a place of healing. Time and again over the weekend, I couldn't help myself thinking, supposing if what happened to me never happened? If I'd actually gone ahead and got to walk down an aisle that day three years ago, would this be me now? If Frank and I had married, would I have been checking into a hotel like ours this weekend and not managing it instead?'

'And do you think you would have?' he asks me gently. 'If I'm not being too cheeky, that is.'

'Without a doubt. Come on Rob, I had a groom who

was at best lukewarm about the whole thing, which would hardly have been a great start to any married life. And even though I've spent the longest time fantasizing about what it would be like to murder him in cold blood for what he put me through . . .'

'Yeah?'

'Well, after seeing him yesterday . . . it was, somehow liberating. For the first time in three long years, I walked away from him with my head held high and better yet, with a sense of closure.'

'Very glad to hear it,' Rob smiles, the eyes twinkling in the dim candlelight.

'Thing is, I can't help thinking that the guy actually did me a favour that day. Because for all the pain and heartache and humiliation I had to deal with, it's absolutely nothing compared to what a lot of couples divorcing go through. And I should know, certainly after this experience.'

Our starters arrive, sautéed garlic shrimp for him, a Caesar salad for me, but while Rob tucks in hungrily, I just play a bit with mine. Because it's now or never really, isn't it? When might I get him on his own again somewhere intimate like this? And it's not like he hasn't asked me enough about my private life, anyway.

Feck it anyway. I'm only dying to know, so I go for it.

'So enough about me, what about you, then?' I prod gently. 'You know all about my sad history, but I'm guessing you must have a lot going on in your own private life too?'

'Less than you might think,' he winks back at me, between mouthfuls. 'Considerably less.'

'But . . . aren't you seeing someone right now? I mean, I thought that . . .'

'No. Single.'

'But what about . . .? I mean, when you were on the phone just now and all those times before . . . not that I was listening in, or anything . . . but it was pretty hard not to overhear you . . .'

And now suddenly he's roaring laughing.

'Oh, that! No, I was on the phone to my daughter.'

'You have a daughter?'

Bloody hell, he kept that quiet!

'Yeah. Eight years of age and the light of my life.'

'But you're not with . . .'

'. . . With her Mum? No. Susan and I broke up before she even discovered she was pregnant. But I very much wanted to be involved in Beatrice's life . . .'

'. . . That's her name? It's so cute . . .'

'Oh, you wanna see her. She's gorgeous. Nothing like me, I'm delighted to say. So I support her of course, and see her every chance I can get. In fact, the child has me wrapped around her little finger.'

I am such a gobshite. An ex and a little girl? Rob reads my thoughts though and keeps on slagging me playfully.

'So to recap, Ms Townsend. You heard me on the phone saying I love you and can't wait to see you and all of that, and presumed I was onto a girlfriend?'

'Well . . .' Pretty much, yeah.

'Young, free and single,' he teases, the eyes dancing now.

I'm wrong footed now, so of course immediately start babbling to make up for it.

'Well of course, in our line of work it's very difficult to meet anyone, isn't it?'

'You said it . . . what with the crazy hours we put in and everything . . .'

'. . . And then when you do get time off, you're just so

wrecked you want to sleep, don't you? I mean, even on my day off, I'm just streeling around the place like a zombie . . .'

'. . . Chloe . . .'

'. . . Because you really have to be married to this job, I think . . .'

'. . . Chloe?'

'. . . Yeah . . .?'

'. . . You're gabbling. I'm not able to keep up with you . . .'

'. . . Oh, right . . .'

'Thing is, you asked me earlier why I kept calling you constantly in the run-up to Hope Street opening . . .'

'And you wouldn't answer me!' I tease.

'Well, here's your answer right now. Did it ever occur to you that maybe I just liked having our chats, no matter how businesslike? That maybe even . . .'

Our hands are side by side on the table now, almost touching. And I've a knot in my stomach just waiting on him to finish that sentence.

'. . . maybe even . . . well, the thing is, a lot of the reason I wanted to ask you here this evening was . . .'

'. . . Emm . . . yeah . . .'

'I mean . . . seeing as how Frank is a thing of the past now . . .'

'Yeah . . .?'

'. . . Well, I suppose I wondered if you'd ever have any interest in having a non-work-related night out sometime . . .'

'. . . Oh well . . .' I stammer, dumfounded.

'. . . Mind you, I take first dates very seriously . . .'

'. . . Of course . . .' I smile.

'. . . They're vital, in fact. They set the tone of the whole relationship to come . . .'

'. . . So . . .'

'. . . So if you're free next Saturday night, is there any chance you'd meet up? Just for a casual night out maybe?'

'Well . . . yeah . . . I mean, thank you. Yes. That sounds absolutely lovely.'

'And Chloe . . .?'

'Yeah?'

'Might just be a good idea to bring your passport.'

SIX MONTHS LATER

Dawn.

'*HAPPY BIRTHDAY TO YOU,*
HAPPY BIRTHDAY TO YOU,
HAPPY BIRTHDAY DEAR DA-AAAAWN,
HAPPY BIRTHDAY TO YOU!'

There's a loud whooping and cheering as Dawn attempted to blow out all twenty-six of her birthday candles on the giant novelty cake her Mum had made for the party specially. A custom-made cake, get this, that looked exactly like the shopfront of Earth's Garden. It was so incredible looking that Dawn thought it a sin to stick a knife into it and start chopping it up. Far nicer just to stare at it, in all its gorgeousness instead.

The function room in her Mum's tennis club was packed out with friends and well-wishers and Dawn looked fondly around at everyone, silently blessing them all for coming. Absolutely everyone she knew was here: Eva, their Mum and all the family, and her mates from work.

Funny thing, it suddenly struck Dawn as she looked around. So many faces here who had the misfortune to suffer through her wedding, almost four years ago. They'd all dutifully turned up that day and they'd all suffered through hemp bleeding wine and a vegan buffet with sitar music in the background. And yet just take a look at her life now! Had she ever thought she'd come out of the tunnel she'd been stuck in? Had she ever even dreamed it possible, not only that life would go on, but that it might, just might, actually take a turn for the better?

Dawn was better, she was healed and she knew it. She was young, free and single and proving that life goes on. She'd even been on a few dates with that cute barman Tommy, from Hope Street. It had all fizzled out after a few weeks, but Dawn wasn't remotely bothered. Because this, she thought, is what being single is all about. Playing the field, getting out there, having fun. Wasn't it? And lately, she'd been having the time of her life.

Next thing Eva bounced over, in a gorgeous black cocktail dress that set off her glossy red hair to perfection.

'Present time!' she said. 'And I'm really proud of this one, so you'd better like it!'

'Wow, thanks so much!' Dawn laughed, gratefully taking the gift from her. A fairly largish box, but which felt really light when she lifted it.

'Well, aren't you going to open it?' said Eva, eyes sparkling with mischief.

So Dawn did. The first layer, which turned out to be an empty box with a smaller box inside, then the second, which again, turned out to be yet another empty box with an even smaller one inside . . . and so on and so on . . .

'Eva! It's like a Russian doll!'

'Just keep going. You'll get there,' she grinned.

So on and on Dawn kept unwrapping until there was just a giant mound of wrapping paper left at her feet.

'Keep going,' Eva laughed knowingly. Eventually, Dawn had peeled the gift down to its last and final layer and all that remained inside this giant box was a slim white envelope. Puzzled, she looked over at Eva.

'Well, are you not going to open it?' she teased. 'After I went to all this bother?'

'Oh my GOWD! Oh my actual God!' Dawn squealed, clearly audible over the music, when she saw what was inside.

'Well, do you like it? Tell me!'

'Eva, I don't believe you did this. Two tickets to Paris, where I've always wanted to go! And an overnight stay at the Hotel du Louvre!'

'Well? Are you up for it or what? Because I'm coming with you!'

'Thank you so, so much,' Dawn beamed. 'I love and adore it. You couldn't have got me anything more perfect or special! I mean that, I really, really do.'

'Two single ladies on a weekend in Paris,' Eva smiled, 'now that's what I call an adventure.'

Dawn's mother bustled over to them, gin and tonic in hand.

'Do you like your gift, sweetheart?' she asked. 'It was Eva's idea, but we both clubbed in.'

'Mum, I can't thank you enough. Both of you,' Dawn grinned, wrapping the two of them in a group hug.

'You deserve it,' her Mum said proudly. 'Oh and by the way, some new guests have arrived. Over there, by the door. You might want to say hello, love.' Then she added a bit sniffily, 'Though why you had to ask that pair is beyond me . . .'

407

Dawn looked over to see Kirk and Shane, standing uncomfortably by the bar, not really knowing where to go or how they'd be received.

'Excuse me one minute, will you?' she said to her Mum and Eva.

She made her way over to the boys and greeted them both warmly. Even Shane.

'This is for you,' Kirk beamed, proudly presenting a small package wrapped in brown paper that stank to high hell. 'It's some goats' cheese my Dad made specially.'

'Thank you, it's lovely.'

'And we brought some elderflower wine too,' said Shane, proffering a bottle. 'Happy birthday.'

'You shouldn't have,' Dawn smiled. 'And thank you both for coming. I really do appreciate it.'

Goats' cheese and elderflower wine, she thought? Eva would piss herself laughing when she heard. But she said nothing, just politely accepted the gifts and thanked them both warmly.

'No reason why we can't all be friends,' Kirk said, calmly and evenly, looking at her softly with the big brown eyes. Dawn grinned back at them both, genuinely pleased they'd turned up. Because life went on, didn't it? But that still didn't mean you discarded someone you once loved from your past, did it?

Besides, her whole life had moved on so happily and being perfectly honest, it was far easier now to think of both Kirk and Shane and to genuinely wish them well from the bottom of her heart.

Then, suddenly distracted, she squealed excitedly at the sight of Chloe coming through the main door to the tennis club. Looking off the scales glamorous tonight and queuing up to check in the most incredibly elegant looking cream, swishy coat, that suited her to perfection.

Dawn ran over to her and hugged her as Chloe instantly lit up and said, 'Hey! Happy birthday! And thanks so much for asking me!'

'Are you kidding?' Dawn laughed. 'After everything I owe you missus, do you honestly think I'd have a birthday bash and not ask you?'

Then Chloe slipped her a beautifully wrapped gift bag with a big white envelope inside, jutting out. Excitedly, Dawn ripped it open and gasped.

'Chloe . . . I can't believe you did this! A voucher for dinner for two at Maxim's in Paris . . . Wow! This is the best birthday ever!'

'Well, a little bird tells me you're taking a trip there very soon,' Chloe laughed. 'And I really hope you both enjoy every minute. No one deserves it more. No one.'

'Thank you,' said Dawn hugging her warmly. 'And not just for this, either. For absolutely everything.'

'You're so welcome!'

'And I can't believe you came tonight . . . and on your own too!'

'Well actually . . .' Chloe said, sounding a bit coy now, and for a second Dawn picked up on something more, something unspoken.

'Yeah?'

'If it's okay with you . . . as a matter of fact, I brought someone with me.'

*

409

Jo.

From: Jo_Marketing_Director@digitech.com
To: davesblog@hotmail.com
Re: The Valentine's Day massacre, as you keep referring to it . . .
February 13th, 6.45 a.m.

Dave! Are you up and about yet? With apologies for the dawn email, but as you know I'm en route to London this morning for a whole day of meetings and my flight is boarding . . . well, now actually. As I type.

So anyway, tomorrow night, or V-Day as you keep referring to it. When you're not calling it the anniversary of the Valentine's Day massacre, that is. Now as you know, it's one subject we're in total agreement on; I too normally loathe and despise Valentine's Day for the poxy, made-up, Hallmark holiday that it is. But this year is different. Like we agreed, new year, new start, new attitude.

So, dinner tomorrow night it is. And no Dave, I'm not leaving you to make all the arrangements again. No offence, but if I do, I'll come home to you saying, 'Ah sure, let's just order in a pizza and have it in front of Strictly Come Dancing.' We're upping the romantic stakes here, if it bloody well kills us. Don't we deserve it?

So leave all the arrangements to me and I'll be in touch,

Stay well, keep safe and have a great day,
Jo xxxxx

From: davesblog@hotmail.com
To: Jo_Marketing_Director@digitech.com
Re: The Valentine's Day massacre, as you keep
referring to it . . .
February 13th, 6.57 a.m.

Oh shite. Is it really morning???? Do I really have to
get up now? Curse my telly job anyway and curse the
frigging alarm clock! How do you do this, Jo? Day in
day out, hop out of the scratcher at 5 a.m., fresh as a
tulip and stride effortlessly through your whole
morning, not a bother on you?

And just as an aside, yes, I'm aware of the irony. I
spent my whole life bemoaning my unemployed
status, and the first time a decent TV series comes
along, what do I do? Whinge and gripe on account of
IT'S SO FREAKING EARLY!!!!

Need caffeine. Urgently. Car's picking me up in
twenty minutes and I'm not even showered yet.

Laters, baby.

Love you. Travel safe.

Dxxxx

PS. I can't find the filters for your fancy Nespresso
machine anywhere. Where'd you put them?
PPS. Think I lost my key again. It's not in its usual
place, i.e., my jeans pocket. Any ideas/clues/hints?

From: Jo_Marketing_Director@digitech.com
To: davesblog@hotmail.com
Re: The Valentine's Day massacre, as you keep
referring to it . . .
February 13th, 7.22 a.m.

*Sweet Mother of God, you'll be the death of me.
Nespresso filters are in the cupboard above the kitchen
sink. Where they always are, Dave. As for your spare key,
suggest you try the washing machine, seeing as how
that's where your last one turned up.*

> *Good luck on set today. VERY proud of you,*
> *Jo xxxxx*

*PS. Will be back to you with arrangements for tomorrow.
Just wear your good black suit from Louis Copeland, turn
up on time and that's all I ask. Leave everything else to
your control freak of a wife and all will be well.*

> *Flight taxiing now, getting snotty looks from passenger
beside me, gotta turn off phone, etc. Xxxxx*

From: restaurant_Patrick_Guilbaud@
merrionhotelgroup.ie
To: Jo_Marketing_Director@digitech.com
Re: reservation confirmation.
February 13th, 9.05 a.m.

Dear Ms Hargreaves,
    Many thanks for your previous email. We're
delighted to let you know that we have indeed had a

cancellation for tomorrow evening, and I can now offer you a table for two in Guilbaud's for 8 p.m. As a long-standing guest, it's been our pleasure to accommodate you in the past, and I'm delighted to be of service to you in this regard.

If you have any additional special requests, then please don't hesitate to contact me,

With sincere thanks for your continued custom,

James Sheridan.

Jo's flight had landed and she was just clipping through arrivals and onto a car that was waiting for her, when that last and final email pinged through. She fastened herself into the back seat, gave her driver Digitech's address and for the first time all morning sat back to really relax.

Wonderful, she thought. Guilbaud's was just perfect. Because tomorrow night was a very special celebration for her and Dave, even though he hadn't the first clue yet. And where better to celebrate in style than Guilbaud's? After every storm they'd weathered, this was it. The big turning point for them. And God, but she was beside herself to see his face when she told him her Big News.

With a broad beam plastered across her face, she scrolled down through her phone and hit on the very email that had her practically dancing a jig, when it came through for her only yesterday. She must have re-read it a thousand times since, but even still it never failed to gladden her heart.

From: National_Maternityhospital@hollesst.ie.
To: Jo_Marketing_Director@digitech.com
Re: Appointment confirmation
February 12th, 4.47 p.m.

Dear Ms Hargreaves,

Further to our meeting earlier today, I'm now delighted to confirm your initial ante-natal appointment for March 10th at 9 a.m. Your husband is, of course, more than welcome to attend with you.

May I take this opportunity to congratulate you and your husband on your impending good news? As we've often discussed, IVF is a lengthy and costly procedure and that cost is frequently emotional as well as financial. I know many times throughout your treatment, things weren't easy for you and yet you persevered and here we are now.

I consider myself a lucky woman, in that my job often entails passing on good news to patients such as yourself, but our meeting this week, when I was in a position to give you final confirmation of your pregnancy, is especially memorable.

Once again, I'm overjoyed for you and know that you and your husband will make the most wonderful parents.

Looking forward to seeing you at your next appointment,

Sincerely,

Dr Katherine Mulcahy, OBS GYN. BMED.

Jo hugged herself and for about the thousandth time since yesterday, patted her tummy gently, wondering how she'd find the right words to tell Dave. Keeping it from him for the past twenty-four hours had been bloody torture, but it would be so worth it, just to see the look on his face in the restaurant tomorrow night.

She sat back against the plush leather seat, thinking about how overjoyed and excited he'd be and remembering her own reaction yesterday when Dr Katherine had first told her. God, she almost had to be given oxygen, she'd been that euphoric! It was a miracle and a dream come true, all somehow magicked together.

Next thing, acting totally on impulse, she grabbed her phone again and quickly bashed out another email.

From: Jo_Marketing_Director@digitech.com
To: davesblog@hotmail.com
Re: The Valentine's Day massacre, as you keep referring to it . . .
February 13th, 9.42 a.m.

Dave, I'm an idiot. Left home without telling you something important.
  I love you.
  But then, you always knew that, didn't you?
  Your,
  Jxxxx

'You're looking mighty chipper this morning then, love?' her driver grinned at her, catching her reflection in the rear-view mirror.

'I am,' Jo grinned happily back at him. 'In fact, at this exact moment in time, I'm officially on top of the world.'

*

Lucy.

'Ready, darling?'

'As I'll ever be.'

'No nerves? Or last minute reservations?'

'Oh come on, how could you even ask?'

'Just remember it's all change from here on in, darling. Because if I have to spend the rest of my life making it up to you for what my family put you through – for what I put you through – then I will. This is it, my love. You and me, except for better this time. We've certainly had the for worse part!'

'So what are we waiting for?'

From the driver's seat of his car, Andrew just beamed over at Lucy, looking all handsome and healthy now that he was fully restored back to himself again. Just like the Andrew of old, the man she loved.

She knew he'd meant every word of what he'd said too. Because this really was a whole new start for them. No more secrets, no more horrible tensions around the stepkids. New start, new beginning. And with Andrew by her side, she knew she wouldn't go too far wrong.

The two of them stepped out into the lashing rain and made a bolt for the Grand Canal Street registry office, just across the street. Tittering with laughter, Andrew held the car door open for her, gamely holding an umbrella over her, so her long, white dress wouldn't get destroyed. Full of energy and vitality, looking so fit and well. Glowing even.

But just inside the door of the registry office, dripping with rain, there was a surprise waiting for them. Because standing there, looking fabulously glamorous, even with soaking wet hair, was Alannah. Carrying two little posy bouquets, no less.

416

'Sweetheart, you came!' Andrew beamed down at her. 'I didn't think you would.'

And nor did Lucy. She grinned over at Alannah, genuinely delighted to see her. The fact was, even though a full rapprochement was still a long way off, ever since Andrew got sick, the two women had somehow grown closer. It was bridge-building at its best and Lucy was bloody grateful for it.

'Thanks for coming, I can't tell you how much it means,' she told Alannah simply, meaning every word.

'Well after all, you're about to renew your vows,' Alannah said, 'and I just figured you could use a bit of support.'

'And will Josh be coming too?' Andrew asked hopefully.

'Not today,' Alannah said, biting her lip slightly, 'but just give him time. He'll come round eventually, I know he will.'

'Ready to move?' an usher from out of nowhere asked them as they all moved inside.

'You're looking absolutely stunning, by the way,' Lucy told Alannah, linking Andrew's arm and waiting for the nod from the registrar. 'I love that shift dress on you. Karen Millen, isn't it?'

'Got it in one. And thanks. I just thought I should make a bit of an effort.'

'Well, it's much appreciated,' Lucy smiled at her. 'By both of us.'

'Thing is . . .' Alannah said. 'I figured you could use a bridesmaid.'

Five minutes later, they were on.

'. . . And do you, Lucy Amelia, take this, Andrew James for your wedded husband? To have and to hold from this day forth, for better and for worse, in sickness and in health, till death do you part?'

'I do,' said Lucy, clearly and confidently. Utterly sure of her answer, this time round.

'Then by the power vested in me, I now declare you man and wife.'

There was no polite handclapping, at least not this time. And apart from a brief 'Well, congratulations to you both,' from the registrar, and a big smiley grin from Alannah, no other well-wishers were even there. Or even knew this was happening. Which was exactly as the bride and groom had wanted.

'Oh, sweetheart,' Andrew said, looking fondly down at the bride he'd just renewed vows with. 'This isn't at all what I'd have wanted for you, you know. I wanted you to have a massive celebration with all your family and friends and a big party for you afterwards, the whole works –'

But Lucy just stood tall, placed her finger over his lips to stop him saying another word and shook her head firmly.

'Now you just listen to me. I may not have got my dream wedding first time round . . .'

'. . . Or indeed your dream marriage, come to that . . .'

'But this time it's exactly what I would have asked for. Just us. Renewing our vows and starting over. Really, properly starting over. Leaving all the crap behind us, once and for all.'

'First time I've head any bride use the word "crap" at the altar,' the registrar laughed, 'but each to his own, I suppose!'

Lucy immediately leaned forward and kissed Andrew on the cheek.

'All change this time?' she asked coquettishly.

He pulled her closer to him and grinned.

'This time, my darling girl, it's all change forever.'

*

Chloe.

So here's what I remember, though he would certainly disagree. Not that there's all that much Rob and I do disagree on, really. However, he does maintain that we should have screening rooms in all Ferndale Hotels on the days that Man U are playing, whereas I think that's a completely mental idea that'll drive female guests completely nuts.

Oh, and he also says that wedge heels on women look like pigs trotters and should all be banned forthwith, whereas I laugh at him, tell him that's a load of Horlicks and a) that they're comfy and b) what's wrong with giving yourself a bit of height anyway?

Oh, and we've had one or two heated discussions about the merits versus flaws of fake tan too . . . but then . . . that's about it, really. In six fabulously romantic months, that's all we've disagreed on really. Man U, wedge heels and fake tan. Not too shabby all told, now is it?

Anyway, back to our famous first date. I remember Rob spent the whole week beforehand calling me from London at the oddest times and asking me the weirdest, most bizarre questions. Did I eat fish? Did I have any other food allergies? Had I been vaccinated for cholera? (Though he later confessed he only threw that in as a red herring, purely to wind me up.)

Sweet divine, was all I could think, getting my knickers more and more in a twist as the weekend drew nearer and our Saturday night first date grew closer and closer. Where was this fella taking me anyway? The Amazonian rainforest?

Anyway, Rob had to go back to London I remember, early that week, and all he said was to meet him at Dublin airport on Saturday at the main information desk. So in I trooped, wheelie bag in tow, wearing a pair of skinny jeans and a pretty floral top I bought especially, fully prepared for all eventualities. Hail, rain, sun or snow, I'd packed just about everything.

And of course he was there ahead of me, looking tall and tanned and gorgeous and absolutely roared with laughter when he saw just how much luggage I'd brought.

'Nothing like packing light, now is there, Ms Townsend?'

'Rob!' I giggled back at him. 'Oh come on, this is mental! You have to tell me where you're taking me . . . please!'

'Surprise,' he said flippantly. 'But by the way, you're looking extremely fetching today . . . loving those tight jeans on you.'

He bent down and kissed me lightly on the cheek and I swear, for a second I actually tingled. Next thing we're checking in at – get this – Emirates airlines in business class!

And never before or since have I experienced anything like it. From the moment we stepped into our beautifully air-conditioned cabin where we were both handed a crisp glass of chilled champagne, followed by course after course of the most unbelievable grub known to man.

'Whoever their head chef is,' I told Rob in between mouthfuls, 'I'm poaching him and bringing him straight back to Hope Street with me.'

'Now, now,' he said teasingly, cocking an eyebrow very sexily at me. 'It's your first weekend off in I don't know how long. Put work right out of your head, relax and enjoy, would you?'

I'd never been to Dubai before, but the minute we touched down that night, I knew I'd adore it. Unbelievable! Kind of like Manhattan except in the intense heat, with some of the most fabulously ornate and exotic looking

420

architecture I'd ever seen. Rob had really pushed the boat out and there was a private limo waiting for us at arrivals to whisk us off to . . . where, well, I hadn't a clue. I kept asking him and he just kept lifting a finger to his mouth and telling me to be patient.

And then finally, we arrived at the Burj al Arab, the world's only seven-star hotel and kind of like a mecca in the hotel business. My jaw dropped from the moment we arrived, as we stepped from the blistering desert heat into the cool foyer. Because this place was actually more like a palace than a hotel, with the most luxuriously ornate interior design job I've ever seen, all that wonderful Emirati design mode of 'more is more'. I've never before or since seen so much glittering gold, from the banisters on the sweeping staircase, to the door of the lift, which we were assured, were twenty-four carat too.

When we both have such a laugh about it now, Rob teases me and said I spent the entire weekend with my mouth gaping like a goldfish, oohing and ahhing over every little thing. But as I remember it, as the evening went on and our dinner date grew ever closer, I started to get nervous and more than a bit antsy.

Ever the gentleman, Rob had reserved two separate rooms, which were right beside each other, but still. I had a knot in my stomach getting showered and dressed for dinner. (A brand new summery Cos number in a pale coral pink. Which sounds a bit bridesmaid-y, I know, but feck it, it was a bargain.)

This, I thought into the mirror as I lashed on mascara, could either turn out to be the most magical night of my whole life or else be an unmitigated disaster. In which case I broke the cardinal rule of dating not only someone I work with, but who's my boss to boot. I could end up either a laughing stock or else a cautionary tale, if this all went skew ways.

In the end though, I needn't have worried. Dinner in the Al Muntaha restaurant, on the twenty-seventh floor of the hotel was like something even no Hollywood studio would ever dare dream up. Rob was there at the door to meet me, for once actually all dressed up in white linen trousers with a pale blue shirt that really brought out his lovely, twinkly grey eyes.

And he looked so handsome, I do remember thinking as he kissed me lightly and handed over a perfect long-stemmed rose.

I remember laughing and jokingly pretending to hit him with it for acting like we were a couple going to a debs but he just smiled at me and said, 'You just better get used to being treated like a goddess, Chloe Townsend.'

He remembers the food as being a bit over spicy, but I clearly remember him woofing back every last bite. He says I got a bit tiddly, with the amount of champagne he kept plying me with, but as far as I was concerned, I was utterly sober and in control, just an awful lot giddier than normal.

But the very end of the night?

Now that much at least, we're in perfect agreement about . . .

*

And now, six months on, it's my first weekend off from Ferndale in a full month and I'm like a bag of nerves sitting in the foyer of the Dorchester Hotel in London. Stomach clenched, palms sweating, the works. Because believe me, this is bigger and far, far more nerve-racking than any job interview.

And then I see them. Rob striding through the foyer and instantly lighting up when he spots me, as I sit tensely under a potted palm tree and try to look all relaxed. Over they come as I stand up to greet them both. Rob kisses me warmly and hugs me tight, then steps aside to introduce me to the other woman in his life.

'Chloe, I'd like you to meet my beautiful little girl, Beatrice. Beatrice, say hello to Chloe.'

She's a little doll of a child too. Beautiful long chestnut hair tied up into the most adorable pigtails and with grey eyes so exactly like Rob's, it's uncanny. She beams up at me, a big gap-toothy smile that makes her look even cuter.

'Well, hello there!' I smile warmly, bending down to her level. 'I've heard so much about you from your Dad, but he never told me you're even more gorgeous than in your photos!'

Beatrice giggles and looks so adorable, I want to hug her there and then.

'Daddy's always talking 'bout you too!' she grins. 'He says I'm the most beautifullest girl in the whole world, but you're the next most beautifullest!'

'Well, isn't your Dad a dote to say that?' I grin over at Rob, who winks back at me. Then I take one of Beatrice's chubby little hands, Rob takes the other and the three of us make for the door.

'Come on, ladies,' Rob smiles happily, 'or else Madame Tussauds will have shut before we get there!'

'Chloe's amazing, Dad!' Beatrice smiles the cutest little gappy smile. 'Just like you said! I really like her!'

'Do you now, love?' says Rob, eyes twinkling in my direction. 'Well then, that makes two of us.'

And so we step outside into the mild spring sunshine. Just the three of us.

THE END

Acknowledgements

Thank you, Marianne Gunn O'Connor. You're so much more than an amazing agent; you're an amazing friend too. And that's the best part of all. I love our chats where we take the whole world apart and put it all back to rights again. Next brekkie is definitely on me!

Thank you, Pat Lynch, who works so hard and is always so positive and uplifting. See you in The Farm very soon, Chicken.

Thank you, to Vicki Satlow in Milan who does such an incredible job with translation right. You're a true star, Vicki.

Thank you, Eli Dryden at Avon. It really has been a joy and a privilege to work alongside you on this book. And I'll keep nagging you till you eventually come back to visit us in Dublin!

Thank you to the fabulous team at Avon, HarperCollins, for your enthusiasm, friendship, hard work and incredible support. I'm so lucky to be part of Team Avon. Special thanks to Caroline Ridding, Claire Power, Sammia Hamer, Helen Bolton, Cleo Little, Lydia Vassar-Smith, Keshini Naidoo and Sam Hancock.

Thanks also to Jo Marino at Light Brigade in London. I'm so looking forward to working with you.

Thanks to Tony Purdue, who works so hard and does so much for all of us.